D0020653

To the
Farthest
Shores

Books by Elizabeth Camden

The Lady of Bolton Hill
The Rose of Winslow Street
Against the Tide
Into the Whirlwind
With Every Breath
Beyond All Dreams
Toward the Sunrise: An Until the Dawn *Novella*
Until the Dawn
Summer of Dreams: A From This Moment *Novella*
From This Moment
To the Farthest Shores

To the
Farthest
Shores

ELIZABETH CAMDEN

BETHANYHOUSE
a division of Baker Publishing Group
Minneapolis, Minnesota

© 2017 by Dorothy Mays

Published by Bethany House Publishers
11400 Hampshire Avenue South
Bloomington, Minnesota 55438
www.bethanyhouse.com

Bethany House Publishers is a division of
Baker Publishing Group, Grand Rapids, Michigan

Printed in the United States of America

All rights reserved. No part of this publication may be reproduced, stored in a retrieval system,
or transmitted in any form or by any means—for example, electronic, photocopy, recording—
without the prior written permission of the publisher. The only exception is brief quotations
in printed reviews.

Library of Congress Cataloging-in-Publication Data
Names: Camden, Elizabeth, author.
Title: To the farthest shores / Elizabeth Camden.
Description: Bloomington, Minnesota : Bethany House, [2017]
Identifiers: LCCN 2016041082| ISBN 9780764230097 (cloth) | ISBN 9780764218804
  (trade paper)
Subjects: | GSAFD: Christian fiction.
Classification: LCC PS3553.A429 T62 2017 | DDC 813/.54—dc23
LC record available at https://lccn.loc.gov/2016041082

This is a work of fiction. Names, characters, incidents, and dialogues are products of the author's
imagination and are not to be construed as real. Any resemblance to actual events or persons,
living or dead, is entirely coincidental.

Cover design by Jennifer Parker
Cover photography by Yolanda de Kort/Trevillion Images

Author is represented by the Steve Laube Agency

17 18 19 20 21 22 23   7 6 5 4 3 2 1

Prologue

U.S. ARMY BASE AT THE PRESIDIO
SAN FRANCISCO, 1898

Jenny Bennett woke as pebbles clattered against her window. She sat bolt upright, trying to get her bearings. As a hospital nurse, she was often called upon in the middle of the night, but always by a knock on her door.

Even as she scrambled from beneath the bedsheets, another spray of pebbles hit the glass. She dashed to the window, wincing at the cold tile on her bare feet. Standing by the lamppost below was the distinctive figure of Lieutenant Ryan Gallagher, his sandy blond hair glinting in the circle of gaslight. Ryan was the most straight-laced man she knew, hardly the type to be flinging pebbles against her window in the dead of night.

She tugged up the window sash. "What's going on?"

"Can you come down?" Ryan called up in a hoarse whisper, trying to avoid waking others in the building. Over two hundred people slept in this army barracks, but only a handful were women. As a civilian nurse, she was fortunate the army let her lodge here.

Otherwise she'd have to make the long cable car journey from the city each day.

"I'll be right down."

April in San Francisco was chilly, so she shrugged into a coat and tugged on a pair of boots. She finger-combed her straight black hair, trying to pull it into some semblance of order before running down to meet Ryan. They'd only known each other for three months, but she'd been in love with him for two.

A glance at the clock revealed it was three in the morning. What on earth was Ryan up to at such an hour? She hastened down the steps, out the door, and straight into the shelter of Ryan's waiting arms. She smiled as he lifted her from the ground, holding on tight as he twirled her around.

"I almost didn't recognize you in those civilian clothes," she said once her feet were on solid ground. "Are you alright?"

"I'm fine," he assured her, drawing back to gaze into her face. He seemed unusually somber—sad, even. He was usually in such good spirits, and his mood worried her. "Let's go somewhere private," he whispered.

The Presidio sprawled over three square miles on the northern tip of the San Francisco peninsula. Most of it was wilderness, but the western side contained an army base, the hospital, and training facilities. The army used only a fraction of the land. The rest of it was blanketed with towering pines, eucalyptus groves, and sycamore trees, making the Presidio feel like a primeval wilderness. The forest also provided plenty of seclusion from the chaos on base.

Normally the Presidio housed less than a thousand people, but since President McKinley declared war against Spain, the base had been mobilizing for conflict. Troops from across the nation streamed into the Presidio, preparing to sail for the Spanish colonies in the Far East. Thousands of pup tents were scattered like mushrooms across the lawns and parade fields to shelter the newly arrived soldiers.

Jenny followed Ryan on a meandering path through the tents, still confused by his strange behavior. Was he ill again? It had been three months since the USS *Baltimore* hobbled into port with half its crew suffering from typhoid. Ryan had been among the stricken, his case bad enough to hospitalize him for two weeks. He finally recovered but was still rail-thin.

During his stay in the hospital, Ryan had been consistently polite, managing a weak smile of gratitude each time she tended him. His warm brown eyes always softened the instant she came into view, and he was the kindest man she'd ever met. He read the Bible before breakfast and murmured a prayer of thanks before each meal.

She'd started calling him Galahad, partly because it was similar to his last name, but mostly because it was how he seemed to her. She secretly gave lots of her patients nicknames: Bossy Man, the Weeper, the Nice Texan, the Rude Texan . . . but from the moment she met Ryan Gallagher, she thought of him as Galahad.

She couldn't imagine why he'd come to see her at such an unseemly hour. He wasn't in uniform either, which was out of character. The Presidio was an army base, but since the declaration of war, the navy had anchored their fleets in the harbor and their officers had moved into Presidio quarters. Ryan had been one of those naval officers, looking wickedly handsome in his crisp, white dress uniform. It wouldn't be long before the ships set sail for the Philippines, and already she ached at the thought of Ryan going to some tropical jungle to fight a war no one understood.

It got darker as they moved into the cool sycamore forest, a carpet of damp leaves cushioning her footsteps and giving off a loamy scent. She startled at a sudden cascade of birdcall, odd at this time of night. She glanced at Ryan with a question in her eyes.

"Night herons," he whispered. "They forage in the hours before dawn, always in groups. They're very social creatures. We must have surprised them."

Ryan knew everything about animal and marine life. It was one of the things she found so attractive about him. Jenny had spent her entire life in the city, but Ryan courted her with walks along the seashore that rimmed the Presidio. During those walks he taught her to see the world with new eyes. He would hunker down on the beach to show her the underside of a starfish. He told her about red rock crabs and how they acted like stewards of the estuary by keeping the bottom of the bay clean. Ryan could explain the difference between a fungus and an alga. Sometimes they simply walked in silence, but even then she felt like singing and laughing at the same time. Ryan touched a part of her soul she hadn't even known existed. It had been easy to ignore the war during those golden afternoons, but it was suddenly all too real.

Ryan pulled her a few feet off the path behind a tree and drew her into an embrace. "I've come to say good-bye," he said, and it felt like she'd been punched in the stomach. None of the ships were leaving until next month, and Ryan wasn't well enough to be sent into combat yet. This didn't make sense.

She pulled back to peer into his face. "Where are you going?"

"I can't tell you. I don't know how long I'll be gone, but I couldn't leave without saying good-bye."

She was speechless. They'd just found each other, and now he was leaving ahead of all the other troops? It seemed impossible for a man as gentle as Ryan Gallagher to be going to war. He belonged in a college classroom or a church pulpit, not a battlefield. They had already begun planning a life together. They were going to buy a saltbox cottage on one of the bluffs north of the city, a place where they could bask in the purity of the sunlight and clean ocean breezes.

"Will you write?" she managed to ask.

"I'll try."

That seemed odd, too. Above all, the military took extraordinary measures to ensure mail was delivered to and from their soldiers. It was one of the few things they could offer to make remote postings more bearable. Writing should be an easy thing to promise, but Jenny knew Ryan wouldn't lie to her.

She grasped his forearms as she tried to memorize each feature of his handsome face. She didn't even have a photograph of him. "Why are they sending you out so early? None of the other men are leaving until next month. I don't want them sending you off when you're still twenty pounds underweight and could suffer a relapse."

He smiled gently. "Jenny, I'm fine."

"You're letting the navy take advantage of you." Ryan was so instinctively generous that he let people exploit his good nature. She didn't know what she'd done to deserve a man as gallant as Ryan Gallagher. She was a girl from the wrong side of San Francisco, and he was a hero straight out of a storybook.

"I can't say anything more, but I don't want you worrying about me, alright? I'm going to be okay. I might even be home before Christmas."

His words were meant to be comforting, but they had the opposite effect. Didn't people always underestimate the enemy? Ever since Congress had declared war, soldiers had boasted it would take only a few weeks to trounce the Spanish, but Jenny wasn't so sure.

"Ryan, it's *Spain*," she said, ashamed of the tremble in her voice. "Spain has been one of the greatest naval empires for centuries. How can you say it won't be dangerous? Even crossing the ocean to the Philippines is dangerous."

"I haven't said I'm going to the Philippines."

Jenny made no answer, but everyone knew the war would be fought in the Philippines, where Spanish soldiers had been entrenched for three hundred years. Even before the formal declaration of war, the navy began funneling men, munitions, and ships into the San Francisco harbor for the grand expedition that would leave next month. Jenny never would have met Ryan except for this war, but she dreaded the thought of his leaving.

"I'm still worried about you," she said. "Something about this doesn't seem right."

He touched her cheek, his face radiating warm sympathy. "I don't want you worrying over me. As I came to see you, I spotted a shooting star. Did you know it's a sign of good luck?" He drew her into his embrace again, holding her tightly. "Don't tell anyone I was here tonight," he whispered into her ear. "It's not something that can get leaked."

"Of course." Civilian employees were warned to keep quiet about all troop movements and activities on the base. It seemed impossible to believe the Spanish would have planted spies among them, but she would keep quiet. Suddenly the war felt very real, and she didn't want it to. She wanted to go on meeting Ryan on the quadrangle, having picnics on the cliff overlooking the bay, and fooling herself into believing their magical interlude would never end. How long would it be before he held her like this again? It seemed so unfair. To have finally found someone, only to have him torn away so quickly.

"Before I go, I want you to know how much I love you," he whispered against her cheek, and her heart squeezed. He withdrew a few inches to gaze down into her face. "As soon as I get back, we'll get married and start the rest of our life together. I wish I'd had a chance to buy a ring, but everything is happening much faster than I thought."

This might be the most wonderful and heartbreaking moment of her entire life. Her heart threatened to split wide open. "That sounds really good," she managed to say.

He fumbled in his pocket, then pressed a heavy gold watch into her hands, the metal still warm from the heat of his body. "At least take my father's watch. Something to remember me by."

"No, Ryan, it's too much." She tried to give it back, but his hands were firm as they closed around hers.

"Keep it safe for me," he said. "I'll be back someday with a wedding ring, and then we can trade, okay?"

"I can do that," she whispered.

"I wish things didn't have to be this way, but it's time for me to go. You won't see me again until this is all over."

"I'll be waiting for you," she said. "I don't care how long you're gone, I'll wait forever."

For some reason, her declaration seemed to make him sad. A shadow passed over his face as he pulled her into his arms, rocking her gently in the moonlight.

"Good-bye, Jenny. I'll never forget you. No matter where I go, your heart and spirit will be with me always."

❦

Months went by with no news from Ryan. Each day Jenny held her breath as she approached the post office on the base. Other people received plenty of letters from the soldiers sent overseas, but Jenny's box was always empty. She checked the casualty lists daily, saying a prayer of relief each time she failed to spot Ryan's name.

The war didn't last long. By September it was all over and soldiers began returning home, but there was still no news from Ryan. As Christmas came and went, she feared he'd been killed and somehow his name was not recorded on the casualty lists. What if he'd been captured and trapped in some foreign land where he didn't know the language? He could have suffered a relapse of typhoid or some other tropical disease. Ryan had no family and no one to sound the alarm that he'd gone missing.

It was impossible to sit by and do nothing, so she wrote to Washington to inquire about a sailor who seemed to have vanished. She wrote to the Secretary of the War Department and the captain of the USS *Baltimore*. She wrote to Admiral Dewey himself. It came to nothing, all of them claiming Ryan was deployed and in good health, but she could not believe it when months went by without a single letter from him.

It took over a year for the first and only letter she would ever receive from Ryan to arrive at the Presidio. Jenny stared at it with disbelieving eyes, but it was short and to the point.

Dear Jenny,

I fear I was too optimistic about our future prospects. I have been offered an important opportunity with the navy and have accepted the commission. I will not be returning to California, but I wish you the very best with whatever your future holds.

I am deeply sorry for any false expectations I may have created during my convalescence at the Presidio.

Sincerely,
Lt. Ryan Gallagher

Jenny stepped outside the hospital, gazing at the sunrise just beginning to light the horizon. While sunrise signaled the beginning of the day for most people, for Jenny it meant bedtime.

Civilian nurses had been reassigned to overnight work after the war ended, and returning soldiers took the desirable day shifts. Working through the night was a struggle, but it was her only option if she wanted to continue working at the Presidio's hospital.

It was still chilly, and she drew her heavy woolen cloak tighter. Normally at this time she returned to her quarters, drew the shades, and slept until noon.

Not today. Her stomach clenched as she anticipated her meeting with Captain Soames, the medical director for the hospital at the Presidio. Once a battlefield doctor, Captain Soames had been working at a desk since the Spanish-American War ended only eight months after it began. He was a humorless, hard-bitten man who had little patience for the civilian employees at the base, but he was the only person who could grant the favor Jenny so desperately needed.

He wouldn't be in his office yet, so she made a quick trip to the barracks where civilian nurses lodged on the top floor. Her room was compact, tidy, and spotless. It ought to be, given that she swept it daily and wiped the windows, the mirror, and the hardware with a mild vinegar solution twice a week.

After scrubbing her face and hands, she changed her collar for a fresh one. All the nurses wore blue cotton dresses beneath a white apron and topped with a starched collar the army supplied to them each week. Jenny paid extra to have a freshly starched collar daily. Cleanliness was important to her, and any time she locked horns with Captain Soames, she wanted to look flawless. She shook her ebony hair free of its pins, brushed it to a high shine, and then coiled it back into an elegant twist. Pinning the folded nurse's cap into place was the last detail before heading to the captain's office.

He didn't seemed pleased to see her, even less so when she explained what she wanted, but she pressed on without letting him shake her composure.

"Skeeter Jones is a bright boy, but unless he has surgery on his eyes, he will be practically blind within a few years," she explained.

"And you want the army to pay for it."

Skeeter was a twelve-year-old orphan who earned less than a dollar a day selling newspapers, so yes, Jenny needed to find someone willing to pay for it.

"Dr. Samuelson tells me that symblepharon surgery is a routine procedure that requires less than an hour in the operating room. I'd be willing to pay any costs associated with medication. . . ."

She let the sentence dangle. Her finances were already stretched dangerously thin since what happened last month, but Skeeter needed this operation. A defect in his system was causing the folds of his eyelids to become anchored to his eyeball, making it hard to see. A simple incision done by a skilled surgeon would change the entire course of Skeeter's life, but it had to be done now, before he grew much older. Operating rooms at the hospital sat vacant most of the day, and it would cost the army very little to perform this operation.

"Find some other benefactor to pay for it," Captain Soames said. "If it becomes known that the army is treating charity cases, we'll have lines stretching to the Embarcadero and complaints about favoritism."

"Or it might improve our reputation with the city."

"Find a way to pay for it, Nurse Bennett. Then maybe I'll hear your request."

"How am I to pay for it when you pay me scarcely half what you pay the male attendants?"

The captain heard the veiled accusation in her tone. "The night nurses get paid less because you do little more than babysit sleeping patients. Of course we aren't going to pay you the same salary as the staff during the day. If you don't like your job here, then quit. If you aren't earning what you need, then quit. If you don't like the way I run the hospital, then quit. Is that clear, Nurse Bennett?"

She met Captain Soames's glower with her chin held high. "Quite clear. The army must be proud their officers can express themselves so forcefully and without resorting to bothersome courtesy."

Captain Soames let out a bark of gruff laughter. He'd had a grudging respect for her since the time he saw her tackle a soldier trying to steal morphine from a supply cabinet. While most nurses hailed from respectable families, Jenny grew up along San Francisco's waterfront and wasn't intimidated by unruly soldiers. Although she liked to pretend it didn't exist, a streetwise toughness from her youth still lurked just beneath her prim, starched uniform.

Captain Soames threw down his pencil and looked at her in frustration. "Why don't you just get married like a normal woman? Then you won't have to work six days a week and still scrounge for money to do a kid a favor."

Jenny tried not to blanch even though she'd heard the question plenty of times over the years. She'd fallen in love once, and it had been a disaster. The most humiliating thing was that even after receiving Ryan Gallagher's terse letter, she couldn't shake free of his memory. Something about it didn't seem right. Maybe it was just her reluctance to face the truth, but she feared something very bad had happened to Ryan and he was trying to shield her from it.

She had clung to that foolish hope for years, even pressuring her friend at the payroll office for information on his whereabouts. All Vivian had been able to tell her was that Ryan's address had been kept confidential for his entire career in the military, but she later learned he had resigned from the navy early last year. His official forwarding address was now in a tiny fishing village near San Diego.

Jenny could no longer delude herself. As a civilian, Ryan was completely free to contact her if he wished. San Diego was only a day's travel by train, and still she heard nothing from him.

"I have no plans for marriage at this time," she told Captain Soames. There had been no one else for her since Ryan, and too many men had let her down over the years.

Only Simon was different. She and Simon both knew what it was to be homeless and hungry. Since the day he took her under his wing when she was a nine-year-old street urchin, they had always looked out for each other.

The gritty world of San Francisco looked askance at a middle-aged man befriending a pretty young girl, so she'd taken to referring to Simon as her father from the very beginning. For all intents and purposes, Simon Bennett *was* her father, the only father she'd ever known. She even took his last name because "Bennett" sounded solid and respectable. He fed her when she was hungry, made sure she went to school every day, and consoled her when kids in the neighborhood taunted her because they knew where she came from. During the boom years, it was Simon who paid for her to attend nursing school.

The boom years were long over, and now Simon needed help. Last month his jewelry shop had been robbed. Thieves kicked in the plate glass window at the front of his shop and walked away with all the jewelry, including Simon's beloved assortment of pearls.

Simon had been collecting and selling pearls his entire life, but the theft left him broke. He didn't even have the money to replace the window and had to nail boards over the opening. Simon's landlord had warned he would be evicted if he couldn't replace the window within the week.

With no other options, Jenny had sold the watch Ryan gave her to buy the plate glass window. Guilt had tugged at her conscience when she laid the watch on the pawn shop counter. It had belonged to Ryan's father, a man who worked as a missionary in the Far East. Both of Ryan's parents had died before she met him, and she felt disloyal selling one of the few keepsakes he had from them.

She hardened her heart. If Ryan cared about his father's watch, he could have asked her for it. She owed Ryan Gallagher nothing and Simon everything.

The sale of Ryan's watch brought enough to install a new window, but it wasn't going to save Simon's shop. Jenny had been funneling all her spare money to help him restock the store, and it meant she had nothing left to help a boy who was quickly going blind.

She needed to play her ace card. When Captain Soames was first appointed to the Presidio, she'd read everything she could find about him. The details of their childhoods were different, but she and Captain Soames both shared the same hardscrabble core, and she knew exactly what it would take to persuade him.

"Your family emigrated from Ireland when you were a baby," she said. "You were one of nine children who grew up in the toughest ghetto of New York City. You didn't have a pair of shoes until you were eight years old. No one ever handed you anything. You joined the army at sixteen and your life got even tougher, but the army gave you the only thing you ever asked for. *A chance.* You labored, sweat, fought, and bled to get where you are . . . but you weren't blind, Captain Soames. You never would have had a fighting chance in this world if you had been blind."

Captain Soames glared at her, and she glared right back. This fight was too important to lose. She waited, counting her heartbeats while he shifted in his chair.

"Go tell Dr. Samuelson to put the boy's surgery on the schedule."

It felt like the sun rose inside her, radiant with light, heat, and hope. She didn't let a trace of it show on her face as she nodded.

"Thank you, sir."

Jenny usually met Vivian Perez for lunch at one o'clock each afternoon. There weren't many female employees at the Presidio, and Jenny and Vivian quickly bonded amidst the thousands of male soldiers stationed at the West Coast's foremost military base.

Instead of eating at the noisy mess hall, they took their lunch to a table outside on the quadrangle.

Jenny twirled a tin drinking cup between her palms. "The surgery for Skeeter's eyes will be in two weeks," she told Vivian. "I'm going to ask Simon to let the boy move in with him after the surgery, because the orphanage won't have the staffing to tend to him. Of course, I can only hope Simon won't be evicted before then."

She sighed as she unwrapped her chicken sandwich on a flaky croissant roll. She didn't have much appetite but needed her strength. Opening her sandwich, she ate the chicken from the middle and left the croissant untouched.

"What about Simon finding some kind of paid work?" Vivian asked as she tucked into her own sandwich.

It would be the easiest solution to their problem. Getting Simon a respectable job somewhere would be practical, efficient, and logical. Sadly, none of those adjectives could be applied to Simon Bennett.

"I would have better luck rerouting the path of the sun than getting Simon to behave logically," she said, unable to keep the trace of fondness from her voice. It was the erratic income Simon earned during her childhood that inspired Jenny to go into nursing. Nursing was a practical skill that would always be needed. People got sick in times of plenty and when the bottom dropped out of the economy. Hospitals could be depended on to pay their wages on time, and she appreciated the steady income.

She leaned her elbows on the table and let the breeze caress her face. She liked this spot because it carried the scent from a nearby patch of eucalyptus shrubs. It was a clean smell. Fresh and crisp. Sometimes she snipped a few twigs to take to her room.

"I wonder what that girl is doing?" Vivian asked, and Jenny followed her friend's gaze.

A few yards away, a little girl in a white smock tugged at a heavy stone bordering the rose garden. She couldn't have been more than three or four years old, and the rock was almost as big as she was. This didn't stop the girl from giving it her all, tugging with her weight.

The child seemed to be alone. Jenny doubted the girl could budge that rock, but it was best to be safe. She rose and approached the child, whose straight black hair had slipped free of its hair clips to obscure her face.

"Are you all alone out here?" Jenny asked.

The girl straightened. She was a beautiful child with distinctively Asian features. There were plenty of Chinese people in San Francisco, but Jenny rarely saw them at the Presidio.

"Papa told me to play here," the girl said in a lightly accented voice. Jenny wondered if Papa knew his daughter was wallowing in garden mulch while wearing a clean white frock.

"Come join us at the table until your father gets back," Jenny prompted, and the girl obediently followed the few steps to the table beneath the cottonwood tree. "Are you hungry? Would you like a bit of croissant?"

The girl looked confused as she studied the croissant. "Bread?" she asked.

"Yes, it's bread."

"Yes please, ma'am." The child swiped at her hair, and a barrette slipped even further, barely hanging on to her silky black strands.

"Come, let me fix your hair," Jenny said. "Your papa won't like it if you lose those pretty seed pearl barrettes."

There was quite an industry in mechanically grinding oyster shells to make seed pearls, so they weren't terribly expensive, but Simon would have a heart attack if he saw a child carelessly lose a pair of seed pearl hairpins while playing in the dirt. The child let Jenny finger-comb her hair, but it was a challenge to get the clips securely anchored in the slippery strands.

Her name was Lily, and once she began chattering, it was impossible to stop her. Lily told them she had two pet cats at home, one of which killed a jellyfish and brought it into their house, which made her papa laugh so hard he had tears on his face. Her papa owned an entire beach, and he had a fancy uniform that sometimes he wore and sometimes he didn't.

"Lily?" A man's voice called from base headquarters on the other side of the quad.

"Papa!" Lily hopped off the bench and went tearing across the quadrangle toward a tall man in a crisp, white naval uniform.

Jenny stared, not trusting her eyes. "Ryan?" she whispered.

He was too far away to tell, but the man reminded her of Ryan

Gallagher. Maybe it was just the navy uniform, when almost everyone else at the Presidio was in the army, but he looked so similar to Ryan it awakened a rush of bittersweet longing.

Without conscious thought she stood and started walking toward him. She'd only gone a few steps when the child reached him. The naval officer squatted down to scoop her up, tossing the girl into the air with a hearty laugh.

She knew that laugh, a golden tenor that came straight from the heart. It was him. It had to be. While she stood mute and motionless, the little girl looked over her father's shoulder and waved good-bye. The man followed his daughter's gaze and glanced back at Jenny.

He froze as if spellbound. There was no doubt.

Ryan Gallagher was back.

Before she could take another step, Ryan hoisted Lily higher into his arms, turned the other way, and set off toward the officers' quarters without a backward glance.

"Jenny?" Vivian asked. "What's going on?"

It took a while to find her breath. "That man reminds me of someone I once knew."

"Ryan Gallagher?" During her brief courtship, Jenny had breathlessly relayed all the details of her whirlwind romance to her friend. It had been painful and embarrassing when she had to tell Vivian that Ryan changed his mind and they wouldn't be getting married after all.

She didn't want to reopen that painful chapter and shook her head.

"He's nobody," she said simply.

2

Jenny arrived for her night shift at eight o'clock, fortified with a large mug of hot black coffee. Staying alert overnight was always a challenge, but there was something deeply fulfilling about taking care of people, and she liked it.

Actually, she loved it. She loved helping make the world a little more comfortable for men in desperate need of compassion. For the past two years she had been assigned to the convalescent ward for amputees. Newly arrived patients needed considerable help changing clothes and preparing for bed. Others had been here for months while learning balance skills and the use of prosthetic limbs. The ward had eighteen patients, with nine beds on each side of the room and a small nightstand, chair, and chest of drawers between each bed.

Although the Spanish-American War had ended in 1898, a rebellion of Filipino insurgents kept American troops on the islands to this day. Far more deaths had occurred in the rebellion than in the actual war, and a steady stream of casualties continued to arrive at the Presidio.

"Our favorite nurse," Ned Jacobsen said as she wheeled a metal cart holding the evening snack through the double doors and into the ward.

"You'd say that to anyone bringing you food," she said with a wink. Most of the men here were so bored they would flirt with a ham sandwich if it answered them back.

"Come on, Jenny, sit down and talk with us."

"Nurse Bennett, please," she said crisply.

"Hey, Nurse Bennett, if I figure out how to use this fancy wooden leg, are you gonna go dancing with me?"

"You can dance with Corporal Johnson. He keeps asking me the same question, so perhaps the two of you can practice together."

Howls of laughter greeted her comment, and the ribbing continued as she delivered cheese and crusty sourdough bread to the few men who wanted an evening snack. Then she began her real nursing duties. Two of the men needed help removing their prosthetic limbs and then changing into nightclothes. All of the amputees needed their wounds inspected for sign of infection. For the recent arrivals, she removed the bandages, cleaned the wounds, and applied a sanitizing ointment to the residual limb. Infection was the biggest danger for these men, and she checked them at the beginning and end of her shift.

Freddie Gibbs winced as she applied ointment. He'd been plagued by periodic skin breaks while adjusting to a new prosthetic limb that fit over his knee. After cleaning and covering the wound, she bent over to pick up a wad of discarded bandages from the bin beside his bed. One of the bandages looked off. Instead of normal splotches of dark blood, it contained traces of pale pink.

She flicked a glance to him. "Is this yours?"

Freddie shrugged, and she inspected it closer. The streaks were blood but heavily mixed with something. Probably saliva.

"Do you have a toothache?"

"It's nothing."

"Not if you're bleeding, it isn't." He'd had cheese during the evening snack but left the crusty bread untouched. "Shall I make an appointment for you to see the dentist tomorrow? If you're bleeding enough to stain a bandage, you should probably be checked out."

"I don't need to go to the dentist. It will go away on its own." He flashed a lightning-fast glance around the ward to see if anyone had overheard, for there was nothing worse for a soldier than being branded a coward. The best thing would be for her to make a joke of it.

"You faced down rats the size of dogs in the Philippines and fended off swarms of mosquitoes for months in the jungle. You endured an amputation by marine medics at a field hospital, not to mention the food on a transpacific voyage. Twice! The dentist is small-fry compared to all that."

Freddie broke into a laugh, cut short by a grimace. He lifted a hand to cup his left cheek. "Okay, make an appointment with the ivory butcher."

"Good man," she murmured with approval before moving on to the next patient.

As much as Jenny loathed the overnight shift, she loved every hour of caring for these men. There weren't many jobs where a woman was so needed, and it went well beyond the distribution of medicine and food. It was a moment of human compassion. A touch, a joke, a fleeting bit of empathy from another human being who understood. Being able to provide that care was what gave meaning to her life.

She continued her rounds, inspecting wounds and refilling everyone's water pitchers for the night, and then retreated to the small table near the door where she made notes of her observations.

It was still too early for most of the men to sleep, and a few started gossiping about a cannon race scheduled for later in the week. A visiting squadron from Fort Bryson was famous for their ability to shove a cannon across the parade field in record time, and the Presidio soldiers were eager to take them on. Most of Jenny's patients planned to observe the race. These men might be broken in body, but their minds were healthy, alive, and competitive.

She tried to ignore the talk as she entered her observations in the journal, but the gossip was lively this evening. Some of the men complained about special housing privileges just granted to a new officer on base. Jenny had worked here long enough to understand the simmering hostility enlisted men harbored toward the officers for everything from the cut of their uniforms to better pay. Nothing was more contentious than the better housing afforded to officers. Most of the enlisted men at the Presidio lived in cramped army barracks with communal facilities, while the officers lived with their families on a handsome street of Georgian brick houses.

"Why can't he have one of the old garrison apartments? The little girl doesn't take up much room. They don't need a whole house for one man and his kid."

Jenny paused. There were almost no children at the Presidio, and she wondered if they were talking about Ryan.

"I never saw him in Manila," one of the patients near the back of the room said. "I checked off every man coming off the troop transports at Manila Bay, and he wasn't there."

"Navy folks," another man snorted.

"You don't really think he was a deserter, do you?"

Freddie propped himself up on an elbow, and others leaned in to listen. "Ever since he got to the Presidio, General Dwyer has been treating him like a war hero or some kind of visiting royalty. He's not. I was in the Army's Eighth Corps, secretary to General Loman, and Loman couldn't stand him. He said that while we were sweating it out in the jungle, that Gallagher fellow was making a killing as a war profiteer."

26

Jenny froze. They *were* talking about Ryan! Her mind reeled, but Freddie hadn't stopped talking, and she cocked her head to listen.

"General Loman said Gallagher lived on a yacht in Tokyo Bay. Said he didn't do a lick of fighting during the whole war."

"There was a fine trade in smuggling contraband from Japan," another patient said. "I guess a navy salary wasn't good enough for him. He had to jump ship for Tokyo."

Jenny's palms began to sweat. She didn't even want to think it, but what they were saying could be true. Ryan was raised in Japan by his missionary parents. He spoke perfect Japanese, and Japan would be an easy place for him to escape to if the pressure of war got too intense in the Philippines.

Thousands of men deserted during the war. Flyers had been posted throughout the base and around the country, seeking news of deserters and promising rewards if any were caught. She cringed at the thought that Ryan could have been a deserter.

The grumbling among the men continued. Every man here had been seriously wounded, and sympathy for deserters was nonexistent.

"You don't really think he was a deserter, do you?" Sergeant Grigsby asked. "Just because no one saw him over there doesn't mean anything."

"Jack Taylor said he looked up the register of naval officers sent to the Philippines. Gallagher was assigned to the USS *Baltimore*, but the officers on the *Baltimore* said he jumped ship before it sailed for the Philippines. I don't think he was ever over there at all. And now here he is, meeting with the top army officers at the Presidio. If Gallagher was a deserter, they deserve to know what we know."

"All I've heard is idle gossip," Major Kinnear said in a voice laced with skepticism. Major Kinnear was the only officer in the ward, and the men tended to instinctively defer to his judgment. "Nurse Bennett, please bring me some writing paper and a pencil."

Good heavens, what was he planning? Her mouth went dry as she fetched a pad of paper for Major Kinnear, who propped it on his one good knee.

"Now then, let's hear your theories, and I'll record them all without prejudice," Major Kinnear said. "If they amount to any-thing more than idle speculation, I shall turn it over to General Dwyer for consideration of a court-martial."

Jenny sat dumbfounded at her table as incriminating details were put forth, mostly having to do with Ryan's absence from any official duties in the Philippines. Some suggested that he'd never even left the country and spent the entire war living the high life in San Francisco. Others said he deserted after the first difficult battle at Quingua.

The bell mounted on the wall behind Jenny's table rang. It was a summons from the nurse in the postoperative ward. Each of the wards had only a single nurse during the overnight hours, and if someone needed an extra pair of hands, the system of bells was designed to summon another nurse. Jenny had just been called, and it might be urgent.

She stood but hesitated in the doorway. Listening to these ru-mors about Ryan was torture, but she needed to hear them. Even now, the scratching of Major Kinnear's pencil recorded detail after detail that might send Ryan before a court-martial.

Oh, Ryan, what have you done?

Feeling protective of Ryan was foolish, but from the moment she'd met him, he seemed too gentle to be much of a warrior. He had poet's eyes. He was compassionate and kind . . . the sort who might crack under the rigor of jungle warfare.

The bell dinged again, and a few men turned to look at her, probably wondering why she lingered.

"I'll be back soon," she said as she reluctantly tore herself away and scurried down the darkened verandah corridor toward the postoperative ward.

A patient recovering from an appendectomy had torn his stiches after falling out of bed, and Nurse Tilden needed help. Jenny helped sanitize the equipment as Nurse Tilden snipped out a few of the old sutures. The patient was sweating and sore by the time the job was complete, and Jenny ran for some ice chips to help cool him down.

An hour later, she was free to leave. She carried the soiled bandages to the laundry before heading to the washroom, where she scrubbed her hands with harsh soap and used a stiff brush to scour beneath her nails. Most people hated the strong lye soap used in the hospital, but Jenny welcomed the clean scent and even the tingle on her hands. It let her know she was getting ruthlessly clean and sanitized.

All was quiet in her ward when she returned. Most of the men slept, and as always when returning from a call, she walked down the aisle to silently inspect for any signs of distress.

Major Kinnear was fast asleep, the folded piece of paper on his stomach, held down by his heavy hand. He was snoring.

She swallowed hard, desperately wanting to get her hands on that piece of paper, but she sensed Corporal McAllister watching her from across the ward. He'd lost both legs above the knee, and the pain always made sleep difficult for him. A book was propped in his lap, the light of a single electric bulb burning softly on his bedside table.

She sat at her desk to document her brief foray into the postoperative ward, all the while thinking about how she could get the note from beneath the sleeping major's hand. Bellyaching from enlisted soldiers amounted to little more than idle gossip, but the note in Major Kinnear's hand was different. Anything reported by an officer would be taken seriously.

She let out a sigh. Why was she so worried about Ryan Gallagher? Ryan cared nothing for her, or he would have tried to contact her after resigning his commission. At the very least, he could have contacted her during the past *week*. She'd heard enough from the gossip tonight to know he'd been at the Presidio for several days.

Well, at least she no longer had to wonder why Ryan had abandoned her so abruptly. Lily was a beautiful little girl who clearly adored her father. Or maybe she wasn't really his daughter. Could Ryan have found an orphaned child in need of care and brought her home with him? It was a tempting thought, but Lily's Asian features had a softness that indicated Anglo blood as well. If Lily was four, it meant she'd been conceived five years ago, around the time Ryan sent the letter severing all contact with her despite their breathless avowals of love.

And she *did* love him during that idyllic spring. She fell for Ryan fast and hard, even though he'd been deathly ill when they first met. The USS *Baltimore* had arrived in port with twenty-three sailors suffering from typhoid. Ryan was placed in the ward she tended. It was six years ago, but she remembered the first words they ever exchanged. She had been restocking the medicine cabinet when he called out from the opposite side of the ward.

"Nurse? Quickly, I need help."

She recognized that tone. By the time she raced to his side with a basin, he'd already thrown up all over himself. He collapsed back onto the cot, covering his face with a trembling hand.

"I'm so sorry," he said.

"My fault, not yours." She tugged the soiled bedsheet away, quickly folding the clean ends over the worst of the mess and rolling it into a ball.

"Truly . . . I'm so sorry." His face was stamped with mortification, a hand shielding his eyes. She tried to tug his hand away so she could get him out of the sopping nightshirt, but he resisted.

"You shouldn't have to do this," he said, struggling to sit up.

"It's my job, Lieutenant. Nothing I haven't done plenty of times before, especially since the *Baltimore* arrived. You sailors must have been miserable."

The effort to sit up sapped his energy, and he collapsed back to the mattress, weak and panting. "Nothing compares with the misery I feel at this exact moment."

Despite his pallor, he was a handsome man with blond hair and warm brown eyes. But such embarrassment! He kept his face averted from her, as though too mortified to be seen.

She sat in the bedside chair and leaned in close so the other patients couldn't overhear. He still wouldn't look at her, so she spoke softly into his ear.

"I puked all over myself on my first day at a new school," she whispered. His head swiveled on the pillow, and she almost laughed at the astonishment in his eyes. "If a nine-year-old girl could handle the embarrassment, you can too, sailor. Arms up! I need you out of that nightshirt."

He complied. As she helped him sit upright, he battled a smile, and she was grateful her childhood humiliation made this moment a little easier for him. Nothing about her childhood had been easy, and the puking incident at school was mild compared to most of it.

Within five minutes, she had Lieutenant Gallagher sponged down, changed into a clean nightshirt, and in a wheelchair so she could push him to a bed with clean sheets. He leaned heavily on her as she helped him out of the chair and into bed. He looked exhausted from that ten-yard journey, lying weakly on the mattress and watching her tug the sheets to cover him.

"Why did you become a nurse?" he asked.

"It pays well."

He seemed surprised by her answer. "That seems a little cold."

"Says a man who's obviously never been cold or hungry."

"True enough," he admitted with a weak laugh. "But really . . . why did you become a nurse? I've seen the way you work with the patients, and you're different from the other nurses. I can't put my finger on it. So I was wondering what made you choose nursing."

Because it was respectable work. No matter how hard or thankless, nursing was an honorable profession that helped blot out memories of earlier years.

She schooled her face into a calm mask. "I told you. It pays well."

Lieutenant Gallagher didn't look convinced. He lay on the bed, pale and exhausted, but his gaze still scrutinized her, as though trying to put the pieces of a puzzle together. As she was leaving, he grabbed her hand. "Again . . . I'm truly sorry about the mess."

"Relax, sailor. I'm the toughest nurse you'll ever meet."

She was probably the toughest nurse in the entire nation. In a profession filled with modest, well-brought-up young ladies, Jenny was different. It was amazing how a little soap and a crisp, starched nurse's uniform could disguise the pieces of her life she wanted hidden.

It was a week before Ryan could leave bed, then another two weeks in a different ward while he regained his strength. It was then that Jenny began joining him on the terrace overlooking the bay as schooners pulled in and out of port. She had never been outside San Francisco's city limits but was enchanted by the stories Ryan told of his life. It sounded like it came straight from the pages of a novel by Rudyard Kipling, but Ryan was never boastful or arrogant. He simply relayed the facts with a soft-spoken humor she was coming to adore. Most of Ryan's childhood had been spent in various rural villages in Japan, following his missionary parents from post to post. He was seventeen years old before he set foot in the United States in order to attend the Naval Academy.

"Do you ever want to go back to Japan?" she'd once asked him.

He paused, gazing into the distance where the sea merged with the sky. If one were to travel due west beyond the horizon, the next landfall would be the rocky coasts of Japan, and Ryan's thousand-mile stare seemed to sense that.

"It's a beautiful country," he finally said. "But no. I have no desire to ever return to Japan." He shook off the momentary disquiet and brightened. "I'd rather learn about you. Tell me everything."

Her life before Simon wasn't worth revisiting, so she skipped to the only part she was willing to talk about. "My father has a jewelry store," she said. When Ryan learned that Simon lived only a few miles from the Presidio, he wanted to meet him.

Jenny had been attracted to Ryan when they walked to Simon's shop in the Latin Quarter, but by the time they walked out, she was in love.

Simon was an eccentric old man who'd always harbored an irrational love of pearls. He could ramble on endlessly about the majesty of pearls, and he'd been in fine form that afternoon.

"The pearl is considered a divine gift with magical healing properties," Simon said as he showed Ryan a pearl ring surrounded by delicate gold filigree. "A grand Austrian empress once fell mysteriously ill," he reported in a hushed voice. "None of the doctors or royal advisers could diagnose her problem, and it seemed the empress was on the verge of dying. Then her lady-in-waiting said it was because the pearls the empress wore around her neck were homesick for the ocean and their grief caused the illness. The empress ordered the pearls carried to the Aegean Sea and tossed into the warm, salty waters. She miraculously recovered at the same hour the pearls were returned to the sea."

"And you believe this?" Ryan asked. Jenny held her breath. She was fiercely protective of Simon and didn't want anyone laughing at his whimsical fantasies, but there was no mockery in Ryan's voice. Quite the opposite—he seemed charmed and curious as he listened to Simon's story.

"If it's not true, it *ought* to be true," Simon proclaimed.

Ryan nodded, staring at the pearl ring as though enchanted. "I agree. There is magic and mystery in a pearl. It's a thing of great beauty, but that beauty came at a cost. It was the oyster's reaction to pain that caused this buildup of calcium carbonate burnished into a luminous masterpiece of nature."

It was that day that Jenny knew she loved him. Ryan was intelligent and educated, but he talked about pearl mythology with as much wistful admiration as Simon.

That had been six years ago. It was hard to reconcile that kindhearted man with the person who ignored her in the quadrangle that afternoon.

She glanced at Major Kinnear, whose hand hadn't budged from the note he'd written. She couldn't make a grab for it until every man in the ward was asleep, but the reading lamp was still on beside Corporal McAllister, who finally seemed to be drifting off. His eyes were closed, and the book still clutched in his hand tilted at a haphazard angle.

She treaded soundlessly toward Corporal McAllister, monitoring his breathing as she clicked off the bedside lamp. He didn't stir. She lifted the book from his hands, marked his place with the ribbon, and set it on his table without a sound.

Everyone was asleep. It was now or never.

She could do this. She'd been trained in picking pockets and covering her tracks since she was a toddler. Getting that letter would be child's play.

There was no change in the rhythmic snores from Major Kinnear as she approached his bedside. She held her breath as she tugged the edge of the note, wiggling it gently from beneath his hand. Just as she got it free, Major Kinnear coughed, shifted, and rolled onto his side.

She froze, the note clutched in her hand. If anyone in the ward awakened, she would simply set the note on the bedside table, just as she had done with Corporal McAllister's book.

No one stirred. She carried the note back to her desk, still barely able to breathe as she surveyed her patients. If she was caught reading this note, it would be bad. She could lose her job. Nurses had to be faultless in both private and professional life. Anything that cast aspersions on her moral character could ban her from the profession for life.

Enough! Whatever happened, she would weather the storm and come out standing tall. She'd been doing it her whole life. She winced at the soft crinkling of the paper as she opened the note. Writing filled both sides. She skimmed it quickly. Most of it was contradictory nonsense, clearly just unsubstantiated rumors from sailors who resented a new officer on base.

But Major Kinnear had marked two spots with stars. One was the assertion that Ryan had been seen in civilian clothes at the marketplace in Manila and was suspected of war profiteering by smuggling goods from Japan. The other was the statement from General Loman's former secretary, stating that the general had reason to believe Lieutenant Gallagher had deserted and fled to Japan. Both sounded pretty bad.

She folded the note, feeling sick at the implications. Desertion was still rampant overseas, and if an officer was suspected of it, the military would have no choice but to make an example of him. She rose silently and returned the note to Major Kinnear's bedside table, wishing she hadn't felt so protective of Ryan from the instant she met him.

She was always friendly with her patients, but something about Ryan had slipped beneath the wall of reserve that guarded her heart. He had unlocked it with his smile. In her world of rough and tumble soldiers, he was quiet and gallant. Tender, even.

It was why she called him Galahad. It had slipped out while gently teasing him about the way he blushed when one of the men told a bawdy story about the dance hall girls down by the docks.

"Don't be so bashful, Galahad," she had joked. She said it quietly, but the patient in the neighboring bed heard it and exploded with laughter.

"Yo, Galahad!" the sailor chortled. "Quit taking up all of Nurse Bennett's time. It's going to tarnish your halo."

All the sailors from the *Baltimore* agreed it was a perfect nickname and started calling Ryan "Galahad." She felt bad and tried to rein it in, but Ryan shrugged it off with a resigned smile. "I've been called a lot worse," he said.

All that seemed like a long time ago, but she couldn't stop feeling protective of him. Despite the terse good-bye letter. Despite the little girl. It would be easy to warn Ryan about what was going on, but why should she risk her career for a man who betrayed her?

She glared at the letter on Major Kinnear's bedside table. Ryan didn't deserve her compassion, and she wished to the marrow of her bones she could extinguish these protective feelings for him, but that would be like trying to stop the tide from rolling in. The memories of her sunlit, halcyon days with Ryan were too precious. She would never regret having known him.

She had only one regret in her life, but it was a terrible one. Jenny would give anything if she could change what happened the night she met the sailor with the scar splitting his left eyebrow. To this day, he haunted her dreams. She didn't want any more regrets like that weighing on her conscience. Life was too short to be tormented by guilt and regret.

Tomorrow morning she would go warn Ryan.

❧

Jenny set off for the officers' quarters as soon as the morning attendant arrived to take over nursing duties. Fog still shrouded the base, and the dampness made the morning seem even colder. At this hour, only she and a few birds were awake. Moving past the barracks of the enlisted men, she arrived at the tidy row of officer townhouses clustered along the hillside. They were pristine, with glossy white paint on the gingerbread columns lining the front porches. The hedges were flawlessly manicured, and their windows sparkled in the early morning light.

Most of the houses had placards with the officer's name and rank nailed to the porch railings, but the houses near the end of the row were reserved for visiting officers. How was she going to know which was Ryan's?

She kept trudging up the hill, the houses looking tidy and uniform as she passed them. It was hard to look at such beautiful symmetry and not imagine that the people inside must be very happy.

She stopped and stared in astonishment. The house at the end of the row had eggs smashed across the front door and windows. Egg yolk streaked down the glass, and broken shells littered the porch.

Well, now she knew where Ryan lived.

Obviously, other soldiers at the Presidio had heard the rumors about Ryan and let him know what they thought of a deserter. Who could have done such a thing? No officer would risk his career over such a reckless act, and none of her patients had been here last night. Civilian employees probably didn't care enough to risk their jobs.

Unless that civilian employee once fancied herself in love with a man who ran off and dallied with another woman.

Jenny pushed the thought from her mind and mounted the steps, surveying the damage. The splotches of yolk on the front door were still wet, and she had to step around eggshells to knock.

Ryan himself answered the door, still wearing his pajamas and a robe. She'd forgotten how handsome he was. His hair was lighter than she remembered, sun-streaked and longer than it had been when she knew him before. A fleeting look of surprise crossed his face before it was masked.

"Can I help you, ma'am?"

She narrowed her eyes, uncertain if she should burst into laughter or scoop up some of the still-dripping eggs to hurl at him. He waited politely, no sign of recognition on his face.

"Do you really intend to stand there and pretend you don't know me?" she demanded.

His breath left him in a gust, and there it was, the flush on his cheeks that happened whenever he was nervous or embarrassed. He swallowed hard, but it took a while before he met her gaze.

"Of course not. How are you, Jenny?"

"I'm fine. I thought it was you yesterday on the quadrangle. Am I so terrifying you couldn't even speak to me?"

"A little bit, yes," he admitted with a reluctant grimace. Whatever he was going to say next got cut off as he noticed the eggs splattered against the door and front window. Obviously he hadn't known about the egging until just now. His brows lowered in annoyance, but he didn't seem all that surprised as he looked at her.

"I didn't do it," she said quickly.

"I didn't think you had. Subterfuge isn't your style."

As he scanned the damage, he stiffened at the sight of a man coming out of the house next door, fastening the buttons on his captain's uniform. Jenny tried not to cringe. She still wore her nurse's uniform, and it didn't look good to be chatting with a man who wore nothing but pajamas, a bathrobe, and bare feet.

The officer looked at them both curiously. "Good morning, Lieutenant Gallagher."

"Captain Ainsworth," Ryan said with a curt nod but made no attempt to introduce Jenny, for which she was grateful.

The captain walked down the steps of his porch and scooped up the morning newspaper that had already been delivered. He loitered on the walkway as he scanned the first page, and Jenny turned impatiently back to Ryan. She hadn't spoken to him in six years, and she had questions that she was helpless to restrain.

"Why didn't you tell me you had returned to California?" she asked. "I thought you would have gone back to Washington, DC, after the war."

His brows lowered and he looked confused. "Why would I live in Washington?"

"It's where you lived for three years after you graduated from college."

"I never lived in Washington."

She blinked, for it was a bold-faced lie. Of course he had lived in Washington! He lived in an apartment right outside the Naval Research Laboratory in the middle of the city. He worked there for three years. She'd been charmed by his stories of visiting the Smithsonian and climbing all the way to the top of the Washington Monument even though it was hot and stifling inside the narrow stairwell.

Eggshells crunched beneath her shoes as she stepped closer. He took a step back, but she didn't let up. "You never worked at the Naval Research Laboratory?" she demanded.

"No."

This couldn't be happening. The man standing before her was Ryan but *not* Ryan at the same time. The Ryan she remembered was kind and tender, not this man who couldn't look her in the eye. It was such a shock to everything she believed that it made her light-headed and confused.

"You never lived in Washington and had an apartment on Danbury Street."

"I already told you. I never lived in Washington."

She swallowed hard, trying to get her bearings. She lowered her voice to an impassioned whisper and used words she knew would cut. "And I never lay on the sand beside a man I adored, gazing up at the cloud formations and dreaming about our future. I never heard that man say I was the only girl he ever felt comfortable with. And I never—even in my wildest fantasies—imagined that man would look me in the face and lie through his teeth."

Only the tiniest flinch indicated he heard her at all, but he recovered quickly, the muscles in his face smoothing out with a look of casual indifference.

"Good-bye, Ryan."

3

Ryan's morning encounter with Jenny haunted him the rest of the day. Nothing about the past six years had been easy, but lying to Jenny was near the top on his list of regrets. Throughout a day crammed with tense meetings, training sessions, and miles of governmental red tape, the memory of Jenny's face constantly intruded, tugging at his conscience.

She looked the same . . . and yet entirely different. Her shiny, dark hair and tilted eyes were exactly as he remembered. She had a heart-shaped face and a smile that lit her whole being. Jenny was still physically beautiful, but he'd never seen the tense, guarded edge she'd showed this morning as she grilled him on his front porch. That was new. A piece of him mourned the loss of the sparkling, wholesome girl he loved so well, but his actions over the past six years had effectively put that woman out of his reach forever. After returning to California he made no attempt to contact her, for what he'd done in Japan was unforgivable. He'd assumed she would be married by now, but none of the nurses were allowed to be married, so she must still be on her own.

The workday was over, and now it was time to be a father. Lily always had difficulty sleeping in a new environment, and tonight was no exception. Ryan held her on his lap in her darkened bedroom, the kerosene lantern turned low, just enough for him to read the haiku poems that usually lulled her to sleep.

He read in Japanese, and Lily's gaze followed his finger as he dragged it across the *kanji* characters. Perhaps she would absorb a little of the Japanese writing system, but he doubted he would teach her. God willing, they would never go back to Japan, but he couldn't be certain. He spoke to Lily in Japanese for an hour every day in case they might someday be forced to return.

He smiled a little as Lily's head drooped and her breathing slowed. He didn't stop reading, as it always took several tries for Lily to finally settle down. It was nearing midnight, and she'd gotten out of bed twice already. Perhaps this third attempt would be the charm.

Not that he minded the nightly ritual, for these quiet moments with Lily were the best part of his day. After he was certain she'd fallen into a full sleep, he carefully lifted her off his lap. As he settled her onto the mattress, an earsplitting crash sounded from downstairs, followed by a string of curses that let him know Finn had arrived home.

Lily started crying.

"Shhhh," he murmured, shooting a glare at the closed bedroom door. Finn was continuing to be a problem. Ryan pulled the covers over Lily, which made her cry harder.

"Don't cry, princess. I'm going downstairs for a few minutes, then I'll be right back."

Lily raised her arms in the universal demand to be picked up. He pushed them down and tucked them under the blankets.

"Stay here, sweet pea."

A wail of grief erupted as he left, but she didn't try to follow. Sweet Lily. She was an obedient child and would stay in bed, which was good, because he didn't want her around Finn at a time like this.

As he suspected, Finn lay sprawled on the floor of the parlor. His clothes were disheveled and his too-long dark hair obscured most of his face except for the sheepish grin. A fake conquistador's helmet dangled from his hand.

"I brought you this," Finn said, trying to hold out the helmet, but it slipped to the floor with a noisy clang. Upstairs another wail of despair came from Lily.

"My daughter is trying to sleep," Ryan said tightly.

"I'm sorry, I keep forgetting," Finn said, looking genuinely contrite. "I would never do anything to hurt that girl. I love Lily. I love *you*. Heck, I love the entire human race. Are humans a race or a species? I can never keep that straight."

Finn rolled onto all fours and tried to stand, but Ryan doubted it would go well. He rushed to prop his shoulder beneath Finn's arm and guided him to the kitchen table, then poured a tall glass of water to start countering the effects of a night of carousing. He set the glass before Finn and took a good look at the younger man's face. Finn's pupils looked like pinpoints.

"Have you been smoking opium?"

Finn held up two fingers pinched together. "Just a tiny bit. The opium dens in San Francisco are world famous. It wouldn't be right not to sample the teensiest bit while I'm in town. I love San Francisco. I love the people here. And the *women,*" he roared. "I love the women here!"

"Quiet. My daughter is sleeping."

Finn gave a shamefaced smile. "Sorry, my friend." He took several gulps from the glass of water, then set it down hard.

"Drain it," Ryan ordered. "When you finish that one, I'll have another for you." He and Finn had a long day of training tomorrow, and he didn't want to do it with a man groggy from a hangover. To his relief, Finn drank both glasses of water and seemed to settle down a bit.

"Our day begins at seven o'clock tomorrow morning," Ryan said. "After a morning of study, we are heading to the bay to practice sailing maneuvers."

"Again?" Finn pressed. "I know how to sail a boat. Why do we have to keep doing it over and over?"

"You won't be accepted into the Tokyo Regatta Club unless you are a master sailor. I don't care what kind of hangover you have tomorrow morning. At seven o'clock you are to be dressed and ready to learn."

"Aye aye, sir," Finn said, nearly poking his own eye out with a clumsy salute.

❧

The next morning Ryan dragged Finn from bed early. Lily and the housekeeper were still asleep, which was good, because he wanted no distractions during his talk with Finn. He set a cup of strong black coffee before the younger man.

"You promised you would quit visiting Maiden Lane," Ryan said. The ironically named street was infamous for its gambling cribs, cathouses, and opium dens.

Finn rolled his eyes as he sucked down a mouthful of coffee. "I haven't been out all week. You can't expect me to live like a monk."

"Look, you have a challenging assignment ahead of you. I need to know if you can do the job. If you're not up for it, I need to know now."

"I told you. I can do anything," Finn assured him.

"Not if you're drunk or strung out on opium. This work is going to be dangerous. If you're having second thoughts, I need to know. It's not too late to back out. We can train someone else."

Ryan clenched his fists beneath the table, sick at the possibility that Finn might back out. If Finn couldn't do this job, the odds were strong that Ryan would be sent in Finn's place. An avalanche of dread loomed at the prospect of returning to Japan, the country where he'd been born and raised.

The rural villages of Japan were a tough place for a white child, where local children viciously bullied anyone who was different. His missionary parents told him to forgive the children, that they didn't know any better. Ryan forgave them, but it didn't ease his loneliness. Growing up, he read novels by Mark Twain and tried to imagine what it would be like to sail on the Mississippi, to play American baseball, to fight for freedom alongside the Sons of Liberty. America was a country he had never seen, but in his boyhood imagination, it assumed a mythical status, as captivating as Camelot or Xanadu.

His parents promised he could go to America for college, and when he was seventeen, he finally set foot in the country he'd always loved but never seen. He arrived at the U.S. Naval Academy wide-eyed and eager to embrace his homeland. Those four years of college were the happiest of his life. He made immediate friends with other students who automatically accepted him even though he was a little different. In America, quirks and individualism were celebrated. In Japan, the nail that stuck up was hammered down.

Within a few months of arriving at college, Ryan was approached by an officer from the Military Information Division, a shadowy organization formed ten years earlier when the government realized they had no centralized agency for collecting intelligence about foreign countries. Although officially a branch of the army, the MID quickly spotted the arrival of a young midshipman at the Naval Academy who spoke perfect Japanese and understood the culture of an island nation traditionally closed to outsiders. They needed an agent in Japan more than another naval officer, and Ryan was recruited into the MID. While the other students took classes in engineering and naval warfare, Ryan was ordered to study aquaculture and marine life. He didn't understand why, but his commanding officers ordered it, and since he had a natural love of the sea, he was happy to comply.

He did everything the MID asked of him. As soon as he graduated from the Naval Academy, he was commissioned an officer and began working for the navy. For a few years he worked in marine research and then served a stint on the USS *Baltimore*. When the war broke out, the MID sent him to Japan as an undercover agent. He didn't want to go, but he took his oath to defend and protect the Constitution seriously, even though it meant leaving the country he so desperately loved. What was supposed to be a one-year mission in Japan turned into a permanent assignment. He'd believed it was going to last a lifetime, but it ended after only six years when the situation with Lily became unbearable.

Last autumn he'd taken Lily to a park in Tokyo to feed the ducks. He stepped away for a moment to buy more food for the ducks, and by the time he returned, a group of children had surrounded Lily. They pelted her with feed corn and taunted her, calling her a *gaijin*. It was the slur for anyone who was not Japanese. Lily had been frightened and didn't understand why she was being ridiculed, but that wouldn't last. Soon she would realize that her American blood made her different, and she would wither beneath the merciless attacks. Ryan had experienced it himself and knew exactly what Lily could expect.

He and Lily returned to California within the month. He hoped to stay in America permanently, but it wasn't his choice. Unless he could get Finn to pass muster with the MID, Ryan and Lily would end up on a ship back to Japan.

Finn Breckenridge was one of the few Americans who spoke fluent Japanese, but that was only the first of many requirements for the overseas assignment. Most important was the ability to be alert, careful, and observant. Finn was smart and good-natured, but he showed no sign of the rigid discipline necessary to operate within the Japanese cultural elite. Although Japanese children could be cruel to outsiders, Japanese adults were wildly curious of foreigners who visited their country and were especially impressed by those who spoke their language. If that visitor was intelligent and respectful, the doors to the universities and social clubs were open to them, but they would slam shut quickly if a foot was placed wrong. The customs were complex and strictly observed.

Ryan set two bowls on the table, one of steamed rice and the other fermented soybeans. A traditional Japanese breakfast. Finn picked up a pair of chopsticks and lifted a chunk of rice to his mouth.

"On a plate, Finn." Ryan tried not to let annoyance into his voice, but it was getting frustrating. Whenever Finn was hungover, he made stupid mistakes like eating out of a communal bowl. That would be enough to get him booted out of the Tokyo Regatta Club.

Finn reached for a plate and assembled the ingredients in the proper order.

"Well?" Ryan asked. "Are you going to straighten up?"

"I'm already perfectly straight," Finn said. He twirled a chopstick through all five fingers of one hand with stunning dexterity, tossed it in the air, and caught it with his other hand. "Trust me," he said with a rakish smile.

That was the problem. Ryan didn't trust Finn, and he had no backup plan should this experiment fail.

4

Was she dreaming? Hunger clawed at Jenny, but she hadn't been hungry since she was a very young child. She hid behind the trash cans, watching the men sprawled on a bench outside the saloon as they ate warm pretzels that smelled so good she was tempted to reach out and snatch one. She'd been watching these men from her hiding place long enough to know they'd been kicked out of the saloon because they couldn't pay for the beer they'd been guzzling all night. Now one of the sailors coaxed a parrot to perform tricks, and his drunken friends roared with laughter.

Jenny drew closer to watch, and the sailor noticed her. A scar split one of his eyebrows, but he didn't seem scary. He had a round, freckled face that looked friendly. If she had an older brother, she'd want him to look exactly like that.

Surprise lit his eyes when he saw her. It was past midnight and few children were out on the streets this late, but he recovered quickly.

"Hey, kid, have you ever seen a parrot wave hello?"

She hadn't, and she moved closer, her heart pounding. A lot depended on the next few minutes. . . .

Jenny snapped awake. Good heavens, she'd fallen asleep at her desk! She glanced around the ward, hoping none of her patients noticed her sleeping on the job, but all the men still slumbered.

She relaxed a fraction, even though her heart still raced from the dream. She ought to be used to it by now, for this nightmare haunted her often. At first she'd tried to stuff the memories away, but it wasn't working. Two years ago, she decided the only way to exorcise this nightmare would be to find the sailor with the scar. It was time to place another advertisement in the newspaper.

As soon as she got off work, she rode the cable car to Fifth Street. Clinging to a brass pole as the trolley lugged her up the cobblestone street, she wished this day was already over. She loathed her regular visits to the offices of the *San Francisco Examiner,* but this wasn't a chore she could hire someone else to do. Some secrets couldn't be shared.

Would this latest advertisement yield any results? She'd been searching for two years but had no leads. She climbed to the fourth floor of the *Examiner* building, where the advertising office occupied an oversized room full of accountants and typesetters. She strode to the clerk who handled the classified advertisements. Roy Tolland had a pencil-thin mustache and overly curious eyes. He smirked as she approached.

"Still looking for your missing sailor?"

"Here is the wording I would like to use," she said primly. She passed a small note card with her newly worded advertisement. She changed the message every few months, hoping that a new wording or specific details might finally yield results.

She tensed as Roy made a great show of adjusting his spectacles and reading her advertisement in a voice loud enough to be heard by everyone in the office.

"In search of Oliver, a sailor with a scar splitting his left eyebrow, who once owned a pet parrot. The first person who provides me with the name of Oliver's parrot, plus news of Oliver's current location, shall receive a reward of two hundred dollars."

Over the years, countless people had contacted her in hope of winning that reward. They had all been liars, but anyone who knew the parrot's name was Knickerbocker could be trusted. Perhaps even Oliver himself would come forward. She alternately hoped and dreaded the day she might come face to face with him again.

"*Oliver,*" Roy said with delight. "So that is the name of your mysterious lost lover. Oliver!"

It was easier to let Mr. Tolland believe that Oliver was a lover than tell him the truth. To this day, the sailor with the scar was Jenny's terrible secret, the one she had never revealed to anyone, not even Simon. Certainly she hadn't breathed a word of him to Ryan.

"Just print the ad, Mr. Tolland." She slid the proper amount of coins across the desk, then held out her hand. "A receipt, please."

Mr. Tolland had never tried to cheat her in the past, but demanding a receipt ensured he wouldn't in the future.

"Maybe you wouldn't be so lonely for your lost sailor if you had the companionship of a real flesh-and-blood man," Mr. Tolland suggested. "We could go out for a drink and a show sometime."

Jenny composed her face into a pleasant mask. "You suggested the same thing the last time I was here. Do you remember what I told you?"

"You said no, but maybe you've changed your mind."

Mr. Tolland's offer was as tempting as a freshly dug grave, especially since he had a photograph of his wife and two children on the corner of his desk.

"Very possible," she said crisply. "It's also possible that your wife won't suspect a thing when her husband comes home late. After all, she will probably tell herself he's working extra hours to ensure the little ones can have new shoes. But at the back of her mind, she fears he might be knocking back liquor with a floozy on Maiden Lane.

She fears having her heart broken into tiny shards that can never really be healed. She fears he might contract venereal disease and doesn't want to get too close to him for fear she will smell another woman on him. She worries he'll put up a fuss if she complains, so she pretends to know nothing even as her skin crawls when he reaches to kiss her, knowing where that mouth has been and wondering how she can stomach his touch."

Jenny closed the top of her reticule and adjusted her collar. "But you're right. Perhaps someday I will change my mind. Good day, Mr. Tolland."

Instead of heading straight to the streetcar stop, Jenny walked behind the building, where the newsboys congregated. Skeeter Jones ought to be there soon. Newsboys arrived early to pick up stacks of newspapers, which they had to personally buy, then sold them for five cents. The strength of their lungs and legs determined how many papers they could sell, and competition was fierce. Newsboys were not reimbursed for the papers they did not sell, and Skeeter often lost money, for failing eyesight made it hard for him to be nimble on his feet. Frankly, Jenny hoped that after his eyesight was repaired he might be allowed to go to school, where any bright twelve-year-old boy should be.

The moment she spotted Skeeter, she pulled him aside to relay the good news about the upcoming eye surgery. He desperately wanted this operation, but he didn't seem as thrilled as she'd expected.

"Will it hurt?" His voice was thin with fear. What intelligent human being wouldn't be terrified of having his eyes operated upon?

"You won't feel a thing during the procedure because you will be deeply asleep. But yes, your eyes will hurt for a few days after the procedure."

He swallowed hard. "That's okay. I don't mind." But he was

shaking as he said it, and she could see the terror in his swollen eyes. She hunkered down so she could be on eye level with him.

"I'll be saying prayers for you the whole time," she whispered. "You're a tough boy, and between the two of us, we're going to get this done, okay?"

He swallowed hard but didn't look very convinced.

She squeezed his hand harder. "I know you're afraid, but there are going to be times in life when you have to stand up to fear, because fear kills more dreams than anything else in the world. Fear kills hope. Fear can paralyze people. Don't let fear make you blind. I am the toughest nurse in the world, and I'll be right there fighting for you. Do we have a deal?"

A glimmer of a smile tilted his lips as he nodded. It was enough.

❦

Vivian couldn't wait to fill Jenny in on the gossip about Ryan when they met for dinner.

"He's been sailing for the past four afternoons down at East Beach," Vivian told her as they headed toward the mess hall. "Daisy Perkins said he's with some civilian no one has ever seen before. They've been racing schooners, and Daisy has been making a point to keep an eye on them when they come off the sea each afternoon. Apparently it's a fine view."

Jenny could imagine. Ryan had always cut a dashing figure, tall and lean with flawless posture that made it hard not to admire him. She had no idea who the civilian was, but the Presidio was not a recreational facility that encouraged leisure sailing among its officers. Was it any wonder Ryan was earning a bad reputation?

She never got around to warning him about the possibility of a court-martial the other day. She'd been too incensed by his lies and had completely forgotten to warn him before she stormed away.

He didn't deserve her sympathy, but she had been the recipient of plenty of kindness she didn't deserve either.

"You run ahead," she told Vivian. "I think I'll head down to the marina."

"To enjoy the view?" her friend asked knowingly.

"Yes. To enjoy the view."

The breeze was fresh as Jenny headed toward the shore. She often came here to watch boats coming in and out of the bay. A few wooden tables and benches had been placed along the bluff overlooking the marina, and Jenny sank onto one of the benches, the wood dry and weathered from the relentless winds.

It didn't take long to spot Ryan and his mysterious companion out on the water. Their sailboat skimmed across the surface of the bay, both sails filled with wind. The two men leaned against the tilt of the boat, looking fit and athletic as their entire bodies were thrown into the effort to keep the boat slicing through the water at a terrific speed.

Yes, the view was indeed fine from here.

Ryan's was the only leisure boat in the bay that afternoon. There were two fishing trawlers hauling in the day's catch and a crab boat. A mighty passenger ship moved slowly toward the port of San Francisco, and farther up the beach a squadron of soldiers practiced marine landings. Only Ryan and his friend appeared to be enjoying the day.

Good heavens, his sailboat was about to tip over. It tilted at an alarming angle while Ryan and his companion leaned out in the opposite direction, dangling by ropes that let them use their weight to counterbalance the boat, which seemed to defy gravity as it sliced through the water. She let out a sigh of relief as the boat righted itself and both men scrambled to adjust the sails.

It took a while for Ryan and his companion to bring their boat to shore. They lowered the sail, secured the main halyard, and tied down the equipment. She was too far away to hear what they were saying, but given the sharp gestures and tense stance, it seemed they were arguing. Finally Ryan stalked off to the side, leaving the other man to finish unrigging the boat on his own. Ryan stood with his arms folded, watching every move the man made. It didn't seem like either one of them was happy.

They headed into a small building beside the marina, and when they emerged ten minutes later, both wore a fresh change of clothing, heavy packs slung over their shoulders. They headed up the wooden staircase toward the main part of base. As they drew closer, Jenny could see Ryan wore his casual service uniform of simple khaki trousers and a shirt. The young man beside him was clearly a civilian. No military man, officer or enlisted, would be caught dead wearing a mauve paisley vest.

Neither man noticed her as they passed the tables. They were engrossed in conversation, heads bent as their discussion continued in quiet urgency.

She stood. "Ryan!"

He froze but didn't turn around. A group of soldiers playing cards on the neighboring table watched curiously. The man in the paisley vest slanted her a curious smile.

She cleared her throat as she scrambled after him. "Lieutenant Gallagher," she amended as she drew closer.

This time Ryan turned around, meeting her gaze across the distance that separated them. He was as handsome as ever, the wind ruffling his hair and brown eyes watching her with caution. His apprehension grew as she closed the distance between them. He wasn't overly rude, but the way he glanced around, as if meeting her eyes was too much to ask, made it clear this meeting was unwelcome.

"Leisure sailing?" she asked.

"Yes," he admitted. "I've always enjoyed it."

"Yes, I remember you telling me how you liked sailing on the Potomac when you lived in Washington for all those years."

His jaw tightened, but he said nothing. She turned her attention to the civilian beside him. He was a young man with a swath of dark brown hair tumbling over his forehead and a reckless grin.

"We haven't been introduced," Jenny said, since it was obvious Ryan had no intention of performing the introductions. "I'm Jenny Bennett, a nurse at the hospital."

"Finn Breckenridge, professor of literature at Stanford." The young man shook her hand and seemed pleasant enough but added nothing more. The silence was excruciating, but she had nothing to be embarrassed about.

Ryan broke the silence. "Professor Breckenridge and I are about to head to dinner. Professor?" Ryan gestured toward the mess hall, and they turned away.

"Ryan, I need to speak with you."

He stopped. "Forgive me, Miss Bennett. It's been a long afternoon, and we are—"

"It will only take a moment. Really, Ryan." Her voice dripped scorn. All she wanted to do was perform a simple act of kindness for a man who didn't deserve it, and he tried to wiggle off the hook with a lame excuse about dinner.

Ryan nodded to the younger man. "I'll meet you in the mess hall shortly."

Jenny waited for Professor Breckenridge to depart before gesturing across the lawn. "Let's go to the cemetery. It's always quiet there, and this isn't something that should be overheard."

"I can imagine," Ryan said.

Was there a note of teasing in that offhand remark? He'd always had a subtle sense of humor, so it was impossible to know if he was jesting or completely serious. At least he followed her.

While most of the Presidio was blanketed with lush plants and towering pines, the cemetery had a neatly groomed lawn with acres of white granite markers standing like soldiers at attention. There was no privacy, but also no place for curious eavesdroppers. Jenny walked down the row of gravestones until they were in the middle of the cemetery. They were alone in a wide open space, and no one could possibly overhear.

"There are a lot of rumors flying around about you," she said. "They're pretty bad."

Ryan stood before her, his hair ruffling a little in the breeze. "Do you believe them?"

How strange that he didn't ask what the rumors were, although he probably already knew. He didn't seem all that surprised when he noticed the eggs smashed against his house.

"I don't know and I don't care," she said. "All I know is that some men are drafting a letter to General Dwyer. They claim you deserted in the Philippines. I don't know if it's true, but I thought it only fair you should know."

His eyes softened. His entire face gentled as the barest hint of a smile curved his mouth. "It's okay," he said quietly.

"It's not okay! They're saying terrible things about you. An officer is helping draft the letter, so it's not just idle speculation. They're talking about a court-martial."

This time he actually laughed. It wasn't a cruel laugh, just a wistful laugh that almost sounded sad. "Trust me, I'm in no danger of a court-martial." He reached out to touch the side of her arm. "But thank you for telling me."

She jerked back, wishing her arm hadn't tingled at the touch of his fingers. "I didn't do it for you, but on account of the little girl. She's your daughter?"

"Yes, Lily is my daughter."

The squeezing in her heart made it hurt to breathe. "And her mother?"

Ryan swallowed hard, and the fist holding the rucksack over his shoulder tightened. He dropped his gaze. "My wife died of pneumonia while she was pregnant with our second child. The baby died as well. Two years ago."

"I see." The slender thread of hope that Lily might be someone else's child had just snapped. There was no refuge from his betrayal by making up silly explanations for his behavior. Ryan had been unfaithful. But he had suffered a terrible tragedy as well.

"And Lily?" she asked. "How old is she?"

"She turned four last month."

She'd been right. Lily must have been conceived around the time that terrible letter arrived. Jenny clenched her teeth so hard it hurt her jaw. All this happened years ago, but it still had the power to scorch.

No, Ryan didn't have that kind of power over her. Not anymore. She'd been tough from the moment she arrived on this earth, and she'd handled bigger disappointments than this. She relaxed her jaw and glared at him, satisfied to see the shame and embarrassment stamped across his face.

"I'm sorry, Jenny," he said in a shaky whisper. "You can't imagine how sorry I am."

"Why did you lie to me about Washington? How am I supposed to believe anything you say when you can look me in the face and lie like that?"

"Captain Ainsworth was standing right next door. I don't want my life's story spilled out for the masses."

"What is the shame of living in Washington?"

"Look, its hard enough being the only naval officer on an army base. I'm already under a lot of pressure, and I don't want to put up with ribbing over a cushy desk job in Washington."

Jenny scowled. "Now that's just a lie. You put up with plenty of ribbing when you were here six years ago." The sailors of the

Baltimore teased him mercilessly for his wholesome innocence. In a raucous world of rowdy sailors, Ryan's shyness made him a misfit. He'd always been a good sport about it, even when she accidentally compounded the problem by dubbing him Galahad.

So why should he worry if an army officer next door teased him about a desk job in Washington? It seemed such a puny thing compared to the more disgraceful rumors flying around about him.

"Jenny, I'm not interested in discussing this any further. I am deeply sorry I've disappointed you, but it would be best if we did not continue our association."

His clipped, formal tone was so out of character with the man she once knew, and yet she could still see a fragment of that man. A hint of caution lingered in his eyes, as though he was silently begging her to simply let it go.

She dropped her gaze, unable to look him in the face when she didn't know what to believe. She didn't want to hear any more lies or excuses—

A stain on his shirt caught her attention. A dark red spot near his ribs. It hadn't been there a moment ago, and it was getting larger.

"Are you bleeding?"

He glanced down and frowned, tugging the fabric away from his chest. "It's nothing."

"It's not nothing, you're bleeding. What have you done to yourself?"

"It's nothing," he said, a little firmer this time.

"Quit being stoic, Galahad. How did you hurt yourself?"

"It doesn't matter," he said, but the curious way he looked down at his ribs was a good indication he hadn't even realized he'd been bleeding until she pointed it out. "I've survived far worse, but look . . . I need to go change my shirt before meeting Professor Breckenridge."

"You ought to go to the hospital and get properly patched up."

He glanced at her, a hint of sympathy in his gaze. "Please don't worry about me, Jenny. I don't deserve it. And I really am sorry about everything."

She stared after him as he walked away, wondering how she could possibly have been so wrong about him.

5

Ryan sat at the kitchen table, Lily on the chair beside him. Before them was a small clock he was using to teach Lily how to tell time. He opened the compartment on the back to wind the hands of the clock to different positions and coaxed her to read the new numbers. Her little face was screwed up in concentration. She was so short the clock was at eye level with her, but still she struggled.

"What time is it, sweet pea?" he coaxed.

"Um . . . I don't know."

He pointed to the hour hand. "What's that number?"

"Three."

"So is it three o'clock?"

She didn't answer, merely looked at him for confirmation. He sighed, wishing he could recall how his parents taught him to tell time. The only memory he had was of playing with his father's watch. He'd been fascinated by the hinged cover that opened to reveal the ivory clockface inside. It made a satisfying click when it closed, and he loved opening and closing it within the palm of his hand, enjoying the reassuring click each time he pressed it.

"Let's try again," he said as he moved the hour hand to another position. The clock was big enough to see from across the room, with large, plain numbers. Very military. Not at all like his father's watch with its miniature face and ornate roman numerals. Wasn't it curious how a watch could convey the owner's personality? His father's watch appeared so plain on the outside, but beneath the cover it was wonderfully complex.

Jenny still had that watch, and he wanted it back. It was the only thing he had left of his father. When he left Japan to go to college, he couldn't imagine it would be the last time he'd ever see his parents. Two years later they died in a house fire with all their belongings. Only his father's watch survived, and it was sent to him at Annapolis.

Asking Jenny for his father's watch was going to be awkward, but it had to be done. He would see her one more time, make another attempt to apologize, retrieve his watch, and then they would go their separate ways for good.

"Sir?" The housekeeper's voice interrupted his painful thoughts. Mrs. Tucker stood in the doorway with a stack of clothes draped over her arm. She held out a small bottle.

"I was preparing these clothes to send out for laundering and found this in Professor Breckenridge's coat pocket."

Ryan rose and took what looked like a small bottle of spice. Cinnamon? He unscrewed the lid and immediately knew he wasn't looking at cinnamon even though it was the same dark brown shade. It seemed sludgy but with a mildly pleasing scent.

Opium.

His lips tightened in anger as he pocketed the bottle. It was no longer possible to deny that Finn had a problem. It was one thing to hit the town for a night or two of carousing, but keeping a personal stash of opium was more serious.

"Could I ask you to mind Lily for an hour? I have a bit of business with Professor Breckenridge."

Mrs. Tucker agreed, and five minutes later Ryan was striding across the grassy lawn toward the Presidio's spacious library. Finn had claimed he was heading to the map room to study harbor and port design in the seas surrounding Japan. Maybe Ryan had been an idiot to trust that Finn was actually going to the library when all the temptations of San Francisco were a quick cable car ride away.

Phineas Breckenridge came from a fine family in New England, but he began bucking his family's expectations early. Whatever his parents wanted, Finn lunged in the opposite direction. When they insisted he learn Latin to study the classics, he learned Japanese to study his samurai heroes. When they nudged him toward the family's banking empire, he dabbled with artists and musicians. They sent him to Harvard with the stern warning to prepare himself for the world of banking. When he chose to study Japanese literature with a minor in violin, they turned to their second son, a man with a genuine interest in finance and a sterling reputation, to take over the family business. Finn was cut off with a check for two thousand dollars and a farewell note. By then Finn had already accepted a job at Stanford University and laughingly spent the money on a custom-made violin.

Three months later he was fired by the college for teaching bawdy limericks to the students. Then he was arrested for taking an axe to the door of a bordello that locked him out. It took a week of legal wrangling before Finn got out of jail, and by that time he had persuaded the police that the bordello should be raided because they were dabbling in underage girls.

In hindsight, Ryan could not be one hundred percent certain Finn's tantrum at the bordello was as heroic as it appeared. Had Finn's attack been on behalf of the underage girls? Or was that merely a convenient excuse once he'd been arrested? The only thing Ryan knew for sure was that Finn was far shrewder than he appeared.

His reputation destroyed, Finn left academia and turned to

journalism, but his career was spotty. His editors praised his work, but Finn had difficulty reining in his impulse to veer off into tangents. He was usually let go for being long-winded and dull.

The MID didn't find Finn's writing dull; they found it extraordinary. Time and again Finn had the knack for predicting future events. Three years before the outbreak of the Russo-Japanese War, Finn predicted exactly what would happen based on his assessment of the personalities of the Russian czar and the Japanese ministers. Finn accurately predicted the month and year in which negotiations would break down and when the war would commence. With his language abilities, wide-ranging interests, and keen perception, they knew Finn Breckenridge had the makings of an extraordinary spy. What no one knew was if he could control himself.

Finn probably wouldn't even be at the library. A group of Russian ballerinas was in town, and in all likelihood Finn had been tempted away to expand his acquaintance with Mother Russia.

The heavy oak door creaked and echoed in the cavernous library. It took a moment for Ryan's eyes to adjust to the dimness, but when they did, he spotted Finn at a corner table, half a dozen maps and books spread out before him.

A trickle of relief loosened the tension in Ryan's spine. At least Finn was indeed studying rather than playing hooky in the city.

Ryan approached and set the bottle of opium on the table, the bottle clicking in the silence of the library. "I believe you misplaced this."

Finn's hand closed around the bottle. "Indeed. Special delivery?"

"I won't have that filth in my house. I've got a four-year-old child who could get into it."

Finn's shoulders sagged. "You're right, of course. I'll be more mindful in the future."

Ryan was about to insist that Finn quit using it altogether, but something on the table looked strange. There were Japanese and

English documents, but at least half of the materials were in German, including a dictionary.

"Why do you have a German dictionary?"

Finn's voice was cool. "I don't speak the language very well yet, but I've been studying. I don't like the look of what I see going on in the port of Yokohama. Japanese newspapers report three of their shipping berths are being dredged to enlarge them."

"And?"

"And the only ship their current ports cannot accommodate is a Brandenburg-class battleship. If the Japanese are widening their berths to accommodate German battleships, we need to know."

This was precisely the reason the MID was so interested in Finn. He could spot a seemingly innocent detail like the widening of a berth and predict a range of possible consequences. This was something that should probably be called to the MID's attention immediately. They had plenty of agents in Berlin who could be asked to be on the lookout for ramped-up relations with Japan.

"Good catch," Ryan murmured.

There was no doubt in his mind that Finn was brilliant. What he didn't know was if Finn could be trusted.

❧

In the coming days, Jenny heard scores of rumors about Ryan and his mysterious companion. Vivian passed on gossip during their regular lunch at the picnic tables outside the mess hall.

"They go sailing every day," Vivian said. "All they seem to do is sail and have fancy dinners on the patio of one of the nicest townhouses at the Presidio. It's causing resentment among the troops."

"Have you learned anything about Professor Breckenridge?" Jenny asked.

Vivian shook her heard. "There's no sign of him on the army's payroll, but there was a note from General Dwyer ordering the paymaster to pay all bills submitted by Mr. Phineas Breckenridge of New York City."

Mister. No military rank or academic title. It confirmed Jenny's suspicions, for she had already checked at Stanford University to see if they employed a Professor Breckenridge, and they did not. She was about to tell Vivian what she'd learned when she saw a familiar figure walking toward her.

"Simon!" She rotated on the bench and kicked her heels up to get to the other side. It had been weeks since she'd had a chance to visit him.

"Look at you, kicking up your ankles like a dancing girl from Maiden Lane. I hope you have clean stockings on," Simon teased.

Vivian snorted. "Are you kidding? Jenny bleaches every item that touches her body within an inch of falling apart."

"I like clean clothes," she defended, taking no offense. She enjoyed the simple task of scrubbing, bleaching, and pressing collars and cuffs into spotless perfection.

Vivian headed back to the payroll office, giving Jenny a chance to visit with Simon in private. At sixty, he was rail-thin but still vigorous enough to walk all the way here from the Latin Quarter.

"Have you eaten?" she asked. "The food is free, and I can get you a meal."

"Not to worry, not to worry," he said in a distracted manner. The way he shifted on the bench worried her.

"What's wrong?"

He brightened. "Nothing's wrong! In fact, just about everything is *right*. But I was wondering if you might have a few dollars for your old dad."

She would gladly open her pocketbook for anything Simon needed, but it worried her that he was coming back for more money after she just sent him her paycheck last week.

"Of course I've got a few dollars. How much do you need?"

"Whatever you've got."

She rocked back on her seat. "What I've got is enough intelligence not to blindly hand over all my money. What are you up to?"

The secretive grin he'd been suppressing widened, and his eyes twinkled. He leaned in and whispered with the excitement of a child on Christmas morning.

"Pearls! Twenty-four perfect, nine-millimeter pearls identical in shade and size. Do you know how rare that is? I've only got enough money for twelve. I need money to buy the rest."

He withdrew a velvet pouch from his battered jacket, but she pushed it away. Of all the silly, stupid, irresponsible things. She worried that Simon didn't have enough to eat and had been taking extra hours at the hospital so she could funnel more money to him, and he frittered it away on pearls? *Pearls?*

She swiveled away, afraid she might unleash a torrent of furious words she'd regret. It was Simon's impulsive nature that led him to adopt a foul-mouthed gutter rat and turn her into something respectable. She would not shout at him. She would not slam her bank account closed or insult his beloved pearls.

She forced her tone to remain calm. "Is it too late to sell them back to wherever you got them?"

"Why would I do that?"

Because she'd already given him more than she could afford. Because the man she would be forever grateful to was spending himself into insolvency over pretty bits of calcium carbonate that could neither feed, clothe, nor house him.

But hadn't she always said she owed Simon everything? She was only nine years old when he found her, and she'd never met anyone like him. He walked along the back streets of San Francisco, preaching God's message about love and hope and forgiveness. He offered her a warm place to sleep for free. He gave her food and shelter and expected nothing in return.

For the first time in her life Jenny had a bedroom of her very own. Simon bought her warm clothes, and she ate three meals every single day. Simon made her go to school and attend church. He helped her with homework and hugged her when she came home crying because girls mocked her back-alley accent. She wanted so badly to be like Simon that she emulated the way he spoke, the books he read, and she tried to graft his cheerful, optimistic outlook onto her own world. At first she felt like a fraud, merely going through the motions, but as the years passed, the habits and behavior of decency sank into the fabric of her world, and she began to believe she might have a chance to become a good person like Simon.

She owed her salvation to Simon, and all he asked for was a little money. She had two pots for her savings. One was for her own security, and the other was to be used should she ever succeed in tracking down the sailor with the scar. That money was untouchable, but the rest was not.

She laid her hand over Simon's. "I'm willing to give you anything I can, but it can't go toward pearls. They're too expensive. You need to restock the store with modest, sensible jewelry. You've got to promise me, no pearls. The money can only go to reopening the store."

"Of course I want to reopen the store," Simon said. "But don't you understand the value of a perfect pearl necklace? Pearls will bring triple the investment."

"And triple the risk!" She yanked her hand away. "I don't want to gamble with everything I've got. I can only give you the money if you promise to use it for restocking the store with sensible products. Garnets or onyx or the like."

He agreed.

She had three hundred dollars saved. It wasn't enough to fully restock his store, but with careful planning, Simon could select inexpensive items that moved quickly, generating enough revenue to buy more stock.

She took a small pad of paper from her apron pocket. "Let's outline how best to invest three hundred dollars, shall we?"

∞

Ryan left the hospital more confused about Finn's condition than when he entered. He had just met with a physician to ask questions about opium addiction. Aside from Finn's refusal to stay sober, he showed none of the obvious signs of addiction. No seizures or trembling, no memory loss, anxiety, or sleep disorders.

It was a relief to hear the doctor's assessment, for a lot was riding on Finn's ability to pass a grueling series of tests required by the MID before they would authorize sending him to Japan. And if Finn failed . . . Ryan's mouth went dry. Well, it didn't bear thinking of.

He headed to the mess hall to grab a quick meal before going home for more lessons with Finn. He'd gladly drill Finn morning, noon, and night to prepare for those tests in September. Anything to avoid—

He was almost upon the picnic table before he spotted Jenny. He froze. Should he turn around to avoid her? She seemed engrossed as she hunched over a small pad of paper with another man, and hadn't noticed him yet. He could easily get away and avoid another painful conversation.

But she had his father's watch, and he wanted it back. He swallowed hard. He could ask for it now and get it over with.

Pine needles crunched beneath his feet as he approached, and he recognized her companion as Simon, the man who'd raised her. It was awkward to intrude but too late to retreat. Simon had recognized him and rose from the bench.

"Lieutenant Gallagher!" the old man said. "I assume it is still

Lieutenant? They haven't gone and thrown a fancier rank at you, have they?"

The older man's voice was polite, but it was in contrast with the suspicion on his face. Ryan couldn't blame him. Twenty years from now, if some man tampered with Lily's affection the way Ryan had done with Jenny, he doubted he could summon even an attempt at decorum.

"I'm still a lieutenant, sir," he responded. "I went off active duty a year ago but have been called to the Presidio on a short-term assignment." He glanced at Jenny, trying to assess her reaction, which was hard since she refused to look at him.

"Have you found any trusting young nurses to sweet-talk while you're here?" Simon asked pointedly.

No hope now of escaping a confrontation. Jenny still refused to look at him, but a gleam of satisfaction lit her eyes as she pretended to scrutinize her fingernails.

Ryan cleared his throat. "Nurse Bennett was always the most exceptional woman on the entire base. Having ruined that relationship through my own stupidity, I'm not eager to compound my sins."

He glanced at the list scribbled on the notepad. It mentioned topaz, marcasite, and other inexpensive stones.

He glanced at Simon. "No pearls?" After all, it was their shared love of the only gemstone yielded by the sea that had been the basis for their immediate friendship all those years ago.

The instant Ryan said the word *pearl*, Simon's hostility melted away, and he reached into his pocket. "Have a look at these," he said as he tipped the contents of a small velvet pouch into Ryan's hands.

Ryan's eyes widened as twelve of the most beautiful pearls he'd ever seen rolled into his palm. He sank onto the bench, mesmerized by their opalescent sheen. He could actually feel his eyes dilate with pleasure. Perhaps his overwhelming reaction came from spending too many years looking at undersized and lopsided pearls, but these were smooth, luminous perfection.

"South China Sea?" he asked.

"Tahitian. I have connections with a captain in the merchant marine who is always on the lookout for me."

Ryan lifted a single pearl to assess the smoothness of the nacre. It glistened with a sheen of silver and a slight peach tint.

"There are twelve more just like that," Simon confided. "I can't afford them yet, but soon."

Ryan met Simon's eyes as the implications set in. Pearls were naturally formed anomalies in an oyster, and their size, sheen, and color varied wildly. Twelve identical pearls was a challenge. Twenty-four was a miracle.

"They match?" he asked.

"They match," Simon confirmed, his voice trembling with excitement.

"Then you *must* get them." Ryan's response was automatic. It would be a crime to separate the group.

"My thinking exactly. The captain is still in port—"

"Would you stop?" Jenny shrieked, standing up so quickly the bench tipped over behind her.

The camaraderie blooming between Ryan and Simon evaporated, and soldiers at the nearby table craned their heads to watch, but Jenny didn't seem to care. She swooped down to stand over Simon like a Valkyrie out of legend.

"You just promised me you wouldn't buy more pearls. You *promised*. The only reason you had money to buy these pearls in the first place is because I've been working and saving for years to be sure we would both be safe, and you still want to squander everything on stupid pearls!"

Simon's shoulders curled in. No man deserved to be publicly berated like this, and Ryan stood.

"Jenny . . ."

She whirled to face him. "And you! How dare you encourage him in this insane foolishness. Look at him! He hasn't bought a new suit of clothes in years because the moment he has a spare dollar, he goes out and wastes it on pearls or rubies or anything else pretty and useless."

Simon continued to wilt beneath the hailstorm of angry words. Ryan didn't know the first thing about Simon's financial situation, but he did understand something about a man's dignity.

He stepped closer to Jenny and whispered softly. "Now isn't the time for this conversation. The man who raised you deserves an apology."

It was as if he'd thrown a bucket of ice water over her. A flash of pain crossed her face when she looked at Simon, who had taken the pearls from Ryan and returned them to the velvet pouch.

"Simon, I'm sorry. . . ."

He waved the apology away. "You're right, of course. Everything you say is entirely correct, but I did not realize how badly my actions have been hurting you. I'll be on my way now."

"I'll come with you," Jenny said.

Simon buttoned his jacket. His badly frayed flannel jacket. "No need, I'll be fine. I've already taken up too much of your time when you should be resting. You have a long night ahead, and I've kept you nattering all through your lunch."

Simon looked like he'd aged ten years in the past minute, his shoulders stooped as he headed toward Lombard Street.

Jenny tried to follow, but Ryan pulled her back. "He wants to be alone. Let him have that."

"I shouldn't have said those things."

"Was any of it untrue?"

"No, but I shouldn't have said it that way." Her shoulders sagged as she righted the bench and plopped down onto it. "I'd do anything in the world for Simon. I want to help him, but I don't understand how a man so wise and generous can live his entire life so recklessly."

Ryan said nothing as he sat opposite her. He understood reckless dreams. They had sustained him in his youth, and it was his own love of pearls that made his adult years in Japan bearable. Yes, he'd done solid work for the government, but an agent needed a cover story for why he lived in a place he had no logical reason to be. And that cover story had been pearls.

The people of Japan had a long-standing love affair with pearls, and there were plenty to be harvested from the warm waters surrounding the island. But that wasn't what made Japan's pearls unique.

For thousands of years people all over the world had been on a futile quest to artificially coax oysters to produce pearls. Countless techniques had been tried; all had failed.

That was about to change. Japanese scientists were fast closing in on a miraculous process using a baffling combination of science and engineering to produce near-perfect pearls. And Ryan had been right there beside them, sharing his American knowledge of marine biology and aquaculture with the Japanese scientists in exchange for the opportunity to watch them in action.

During his years in Japan he'd become an expert on pearls, including their value and their risks. Jenny had been right to warn Simon away from them if he didn't have a healthy financial nest egg.

But he wasn't here to discuss pearls. All he wanted was his father's watch.

He cleared his throat and braced himself for the uncomfortable request. "If convenient, I'd like to pick up my father's watch this afternoon. Could I come to your barracks for it?"

She looked as if he'd just slapped her. The shock was soon replaced by a hard glint in her eyes. "If I remember correctly, you were supposed to return with a wedding ring, and we would trade the ring for the watch. Is that offer still on the table?"

The rancor in her voice should come as no surprise, but it stung anyway. Of all the people he'd hurt by his weakness in Japan, Jenny had surely suffered the most.

"You have every right to resent me," he began.

"Oh, Ryan, *resent* is such a pale word for what I feel."

"I'm sure." He waited for her to continue berating him, but her next words were unexpected.

"Who was she?"

The venom in her voice made it obvious she was asking about his wife. He didn't want to talk about this, but he owed her some sort of explanation.

"She was the daughter of a silk merchant. Her name was Akira."

"How long did you wait before you were unfaithful to me?"

It was the night he received orders that he was to remain in Japan for the rest of his life. The night he fell into despair. The night he saw the future he wanted so badly crumble away.

"It was August of 1899."

"Why?" she asked in a shattered voice. The venom was gone, replaced only with bewilderment and pain. "Why did you throw me away like that?"

He wished he had an answer for her, but anything he said about why he had to stay in Japan would compromise an ongoing mission. Besides, it would only sound like a justification to her.

"I have no excuse," he said simply.

"I sold your father's watch."

He rocked back on the bench, stunned. Jenny was good down to the marrow of her bones, and he hadn't expected this of her. The triumph in her voice sounded wrong.

"I see," he said quietly, but he didn't. When he'd pressed that watch into Jenny's hand that night, it felt like a promise. It had been a beautiful night, tense with excitement and fear, but most of all love. He'd set caution aside and poured his heart out to the woman he'd started to love within moments of meeting her. It was a communion of souls, and the watch had been its symbolic promise.

It wasn't an expensive watch. It had no gemstones or fine craftsmanship. It was the watch of a humble missionary who dedicated his life to his faith and his family. Ryan had hoped to pass that watch on to his own son someday.

"I got twenty dollars for it," Jenny said. "I used it to buy new window glass for Simon's shop, and then we spent what was left on a fine steak dinner on Market Street."

All he could do was nod.

"I wanted to hurt you," she said with no shame in her voice.

He looked away. "You did."

Jenny had always seemed so resilient. Strong and confident, but it was underscored with a grounding of humor and compassion. This hardness in her character was new, and it hurt because he was the cause of it.

"I hope it helped Simon," he said. "He is a man of true valor." He still didn't fully understand the bond between Jenny and Simon but knew it was rock solid. Not like him, a man who collapsed within six hours of learning bad news. A man who gave in to temptation. Stumbled, fell, and brought down others with him.

"The men say you abandoned your post in the Philippines," she continued. "That you were either a war profiteer or a coward. Which was it?"

He hadn't expected her to believe the rumors, but she probably hadn't expected him to be unfaithful to her either.

"Well?" she demanded.

"I'd rather not discuss what happened in the Philippines," he said, knowing he was giving her the wrong impression, but it was important to keep Japan out of this conversation.

Her eyes narrowed. "Still? After all these years you can't tell me why you disappeared from the military and acted like a traitor?"

He couldn't because the Americans were still spying on the Japanese.

"I'm sorry. No, I can't." Even though he longed to bare his soul to her. Tell her about the loneliness and demoralizing isolation he'd felt during those years in Japan, but it would only sound like an excuse. He *had* been unfaithful, and there was no excuse for that.

"Just go away, Ryan. You don't belong here anymore." Her voice sounded tired and sad, but she still looked at him with guarded curiosity. "I can't figure you out. You *seem* like a good man, but you don't act like one."

He stood. "Take care, Jenny. I wish I could find a way to express how sorry I am, but I don't think Shakespeare himself could find the words. But please know, I am truly sorry. On the hour of my death, the greatest regret of my life will be what I did to you."

It was a relief to escape the searing disappointment in her gaze.

6

The people of Japan had eleven different expressions for saying "I'm sorry." Its culture elevated apologizing to an art form, and it was essential that Finn learn all the shades of meaning and techniques for delivering apologies across the range of social situations. While westerners often considered apologies a sign of weakness, the Japanese considered a beautifully delivered apology a virtue.

Finn barging into the house near midnight and disturbing Lily's sleep created a perfect opportunity for Ryan to counsel Finn the next evening in the technique of expressing regret. Lily thought it highly amusing, sitting in the parlor with her feet not even reaching the edge of the sofa.

Finn stood before her and executed a slight bow. "*Gomennasai,* Lily," he said formally. It was the correct term to use, a polite expression of regret but lacking the slavish formality required were he apologizing to a superior.

"Lily?" Ryan prompted.

Lily scooted off the couch and returned the bow. "*Watashi wa anata no shazai o ukeiremasu,*" she said, then spoiled the solemnity of accepting the apology by hurling herself facedown onto the couch in a fit of giggles.

"And now the proper apology to Mrs. Tucker," Ryan said. The housekeeper was in the kitchen, drying dishes from the evening meal, but Ryan summoned her into the parlor. They often recruited Mrs. Tucker to help during etiquette lessons. The old housekeeper didn't know a thing about Japan but had been gamely following Ryan's lead.

As a housekeeper, Mrs. Tucker was a subordinate to Finn, and that was important to remember in a society as stratified as Japan, but her age meant she was worthy of a more formal apology than the one tendered to Lily.

Finn bowed at a forty-five-degree angle, holding it to the count of five. "*Moushiwake arimasen deshita*, Mrs. Tucker." He went on to outline his offense of disturbing the household while others were trying to sleep, even though Mrs. Tucker did not understand a word of Japanese. Finn's apology was flawless. He selected an expression of serious remorse, and the lengthy bow indicated respect for the housekeeper's age. Perfect.

Mrs. Tucker stood frozen, the dish towel hanging limp in her hands, uncertain how to respond.

"Thank you, Mrs. Tucker," Ryan said to the bewildered housekeeper. "Your help is appreciated." He waited until she went back to the kitchen before turning his attention back to Finn. "You might lower the bow a little more," he said. Normally Ryan would demonstrate the appropriate angle, but his ribs were hurting again, so he remained seated.

They were just about to practice their nightly tea ceremony when a knock at the door surprised him. Rather than disturb the housekeeper again, Ryan answered the door himself and was stunned to see Simon Bennett standing on the front stoop, wearing the same threadbare suit from that afternoon. He looked nervous, and Ryan instinctively feared for Jenny.

"I hope my visit is not disturbing you," Simon began.

Ryan beckoned him inside. "Not at all. Is everything alright?"

"Fine, fine," Simon said hastily. He looked curiously at the elaborate tea service set out on the parlor table.

"We are practicing Japanese," Lily said in English, and Ryan winced. The less people associated him with Japan, the better. Most people assumed Lily was part Filipino, and that was fine with him.

"Very nice, very nice," Simon said, still glancing around the room in distraction. He seemed edgy and uneasy, and whatever drove him here probably wasn't something he'd be willing to discuss in front of Lily and Finn.

"Lily, why don't you take Mr. Breckenridge to the garden in the backyard. You can show him the bird's nest you found this afternoon."

Lily knew a dismissal when she heard it, and as soon as they were alone, Ryan offered Simon a chair.

"Tell me what's going on."

A Cheshire cat smile spread across Simon's face. "You remember the pearls I showed you?"

Ryan wasn't likely to forget. "I do."

"The captain who brought them is leaving port on Friday. If I can come up with eight hundred dollars, I can buy the rest of them. Would you be willing to go in on the investment with me?"

Ryan tried not to let the surprise show on his face. Unlike Jenny, he understood the value of keeping identical pearls grouped together, but that hardly meant he had a spare eight hundred dollars he was willing to invest. Besides, he knew a lot more about pearls than Simon Bennett, who had no idea of the avalanche of change coming to the pearl industry.

Ryan braced his elbows on his knees and stared at the hardwood floor. This was a delicate situation. If he did anything to encourage Simon's obsession with pearls, it would infuriate Jenny. She had a right to be frustrated with Simon, and Ryan didn't want to intentionally hurt her . . . but it was hard to pass up an opportunity like this.

Were he a man without responsibilities, it would be tempting to buy the pearls, but it was too big a risk right now. Especially since technology might soon slash the value of those pearls. The more Simon invested in pearls, the more likely he was to be financially destroyed. It all depended on how quickly the Japanese perfected their cultured pearls. Once that happened, the world of pearls would never be the same, and anyone heavily invested in genuine pearls risked financial devastation. Simon didn't seem the type of person who could withstand the tsunami on the horizon.

"Well?" Simon asked, a world of hope crammed into that single word.

"Give me a moment," Ryan said.

A far more dangerous, potentially lucrative opportunity loomed. If all panned out well, Ryan was going to need to form an alliance with a jeweler soon. Could he trust Simon to be brought in on the secret? There were so many things about this that were risky and farfetched, but he liked Simon and knew the old jeweler would be dazzled by what was sitting in Ryan's top desk drawer.

"Wait here," he said, wondering if he was making the biggest mistake of his life or an unbelievable coup. He worried the entire time he walked to the office, unlocked the top desk drawer, and retrieved a compact box. It was light in his hands even though it carried the weight of a thousand dreams.

Simon looked at him with curiosity as he returned to the room. He pushed the tea service aside and opened the box, tipping out its contents. The keshi pearls clattered and bounced onto the glossy mahogany table.

"What are they?" Simon asked, staring. Instead of perfectly round spheres, the keshi pearls looked like misshapen disks. Some were formed like teardrops, some like buttons, and a few looked like large grains of rice.

"They're real pearls," Ryan confirmed. "The Japanese have figured out how to seed oysters and farm them. This is an example of what they can produce. They're close to creating perfectly round pearls, but I messed up with this batch. The seeds weren't properly set."

"Impossible," Simon said. "People have been trying for centuries to force oysters to produce pearls. It never works."

Ryan couldn't resist smiling. "It does now."

Natural pearls were formed when a tiny irritant found its way inside an oyster and secretions of nacre formed layers of smooth, iridescent calcium to cushion the irritant. The logical way to make a pearl was to force the same conditions on an oyster and hope for the best. It never worked. The oyster either expelled the irritant or died.

Until now. A British biologist first suggested a grafting technique that used muscle tissue clipped from a donor oyster to stimulate the nacre production of the host oyster. Japanese scientists seized on the idea and began experimenting.

"Instead of grains of sand, they've been using tiny beads made of natural oyster shell," Ryan told Simon. "The oyster seems to recognize the material and is less likely to expel it, but it's still not enough to make the pearl form. The trick is to use a snippet of fresh mantle, the organ that produces pearl nacre when an irritant gets inside the shell. No one knows why a bit of foreign mantle helps spur the growth of a pearl in the host, but it does."

Simon's eyes grew round as the implications set in.

"And, my friend . . . the pearls they are growing in Japan are beautiful."

Simon's gaze flitted to the array of cultivated pearls on the table. "So where did these come from?"

Ryan hedged. "I told you. They were grown with the Japanese method."

"You grew them."

"What makes you think that?"

"You said the Japanese were getting close to creating perfect spheres, but that *you* messed up with this batch. You've got your hand in this game."

He had more than his hand in it. He had his heart, his career, and his life's savings in it. The first thing he did after returning to America was buy a plot of oceanside land suitable for raising and harvesting his own pearl oysters. The land came with a house and a pier, but he had to buy a boat, nets, and other equipment. He already had two thousand oysters living in his crescent-shaped cove, each of them treated with the Japanese technique for growing pearls. It took time, patience, and delicate handling to yield a pearl, but someday Ryan hoped his oysters would produce pearls as perfect as the ones Simon had showed him this afternoon.

But his experiment with the oysters needed to stay a secret. He hadn't exactly asked the Japanese for permission to emulate their techniques in America.

"Yes, I'm up to my neck in it," he acknowledged. "Those pearls came from Japan, but my most recent attempt is still growing off the coast in southern California."

Simon looked delighted enough to levitate. "I want in on it. I never imagined this could happen in my lifetime. It's the most thrilling—"

"Any man who dabbles in pearls is risking ruin." Ryan didn't mean to sound so blunt, but Simon needed to know. "You must understand what is about to happen to the pearl industry," he continued. "The Japanese are closing in fast on the ability to make perfectly round pearls. When that happens, the cultured pearls will be indistinguishable from the real thing, because they *are* the real thing. They will flood the market. The entire pearl industry is about to change. It's too risky to sink a fortune into natural pearls. I didn't realize you were short of funds when you showed me those Tahitian pearls. It's impossible to know when the Japanese will have the technique perfected. It could be in the next year or maybe it won't happen for another decade . . . but it's coming, and you need to be ready."

Simon's face was thoughtful as he stared at the array of pearls scattered on the table. With a connoisseur's eye, he selected one of the larger pearls, almost the size of a thumbnail but shaped like a kidney bean. "A pearl like this would make a magnificent centerpiece for a brooch," he said. "I could smooth the edges, surround it with gold filigree, and possibly a few accent pieces of garnet. It would be a showstopper."

Ryan's eyes widened. He'd never considered such an oddly shaped pearl could be anything more than a curiosity, but before he could even finish the thought, Simon grabbed a piece of paper and sketched out his vision.

"I can grind down the back side of the pearl so it will lay flat against the mount. Or maybe . . ." He began poking through the smaller keshi pearls on the table. In short order he flicked five into a separate pile. "These! I can shape these into teardrops and surround the larger pearl. Alternate the accent pearls with garnets, and it will look like something a duchess would wear."

The prospect was dazzling. Ryan's partners in Japan had been scientists focused with single-minded determination on creating round pearls. None of them had the soul of an artist who could look at a badly deformed pearl and see its potential.

His confidence grew. "Take them. Turn them into something beautiful, and we can split the proceeds."

"I like the way you do business!" Simon gave him a hearty handshake.

"Don't tell Jenny about this," he said, and Simon froze.

"Jenny and I have no secrets from each other," the old man said slowly.

Whereas Ryan's life was full of them. It didn't matter how much he longed for a simple life, he'd made his decision at age seventeen when the American government asked for his allegiance. Ever since, his life had been concealed behind layers of deception, illusion, and secrecy.

"Look, the marine biologists I worked with in Japan were generous by allowing me into their research labs. It was a two-way street, for I knew plenty about coastal biology and translated entire volumes of English-language research materials for them. Scientists understand that sort of reciprocity, but it's not how Japanese investors think. The men who funded our research will not be overjoyed that I'm trying to replicate it here in America. I need to keep this quiet."

"And you don't think Jenny is trustworthy?" It was a simple question, but Simon's words were heavy with irony. Ryan's betrayal of Jenny could not be more blatant, for the evidence of his infidelity was playing in his backyard.

"Jenny has no reason to think fondly of me." It hurt to even say the words. There was a time when Jenny had looked at him as though he were a knight out of the old legends, and he wanted to *be* that knight. Instead he'd crushed her dreams.

Simon pierced him with a keen gaze. "Do you know that every week for the past six years Jenny checked the casualty lists as they arrived at the Presidio? Yours is the only name she ever looked for."

It was like a punch in the gut. He knew she would be hurt when she received his letter, but he'd assumed she would recover quickly, like a buoy springing back to the surface after being briefly overcome by waves. Jenny was a survivor, strong and beautiful. It was stunning that she would still care about him, but Simon hadn't stopped speaking.

"Even after she heard you were back in the United States, she still checked those casualty lists each time they were sent in from Manila. She admitted it was insane, but a part of her refused to accept what all the evidence indicated. A part of her was still hoping it was all wrong and that you would someday come back to her."

Ryan closed his eyes against the anguish, but the back door opened and little footsteps came running inside.

"Look, Papa, I picked these," Lily said, holding out a fistful of dandelions.

His heart turned over. He couldn't regret what happened in Japan because it had brought him Lily. He regretted hurting Jenny. He regretted that Akira's family turned their back on her when she conceived a child before wedlock. There were so many regrets, and yet there was also this beautiful child whose smile lit up his world.

"Let me get a glass of water," he said, rising with care to avoid reopening the wound in his side. He had just filled a glass and set the dandelions in it when he realized there was no sign of Finn. "Where is Mr. Breckenridge?"

"He said he had to go downtown," Lily replied. "I don't know what that means. What's downtown?"

Downtown was trouble. It was gambling and opium dens and everything else Finn should be avoiding.

"When did he say this?" he demanded.

Lily's face crumpled at the anger in his voice.

He hunkered down to put an arm around her shoulders. "I'm not mad at you, sweetheart, but when did Mr. Breckenridge leave?"

"I don't know."

"Did you show him the bird's nest?"

"Yes. Then he said he had to go downtown. I picked some dandelions, and then I came inside."

There might be time to intercept Finn, but not without a carriage. He dashed to the kitchen and asked Mrs. Tucker how quickly she could get a carriage and driver here.

The old housekeeper looked confused. "Within an hour, I suppose. Will that do?"

"I need to intercept Finn before he gets to the nearest cable car stop. Have you got any ideas?"

Mrs. Tucker glanced out the window. "Cutting across the lawn behind the quartermaster's house should get you there quickly."

He nodded and returned to the front room, then shoved the box of pearls at Simon and grabbed his coat.

"Come see me as soon as you've developed something," he said, then kissed Lily on the forehead and headed outside.

He might be able to intercept Finn tonight, but what about when Finn left for Japan? There was plenty of opportunity for carousing in Tokyo, and the MID could not afford to have one of their agents running haywire. Ryan could still get Finn straightened out before the tests in September, but time was growing short.

Because if Finn couldn't do it, Ryan would have to leave behind his home, his pearl farm, and Lily's chance to grow up in America.

7

Jenny bolted upright in bed at the sound of a cannon blast. She dragged off her sleeping mask, wincing at the sunlight as she squinted at the bedside clock. It was only noon. She groaned as another series of cannon blasts boomed from the artillery range. She'd gotten less than four hours of sleep, and there wouldn't be any more on a day the soldiers were doing artillery drills.

Maybe it was just as well. She hadn't been sleeping well since Simon's store had been robbed, and today she was going to turn over most of her remaining savings to him. She could only pray he would use it sensibly. Giving this money to Simon might be a huge mistake, but if he hadn't rescued her from the streets . . .

Well, it didn't bear thinking about. He *did* rescue her, and she *would* hand over her savings to restock his store.

She dressed in her nurse's uniform to visit the bank. Most nurses wore street clothes when they were off duty because high-stand collars were uncomfortable, but Jenny liked her uniform. People looked at nurses with respect.

Simon leased a compact shop tucked between a bookstore and a café. The new glass window, purchased with a missionary's watch, sparkled in the early afternoon sun. A little bell above the door dinged as she stepped inside.

Simon was hunched over his worktable, one eye covered by a jeweler's loupe as he worked at the grinding wheel. His display cases were empty, but at least he had bits of gold and other items spread out before him.

"Jenny, my love!" he said, peeling off the jeweler's loupe and coming around the worktable to embrace her.

"What are you working on?" she asked, drifting over to see odd bits of white scattered across the table.

Simon gave her a nervous smile. "They're pearls," he said. "Not like any I've ever seen before, but I think I can make a real go of them. Have a look at this brooch."

The instant he said *pearl*, every muscle in her body tightened. The drawing he tried to press into her hands slipped onto the table. She didn't even want to touch it.

"You said you were going to sell sensible jewelry. Beads or silver or factory-made watches. Pearls are too expensive!" She clutched her reticule, more reluctant than ever to turn over the money she'd just withdrawn from the bank.

"I didn't pay anything for them," Simon hastened to add. "You can see they're deformed. A man gave them to me for nothing, just a request to split the proceeds if I can sell any of it. And I know I can! Would you just look at the drawing for my brooch? It's going to look spectacular even though I'm starting with lop-sided pearls."

The drawing lay faceup on the table. Yes, it looked like an impressive piece, but entirely unlike the modest jewelry they'd agreed he would work on. She picked up one of the tiny, misshapen stones. It had the luster of a pearl, but she doubted it was the real thing. Simon was too trusting. Some smooth-talking swindler was trying to take advantage of him.

"Who?" she demanded. "Who told you these bits of stone were valuable?"

"They're real pearls, Jenny. Ryan said—"

"Ryan? Ryan Gallagher?"

His guilty flush let her know she had guessed correctly. It felt like a double betrayal. Ryan knew she was frustrated by Simon's thirst for pearls, and yet he'd gone and stoked that obsession to life. It was worse than pushing liquor to an alcoholic.

"Why would you do business with Ryan Gallagher?" she asked, trying to keep the hurt from her voice.

"I feel like Ryan and I are kindred spirits," Simon said. "He understands pearls. He appreciates the—"

"Oh, stop it! I once thought the same thing about Ryan, and look at the fool he made out of me!"

Her hands shook as she extracted the roll of bills from her reticule. How many nights had she struggled to stay awake to earn this money? She'd lived most of the past five years in a fog of groggy exhaustion so that she and Simon would have a secure future.

She held up the bills. "Can I trust you with this?"

"It doesn't appear you do."

"Don't give me that wounded look; you know what I'm asking. If I give you this money, are you going to restock your store with sensible items, or will it get wasted on Ryan's malformed pearls?"

Simon took the roll of bills from her hand, but instead of pocketing it, he tucked it back into her bag. It made her feel even worse. Now Ryan was driving a wedge between her and Simon.

That wouldn't happen. If she had to crawl over broken glass, she was going to protect Simon from whatever Ryan had up his sleeve.

Jenny headed straight to Ryan's house after Simon booted her from the shop. Maybe she couldn't persuade Simon to stifle his obsession with pearls, but she could tell Ryan to leave him alone. She instinctively slowed as she approached his front porch. The egg yolk and broken shells had been cleaned away, but she'd do a lot worse than fling eggs at his house if he dared tamper with Simon.

She raised her hand to knock but paused. A window must have been open somewhere, for she could hear voices from inside. She cocked her head to listen.

It was two male voices in conversation, but they weren't speaking English. As far as she knew, Japanese was the only foreign language Ryan spoke, but who else at the Presidio knew Japanese? The conversation sounded angry, as though they were arguing about something. Or was that merely the natural cadence of the language? She recognized Ryan's voice even though it sounded odd rattling out the strange syntax in such rapid-fire conversation. He had a soothing tenor in his voice, a rich warmth that appealed to her even though she couldn't understand a word he said.

She shook herself. It was beyond foolish to let Ryan weave that golden web of fascination around her. She knocked, and the conversation abruptly ceased. A moment later Ryan answered the door. Before he could say a word, she pushed inside.

"What is your business with Simon?" she demanded.

"Hello, Jenny," he replied calmly. "Perhaps you remember Professor Breckenridge?"

This was the man Ryan was arguing with? The professor who wasn't a professor? It was tempting to confront him about the deception, but she smelled something odd. She paused, sniffing the air.

"Why are you using mercurochrome?" she asked.

That surprised Ryan. "What makes you think I'm using mercurochrome?"

"Because the other day a wound on your chest opened up, and my guess is that you've got bandages soaked in it under your shirt. I can smell it."

"Ah." That was all he said. No denials, no explanation, but it was obvious he was trying to treat his own injury. Staff at the hospital had quit using mercurochrome to clean wounds years ago. Tincture of iodine was just as effective and less caustic to the skin.

"You really ought to go to the hospital about that wound. Infection is dangerous, and you don't know what you're doing."

His face softened with affection. "I'll be alright, Jenny. Now tell me what I can do for you."

She didn't know who Professor Breckenridge was, but she didn't trust him. She certainly did not want to spell out Simon's obsessive weaknesses in front of a stranger. "I need to speak with you privately."

Professor Breckenridge gamely rose to his feet. "I was just off to the mess hall for some lunch." He flashed her a wink on the way out the door, and it set her teeth on edge.

"Yes?" Ryan asked, his tone courteous.

"I want you to leave Simon alone," she said. "I know you've given him some strange little stones you claim are pearls, but—"

"They *are* pearls."

"But I want you to stop. He can't afford to squander what few resources he has on overpriced jewelry that is hard to sell quickly. I want him to buckle down and—"

"Don't you think this is Simon's decision?"

"Not when he's using my money."

"He isn't. I gave him the pearls free and clear. Aside from a bit of mounting material, Simon's only investment is his time and expertise. It's none of your business, Jenny."

His tone was soft, but the words were firm. It was maddening that he wouldn't yield to her on this. She stepped closer and lowered her voice. "Let me be very clear. Simon's nature makes him vulnerable to scoundrels and cheats. I will stand between him and anyone who dares to take advantage of him. Simon may be a babe in the woods, but I am not. I will cheerfully strangle anyone who hurts him."

"I don't doubt your love for Simon, but you haven't a mean bone in your body."

He didn't really know her. For years she'd worked to transform herself into a proper feminine ideal, but she had claws and teeth and wasn't afraid to use them. She didn't know why Ryan had come back to the Presidio, but he seemed to have the favor of General Dwyer, and the mysterious Finn Breckenridge was involved in all this.

"I don't know what to think or believe about you," she said. "When other men were fighting and dying in the Philippines, rumor has it you were yachting in Tokyo. Even now, while other men drill and train, you go sailing with some civilian who seems to have no purpose here."

Instead of taking offense at her words, Ryan's expression softened with understanding, and she had to battle an instinctive urge to step into his arms and pretend the past six years hadn't happened. Something deep in her soul awakened and responded to him, like a flower seeking the warmth of the sun.

"I wish I could hate you," she said softly.

He sucked in a quick breath. "You don't?"

"No," she said simply. "Everything would be easier if I could, but I loved you so much that I'm not sure anything could ever blot it out. Those few months with you echo in my mind like a golden chord, a symphony I can never forget. I remember walking along the seashore when we found a starfish. You turned it over and showed me how they breathe through the tiny little tubes on their underside. Do you remember that day? I loved those seaside walks with you. Beneath all the lies and deceit is a man who has qualities I will always adore. If I could only forget *that* man, my life would be so much easier. So no, I don't hate you."

The oddest expression crossed his face, so quickly she thought she imagined it. It was hope. Wild, barely restrained hope that looked ready to burst forth with the heat of the sun. Then it was gone.

"What I did was unforgivable. There's nothing I can ever do to heal that wound."

"Try."

There it was again, a fleeting look of hope that was barely restrained. He swallowed hard. "How?"

She didn't know. He couldn't turn back the clock or wish Lily out of existence. He couldn't make her forget his infidelity or his broken promises. The only way he could possibly mitigate the damage was to stop being so evasive and simply answer her questions.

She glanced at his chest. "How did you injure yourself?"

He snorted. "Someone tried to mug me last month. A knife was involved, and it got a little messy."

"A *knife?* Where did this happen?"

"Down in Summerlin, a small fishing village on the southern end of the state. I moved there last year."

"And does this fishing village have an underclass of hardened criminals?"

He laughed a little as he shook his head. "No, Summerlin is the closest thing to paradise I've ever seen. It's just a few dozen shops and a lot of people who make a living by casting their nets into the sea. The mugging was a fluke. Probably some transient from the city desperate for cash."

His voice was entirely void of deception, but she was beginning to suspect Ryan was a much better liar than she'd ever imagined. Her gentle, innocent Galahad who blushed when teased and read the Bible each morning before breakfast was only a fantasy she'd spun out of unfulfilled daydreams.

It was time to dig deeper and ask what she really wanted to know.

"What did you do during the war to start the rumors about

you? Why did you leave San Francisco a month ahead of all the other soldiers?"

His mouth tightened into a flat line, and it seemed every muscle in his body tensed, as if pulled by an invisible string. "You know I can't answer that."

"I know you don't *want* to."

He folded his arms but remained silent. All that could be heard was the ticking of the clock on the mantel, but she wasn't going to back down. The war with Spain was long over, and there was no reason for Ryan to maintain this ridiculous secrecy.

Unless . . . unless it had nothing to do with the war at all and he left for entirely different purposes. Perhaps the mysterious Akira had been part of his life all along. He'd lived overseas until he was seventeen, after all. He would have been old enough to form ties, fall in love. . . .

"Was it a woman?" she asked in a choked voice.

"What?"

"A woman," she repeated. "You told me Lily's mother was named Akira. Was this whole thing over a woman you couldn't bear to be apart from?"

The pain in his eyes deepened, but he still refused to answer. His silence allowed her to fill in the blanks with images of a lovely woman who probably knew Ryan far better than she did. A laughing woman named Akira who married Ryan and shared his bed. Who carried his child, nursed his child, loved him.

"You were the first man I ever let kiss me, did you know that?"

He winced a little, but had the decency not to look away.

"I trusted you. I grew up in a world where children stole and the police couldn't be trusted. Where men drank and gambled and bought prostitutes. Where they knifed each other over a hand of cards. I thought you were different. The kind of man who only fought for a principle. I thought you were an honorable man willing to die for a cause, be it your country, your faith, or your family. I thought you were *that* kind of man. What a mistake I made."

She waited for him to speak, but he said nothing. She glanced at his chest and continued her accusation. "Now it appears you are a man who gets in knife fights, consorts with charlatans who pretend to be college professors, and has a woman in every port. Am I wrong?"

Ryan met her gaze and absorbed every hurtful word without flinching. He did not utter a single word of explanation, he simply turned the other cheek and let her rant. It made her feel like she was the guilty one, not him. And she had lost sight of what she came here to do.

"Just don't hurt Simon, okay? He saved me when I was only a child, and now it's my job to return the favor."

"What you value, I value," he said formally. "I will honor your request."

He spoke with heartfelt sincerity, with an echo of that Japanese formality she always found so appealing. The reluctant attraction stirred to life again. Why couldn't she figure him out? Beneath the lies and evasion, she still believed Ryan to be an honorable man, and it terrified her. It was impossible to hate Ryan, and that made her vulnerable to him again.

"Thank you," she said softly, then turned and fled the house as though it were on fire.

8

Ryan squatted before Lily in his third attempt to wrap the complicated sash that secured her kimono. There wasn't much room in the cramped photographer's studio, and they were already ten minutes late for their portrait sitting, but he'd forgotten how long it took to put on the robes, collars, and panels of a formal kimono.

This kimono was the single most expensive item Ryan owned. Made of pure ruby red silk with white cherry blossoms woven into the fabric, it ought to belong in a museum. In Tokyo this kimono would cost upwards of two thousand dollars. It had been a gift from Akira's father, who doted on Lily.

"Keep turning," he instructed Lily, continuing to wind the twelve-foot length of the *obi* sash around her waist. Her wooden sandals clomped on the floor as she rotated.

"It's too hot," she complained. "I want to go home."

Finn stood against the wall on the other side of the studio. "But you look so pretty," he said. "Think how happy your grandfather will be to see your picture in that fancy kimono."

"I don't like these shoes," she said, and it was hard to argue with her. The sandals were made from flat wooden boards and were hard to walk in, but once again, Finn knew the perfect thing to say.

"I'll bet you are the only girl in California who has such special shoes. Only a girl of tremendous grace and skill can walk in authentic Japanese *geta,* right?"

Lily stopped rotating to beam at Finn, who had been on good behavior ever since the incident with the jar of opium. He put in extra hours of study every day, helped Mrs. Tucker with the heavier housekeeping chores, and even volunteered to help Lily with her lessons. Today he'd carried the expensive silk kimono so it wouldn't get crushed on the cable car.

Every detail of this photograph needed to be perfect. It was important for Lily's grandfather to see that Ryan was not completely severing Lily from her Japanese heritage. The silk panels rasped between his fingers as he secured the large sash over her waist. Twelve feet! Who could imagine that a sash for such a small girl would be twelve feet long, but it was finally wrapped properly, and now he could tie it down.

"Hold still while I tie the knot," he instructed, struggling to remember how to tie a butterfly knot at the small of Lily's back. At last he had the sash tied into place. "Turn around and let's have a look."

Lily rotated slowly to face him, holding her arms out to display the oversized sleeves falling to the center of her hands. He wanted to say something, but the sudden lump in his throat made it impossible. She looked so grown up in the elegant kimono, and an embarrassing sheen blurred his eyes.

"Your grandfather is going to be so pleased at how pretty you are," he managed to choke out.

Ryan had no fondness for his former father-in-law, but Harue adored Lily. A surprise, considering Harue shunned Akira the moment he learned she was consorting with a hated foreigner. Harue refused to attend their wedding, and to this day he had never looked Ryan directly in the face. Yet when Lily was born,

Harue swallowed his pride and paid a visit to their home. His face broke into a smile as he leaned over Lily's crib to poke the baby awake, then beamed in pride over her little whimpering noises. Ryan prayed this newborn baby might somehow mend the rift between father and daughter.

It had not happened. Harue began to reluctantly accept Ryan and Akira as guests in his home in order to see his only grandchild, but there was no softening of the old man's contempt for Ryan, a gaijin, a foreigner, not worthy of being part of his family.

Nevertheless, even after moving to California, Ryan continued to send Harue letters about Lily's progress, and in his next letter, he would send this photograph of Lily in full Japanese regalia, complete with wooden sandals and her silky hair in a formal bun and held in place with two lacquered hairpins that once belonged to Akira.

"Are we ready?" the photographer asked, barely masking the impatience in his voice.

Ryan nodded and guided Lily to the platform. "I'd like to photograph her standing beside the chair to get the full effect of her kimono," he told the photographer.

"Certainly," the man responded. "And will the father be joining the young lady in the photograph?"

Ryan could just imagine Harue's reaction should his hated son-in-law mar the photograph. "Only Lily."

It took a while to take the photograph, for Finn could not resist the impulse to make Lily laugh. Giggles were the enemy of a clear photograph, and each time Lily schooled her face into a somber look, she risked a glance at Finn, which spoiled everything. Ryan finally had to ask Finn to step outside so Lily could remain motionless for the five seconds necessary for a clean shot.

After the photographer finally got a clear image, Ryan made arrangements for two copies of the photograph, one for him and one to send to Harue.

Finn stepped back into the shop before the transaction was complete. "Order one for me, too," he said. "I'll pay for it."

Ryan glanced at him in surprise, but Finn's expression was unusually sad. "I'll miss Lily once I get . . . well, once I get where I'm headed."

Once he was in Japan. The wistfulness in Finn's tone was unmistakable and caught Ryan off guard. It was the first time Finn seemed to comprehend the magnitude of the mission. He would not only be heading into a strange and foreign land, he'd be leaving the United States and every person he knew to venture into the unknown, carrying only a few photographs to remember what he was leaving behind.

"I'll pay for the photograph," Ryan said. After all, it was the least he could do for a man who was making it possible for him to remain in America and raise Lily in a place where she had a chance at acceptance. Even in California, Lily was going to confront her share of bigotry and cold shoulders, but it was better than the alternative.

Lily still wore the kimono and clomped over to Finn in her wooden sandals. She reached up to touch his hand. "You want a picture of me?"

"Who wouldn't want a picture of the prettiest girl in all of California!" Finn said, and Lily blushed, racing to bury her face against Ryan's leg.

It was days like these when Ryan could taste the sweetness of the future coming within reach. Finn had been exemplary all week. He was clear-eyed, studious, and Ryan's confidence in his ability to pass the MID tests in September was gaining strength.

If Finn passed, it meant Ryan could have a chance with Jenny again. He dared not court her as long as he might be forced to return to Japan, but if Finn could take his place?

I wish I could hate you, she had said. The irony was that Jenny's backhanded insult filled him with exhilaration. It meant he had a chance, that a piece of her remembered the radiant happiness of what they once had together. It meant he could fight for a future with her . . . but it all depended on Finn being able to pass those final exams.

The tests to pass the MID's requirements were extensive, covering Japanese language, customs, diplomacy, and military prowess. Finn would need to demonstrate fluency in Morse code, Bacon's cipher, and Baudot's 5-bit code. And those were only the tests they knew about. The MID had a nasty habit of springing bizarre challenges on their candidates unannounced, and Ryan didn't know if Finn would pass the unknown hurdles ahead.

And until he knew for sure, he dared not include Jenny in his plans.

❧

It was the middle of the afternoon as Ryan walked back toward the house, Lily clutching one hand and the folded set of kimono robes in his other. The weather was perfect, and he looked forward to an afternoon with Finn sailing their cutter-rig sailboat. The cutter-rig was popular at the Tokyo Regatta Club, and if Finn could gain admission to the club, it would open many doors in the city.

Their footsteps thudded on the porch as they approached the front door of their house. The scent of simmering lamb surrounded them as they stepped inside.

"Lamb stew!" Finn proclaimed. "I haven't eaten this well since I was kicked out of Stanford."

Mrs. Tucker stepped out of the kitchen, drying her hands on a towel, a look of uncharacteristic disapproval on her matronly face.

"Did we miss a lunch you had prepared?" Ryan asked. They always dined in the Presidio mess hall for lunch, but perhaps there had been a misunderstanding and Mrs. Tucker had expected them home for a fine meal.

"No," she said with no change in her unsmiling demeanor. "The stew is for tonight's dinner. My husband is here."

That was a surprise. He'd assumed Mrs. Tucker was a widow. Weren't most live-in housekeepers widows?

He recovered quickly and tried to present a welcoming face. "Excellent. I hope you invite him to dine with us." Perhaps that wasn't the correct protocol, but he wasn't sure how to handle the unexpected arrival of a housekeeper's husband.

"Oh yes, he will be dining with you," she replied. "This is probably the right time to tell you that 'Tucker' is actually my maiden name. My husband is Colonel Theodore Standish, and he is waiting for you on the back patio."

Ryan's breath left him in a rush. Colonel Standish was the head of the MID, the man Ryan had been working for since his second year in America but had never met in person.

And the colonel's wife had been spying on the spies.

Mrs. Tucker—rather, Mrs. Standish—had seen *everything*. All of Finn's late-night carousing and early morning hangovers. Ryan had hoped to straighten Finn out before the MID got wind of his problems, but that was obviously a lost cause now.

He still held the kimono in his hands, two thousand dollars of handwoven silk and the only thing of value Lily was likely to inherit from him. "Let me put this away, and I'll join you shortly," he said to buy a little time.

Mrs. Standish deftly took the kimono and reached for Lily's hand. "I know where this is to be stored, and I'll put the little one down for her nap. I suggest you go out to the back porch immediately."

Ryan nodded grimly to Finn. "Let's go."

The back patio was entirely enclosed in glass, making it warm year-round. The colonel sat in one of the patio chairs, his back to them, a newspaper held up with both hands and a smoking pipe resting on the table beside him.

"I gather the charms of San Francisco have been unusually tempting, Professor Breckenridge," the colonel said in a flat voice, not turning his head or lowering the newspaper.

"Nothing I can't control, sir," Finn said with typical confidence.

The newspaper snapped shut, and Colonel Standish shot to his feet and turned to face them. With a steely glare and posture like a bayonet, he got straight to business.

"My wife reports that you have come home drunk or incapacitated four times in the past two weeks. You refused to obey direct commands from Lieutenant Gallagher and have been negligent in studying Morse code. Finally, you failed to notice that my wife was no ordinary housekeeper. All in all, a shabby performance."

Finn shrugged. "I suppose so."

Ryan tried not to wince. Finn had no formal military training, but basic courtesy required more respect.

"You suppose correctly. Now get out of here. I need to speak to Lieutenant Gallagher privately."

Ryan waited as Finn's footsteps trailed away. Perspiration gathered beneath his shirt, and he tried to block the tension from showing on his face.

The colonel's glare did not soften as he pinned Ryan with a stare. "How bad is he?"

"I don't know," he answered truthfully. "I think he can control it when he wants to, but he doesn't always care enough to try." With every ounce of his heart, Ryan wished he could provide a better answer, but he could not lie, and he didn't know Finn well enough to vouch for him.

The colonel's mouth tightened as he reached for his pipe and began filling it with terse movements. "We just got word that the

Japanese invaded China to launch a surprise attack against a Russian fleet docked in harbor."

A wave of guilt hit Ryan. If he'd been in Tokyo, he might have seen the ramping up of operations, not let his government be taken unawares by the attack.

"The Russians are in full retreat and desperate to sue for peace," Colonel Standish continued. "Once that happens, Japanese imperial ambitions will be unchecked, and they might start to covet the Philippines. We've got three thousand troops stationed in Manila who need protection. We need someone on the ground in Tokyo who can be relied upon."

The colonel set down his pipe without lighting it. Ryan dreaded the next words out of Colonel Standish's mouth, but heaven help him, he knew what was coming.

"Finn Breckenridge can't be relied upon. He's out."

Ryan blanched. He reached for the back of a chair for support, seeing everything he'd worked so hard for slipping away. A safe home for Lily, his pearl farm . . . Jenny. Leaving her again would hurt most of all.

"I want you to return to Japan," Colonel Standish said. "You have no legal obligation to go, but your country needs you. You gave an oath to support and defend the Constitution of the United States against all enemies, and that oath does not expire when it is no longer convenient."

Ryan could refuse the request. It would be the easiest thing to do. He could walk away with no harm or legal ramifications.

"Will you go?" the colonel asked. The slight catch in his voice betrayed his anxiety. Both of them were sworn to protect this country. Both of them knew the best way to make that happen.

This mission was more important than one man. The ideal of America had been grafted onto Ryan's soul when he was younger than Lily. It happened listening to his mother's stories about hayrides and apple picking in a place called Ohio. It happened when he read about a man who grew up in a log cabin but still became a great president. It happened when he opened a book showing pictures of Nebraskan wheat fields and patriots gathered in Boston coffeehouses while drafting plans for a new nation. America was a place where a man was judged by the size of his heart and the sweat of his brow, not the shade of his skin. It wasn't a perfect country. They had made mistakes, but they could work to correct their course. He loved America down to the marrow of his bones and would fight for her, even if it meant leaving its shores.

But he loved Jenny, too, and he wasn't ready to give up yet.

"Finn is scheduled to take the MID tests in September," he said. "I want you to let him take those tests."

The colonel shook his head. "Breckenridge is out. He's an opium fiend and can't be trusted."

Finn might have a problem with opium, but he was also cunning, shrewd, and probably the smartest person Ryan had ever met. While Ryan knew Japan inside and out, he didn't have the natural qualities of a brilliant spy. Finn did.

He braced himself and met the colonel's gaze. "I don't want an agent clouded by opium any more than you, but I want Finn to have the chance to prove himself. I'll get him ready for the tests in September. I'll train him to buckle down and live a sober life that would make a nun proud."

The colonel sat, lit his pipe, and pulled in a deep draw. Curls of pungent smoke climbed and dissipated in the air before the colonel finally answered.

"You've got two months," he bit out. "We'll be watching. We won't lower the bar for him, but if Finn can prove himself in September, we'll send him. If Breckenridge fails, do you understand you will be our first choice to send back to Japan?"

"I understand, sir."

He was their *only* choice if Finn didn't work out. The first agent the MID sent to replace Ryan last year had failed for lack of understanding Japanese culture. They didn't have time to find another qualified man. If Finn couldn't pass muster, Ryan would do whatever his country asked of him, no matter what the cost.

❧

There were too many temptations in San Francisco to train Finn here. Ryan needed to get him in an isolated environment where he'd have no access to drugs or alcohol, and he knew just the place.

Ryan's house in Summerlin was on an isolated promontory on the coast. There were no taverns, no dance halls, and none of the myriad distractions that could be found on every square block of San Francisco. The peace and isolation of Summerlin was the best place to dry Finn out.

But Ryan had business to finalize before leaving the city. He'd given Simon a box of keshi pearls, and he wanted to see if the old jeweler had been able to make anything with them. To his surprise, when he entered Simon's jewelry shop, he saw that Simon had almost completed the brooch. The large pearl had been filed down to sit beautifully in a gold filigree mount, with tiny garnets set in the rim.

Ryan smiled in satisfaction. "It looks spectacular. How much do you think you can sell it for?"

"I'll price it at one hundred dollars and see if I get any takers. When can you get me more?" Simon asked.

That was the rub. At this point Ryan couldn't promise Simon more pearls without endangering his quest to win Jenny back.

"Jenny would be less than enthused if I sent you another batch," he said.

Simon snorted. "Jenny is a worrisome old woman. When will you have more pearls?"

"I'm not sure. I'm heading down to my pearl farm soon and will seed another batch of oysters if all goes well. A friend is going with me, and he might be able to help me with some of the work."

There was almost nothing to do at Summerlin *except* tend to the oysters, but it was impossible to predict how Finn would cope with sobriety. Opium might be a simple habit Finn could quit at will, but he could be in for a messy medical withdrawal.

"That dodgy friend Jenny told me about? That Finn fellow?"

Ryan nodded and sat in the seat opposite Simon. "You once worked with the Salvation Army, didn't you?"

"Still do," Simon acknowledged.

"Then you know a little something about drying a man out?"

Simon's laugh was ironic. "I've had some personal experience with that one."

This could be good. Ryan didn't know the first thing about the challenges of leading a man to sobriety. He began picking Simon's brain for insight, confessing that his primary reason for returning to Summerlin was to get Finn away from the temptations of the city.

"It sounds as if your friend's problem is with opium, not alcohol. That requires an entirely different approach."

"It does?"

Simon nodded. "One I have no experience with. Whiskey was my demon, and I beat it more than twenty years ago. Opium is different. You might want to talk to Jenny about it. Some of the soldiers in the amputee ward get too fond of morphine. She knows how to spot the signs and straighten them out."

Ryan grimaced. Jenny had no fondness for him and already distrusted Finn. When he told Simon as much, the old man shook his head.

"Jenny wants to save the world. Maybe when the two of you were courting, you never figured that out about her, but if she sees someone in pain, she wants to fix it. If you ask her for help, she'll give it to you."

Ryan shook his head. "I don't think Jenny would give me a glass of water if I was on fire. I think the manner in which I betrayed her is fairly obvious."

"Do you still love her?"

Ryan looked away and refused to answer. This was a humiliating and painful conversation veering in a direction he never expected, but Simon had not stopped talking.

"There is a piece of her that still cares for you," Simon said. "She's furious with you, too, but that doesn't have to be a permanent condition. Maybe you could earn her forgiveness."

"I don't deserve her forgiveness."

Simon snorted. "You'll never earn forgiveness by sitting around feeling sorry for yourself or running away to southern California. How hard are you willing to fight for what you love?"

He'd fight to the ends of the earth if there was a chance to win Jenny back. It was hard to imagine she might even consider it, but why had she tried to warn him about the rumors of a court-martial? Why hadn't she married? Why had she checked the casualty lists each week for the past six years?

A new idea began to take shape. Depending on the extent of Finn's addiction, they might be in for a bumpy ride in the coming weeks, and there were no doctors he could turn to for help in Summerlin. What if Jenny came with them?

His heart started thudding and hope flared within him, but he carefully kept it from showing on his face. Simon was loyal to Jenny, and any hint of emotion Ryan betrayed would find its way back to her.

He glanced around the shop. The display cases were empty, and Simon had only a few pieces of jewelry, not enough to reopen the store. Ryan could hardly persuade Jenny to come to his remote house with two adult men and no chaperone, but what if Simon came with them?

Ryan had a perfect excuse for luring Jenny to Summerlin. The MID would authorize a nurse to accompany him, and for some reason, Simon seemed willing to help him win Jenny back. He met Simon's eyes.

"How would you like to see pearl farming up close?" he asked.

Given the slow smile that spread across Simon's face, they were thinking along the same lines.

❧

It had been a week since Jenny's latest advertisement for the sailor with the scar, and this was usually about the time people came crawling out of the woodwork in an attempt to get the reward. Two hundred dollars was a lot of money, but unless they could produce the name of the sailor's parrot, they were nothing but frauds trying to swindle her.

Even knowing the letters were likely to be of no consequence, her stomach clenched and her head pounded as she approached the Presidio's post office. What would she do if one of her advertisements finally brought her face-to-face with the sailor? Even thinking about it made her apprehensive, but she'd lived with the guilt long enough to know that seeing him again would be the only way to close the door on her wretched childhood forever.

At nine o'clock in the morning most soldiers were already at work, so the lobby of the post office was empty. Strangely, there was no one standing behind the service window either, but peals of feminine laughter floated out of the sorting room.

Jenny rang the bell on the counter, and the laughter immediately ceased. Daisy Perkins scurried into place.

"Can I help you?" Daisy asked as she finger-combed some loose tendrils back into her auburn bun.

Before Jenny could reply, a familiar figure sauntered in behind Daisy. Finn Breckenridge, the professor who wasn't a professor, looked flushed, guilty, and happy. A swath of dark hair flopped forward over his eyes, but his devilish grin was out in full force.

The last thing she wanted was an audience. Picking up her mail the week after she placed a new advertisement was always stressful, but Mr. Breckenridge's rude scrutiny made it even more so. He didn't seem like the sort of person Ryan would consort with, but given Ryan's shocking change in demeanor, nothing surprised her anymore.

"What are you doing here?" she asked.

"Just helping file the mail," he said casually.

"It's a violation of federal postal regulations to have unauthorized personnel handling official mail." She didn't know if that was true, but she didn't trust this man and wanted to see how he'd react.

He clutched his hand to his chest in mock dismay. "Heavens," he murmured, "I ought to be taken out and shot at dawn. But you'll forgive me, won't you, Daisy?"

The girl giggled like an idiot but had the sense to look a little embarrassed. "She's right, you probably shouldn't be back here. Let me go fetch your mail, Jenny. You've got quite a pile built up."

It was an understatement. When Daisy returned, she carried a stack of letters nearly two inches thick.

"Someone has a lot of admirers," Mr. Breckenridge said. "At least I hope they're admirers and not bill collectors."

She left the post office without acknowledging Mr. Breckenridge's rude remark. All she wanted to do was get home and read through these letters, for even now she could be holding a note from the sailor with the scar himself. She alternately prayed for it and dreaded it, too.

By the time she got back to her room at the barracks, her mouth was dry, her fingers trembled, and anxiety made it hard to see straight.

It turned out not to matter. Letter after letter made ludicrous guesses about the parrot's name. Most went for the obvious: Polly, Birdie, Frisco, or simply Parrot. Others were more creative: *I remember Oliver the sailor, and he didn't have a parrot, he had a pet squirrel.* When she opened the last letter and read its wildly inaccurate guess, a sigh of relief escaped her. It would be easier if she could forget about the sailor with the scar and just go on with her life. What good would come of tracking him down, anyway?

It would be easier, but not better. Somehow Jenny knew that unless she found Oliver and made peace with what happened, he would continue haunting her. Would he ever be found? Was he dead? Conflicting emotions rolled through her as she pulled the blinds shut, changed into her nightgown, and put on her sleeping mask.

As she expected, the sailor with the scar plagued her restless dreams.

9

Each Sunday morning, Jenny forced herself to stay awake after breakfast so she could attend church at ten o'clock. It would be easier if she could indulge in a cup of strong black coffee like all the other people having breakfast in the mess hall, but if she succumbed to temptation she would never be able to sleep after church. She sat slumped over her bowl of oatmeal but savored the scent of percolating coffee, hoping it would be enough to rouse her for a few more hours. Maybe someday she'd find a job with normal hours and would not need to struggle with this endless craving to crawl into bed and sleep for a week.

As she sat in the pew each Sunday, she wondered if what Simon told her about salvation and forgiveness was really true. Intellectually, she understood that the things she'd done as a child would probably not be held against her by God, but it was hard to accept. She still wasn't really clean.

When she arrived at church, she gazed at the simple wooden cross behind the altar. Simon had taught her that Christ died so that her sins might be forgiven. But how could Christ forgive her if she'd never forgiven herself? The sins she carried were a blot at the very center of her core. They could never be expunged, only painted over. Even thinking about it was demoralizing. Or maybe it was just the exhaustion of working overnight. Sometimes the chronic lack of sleep made her weepy and weak. She'd feel better once she had a few solid hours of rest.

When the service was over, she rose and walked down the aisle . . . and froze at the sight of Lieutenant Ryan Gallagher in full uniform, watching her from the back pew. The white of his uniform was in sharp contrast to the dark blue and gray of the other men, and she averted her eyes, continuing down the aisle without stopping. If she stopped to speak with him, it would churn up bitter feelings. A better woman would extend forgiveness and be happy for Ryan and his beautiful daughter, but she couldn't do it.

After stepping into the sunshine, she headed north toward her barracks and sleep while almost everyone else was off toward the mess hall or out through the Lombard Gate to enjoy a day in the city.

Ryan was following her. His footsteps were gaining on her, but she quickened her pace, hoping he would get the message that she wanted nothing more to do with him.

He didn't. With an easy jog he pulled up alongside her. "Good morning, Jenny. Lovely day, isn't it?"

"I wouldn't know. I'm about to go get some sleep." The pace made her a little breathless, and she stopped. "Should you be scampering about like this? What about that knife wound in your side?"

Ryan grinned. "Walking isn't a problem. It was hanging from the racing schooner the other day that opened it up. I'd like a chance to speak with you about something. Could we go get a cup of coffee?"

"Thank you, but I would prefer to get some sleep. Night shift, you know."

"How would you like a chance to get off the night shift for a while?"

That got her attention. She scrutinized his face, looking for some sign of a trick. "Doing what?"

"Working as a private nurse. The government is interested in helping a particular man through some difficulties, and the attentions of a skilled nurse may be required."

"Here? At the Presidio?" Plum opportunities like that almost always went to the enlisted medical corps, not the civilian nurses.

Ryan shifted his stance a little. "Are you sure I can't get you something to eat? If not coffee, maybe we can just go to the Officers' Club and talk."

The Officers' Club was almost a mile away, and she could barely hold her eyelids up, but if there was an opportunity to get off the night shift, she wanted to hear it.

"We can talk as I go back to the barracks."

He followed as she set off toward home. "The patient I'm speaking of is Finn Breckenridge," he said in a low voice, his head tipped down.

"Hey, Sally!" a voice hollered from the other side of the stables. "Look, there goes Sally, off to hide behind a nurse's skirt!"

"Come on over and pet our yellow dog, Sally!" another voice shouted.

Jenny turned to see who was being so obnoxious on a Sunday morning, but Ryan grasped her elbow and kept prodding her forward.

"Ignore them," he said.

"Sally!" another obnoxious voice wailed. "Don't leave us, Sally!"

"Who are they?" she asked. "Why are they calling us Sally?"

"They're calling *me* Sally. It's a term for coward. They've heard the rumor that I deserted in the Philippines." He didn't flinch when he said it, but the tension in his voice was plain.

"Well . . . did you?"

The glare he shot her could scorch paint from a wall.

"If you didn't desert, why don't you just say so? Why all the mystery?"

"I'd rather not talk about it."

The heckling continued as they crossed the quadrangle. She didn't know how he could tolerate such abuse. She'd been on the receiving end of cruel taunts as a child, and she could unleash a savage attack in retaliation. She'd had to stop when she went to live with Simon.

"Ladies don't curse," Simon had gently soothed. "They don't bite. They don't kick, and they don't tackle boys and rub their face in the mud, even when that boy is being very mean."

Boys rarely expected girls to fight with the ferocity Jenny could unleash, but she had reined it in for Simon. Instead, she stood there and took the abuse, just like Ryan was doing now. When she was a child, she used to run home and sob in Simon's arms. Somehow she couldn't see Ryan doing the same.

"Let's step inside the hospital," she said quietly. "They can't follow us there."

She led him down the corridor of the first ward and out into a courtyard. The hospital was built around a series of courtyards, each with a wide verandah and plenty of rocking chairs for the convalescents. They sat on a pair of chairs and watched a group of patients being led through calisthenics in the exercise yard.

"Out with it," she said abruptly, and it annoyed her that he smiled at her command. He glanced around the courtyard, but they were far away from everyone else, and yet still he leaned in close and lowered his voice.

"What I am about to tell you needs to remain confidential. You understand that?"

"Of course."

He still seemed pensive and uncomfortable as he lowered his voice even further. "Over the years I've done some work for the government overseas. Finn Breckenridge has been tapped to take over the assignment. The first man the government sent over to replace me didn't function well in Japanese society and caved under the stress. He came back after less than six months. Finn is our last hope."

"What kind of assignment?"

There was a long pause, broken only by the rasping noise of the rocking chair treads as she slowly pushed with her foot.

"It's a job where he needs all his senses about him. He can't be drunk or intoxicated on opium. I'm taking him to my home in Summerlin, where I can get him straightened out. I need a competent nurse to help."

"And you want *me*? Have you lost your mind?" It was the most ridiculous suggestion she'd ever heard. She had a job with responsibilities, and Ryan lived in the middle of nowhere. She knew because she had looked it up on a map after Vivian tracked down his address. It would take a full day's travel by train just to get there.

"I want a nurse who is familiar with opiates. I don't know if Finn is just dabbling or if he has a more serious addiction. You know how to deal with this issue—I don't. General Dwyer has agreed to have you assigned to this mission until we can demonstrate that Finn is fit for service."

She looked away. Yes, she could spot signs of men indulging in opiates and the tricks they used to get their hands on it, but there were plenty of people who could do this job. Ryan was up to something. Her blind faith in him was gone forever, but even now a whirlwind of emotion stirred, making her long for things best forgotten. Some dreams were too dangerous to toy with.

"Why me?"

Once again a silence stretched between them. Ryan stared at the men performing calisthenics on the other side of the yard, but she sensed his mind was riddled with turmoil. His brow was furrowed, and the corners of his mouth were turned down.

"Jenny, are you happy?" he finally asked.

It wasn't the kind of question she ever contemplated. She had a respectable job that gave her life a sense of purpose. She was good at it. And if she sometimes mourned that her life wasn't everything she hoped . . . well, that was alright. After all, her life was much better than any gutter rat had a right to expect.

She didn't answer Ryan's question, just kept up the lazy rocking in her chair as she stared at the wounded soldiers struggling to regain their health.

"Summerlin is in the southern part of the state, nestled into an inlet north of San Diego," Ryan said. "I have a house that faces the ocean. It's like a piece of Eden forgotten by time. Your only responsibility will be to look after Finn, and it's anyone's guess how things will go. I realize I'm asking you to venture into the complete unknown. It might be wonderful or it might be a disaster, but Jenny . . . you know what you will get if you stay at the Presidio."

She swallowed hard. She would eat nails before admitting it, but the prospect of having a decent night's sleep was more tempting than all the jewels in the Indies. Already her body longed to crawl into bed and sleep straight through until dawn. Following Ryan meant a few weeks of undisturbed sleep during the overnight hours when the human body was designed to rest. Even now, her exhausted body quivered at the possibility.

Ryan kept speaking. "I've already talked to Simon. He's willing to accompany us, so you need not fear I will expect anything . . ." He paused and a flush stained his cheeks. "Anything unseemly."

It was probably exhaustion that made her laugh, but she always found it amusing how abashed Ryan could be regarding anything *unseemly*. Even when they were courting six years ago, she had been far more forward than Ryan, who always seemed so touchingly hesitant.

Which was ridiculous. He certainly got plenty of experience with at least one woman after he left her, and she must never forget that.

"How much will you pay me?"

He blinked. "I hadn't thought that far."

Honestly, for a man as well-traveled as Ryan Gallagher, he was so naïve about the ways of the world.

"I'll need twenty dollars a week," she said bluntly. It was what the hospital paid the enlisted men who had her same job during the day, and she'd always resented how women on the overnight shift were paid less. "Twenty dollars and confirmation my job will be waiting for me when I get back."

Ryan nodded. "General Dwyer has already confirmed your job will continue."

"It needs to be in writing. I don't trust verbal promises."

He flinched a little, a sign her arrow found its mark. "I can get that as well."

There would be no better time to bargain for what she wanted than right now. It seemed the government was unusually invested in whatever they had planned for Finn Breckenridge, and if they wanted her help, she was prepared to drive a hard bargain. She clenched the arms of her chair so hard it made the palms of her hands hurt, but hope was beginning to take root, and she was going to fight for it.

"Days," she said bluntly.

"What?"

"I want to work *days*," she said. "In the document promising I will have a job when I return, I want it specified that I will be working during the day. No more night shifts. Ever. And I will be paid at the same rate all the male medical attendants are paid."

"That might be difficult," Ryan said.

She stood so quickly the rocking chair tilted crazily behind her. "Then this conversation is at an end." She walked down the verandah without a backward glance.

"Wait!"

She paused but didn't turn around. The tension in Ryan's voice was all the indication she needed that she was in charge here. He drew up alongside her.

"I'll speak to General Dwyer, but I can't make any promises."

"You know my conditions. Make it happen, Ryan."

⁂

What had she just done? It was either the most brilliant or potentially catastrophic decision of her life. Stepping back inside Ryan Gallagher's orbit was like sticking her heart in a vise and asking for it to be stomped flat. Her armor was no good where Ryan was concerned. All it took was a flash of that tender, hesitant smile, and her heart turned over.

Back in her room, Jenny cradled a cup of chamomile tea in her palms as she gazed mindlessly out the window at the people enjoying a Sunday morning on the grounds below. If Ryan could get her moved to the day shift, perhaps someday soon she could take part in normal activities like those people.

Among the dozens of soldiers she spotted a man who didn't blend in with the others. She hoisted up the window sash and leaned out to get a better view. She could only see him from the back, but on a base where every man wore a sober uniform, the yellow velvet smoking jacket stuck out like a sunflower in a field of rye. Finn Breckenridge was the only person affiliated with the Presidio who'd be caught dead in such a getup.

He was the exact opposite of Ryan's straight-laced, reticent personality, and if she was going to be his nurse, she needed to figure him out. The teacup clattered as she plunked it on the bureau then dashed through her door, down three flights of stairs, and outside to catch him. Ryan might be a babe in the woods, but she could sense a charlatan from yards away, and Finn set off all her warning bells.

It was easy to overtake him as he shambled down the path. Her nose wrinkled at the scent of whiskey coming off him.

"Late night?" she inquired in a polite tone.

Finn shot her a glare. "What are you doing here? Shouldn't you be tending the brave boys in blue?"

"Rumor has it I'm going to be assigned to tending you. Something about a temperance problem."

That stopped Finn in his tracks. He whirled to look at her, anger in his eyes. "First of all, I don't have a problem. If Ryan Gallagher wasn't such a prude, he'd know that it's perfectly normal for a healthy young man to indulge in the joys of life. Second, who said you'd be assigned to me? This is the first I've heard of it."

They were blocking the path, and a pair of soldiers had to step on the neatly manicured lawn to navigate around them, but Finn didn't seem to care as he glared at her from an unshaven face with bleary eyes.

Eyes that were watering badly. It was a classic sign of opiate withdrawal. She softened her attitude. It appeared he was already trying to straighten up, and that deserved some sympathy.

"If General Dwyer agrees, I've been assigned to go to Summerlin until you're healthy."

"I don't want you there," Finn snapped. "Ryan had no right to blab about my private business to you. I don't want or need your help."

"Pipe down," she ordered in a low voice. "You're announcing your weakness to the entire base by standing here and yelling at a nurse. Believe it or not, people actually like me here, so pretend you have more self-restraint than a drunken sailor."

A hint of respect gleamed in his eyes, but he couldn't resist the opening. "Known a lot of drunken sailors, have you?"

"What does the army see in you?" she asked.

"My undaunted brilliance." The effect was spoiled when he hiccupped. This man was definitely *not* someone Ryan would choose to associate with under normal circumstances. Something was wrong here, and she wasn't blindly going to join forces with these two men unless she understood exactly what she was getting into.

"You aren't what you seem," she challenged.

"And you are?" His voice dripped with sarcasm, and she hoped he didn't notice her flinch. The veneer she'd built up over the years was solid, but the way he inspected her made her wonder how she'd slipped.

"What's that supposed to mean?" she demanded.

He smirked as he glanced at her throat. "What's with the prissy starched collars? Men on the base talk, and rumor has it you pay to have a fresh collar every day of the week, and that's not normal. My guess is that you're hiding behind them, compensating for gross inadequacies."

"That's all you've got to prove a shifty character? The fact that I like to be cleanly turned out each day?"

"That and the fact that you've placed an advertisement in the *San Francisco Examiner* looking for some strange sailor."

She flinched and he pounced.

"I saw that stack of letters in response to the advertisement you posted," he continued. "Did you think using an anonymous box number and having the letters forwarded to the Presidio was a clever way to cover your tracks? So touchingly naïve. All I had to do was take your box number to the *Examiner*, do a little reverse engineering with their payroll department, and figure out who was placing the advert and what it said. So tell me, Nurse Bennett, who is this missing sailor you're looking for? I'm sure there's a juicy story there, and it's nothing good."

Jenny kept her face schooled in a carefully blank mask. She

didn't want her shameful history bandied about in public, but Finn gloated at her discomfort. The old Jenny would have kicked him in the back of the knees, then shoved him onto the ground to rub his face in the dirt.

But she wasn't the old Jenny. She was a nurse with an unblemished reputation, and unless the sailor with the scar was found, no one would ever know otherwise.

"My story is quite dull," she said quietly. "I am a highly qualified nurse with no unsavory dependencies on opiates or alcohol. I have the complete confidence of the army and need prove myself to no one. Those are the most significant differences between you and me."

She turned her back and headed toward her barracks, hoping Finn didn't notice the tremble in her voice. Although everything she'd said was true, should her shady past ever become common knowledge, she would lose the trust of the army and any other hospital that considered hiring her. Nurses were required to be morally above reproach, and the sailor with the scar could blow Jenny's cover to smithereens.

10

Ryan contemplated his return to Summerlin with a rush of anticipation mixed with anxiety. He sat at his desk, trying to focus on the analysis Finn had written about Japanese trade regulations, but it was impossible to concentrate. So much depended on the next few weeks. He and Jenny would be in constant contact. There would be no way to avoid each other, and the stakes of the mission couldn't be higher. His heart and his entire life savings were invested in California. All of it hung in the balance until Finn could pass those tests.

He was eager to get started, but Jenny refused to leave San Francisco until she had a signed letter from General Dwyer guaranteeing the security of her position and her shift to daytime hours upon her return to the Presidio. She refused to pack her bags or even meet with Finn until she had that letter. At first he thought her behavior a little paranoid, but perhaps she was right to be skeptical. Apparently his request to adjust Jenny's schedule had stirred up a stink at headquarters.

Footsteps on the front porch and a brisk knock interrupted his thoughts. He set the paper down and opened the door to a young corporal, who handed him an envelope.

"From General Dwyer, sir."

"Thank you, Corporal," he replied as relief rushed through him. As soon as he got this letter of approval to Jenny, she could start packing. They could be on a train first thing in the morning and home at Summerlin by tomorrow evening. They'd wasted so much time already.

He pulled out the letter, scanning it quickly.

This was unbelievable. The hospital director had appointed a different medical attendant to monitor Finn. *Corporal Jervis is well trained in the needs of patients ranging from stopping hemorrhage, the relief of shock, setting fractures and dislocations—*

Ryan dropped the note. Did Captain Soames even know what the mission was, or was he so adamant to avoid a staffing disruption that he didn't care?

Ryan strode to headquarters, his footsteps echoing down the whitewashed hallways. "I need to see General Dwyer," he informed the officer on duty at the front desk.

"The general is at lunch, sir."

"The officers' dining room?"

"Yes, sir."

He didn't care that he would be disrupting the general's lunch. He'd been waiting three days for this letter, and he had been explicit in his demands. Rather, Jenny's demands. But it didn't matter, he wanted them met. They *owed* him that. He was willing to disrupt his entire life on behalf of this country, and his request wasn't unreasonable. He was going to get it today.

The officers' dining hall was in one of the elegant old buildings built when the Presidio was still a Spanish outpost. The floors were of cool Spanish tile, and the ceiling consisted of exposed beams and whitewashed adobe. The sounds of cutlery and clinking glasses filled the dining room. With only a dozen tables, it was easy to spot General Dwyer by the window with a number of his company commanders.

General Dwyer saw him approach and rose. "Still here?" he asked cordially. Although the general was polite, Ryan could feel the suspicious stares from officers at neighboring tables. No one here knew of Ryan's service in Japan, but most had probably heard the rumors that he was a deserter.

"Still here," he confirmed. "And I will be until I get the authorization for the request I put in three days ago."

"I turned that over to Captain Soames. Hasn't he delivered it?"

Ryan handed the note to the general, who read it quickly, his mouth clenched in annoyance.

"It may not be what you asked for, but it still meets your needs, Lieutenant."

It did. There were probably dozens of people on base who could look after Finn, but Ryan didn't want any of them. Only Jenny. He was already mentally bracing himself for another difficult posting in Japan. If he had to upend his entire future once again, he would leave with the knowledge that he'd helped give Jenny a better life here in America. It was the least he could do for her.

"I would like my original request resubmitted to Captain Soames." A dozen officers at neighboring tables could hear every word, but Ryan continued. "It will be difficult to summon the necessary concentration if I don't have a nurse I can trust."

"Are you refusing an order?"

The stunned question hung in the air. From the moment Ryan had arrived in America as a wide-eyed seventeen-year-old, already infatuated with the nation he'd never seen, he wanted only to be a good and loyal officer. He'd done everything his government asked of him for twelve years. Only when he saw what was in store for Lily in Japan did he ask to be relieved of duty. No agent in the history of the MID had stayed in an undercover assignment as long as he had. He was prepared to go back, but he wanted something in return.

"I would like my request resubmitted to Captain Soames. I am prepared to do whatever my country asks of me. I would expect no less of Captain Soames." He met the general's gaze squarely, the implication obvious. General Dwyer could easily order Captain Soames to honor Ryan's request, but he would have to spend some political capital to do so.

It was a staring contest. General Dwyer's steely gaze did not waver, but neither did Ryan's. He had been an even-tempered man his entire life, but not when a woman he cared for was involved.

"You will have a decision by the end of the day," the general said.

≈≥

It was ten o'clock that night when the new orders arrived at Ryan's house. A soldier delivered two copies of letters that had been signed and notarized by both Captain Soames and General Dwyer. Ryan smiled in satisfaction as he read the document. Jenny would get her raise in salary and a promotion to the day shift upon her return to San Francisco.

He slid the letters back into their envelopes. Even if the worst happened and he ended up going to Japan in place of Finn, at least he had won this victory for Jenny. He wanted to deliver it to her in person. And despite the late hour, he knew exactly where to find her.

The hospital was eerily quiet at night, and his footsteps echoed in the tile hallways. The floors had just been swabbed down with an antiseptic solution that gleamed wetly in the dim electric lighting. The scent was familiar. He'd used the same weak solution on the wound in his ribs.

How odd that despite twelve years of active duty in the military, the only time he'd ever been seriously injured was in the tiny, idyllic fishing village of Summerlin. Ryan had just stepped out of the hardware store after purchasing some rope when a bull-necked man dressed like a common sailor barreled directly at him, knocking him to the ground and slashing wildly with a knife. Ryan blocked the first few attempts, but a blow finally struck home in his ribs with a searing rush of pain. A couple men at the feedstore across the street came to his aid. The sailor ran off, but several people got a good look at him, and all agreed he was a stranger to the village.

The worst thing was that Lily saw the entire incident. She'd screamed in terror, and Ryan wanted to reassure her, but he'd just been stabbed, and Jack Brewster from the feedstore held him down while they pressed a rag into his ribs. Jack made a living mending sails, and he set a row of ten stitches in Ryan's wound since Summerlin had no doctor. The wound was long but not deep, and Jack said one of Ryan's ribs had prevented the blade from sinking in enough to puncture a lung.

All that had been more than a month ago, and the wound had been healing well until Ryan tore it open while hanging like a gymnast off a sailboat careening through the waves. He didn't look forward to a fourteen-hour train ride with the itchy, tender wound, but all things considered, he'd escaped lightly.

A light at the end of the hallway lit the entrance to the amputee ward where Jenny worked. Ryan tried to hold down his sense of anticipation. He had no right to expect anything from Jenny, even gratitude, but he still looked forward to letting her know of his success.

He tapped softly on the door before twisting the knob and entering. The ward was a long, narrow room with nine beds on either side. Immediately to his left was the nurse's station. Jenny was making notes in a register, the folded nurse's cap pinned atop her glossy black hair.

She looked up in surprise, then quickly rose and came around the desk. "What are you doing here?" she whispered.

"I came to deliver a message. Can you step into the hall for a moment?"

She glanced quickly at the patients, most of whom were sleeping. "I've only got a moment," she said as she stepped into the hall.

Ryan held the envelope aloft. "The document you requested just arrived a few minutes ago."

Her eyes widened, staring at the letter as though she feared it would vanish if she touched it. Finally she snatched it and yanked the pages from the envelope. He studied her face as she read, her eyes scanning the lines of text over and over.

"I didn't really think you could do it," she stammered. The amazement in her voice filled him with pride. "Thank you, thank you so much."

Then she grabbed his face with both hands and pulled him down for a kiss directly on the mouth.

She pulled away quickly. "I'm sorry," she stammered.

"I'm not. You can kiss me anytime."

"You can't imagine what this means to me."

"I think I can," he said, still too stunned by her kiss to form a coherent sentence.

Jenny had always been pretty, but her face practically glowed with delight as she scanned the note again. It was astonishing that so much passion could be contained in such a petite body. She turned to face the wall, dabbing her eyes with the cuff of her gown.

"Are you crying?" he asked in amazement.

"Of course not," she choked out. "I'm just tired and hadn't really expected this." She sniffled and straightened her shoulders. She adjusted her collar before turning back to him, her face composed. "What happens now?" she asked. "Quite frankly, I haven't done much to prepare."

"Can you be ready to leave on the morning train? The letter says you must continue your overnight shift until you leave for Summerlin."

"Then I'll be ready to leave tomorrow morning!" she said, her voice sparkling with delight.

She was looking at him the way she used to, like he was Robin Hood and Hercules rolled into one person. As though he were a man worthy of her. It stirred old hopes he'd long since abandoned. Hope was a dangerous thing, for it unleashed his inhibitions and prompted him to speak straight from the heart.

"I wish we could run away together," he said. "Just the two of us. Escape to my house and build our own isolated kingdom by the sea. We could forget about obligations and responsibilities and just be two people free to write our future the way it always should have been."

She stiffened and drew a step back. She looked as shocked as if he'd just yanked the ground out from beneath her. "Don't talk like that," she said. "I'm not following you to Summerlin to rekindle the past. I'm going because I want to work the day shift, and this is the price I need to pay. That's all, Ryan."

Her words were a kick in the teeth. The wild, nascent stirrings of hope crumbled to ash inside, but he kept his shoulders back, head held high. "I understand," he said, even as he wished it could be otherwise.

When she turned to leave, his arm shot out to stop her. He needed to tell her about the MID. Once they were in Summerlin it would be impossible to hide it from her. Jenny would see Finn cramming to learn Morse code, military armaments, and the myriad topics required of any foreign agent.

When Jenny understood why he abandoned her all those years ago, would she forgive him? He hadn't asked for the assignment that had been thrust upon him. He hadn't *wanted* it. Six years ago, the only thing he longed to do was grab Jenny's hand and run toward a beautiful, sun-filled future with her at his side. Perhaps when Jenny learned why he acted as he had, she might soften toward him.

"I need to tell you something," he said.

Jenny paused and looked at him curiously. "Why do you look so serious? You're making me nervous."

She was nervous? This was the moment he'd alternately longed for and dreaded for the past six years. He glanced up and down the hallway. They were completely alone.

"I was in Japan for most of the war," he said softly. "Ever since graduating from college, I've been working for an agency in Washington that most people don't even know exists."

That got her attention. She took a step back and stared at him with incredulous eyes.

"When I was accepted into the Naval Academy, I assumed I would become an officer like everyone else, but during my first year a man from the government visited me on campus," he said. "They wanted my knowledge of Japan."

He explained that America's newly claimed territory in the Philippines had angered Japan. The growing tensions meant the government needed someone in Tokyo to have their ears open, befriend Japanese industrialists who might be involved in gearing up for war, and be on the lookout for increased military operations.

Jenny gazed at him in growing bewilderment as he continued. "I never went to the Philippines. From the outset I was sent to Tokyo, and I thought I'd be free to return home after the war. I truly believed I'd return to you quickly, but the rebellion in the Philippines complicated matters. Once it became clear the Americans intended to stay in the Philippines, my mission was extended indefinitely. The government asked me to stay in Japan permanently. Forever."

Jenny's face was a mask of white as she gaped at him, speechless.

"So now you know," he said. "I wanted so badly to tell you everything, but I couldn't."

Jenny finally found her tongue. "So you were a spy?"

132

"That's not a term any of us use. I was just keeping an eye on things."

Sorrow filled her eyes and she reached out to touch his cheek. "Oh, Ryan," she whispered in an aching voice. "I always knew something was very wrong, but I never imagined this."

He turned his face into her palm. Six years of longing and regret began draining out of him, finding comfort in her touch. "You can't imagine how much I've always wanted to tell you . . . to confide in you . . ."

"Shhhh," she soothed. "It's alright. I understand."

"You do?" Hope rekindled, even as her face further clouded in despair.

"I've always understood about your loyalty to this country. It all makes perfect sense now. When the soldiers taunted you for failing to fight in the Philippines, for living on a yacht in the Tokyo Bay—"

"It was true. All those things were true, but if I tried to defend myself, I would put any future agent assigned to Japan in danger."

Jenny withdrew a few feet and wrapped her hands around her middle. "And Akira? Where does she fit into this?"

He froze, not wanting to reveal anything else that would hurt Jenny. Far from the man of honor he'd always tried to be, the night he agreed to stay in Japan permanently he had wallowed in self-pity and fallen into despair. He'd turned to the only real friend he had in Japan, a girl he'd known since childhood. He'd sought out Akira for help, but all he'd done was dishonor them both.

"Akira was a good friend," he admitted. "I turned to her for comfort, and she became pregnant. I had already agreed to stay in Japan for good, so I married her. It wasn't that I stopped loving you . . . but I needed to do the honorable thing."

Jenny withdrew farther, crossing her arms over her chest and looking sick. The acrid scent of cleaning solution from the floor made it suddenly hard to breathe, but nothing was as uncomfortable as the expression on Jenny's face.

"Did you love her?"

He hated this discussion. His infidelity was long past, and he didn't want to shove it in Jenny's face. The less said about Akira, the easier it would be for Jenny, but she'd asked a direct question and deserved an answer.

"Akira was a good woman, and she was Lily's mother," he said slowly. "She's also part of the past." He held his breath, hoping this would be enough. No good could come from this conversation, only pain.

"And that's all you have to say about her?" Jenny's voice had turned hard.

"Yes. That's all I have to say."

Jenny's movements were jerky as she crossed and uncrossed her arms. "Well," she finally said, "I'm proud that you did your duty. I'm humbled at the sacrifice you made, but I still can't reconcile the man I loved with someone who would cut me off with a four-sentence letter—"

"I couldn't explain more without endangering the mission. Letters from Japan could be censored."

"Am I expected to overlook the four-year-old girl you brought back with you?"

"Be careful, Jenny." He tamped down the impulse to retaliate at the hardness in her voice. He deserved her anger. Lily did not.

Jenny must have sensed the warning in his voice, for she sighed and glanced away. She seemed to age ten years as her shoulders slumped and the fire died from her eyes.

"Lily is a beautiful child," she said in an aching voice. "She is smart and cheerful, and you must be so proud of her, but don't you understand she is painful to me? She is living proof of what happened in Japan and a woman named Akira. I feel low and petty for resenting her, but I can't help it."

Anguish settled over him. What Jenny said was true. It was

impossible to look at Lily and not see Akira in his daughter's silky black hair and almond-shaped eyes. He would lie down before a speeding train to protect Lily from harm, but already she was the recipient of sidelong looks in California. People who met them for the first time would glance between him and Lily, speculation rampant on their faces as they stared. Most were polite, but a few were disdainful. It made Ryan ferociously protective of Lily.

"You're human, Jenny. I can't blame you for harboring resentment toward me and Akira, but I need to know if that will extend to Lily."

Jenny looked exasperated. "I'd cut off my hand before I'd knowingly do anything to hurt a child. These ugly feelings are my shame, not hers."

It wasn't exactly a ringing endorsement, but Jenny had always been honest. "I'll meet you tomorrow morning at the train station, then."

Jenny kept her face averted, arms still folded across her chest. She did not reply.

He repeated his question. "I'll see you at the train station tomorrow morning, then. Right?"

"Alright," she finally said, barely loud enough to be heard before she turned away and left him standing alone in the hallway.

The cool night air was a relief after the tense scene outside Jenny's ward. It had been naïve to hope she might be able to overlook Akira. It was still difficult for him to discuss Akira, the girl who had been his only friend during those difficult childhood years.

His parents arrived in Yokohama as Christian missionaries just as Japan was beginning to open up to the West. It was a difficult assignment, and most of their words about Jesus and love fell on rocky soil. A handful of Japanese listened to them but mostly as a way of establishing valuable trading ties with the West. Akira's father was one such man. Harue was already one of the richest silk merchants in Japan, but if he could export his silk to America and Europe, he would become rich beyond all imagination.

Just because Harue allowed missionaries to distribute Bibles in his silk factory did not mean Ryan was accepted by the children of the village. The kids at school had been brutal in their harassment, but like other Japanese children, Ryan learned to suppress his emotions, lock them down, and put on a stoic face of indifference. On occasion it cracked and his parents sensed his profound alienation, but they told him to forgive his tormenters.

He did. He tolerated, endured, and ignored. Over time he became a master at hiding his emotions.

There was only one place he felt entirely safe. Harue's silk factory was a cavernous building with plenty of hiding places, and his daughter Akira was always there. They were the same age, and they escaped to the factory after school to feed the ravenous silkworms in the huge breeding frames and watch the miracle of nature as the worms spun their cocoons.

Those hours in the silk factory were Ryan's only happy memories of childhood. While they fed the silkworms, he shared tales of America with Akira and prayed for the day he would be allowed to travel to that distant land where his real life could begin.

When he returned to Japan as an adult, Akira was still at the silk factory, for while her father's dabbling in Christianity was only a business strategy to open doors to the West, Akira's conversion was genuine, and there were precious few Christian men in Japan. Rather than marry a man who did not share her faith, she found her calling in her father's factory, overseeing the artisans who created the magnificent silk kimonos.

The day he accepted the MID's mission to remain in Japan, Ryan rode to Yokohama and turned to Akira for solace. He could not tell her why his heart was so wounded, and she did not ask. He simply needed her smiling presence, the reassuring thump and rhythm of the silk looms that had been the only happy place of his boyhood. There was good in Japan, and he would find it.

When he reached out to embrace Akira, she did not turn away.

Lily was conceived that day, and he married Akira two months later. Harue went into a rage, breaking the Japanese taboo against public displays of anger as he banished Akira from the silk factory, her one source of pride and accomplishment. They went to live in Tokyo, where she found work as a seamstress.

Akira lost everything when she married Ryan. Her wealth, her family, her status as a silk artisan. She was a regret he would carry for the rest of his life, but there could be no going back to correct his mistakes. All he could do now was protect Lily. That meant he had two months to get Finn healthy and ready to pass the rigorous tests in September, or else his American dream would come to an end once again.

11

Ryan paced on the platform at the railway station. The train was leaving in ten minutes, and Jenny still hadn't arrived. Her shift ended two hours ago, and Simon had already brought her luggage, so she hadn't needed to pack a bag. She ought to be here by now.

During the hour they'd been waiting at the station, Ryan had taken Simon aside to explain his association with the MID and the need to train Finn for a rigorous series of tests. Part of him hoped that once Simon understood why Ryan acted as he had in Japan, the older man would help soften Jenny's mistrust. He was disappointed.

"Jenny has always been gun-shy," Simon said. "She grew up with a guarded heart, and it takes a lot for her to lower her defenses. She did it for you once, and I doubt she'll be able to do it again."

Ryan did too.

The train was on the verge of pulling out of the station. Had Jenny decided to back out after all? Finn, Lily, and Simon were already aboard, and Ryan strained to see through the early morning fog. Porters loaded the last of the luggage, and a few family members loitered to see the train off.

At first he didn't recognize Jenny. He'd been looking for her nurse's uniform, and the woman walking toward him in a slim-fitting maroon dress took him aback. She looked so different in civilian clothes. Lovely but different.

Relief flooded him and he gestured to the open compartment door. "Ready?" he asked, hoping his impatience didn't bleed into his voice.

It must not have, for she continued strolling at that leisurely pace until she was finally climbing up into the train ahead of him.

Lily suffered from a queasy stomach if she traveled backward, so Ryan put her on the forward-facing bench. He wanted to offer the other forward-facing seat to Jenny, but Lily was anxious and insisted he sit beside her. It was going to be a fourteen-hour journey to Summerlin, and it was best not to begin the ride with a crying jag from Lily.

"Jenny, will you be alright in a rear-facing seat?" he asked.

"It makes no difference to me," she said as she plunked onto the bench opposite him. She tucked a small pillow beside her shoulder and leaned against the window. "I intend to get as much sleep as I can."

This was going to be awkward. Finn was grouchy and hungover, Lily anxious, and Jenny's attempt to sleep was surely going to be foiled by a chatty four-year-old sharing the small compartment. Only Simon appeared chipper as he made room for Jenny, commenting favorably on the padded benches and door that gave their compartment a private feel.

The stationmaster walked down the platform, calling out the departure commands. Steam from the engine hissed as the train chugged out of the station, gathering momentum as they pulled away. Against Ryan's will, a surge of anticipation stirred to life. He missed Summerlin. It was the first home of his choosing, and he longed for it like a compass needle seeking true north.

He leaned down to Lily. "We're on our way," he whispered in her ear.

She shrieked in delight and pumped her legs with enthusiasm, causing Jenny to open her eyes and glare.

The glare was uncalled for. He tucked a protective arm around Lily's shoulders, who was too busy looking out the window to have noticed the ire from Jenny. Naturally Jenny was exhausted from her overnight shift, but it was unreasonable to expect silence in a tight carriage compartment with four other people.

"Lily will settle down in an hour or so and take a nap," Ryan said. "Perhaps it will be easier for you to sleep then."

Jenny said nothing, but surely she understood the wisdom of his suggestion. Or did she? Jenny had no children of her own, so perhaps she couldn't appreciate that there was only so much one could order a small child to do. Lily was a remarkably well-behaved girl, but she still had the heart of a four-year-old.

Lily didn't settle down. She plastered her face against the window and stared at the city streets as the train rumbled through town. After getting bored with the passing scenery, she mimicked the shunting cadence from the engine by thumping her feet. Ryan hauled her onto the bench to settle her down, but it didn't last even a minute. Lily stood up and decided it was time to introduce her doll, Zuzu, to everyone in the carriage. Lily even asked Jenny if she would like to play with Zuzu.

"No, thank you," Jenny said stiffly.

Lily must have sensed the tension in Jenny's voice, for she grew somber and started sucking her thumb. She backed up until she leaned against Ryan's knees, wrapping one arm around his legs for security. He placed his hands protectively on her narrow shoulders, rubbing gently and hoping her feelings weren't hurt by Jenny's rejection.

Lily stared at Jenny with the intense scrutiny only a child would dare. Lily was not accustomed to being around women. There were almost no women at the Presidio, and they lived an isolated life at his house in Summerlin. A local girl sometimes helped around the house, but Abigail was very different from Jenny, and it was only normal for Lily to be curious.

And Jenny was unusually beautiful, with refined features and her smooth, black hair swept into a neat bun at the back of her head. Her face was an expressionless mask as she gazed out the window at the countryside rolling past. They'd left the city behind, and now the golden hills of California rolled out in an endless sea of grass.

Lily moved forward and set a hesitant hand on Jenny's knee. "You look like my mommy."

Ryan tensed but relaxed when he realized Lily had spoken in Japanese. He tugged Lily back onto his lap, his arms folding protectively around her compact body.

"What did she say?" Jenny asked.

"Nothing." The last thing he wanted to discuss was Akira. Jenny was already exhausted and annoyed with Lily, and bringing Akira into this overcrowded compartment would be like poking a wounded lion.

The odd thing was, Jenny *did* look a little like Akira. Their coloring was similar, as was their heart-shaped face and narrow chin. Lily was only a toddler when her mother died, but there was a photograph of Akira in her bedroom, and he knew by the way Lily often stared at it that she was hungry for the kind of maternal love Akira had provided in abundance.

Jenny turned to Finn. "What did she say?"

"She said you look like her mommy," Finn translated before Ryan could stop him.

Jenny said nothing, but the tightening around her mouth spoke volumes. Ryan glanced at his watch. They'd only been traveling for an hour, but it felt like days. And they still had thirteen more hours before reaching Summerlin.

Jenny was bleary-eyed and exhausted by the time the train arrived in Summerlin. It was after midnight and everyone was drowsy, but Jenny was the only person who'd worked through the previous night and had gone close to thirty-six hours without sleep. Her cramped muscles screamed in protest as she stepped down from the train.

The railway depot was shuttered and dark, but Ryan's cook waited for them with a wagon to take them home. At first glance Jenny assumed the cook was Japanese, but he introduced himself as Boris Lu, a man whose grandparents were among the first wave of Chinese immigrants to California in the 1850s.

Jenny wanted to get to Ryan's house as soon as possible, but apparently they had to walk two miles to get there. The wagon was overloaded with luggage, and with only a single horse to pull it, all the adults were expected to walk alongside. Only Lily rode in the back of the wagon, and she soon fell asleep amidst the baggage.

Jenny bit her lip, reluctant to admit the sudden fear that settled on her the moment they walked beyond the circle of light from the train depot. It was so dark here! She'd never set foot outside the city of San Francisco, where streetlights lit up every block. There was no moon tonight, only the barest glimmer of starlight.

Would it be pathetic to admit she was frightened of the dark? She'd had no experience with real darkness before this very moment. Thankfully, Boris lit a lantern attached to the side of the wagon. Its light was dim, and she stayed close as they trekked into the countryside.

Very little could be seen as they walked on the hard-packed dirt road, but she smelled pine from the surrounding trees, and soon there was a tang of salt in the air. The faint roar of surf sounded in the distance as they approached Ryan's home after an hour of walking. The darkness made it impossible to see much of the house silhouetted against the starlit sky. Jenny was so tired she'd sleep in a dustbin if she could just lay her head down and close her eyes.

But the unpleasant surprises did not stop once she got to the house, for as Boris helped carry the luggage inside, she learned she would be expected to share a bedroom with Lily.

"I hope you don't mind," Ryan whispered. Lily's head rested on his shoulder as he carried the slumbering child upstairs. "Finn needs his own room for the duration of his recovery, and Simon can share a room with Boris. That leaves only Lily's room, but don't worry. She loves the chance to use the trundle bed."

It didn't seem she had much choice in the matter.

It was dim inside the house, which smelled of cedar boards and lemon polish. Jenny walked up the creaky staircase to the second floor, which had four bedrooms tucked beneath the slanted roof.

Lily roused, and the moment she noticed Ryan pulling out the trundle bed, she perked awake and began jumping up and down.

"Oh, good! Can Zuzu sleep in the trundle bed, too?" Lily was already trying to tuck her doll beneath the sheets. "Zuzu likes the trundle bed. She likes things that are small like her."

"Shhh, shhhh," Ryan soothed. "Everyone wants to go to sleep, so we need to use our sleepy-time voice."

"Okay!" she said happily. "I can show Miss Jenny where to put her things. See how this bed can fit right under the big one? Usually I sleep on the big one except in special times. I love the little bed! I can't wait to sleep in the little bed! Zuzu can't wait either."

Why had Ryan let Lily sleep during the wagon ride? The child was now wide awake and thrilled down to her foundation by the rare treat of using the trundle bed. It was almost amusing to watch how eagerly Lily tore off her dress, yanked on a nightgown, and lunged into the small bed. Her head barely touched the pillow before she rolled back onto her feet.

"Look, Miss Jenny, even the sheets are small on the little bed. See?" She peeled back the sheets and started tugging them off before Ryan could stop her. He tucked the sheets back in and tried to guide Lily back onto the mattress.

He cast an apologetic glance at Jenny. "This may take a while."

"I can imagine."

The girl's boundless enthusiasm for the trundle bed was sweet, and Jenny watched as Ryan perched on the side of the squat little mattress to read Lily a bedtime story. It hurt to even look at such homespun tenderness. In a perfect world, Ryan would be reading to *her* child. This would be *her* home. She wouldn't be standing here feeling awkward and out of place.

"I think I'll step downstairs for a spell," she said, and Ryan met her gaze gratefully.

"This might take twenty or thirty minutes," he said, rocking Lily gently against his chest with the book still balanced on his knees.

She nodded and turned away. Anything to avoid the sight of the man she once loved so desperately and yet knew so little.

Coming here was a mistake. Seeing Ryan read his daughter to sleep was like tearing a scab from a wound, and this close proximity was going to continue for weeks, maybe even months. The night shift hadn't been so bad. She shouldn't have let a momentary weakness caused by lack of sleep cloud her judgment, and now she was here and already regretting it. She needed air. She needed to escape.

Everyone else had gone to their rooms, and downstairs it was dark save for a ship's lantern burning softly on the kitchen table. A combined kitchen and dining area stretched across the back of the house, with the stove and cook surface on one side and a dining table on the other. A door between the two areas led out to the beach, and she grabbed the ship's lantern as she headed outside.

The rhythmic roar of the surf and warm sea air surrounded her as she stepped onto a short landing outside the door. She padded toward the edge of the patio where a staircase led down to the beach. Even with the lantern, it was too dark to see much, so she sat on the top step and leaned against the railing. The boards were dried and cracked in the sea air. Ryan really ought to do something about that. If she had a house like this, she would baby every square inch of it.

She must have dozed, for she startled at the creak of the screen door, and a moment later Ryan joined her on the step.

"I think she'll sleep now, but it would be best to wait a little longer before going up," Ryan said.

"She sure loves that trundle bed."

"Lily is easy to please. She always has been." His voice carried a note of humor mingled with admiration. Something about a man who doted on his child was irresistibly attractive.

Her stomach let out a mighty growl, the embarrassing noise curling and squeaking with surprising volume. She clamped a hand over her stomach, but it was impossible to drown the noise, and Ryan smothered a laugh.

"Can I get you something to eat?" he said with a grin. "The cheese sandwiches on the train seem like a long time ago."

She wanted to deny her hunger, but another rumble from her stomach split the silence. "I could eat," she admitted and followed Ryan inside.

"I enjoy cooking, but it's a little late to prepare anything but the basics," he said. "I can scramble some eggs, though."

"That makes one more dish than I can prepare."

The single lantern cast a circle of light around Ryan as he moved through the kitchen, cracking eggs into a bowl and heating a skillet. Soon the sizzling aroma smelled so good she feared her stomach might send out another embarrassing howl.

She glanced around the kitchen, feeling a nostalgic stab of longing as she noticed the white shelves and wainscoting, the wooden counters, and even blue-and-white china dishes stacked on the shelves. This was precisely the sort of home she and Ryan once dreamed about.

"What kind of meals does Boris cook?" she asked. "Is it mostly Chinese food?"

Ryan nudged the eggs around in the pan a bit before answering. "Boris is as American as you or me. His grandparents emigrated from China fifty years ago, but he was born and raised in San Francisco."

A tiny hint of warning underlay Ryan's tone, and she immediately backpedaled. "I meant no offense. When I first saw him I assumed he was someone you met in Japan."

Ryan shook his head. "We met on the *Baltimore*. He was the ship's cook, and he is a miracle worker in the kitchen. His chili made him famous in the navy. One time a warship coming in from Taipei spotted the *Baltimore* and sent a semaphore message asking Boris to prepare the ship's officers a pot of his chili. When I resigned from the navy, I immediately sought him out."

"And he left just like that?"

Ryan continued stirring the eggs in the pan, taking so long to answer that she thought he might not have heard her question. He tipped the eggs onto a platter, added some salt and a heavy grind of black pepper, then finally answered her.

"Boris and I both know what it is to be an outsider. The navy was willing to hire people like Boris to work belowdecks, but he could never rise in the ranks. Boris is far more than just our cook. The pearl farm is a lot of work, and then there's Lily, who needs looking after as well. So he's part cook, part nanny, part farmhand, and full-time friend. When Boris agreed to come live here, I gave him a ten percent stake in the pearl farm."

She nodded, even though she didn't understand what he meant by a "pearl farm." The lopsided pearls he showed Simon were surely no more than strange curiosities.

"Why pearls?" she asked. "Of all the things for a former naval officer or a foreign spy to be interested in . . . why pearls?"

He smiled while he served himself. "I needed an excuse to befriend scientists and other men working along the harbors in Tokyo. Becoming involved in the pearl industry was a perfect opportunity for me to be at the ports and make connections. The more I learned about pearls, the more they appealed to me. I find it fascinating that such beauty could evolve as a defense mechanism from pain. You remind me of a pearl . . . lovely and luminous on the outside, but tough, too. As though it's all a veneer covering something very deep. I've always known that about you."

She set her fork down and pushed her plate away. Ryan was about to stray into dangerous waters, and she wasn't ready for it. "Thank you for the impromptu snack. Do you think Lily is asleep by now?"

Ryan's hand shot out to cover hers, freezing her in place.

"Jenny, have you ever made a mistake? Not a blunder like buying a pair of shoes you regret, but a huge, howling mistake that haunts you for years?"

The image of the sailor with the scar immediately popped into her mind, but she tamped it down. Ryan's hand still clasped hers, and it was obvious where he wanted to lead this conversation. She hadn't even been in his house for an hour and already the magnetic attraction was flaring to life between them. She wouldn't permit it. She had a good job awaiting her back home. A *day* job.

"I've made plenty of mistakes—thousands—but no matter what mistakes I've made, I was never disloyal to you. There was a purity to what we had, and you threw it away."

He sighed and looked away. "I did," he admitted. "I did and I'm sorry, but I cannot regret it because it brought me Lily—"

"Oh, stop!" she said in a harsh whisper. "It brought me years of bewilderment and confusion and heartache."

Ryan lowered his head, and she hated that she'd just hurt him, but it seemed the past was a minefield ready to detonate at the least provocation. This wasn't the kind of person she wanted to be. For pity's sake, every instinct in her wanted to comfort him, stroke his hair and whisper that all was forgiven. Anything to soothe that wounded look in his eyes.

It would be a mistake. He betrayed her in a way that would be impossible to forget, for Lily was a constant reminder of it. Ryan Gallagher was the wrecking ball that could smash her safe world to the ground. She survived it once but didn't know if she could manage it again.

"Ryan," she began hesitantly, "might we declare a ceasefire? We both have a challenging task ahead of us, and we both want nothing so much as to return to our normal lives. Please . . . can we forget the past? Leave well enough alone?"

He didn't say anything, but her words seemed to sadden him as he collected the plates and carried them to the sink. "Yes, of course," he murmured politely.

She tried to blot out his dejected expression as she tiptoed upstairs.

12

Jenny awoke in unfamiliar darkness. The mattress was different and the air smelled like cedar. It took a moment to get her bearings. For the past seven years she'd awakened in the barracks at the Presidio, but she was in Ryan's house now. In Lily's bedroom.

Jenny turned her head on the pillow to see Lily's outline in the darkness, the steady sound of the girl's breathing indicating she was still deeply asleep.

It was time to get up. She had a patient to look after.

Finn Breckenridge might look charming on the outside, but she wouldn't trust him if he told her the sun rose in the east. Addicts were notorious liars, and in the early stages of withdrawal, they often suffered from insomnia. She tried to be silent while lifting off the mattress. The last thing she wanted was to wake Lily, whose supply of energy seemed to be drawn straight from the molten center of the sun.

Jenny's dress lay draped over the bedstead, and it didn't take long to pull it over her head and tug it into place. She tiptoed to the single dormer window in the room. The sky was beginning to lighten to gray, just enough to spot a man walking along the beach, hands plunged into his pockets, head down low. Finn. The tense way he stalked along the beach showed all the symptoms of a restless spirit.

She scooped up her shoes and stockings, crept to the door, and was about to escape when Lily rolled over in the trundle bed and stopped her.

"Where are you going? Can I come?"

"Shhh, go back to bed," Jenny whispered. "It's too early to get up."

"I want to come with you. I'm hungry." The longing in the little girl's voice was impossible to ignore.

Jenny fumbled in her canvas bag for the last wedge of a cheese sandwich and handed it to Lily. "You can eat that, then go back to sleep," she whispered before slipping out the door, down the staircase, and outside onto the porch behind the kitchen.

She sat down to tug on her stockings and shoes, then trudged through the mounds of soft sand toward the beach. Finn was some distance ahead of her, but given the tracks in the sand, he'd been pacing this stretch of beach for some time.

She scampered until she caught up to him. He spared her a single baleful glance but said nothing.

"Have you been able to sleep at all?" she asked.

"No." The terse response was a sign that withdrawal was already setting in. She walked alongside him for a while, curious to see if he'd try to start a conversation, but he said nothing.

"Would you like to know what to expect?" she asked.

"Trust me, Jenny, I already know."

"So you've walked this road before?"

It seemed a little odd to have such an intimate conversation with a man she barely knew, but in the coming days and weeks they would be in constant contact, and there was nothing pretty about opiate withdrawal. They were going to have to lean on each other as they plowed through the difficult physical and emotional challenges ahead.

"I've done it once before. I went through a brief phase when pleasing my parents became important to me, and my father wagered I could not abstain from all forms of alcohol and intoxicants for six months. I proved him wrong."

She nodded as they continued walking along the beach. They were near the water, where the dampened sand made for easier walking. Backsliding was not uncommon for addicts, but the first step was admitting there was a problem. So far, Finn had failed to do so.

"Jenny, don't take this the wrong way, but your presence here is a waste of time. Ryan is a gigantic force of prissy disapproval who doesn't understand that it's perfectly normal for a man to have a drink or perhaps something a little stronger now and again. I've never done anything stupid while indulging. I've never gambled or gotten sloppy and irresponsible. This entire trip to this nowhere village is pointless."

"And yet we are here. And I am under orders to see you on your road to recovery."

He stopped, and she did too, turning to face him.

"What's in it for you?" he asked.

"I've never enjoyed working overnight. As soon as you are declared fit, I've been promised a transfer to the day shift. Plus a raise in pay."

"Then declare me fit, and let's be done with this. I'm ready to go to Japan. I'm in perfect control of my mind and spirit. Ryan won't agree to that until he has your medical stamp of approval. You'll get to move to the day shift, and I'll go to Japan."

His voice was confident, free of the tremors she thought she'd heard a few moments earlier. He projected self-confidence and determination.

"Let me sweeten the deal." Finn withdrew his wallet and cracked it open, flipping through some bills in the back. He pulled most of them out, folded them into a tidy packet, and held them up.

It was a lot of money, and this wasn't something she'd seen coming.

"Two hundred dollars," he said. "I'm willing to go through the motions with you for a week or so, then you declare me fit, and we can both get out of this wasteland."

She practically started salivating at the sight of that much money. Money meant security for both her and Simon. It was embarrassing, but she felt dizzy just looking at the crisp, clean bills in Finn's hand.

She held out her hand, palm up. He slapped the wad of bills into it, and she closed her fist around the money. Her heart pounded so loudly it could probably be heard over the soft rush of the surf against the beach.

But he had more where that came from. She hadn't earned her reputation for being the toughest nurse in the world by being sweet and polite. Finn Breckenridge was someone she understood. He was cagey and tough, but she was a match for him.

"I'll need the rest of it," she said, glancing at the wallet he still held in his other hand.

Finn's eyes narrowed in displeasure. "I'll pay you the rest when you declare me fit."

"No deal," she said. "Addicts are notorious liars and backstabbers. I need it all right now."

His glare grew colder. "I really loathe women like you." But he opened his wallet and handed over the rest of the money.

She smiled softly. "We have a deal."

Finn glanced over her shoulder and cursed under his breath. "Here he comes. Hide that money."

She didn't need to turn around to know who was coming, for already she could hear Ryan's voice.

"What's going on?" Ryan asked. "Is everything alright?"

She managed to get the fat wad of bills tucked into her skirt pocket before turning to face him. With disheveled hair and no shoes, Ryan must have come tearing out of the house the instant he saw Finn was gone. Against her will, a tug of affection stirred at the sight of him. He was always so relentlessly good and caring. She instinctively stood in front of Finn, almost like she could serve as a buffer between Ryan's innocence and Finn's treachery.

"Everything is fine," she said smoothly despite the fat wad of bills bulging in her pocket. "Finn couldn't sleep, and neither could I. Nothing to worry about."

Ryan glanced between the two of them, relief and mistrust warring on his handsome face. She angled her body away so he'd have no chance of seeing the lump in her skirt.

It was dawn now, and she looked past Ryan to get her first real glimpse of his house on the bluff.

"Oh, Ryan," she whispered. She would have fallen to her knees, but Ryan's hand shot out to grab her elbow, steadying her. She couldn't tear her eyes from the house.

It was nestled in the bluff and surrounded by acres of sea grass. It had dormer windows and white clapboard siding. The verandah across the back was the perfect place for a cup of coffee in the morning. It was a house where someone could be safe and happy, buffeted by cleansing winds and the comforting sounds of the sea. It was the house they once dreamed of owning.

"Are you alright?"

Ryan's voice sounded like it came from a distance, but no, she wasn't alright. It hurt to see his house. It was the embodiment of the youthful dreams they once shared, back when she believed he was the answer to all her prayers. Ryan had managed to find his perfect seaside house, a wife, and a lovely daughter. She was still alone with nothing but daydreams.

"I'm fine," she said. "And hungry. Is it too much to hope that Boris is awake?"

Ryan nodded. "Yes, I expect he will have breakfast soon."

She and Finn followed Ryan to the house, where Boris had indeed started breakfast. As the morning lightened, she had a better view of the kitchen. The dining table sat beside a window overlooking the beach. She trailed her finger across the well-worn surface. It seemed like the type of table that had been the gathering place for generations of happy families.

Ryan and Finn both helped themselves to glasses of milk, then took seats at the table. Should she offer to help Boris? It seemed rude to sit while another man performed all the work.

"Good morning," she said to Boris. "Is there anything I can do to help?"

"Can you make coffee?" Boris asked, nodding to a percolator on the countertop.

"I can make coffee," a feminine voice chimed in behind Jenny. She whirled to see a young blond woman with a fresh, homespun prettiness already reaching for a jar on one of the kitchen shelves.

"I'm Abigail Mayberry," the woman said. "Who are you?"

Abigail's smile was wide and her blue eyes innocent, but a note of challenge lurked in the younger girl's voice.

Ryan spared Jenny the reply. "Abigail, this is Nurse Bennett, who will be living with the family for a while." He went on to introduce Abigail as a girl whose family lived at a neighboring house farther down the beach. Abigail often came to look after Lily when both Ryan and Boris had to be away.

It seemed that Abigail wanted to look after more than just Lily as she went about the business of making coffee, rearranging the table settings, and pouring Ryan a cup of coffee with exactly the right amount of milk and one sugar cube.

Well, well. It seemed Ryan wasn't quite the lonely bachelor Jenny had been led to expect.

Ryan watched with bated breath as Abigail waltzed through the kitchen, helping to set the table and adding an additional place for herself. He wished she wouldn't join them, but he could hardly tell her to leave. Abigail had been a tremendous help over the past year and asked precious little in return. It would be petty to begrudge her breakfast, but this morning was already tense enough without her here.

"Who is in need of a nurse?" Abigail asked brightly.

"It's private," Ryan replied. It was a blunt answer, but he'd been battling a ferocious headache since he awoke. Besides, Finn's shortcomings weren't his to share.

The response didn't go over well with Abigail, who cast a sidelong glance at Jenny before setting a bowl of muffins on the table.

Before long the scent of bacon and sizzling eggs summoned both Lily and Simon to the kitchen. Lily came hurtling into Ryan's arms, and he hoisted her onto his lap. Even the act of lifting Lily left him weak and dizzy, and he again wondered at the strange feeling of malaise. It must have been all the travel yesterday and then the difficult conversation with Jenny last night. His first tentative steps at reconciliation had been flung back in his teeth, and he hadn't been able to sleep much after that.

He leaned over to kiss the top of Lily's head. "How is my sweet pea this morning?"

She was chatty. With this many new people in the house, she couldn't stop talking and soon pushed off his lap to show Simon the basket of seashells and driftwood she had collected. Then she showed him the bowl where they kept cat food for the two strays who wandered in and out of the house. The chatter stopped only when Boris brought platters of steaming eggs, cheese, and bacon to the table.

Ryan usually said the blessing before each meal, but he still felt ill from the difficult night. Even the scent of the food made him nauseated, and his mind was foggy.

"Simon? Can I ask you to say the blessing?"

The old man confidently held out both hands, and soon everyone joined hands around the table while Simon prayed.

"Lord, we thank you for our safe arrival here and for the blessing of good food and friendship. We ask for good health for our friend Finn and for all who are gathered here today. And the oysters. May I be so bold as to make an appeal for the pearl oysters Ryan is raising, for they are a miracle of nature, and I am looking forward to making their acquaintance."

Ryan had to laugh a little, and he wondered how long he'd be able to keep Simon from darting down to the beach and asking him to haul up one of the baskets of oysters happily living in the surf.

Silverware clinked, and Simon groaned with pleasure at the first taste of Boris's scrambled eggs. It was then Ryan noticed that Jenny was not eating. She met his gaze across the table, then rose to her feet as she reached into her skirt pocket.

"Everyone needs to know that Finn tried to bribe me this morning," she announced as she calmly set a fat roll of bills on the table.

Finn lunged for the money, but Jenny scooped it up just in time, angling her body away and holding the roll of bills out of his reach.

"I'm telling everyone so that we all know not to trust him," she said. "He bribed me to sign off on a clean bill of health, when any fool can see he's barely hanging on by his fingernails. Ryan, you need to hide this money or else Finn is likely to use it to get his hands on opiates. It's best to remove all hint of temptation."

This was unbelievable. Ryan felt hot and dizzy and outraged. He had *trusted* Finn! Finn had sworn he would do everything possible to demonstrate sobriety and earn his opportunity to work for the government.

Jenny walked around the table and pressed the money into Ryan's hand. He didn't know what to do. He stared stupidly at the money in his palm, confused and disoriented. He rose to his feet, but everything tilted and swayed, and he was so thirsty he couldn't think straight.

"Ryan, are you alright?" It was Jenny's voice, but it sounded tinny, like it came through a telephone wire.

Water. He needed water. He reached for his glass but knocked it over, the water spilling across the table. The glass rolled onto the floor and shattered.

Everything went black.

13

Jenny tried to break Ryan's fall, but they both crashed to the ground. Her hip smacked hard, taking the brunt of Ryan's weight as he collapsed on top of her. It knocked the air from her lungs. She saw stars and couldn't breathe, but someone rolled Ryan's weight off her.

"Are you okay, Jenny?" Simon leaned over her.

Pain shot up from her hip. Everything hurt. It took a moment before she could drag air back into her lungs. "I'm fine," she managed to gasp. "What's wrong with Ryan?"

Finn had rolled Ryan off her, but he was still unconscious and lying flat on his back, his complexion a waxy sheen that didn't look good. She struggled to her knees and pressed two fingers to the pulse in his throat. His heartbeat raced with an unsteady rhythm. She had no idea what was wrong with him, but this was bad. It seemed he was on the verge of a heart attack.

"Go get a doctor," she ordered the cook.

"There is no doctor in Summerlin."

"Where is the nearest doctor?"

"Gleaner's Point," Boris said. "It's about a thirty-minute ride by horseback."

What was she supposed to do? She had no experience with this sort of emergency and couldn't begin to guess what was wrong with Ryan, so how could she provide aid?

Mercifully, Ryan twitched and opened his eyes. "What happened?" he asked, struggling to rise.

She pushed him gently back down. "You fainted. I'm going to elevate your feet to make sure enough blood is getting to your head."

He didn't argue with her, just stared blankly at the ceiling as though he were losing strength again.

Jenny glanced at Abigail, who twisted her hands and watched helplessly. "Do you know how to get to Gleaner's Point?"

Abigail nodded.

"Go get the doctor," Jenny ordered.

"I can't ride a horse."

Neither could Jenny or Simon. Finn watched the unfolding events from the rear of the kitchen, his eyes sharp.

"Finn, I need you to ride to Gleaner's Point and bring back that doctor," she ordered.

"Wouldn't Boris be a better person for that?" Finn asked.

Boris was the logical choice to send, but she wasn't going to admit it. It was possible Finn had some role in Ryan's illness. Something had caused a man in perfect health to keel over, and to the best of her knowledge, Finn was the only person here with a motive to want Ryan out of the way. She would ask Boris to scour the house for any toxic medicines while Finn was gone.

"I need Boris here to help me find supplies in the house. He can give you directions to the doctor's house, but I want him to stay here." She looked up at Finn with a hard expression. "If you take a single step off the path to Gleaner's Point or do anything other than return directly here with a doctor, I will personally hunt you down and tear you limb from limb. Is that clear? There won't be a back alley or opium den in the state that is safe from me smashing into it and dragging you out for a public flogging."

"I get it, Jenny," he retorted.

"Papa, what's happening?" Lily asked in a shaky voice, trying to nudge around Jenny and get to her father, who still lay on the floor.

Ryan tried to rise, but Jenny pushed him back down. "I need you to stay down," she said.

Panic set in as Ryan's eyes rolled back into his head and he seemed on the verge of passing out again. What was she going to do if his condition worsened? His breaths came so fast he was panting, like he wasn't getting enough oxygen.

"Ryan, are you allergic to anything?"

He blinked a few times, and she had to repeat the question twice before he understood.

"No," he said.

"Have you taken any medication? Anything new?"

He shook his head, apparently too weak to even speak.

The next few hours were among the most harrowing of her life. Simon and Boris were able to get Ryan into bed, but his condition showed no sign of improvement. He was confused, dizzy, and continually out of breath. Abigail made a pest of herself, hovering in the open doorway of Ryan's bedroom and suggesting that her raspberry lemonade was world famous and could cure anything. Boris got her out from underfoot by ordering her to go home and help bring in her father's crab traps. Then he scoured Finn's room and baggage, looking for anything suspicious, but came up empty.

The doctor finally arrived two hours later and was as baffled as Jenny. A stocky man with steel-gray hair, Dr. Keselowski was all business as he measured Ryan's pulse and examined his pupils. He ordered Jenny from the room so he could inspect every inch of Ryan's skin, looking for an insect or spider bite that might have injected some strange toxin. She'd been a nurse for seven years and tended thousands of men without suffering a case of the vapors at the sight of naked flesh, but she obeyed the doctor's orders without question.

Since Ryan's collapse, she had been strangled with a sense of helplessness unlike anything she'd ever known. Rarely had her patients suffered from life-threatening illnesses. The few times her patients contracted dangerous infections, there had always been a competent doctor on hand who knew exactly what to do.

Across the hall, the door to Lily's bedroom was open, the trundle bed still pulled out, the sheets unmade. Had it only been a few hours ago when everything seemed normal? Now Jenny sweated out each minute, the silence from behind Ryan's closed door ominous.

Dear Lord, please let him live through this. If you've got to take someone, take me. Ryan has responsibilities, he's needed here. I'm not.

Even now she could hear Lily's voice downstairs as she played with one of the cats that had come inside for water. With her father out of sight and the limited attention span of a child, it seemed Lily had completely forgotten the terrors of the morning.

It was another twenty minutes before Dr. Keselowski finally emerged from the sickroom, reporting that Ryan's pulse had stabilized and his breathing was normal. He still suffered from body aches but seemed to be out of immediate danger. The doctor had no explanation for what might have caused the sudden illness.

"Could it have been poison?" Jenny asked quietly.

Dr. Keselowski's shrewd eyes narrowed. "Do you have any reason to suspect someone might have poisoned him?"

"Aside from the fact that his symptoms seem to indicate it? I know at least one man in this house has cause to resent Ryan." Although if Finn wanted to poison Ryan, it would have made more sense to do it at the Presidio, where they were surrounded by hundreds of other people, many of whom suspected Ryan of desertion or even treason.

"Poisoning can happen from natural causes," the doctor said. "Food can go bad. Spores in the air can be toxic to people with allergies."

But Ryan had lived in this house for over a year and never suffered from any such anomalies. All the doctor could recommend was to throw out any food, drink, and toiletries Ryan had used and buy new.

"If you need me again, there is a telegraph operator at the apothecary shop in Summerlin. They can send a message to the store next door to my house quicker than you can send a man for me. I will be on the lookout for any message."

After the doctor left, Jenny stepped inside Ryan's room, relieved he was breathing normally. It was a spacious room. One side had a steeply angled roofline with two dormer windows cut into the slanted ceiling. Creamy yellow walls made the room feel flooded with sunlight. A brass four-poster bed stood on one side, a huge sailor's trunk at its base. With thick strapping and battered leather, that trunk had probably traveled over half the surface of the earth.

As she drew closer, Ryan opened his eyes, a faint smile on his mouth.

"This seems like old times," he said.

A lump rose in her throat as she sat on the trunk at the end of his bed, for it was true. The first few weeks they'd known each other was in just this sort of situation, with her caring for him while he tried to be the perfect patient. It would be so easy to slip back into those halcyon memories and let him flirt with her while she tended him.

"The doctor advises me to rummage through your toiletry bag and throw everything out. I hope you don't have any expensive French cologne or pearl-dust tooth powder."

He let out a weak laugh. "That's an old wives' tale . . . about pearl dust. It doesn't clean teeth any better than plain old baking soda."

"I hear they pay a fortune for it in the Far East."

"They do, but don't worry. I love my pearls too much to grind them up for tooth powder. You can throw out anything you find in that bag."

He hadn't unpacked from San Francisco yet. She opened his luggage and landed on the toiletry bag. It seemed terribly intimate to poke through his belongings, but she tossed his tooth powder, a bar of soap, and a small bottle of cologne into the trash. She sniffed each item first, trying to find something that smelled as if it might have gone bad. Everything seemed fine, but the bayberry cologne summoned a rush of old memories. It reminded her of stolen hours wandering the Presidio grounds, of lying beside him on the bluff, staring at cloud formations and dreaming of their future. She set the cologne carefully into the bottom of the wastebasket to avoid breaking the bottle and flooding the room with that poignant scent.

"Are there any toiletries in your bureau you've used since we got here?" she asked.

He gave a drowsy shake of his head. "I don't think so. I don't remember."

"Can I look?" The bureau probably didn't have toiletries, but Ryan didn't appear to be thinking very clearly, and she needed to get to the bottom of what had caused this malaise.

"Go ahead," he said.

The bayberry scent grew stronger as she opened the drawers, but all she saw was neatly folded clothing stacked with military precision. The bottom drawers contained clean linens and a scratchy wool blanket. There was only one drawer she could not inspect, a narrow drawer at the top held shut by a little brass lock.

"Is there anything in here I should know about?"

He shook his head but made no comment. What was in there? She once thought Ryan was an open book, but she must never forget he had layers of secrets and a past she knew very little about.

ELIZABETH CAMDEN

She'd bet her bottom dollar there was plenty of insight to be had
in that small, locked drawer. Curiosity got the better of her, and
she gave the knob a tug.

"There's nothing in there," he said in a weak voice. "Promise."

"Secret spy stuff?"

He only shrugged. She let go of the drawer, feeling guilty for
prying. Of course Ryan probably had documents from the government that ought to remain private. He was a good man. Not
perfect, but neither was she. Whatever had clobbered him worried
her and made it easier to put his sins in perspective.

She sat on the trunk at the foot of his bed, wishing his limp
figure didn't stir that rush of old, protective feelings. "If you had
died, I would feel really lousy about the bratty way I've behaved
over the past few days."

He laughed a little. "I'm not on my deathbed yet."

"I want to say I'm sorry for selling your father's watch. I needed
the money, but I should have found another—"

"It's alright, Jenny."

"It's not. I gloated when I did it. That was a low and petty emotion, and I'm sorry I gave in to it. I thought that sort of cruelty was
behind me, but I guess a piece of it is still there."

"Shhhh . . ." Ryan soothed. "We've both hurt each other. We've
both done things we regret, but I only have the highest regard for
you. I don't want you feeling guilty over that watch. Life is too
short, Jenny."

The gentle expression on his face cut through every one of her
defenses and wiggled straight into her heart. How could he reel
her in so quickly? She came here on an assignment, and within
hours she was falling headlong back into an irrational infatuation
with Ryan.

She straightened. She had a job to do, and she wouldn't get
distracted by a dangerous rekindling of old romantic dreams.

"Ryan, I think Finn might have tried to poison you."

"Finn is harmless. He may be self-destructive, but he'd never hurt another person."

"He tried to bribe me this morning. He's no angel."

"I am aware of Finn's many shortcomings. We've locked horns because I've been driving him hard, but trust me, Finn wants my help getting to Japan."

"And he wanted my help getting him sprung from Summerlin. All of us have been eating and drinking from the same communal pot. We all ate cheese sandwiches and apples on the train. This morning we all ate from the same meal Boris prepared."

Ryan shook his head. "I already felt ill when I woke up this morning. I don't think it could have been anything I ate because we all . . ."

His voice trailed off, his eyes widening as his gaze drifted out the window.

"What?" she demanded. "What are you thinking?"

He swallowed hard. "Last night after we talked, I couldn't sleep. I had a lot on my mind, and I took a swig or two of apple brandy. Maybe more than a swig or two." His face flushed with embarrassment, and he couldn't meet her gaze.

She was flabbergasted. "Are you telling me you're hungover?"

He shrugged helplessly. "I didn't drink very much. I wasn't drunk, I swear it, but maybe the brandy had gone bad. I always thought brandy got better with age and couldn't go bad. I bought that bottle the first week I came to Summerlin, and there is still more than half a bottle left."

"Your symptoms weren't those of a hangover," she said. "Where do you keep the apple brandy? I need to see it."

"There's an oyster shed out near the barn. I keep it on top of the cabinet where I know Lily can't accidentally get into it."

His eyes drifted closed. At first she feared he was feeling poorly

168

again, but she could tell by the way he rubbed his brow that he was embarrassed. Ryan was always so straight-laced, and now he was mortified for having been caught tippling. She battled the temptation to smile in sympathy but couldn't stop it from leaking into her voice.

"Get some sleep, Galahad," she said before slipping out the door.

She heard the argument before she got all the way down the stairs. Jenny loitered in the hallway leading to the kitchen, cocking her head to eavesdrop. The doctor must have spoken to the men downstairs, for Boris was clearing the kitchen of anything that had been used to prepare that morning's meal. Finn was ripping into the cook, accusing him of "destroying evidence."

Boris gave as good as he got. "I'm not the opium-eater here. I'm not the person guilty of bribery and prowling around this kitchen in the middle of the night. Someone used my kitchen after I went to bed, and I know for a fact that you were up hours before dawn."

Jenny stepped inside the kitchen, and all heads swiveled to look at her. Simon sat at the table, twirling a mug of tea between his hands and looking like a soldier caught in the middle of cross fire.

"Ryan used the kitchen last night to make us both scrambled eggs," she admitted. "But it's true that Finn was up before anyone else. What were you doing?"

Finn planted his hands on his hips, looking like he wanted to lunge across the space between them and strangle her. "I was pacing on the beach, and you know why!" he roared.

That much was true. Finn's eyes were watery and his hands trembled, both classic signs of withdrawal. At least he wasn't denying his condition anymore, but men in his position could be unstable and erratic. She would trust a snake offering an apple before trusting Finn.

"Were you ever in the kitchen alone?"

"Why would I poison Ryan?" Finn demanded "He's the only man who's ever believed in me. I'd step in front of a bullet for him!"

"And yet only a few hours ago you were suggesting Ryan was a hopeless prude," she said. "To suddenly spout such avowals of loyalty sounds a little suspicious, don't you think?"

Boris smirked, but Finn quieted. He looked tired, beaten, and exhausted. "Jenny, haven't you ever wanted to prove yourself to the world?"

She flinched, for it was what she'd been trying to do since she was nine years old.

"Ryan is offering me a chance to redeem myself," Finn continued. "I'm likely to stumble and fall a dozen times before I get there. I'm the most flawed person in this house, and everyone knows it, but I'm not going to poison the only man willing to give me a chance to do something really great."

She locked gazes with him. She could detect no deceit, and she was good at spotting it. Only a fool would trust a drug addict in the throes of withdrawal, but she couldn't see a motive for Finn to poison Ryan.

She dropped her gaze. "I need to go to the oyster shed on the side of the house. Come with me?"

The tension in the room loosened just a fraction. Finn unclenched his fists and gave a brusque nod.

She didn't expect him to light into her the moment they set foot on the porch, but he did.

"You could be a lot nicer to me," he groused. "We're going to be trapped together like sardines in a tin for the next few weeks, and I can't abide screechy, sanctimonious women."

Their footsteps thudded on the badly weathered planks leading down to the beach. "Are you suggesting I shouldn't have made a public show of your bribery attempt?"

"No, I suppose I deserved that one. Just ease up on your tone. It's like an ice pick straight into the center of my brain."

Heightened sensitivity was another sign of withdrawal. "I have a normal female voice," she said softly. "It sounds irritating to you because your nerve endings are strung tight as a drum. Trust me. Once you're through all this recovery business, you'll appreciate that I have a beautiful voice. Men fight for the chance to be placed in my ward."

He snorted. "You've got a high opinion of yourself."

"Entirely warranted."

The shed Ryan mentioned was a modest structure covered in fading red paint and surrounded by tufts of long grass swaying in the breeze. It was dim inside, with a musty scent of damp canvas. Enough light leaked through the single window to illuminate the shelves weighed down with coils of rope, fishing tackle, and equipment Jenny could not begin to name.

"What are we looking for?"

"A bottle of apple brandy. Ryan took a swig or two late last night. It's the only thing we can think of that others didn't drink, too."

She spotted the half-empty bottle on top of the only cabinet in the shed. She unscrewed the cap and sniffed. It was pungent, but brandy was supposed to smell pungent, wasn't it?

She sent a cautious glance at Finn. "Do you know what normal apple brandy smells like?"

He shrugged. "Apple brandy is a sissy drink. I have no idea."

She carried the bottle outside into the sunlight so she could have a better look at the golden amber of the liquid. Holding it aloft, she immediately noticed sediment at the bottom of the bottle.

"Is brandy supposed to have solids in it?" she asked. For the first time in her life, she regretted not having experience with hard liquor.

Finn stared at the grit in the bottom of the bottle. "I'm no expert, but it seems odd," he said in a worried tone.

"Simon might know."

He did. Simon confirmed her suspicion that properly distilled liquor should have no sediment gathering in the bottle. Something was seriously wrong with this brandy.

❧

Ryan spent the rest of the day in bed, but even from the second floor he could hear Finn bickering with just about everyone in the household. Finn was obviously miserable, but Jenny's calm voice could often be heard ordering him to finish his meal or go for a walk with her along the beach. He loved the way she didn't take guff from anyone but still managed to be relentlessly compassionate. She always had been.

The mysterious illness had faded by the next day, which was a blessing because he worried about his oysters. Boris had been looking after the oysters while he and Finn were in San Francisco, but like a worried parent, Ryan wanted to check on them himself. Spawning season was drawing near, and the nursery he'd been building for the new crop of oysters wasn't finished. There were a million things he ought to be doing, and lying in bed wasn't one of them. He was determined to join his family for breakfast and then head out to check the oysters.

His head throbbed with each footfall as he carefully lowered himself down the staircase, but the scent of warm vanilla and cinnamon beckoned him to the kitchen.

"What are you doing out of bed?" Jenny asked in concern, but Lily was far more welcoming, hurtling across the kitchen and wrapping her arms around his legs.

"Have you been behaving for the grown-ups?" he asked as he ran his fingers through her hair.

"She's been an angel," a voice purred from the far side of the kitchen. Abigail had just taken a tray of cinnamon rolls from the oven. His mouth watered at the scent, but he wished Abigail hadn't made them. Lily's sweet tooth was bad enough, and he rarely indulged it at breakfast, but he could hardly say anything negative since he was grateful for Abigail's help looking after Lily.

"Can I have a cinnamon roll, Papa?" Lily begged. "Please?"

"You'll have to ask Miss Abigail. She's the one who was good enough to come over and bake for us."

Abigail preened at the compliment. "Just as soon as they are cool, sweetie. Boris had to run into town on an errand, so thank goodness I came this morning and can prepare a little something fresh for you all."

"What sort of errand?"

Jenny supplied the answer. "He's riding to Gleaner's Point. He wants to see if Dr. Keselowski can figure out if there was something wrong with the apple brandy."

Ryan nodded, even though it seemed like a waste of time. He was almost completely recovered, and it would have been quicker simply to throw the bottle away.

"Your father is doing well, I take it?" he asked Abigail. He and Chester Mayberry had gotten off to a difficult start. During the years this house was vacant, Abigail's father had used Ryan's cove for crabbing, but when Ryan bought the place, that had to stop. It was an awkward situation, but after Ryan explained the exacting requirements for an oyster nursery, Chester agreed to quit using the cove.

"Papa is fine, except that he makes me spend all my time sorting blue mussels from rock scallops and pectin scallops until I'm practically blind." Abigail put on a bright smile. "Not that I mind, of course. I'd just rather have a chance to come visit and bake a little something for you."

He managed a polite smile as Abigail set a plate of cinnamon rolls before Lily's delighted eyes.

"I need to check my oysters," he said. "Does anyone want to come?"

Simon shot to his feet. Jenny was curious too, and where Jenny went, Finn needed to follow. Ryan glanced at Abigail. It would be rude to leave her out, but she simply went about tidying up the kitchen.

"You run along," she said. "I'd rather stay here and look after this little one."

Ryan sent her a grateful smile before leading the others out to the beach.

He'd been lucky to find a stretch of beach suitable for growing oysters. The crescent-shaped cove was protected from the stronger tides and had a substantial pier stretching twenty yards into the water. To a casual observer, it looked like a serene, sheltered cove, no different than hundreds of others along the wild California coastline. To him, it looked like the future.

The house sat on one end of the land spur that created a sheltered cove behind it. With the cove on one side of his house and the ocean on the other, it was an ideal spot for growing oysters. It was hard not to be proud of everything he'd accomplished during the short time he'd been here, and he was helpless to stop the smile breaking across his face as he nodded toward the pier.

"That's where I've got my first season of oysters living."

Only a seasoned observer would spot the line of buoys stretching out from the pier. Each buoy held a lantern net exactly like those he'd used in Japan. The column-shaped nets were made of mesh wire with plenty of room for oysters to latch on and water to circulate. The lantern nets were suspended from a buoy and tied to the loglines below. The only real danger was if the ties broke free and the lantern net was carried out to sea.

It didn't take long for his gaze to track along the five rows and count each of the eight buoys. They were all still there, gently bobbing in the water. As soon as he felt well enough, he'd go for a swim and inspect the loglines to be sure the ties were still secure.

Satisfaction filled him as he gazed at his oyster farm. He had laid those loglines and buoys himself. He and Boris had seeded two thousand oysters, using slightly different techniques in each net, hoping that at least one net might yield a batch of round pearls. Each net was coded with colored ties to identify the variations in seed placement and type of mantle used.

His feet thudded on the planks as he led the others onto the pier. From here he had a good view of his house and the shed, but his real pride was his oysters.

"Here is my farm," he said, gesturing to the stretch of ocean. It looked so ordinary, yet beneath the waters it harbored a grand scientific experiment. He loved it. Aside from Lily, this was the proudest accomplishment of his life, and he wanted to dive into the water, haul up an oyster, and pry it open to bestow Jenny with a beautifully formed pearl of his own creation.

All of that was nonsense, of course. Jenny probably wouldn't want anything he could offer her, and it would be another two years before any of these oysters could yield a pearl large enough to be of value.

Simon seemed to appreciate the magnitude of the endeavor and looked dazzled as he gazed over the harbor, but Jenny folded her arms across her chest and scrutinized the floats.

"It doesn't look very practical," she said in a voice heavy with skepticism, and Ryan burst out in laughter.

"No, it's not practical," he agreed with a reluctant smile. It was the biggest risk of his life.

Japanese scientists had been trying for more than a decade to produce round pearls, and his own experiments so far had produced nothing but oblong and lopsided pearls. Each year he would seed more oysters, using different variations until he finally stumbled on the magical combination to yield a round pearl.

"They keep me busy," he continued. "I go down most days to pull up a net and make sure everything looks good."

"But do they have pearls?" Simon asked.

"They do! I know how to coax them into making pearls, I just don't know how to make them *round*," he said with a mild laugh. Even that caused the ache in his head to pound again. "As soon as I feel better, I'll pull up one of the nets and show you what's down there."

Finn kicked at the pier with the toe of his shoe, causing a splinter of wood to break free. "This dock is a piece of trash," he said. "When was the last time you put a decent coat of varnish on it?"

"There hasn't been much time for basic maintenance," Ryan admitted. He squatted down to rip off the splinter Finn had kicked loose. Lily liked to run around in bare feet while outdoors, and he was not a careless man.

"You won't have a pier if you keep neglecting it," Finn said sourly. He thumped three times with the flat of his foot. Each thud caused the ache in Ryan's head to roar anew. "Hear that? That's the sound of stick-dry wood. Ash from a cigarette butt could send this whole pier up in flames if you don't take better care of it."

"There won't *be* any smoking on my pier," Ryan said tightly.

"Oops," Finn said in mock contrition. "I forgot we're dealing with the epitome of a straight-laced Puritan. Of course there won't be any smoking on your dock. No foul language, no naughty thoughts. Certainly not a breath of fun."

"Oh, Finn!" Jenny teased. "Your company is unmitigated fun for us all."

"Why don't I show you the barn and the oyster shed," Ryan said tightly. He wouldn't let Finn's barbs sting. Maybe his pier needed a coat of varnish and the shed looked a little weather-beaten, but this farm was still a rare accomplishment, the only one of its kind in America.

They trudged up the beach toward the shed. It was low tide, so the sand was damp and hard-packed, but soon they reached the mounds of soft, white sand warmed by the summer sun. Above the berm were clumps of tall bluestem grasses, their stiff fronds blowing in the breeze. Ryan loved this land. Just the sound of wind rustling in the grasses, the call of sea gulls, and the scent of salty air made him proud to own this remote stretch of paradise.

"What's this?" Jenny asked, gesturing to the lagoon behind the shed.

It had taken him a month to build the short pier and dredge a pool deep enough for the oyster frames. It might not look like much now, but by the end of the summer, it would be an oyster nursery. He'd already built a dozen box frames and lined them with mesh screening small enough that baby oyster spat wouldn't fall through. Oyster spawning was a natural process he had no control over. All he could do was keep careful watch and be ready to spring into action when it occurred. It usually happened in late summer when the water was at its warmest.

"If all goes well, within the next month this is going to be the oyster nursery," he explained. "When the female oysters release the larvae, they float in the water for a while. The male oysters sense it and release . . ." He swallowed. In Japan, all the scientists he worked with had been men, and they could discuss the process of fertilization without worrying about indelicate words. "The male oysters release . . . um . . . they do their part, and then . . . um . . ."

"Oh look, he's blushing," Finn said.

Sure enough, heat was building in his face, and both Finn and Jenny choked back laughter. Ryan needed them to understand how this process worked, for it would be nice to have some help once spawning occurred, but this was extremely awkward. For pity's sake, Jenny was a highly trained nurse and understood how reproduction occurred. He just wished he found it easier to discuss in mixed company.

He cleared his throat and started again. "The larvae become fertilized and turn into 'spat.' At first the oyster spat will be smaller than a poppy seed, but it floats and will be trapped in the cheese-cloth I've attached to the top of each lantern net. We'll scoop up as much as we can and transfer it to the nursery."

He opened the door of the shed and nodded to the large boxes leaning against the far wall. "I built those boxes to protect the spat from being swept off in the tide."

He rubbed his thumb across a hard buildup of callouses on his palm. He'd gained them while building those boxes and the nursery pier. He'd pulled splinters from his hands for a solid week after the task was complete.

Jenny took a few steps inside to look around. "It smells bad in here." Her nose wrinkled as she peered skeptically at the sacks of fish meal mounded on the far wall of the shed. True, fish meal had an un-pleasant odor, but he needed it to ensure his oyster spat would thrive.

He kept silent. He loved every square inch of this seaside farm. It was the laboratory where he could pursue his wild, ambitious dreams, but Jenny didn't see it as he did. There was a time when she had listened with rapt attention to everything he shared about life along the seashore. She had been curious and excited, willing to dream alongside him with reckless abandon. That Jenny was gone, replaced by a guarded woman interested only in completing an assignment so she could return to her life in San Francisco. Could he blame her? It had been his doing that kicked the foundation out from beneath their castles in the air.

A tiny piece of him had hoped she would see the oyster farm through his eyes. It would have been nice to share it with her.

"Let's head back to the house," he said, wishing this morning had been different.

He was completely exhausted by the time he climbed the steps back to the house. Abigail left after lunch, and he spent the afternoon teaching Lily her letters. By dinner time, Boris had still not returned from taking the apple brandy to Dr. Keselowski in the hope that he could diagnose it.

Which meant someone needed to prepare dinner. Ryan's head throbbed, and he was still smarting over the way Jenny and Finn had disparaged his farm, but at least he was no longer dizzy and could cook dinner without burning the house down. He banged the skillet on the stove louder than he intended. What did Jenny or Finn know about responsibility, anyway? Everything was a joke to them.

When they joined him in the kitchen, they were bickering about how fast an automobile could travel. Jenny was adamant that an automobile couldn't outpace a streetcar, but Finn was just as determined that it could. Jenny was going to lose this one, but it wasn't in her nature to back down. She and Finn went at it like banshees, making Ryan's headache even worse. He could understand why Finn's withdrawal put him in a bad mood, but why did he have to be so aggressive? Suffering in silence had been instilled in Ryan since infancy, and by now it was second nature.

Lily entered the kitchen, clutching her doll to her chest. She smiled at him from across the room, and instantly his irritation evaporated.

"Do you want to help me make something for dinner, sweet pea?"

"Pie?" she asked.

He stifled a smile. "No, we can't have pie for dinner." Although heaven help him, sometimes he was tempted to spoil Lily with whatever her heart desired. He was complete putty in her hands and loved nothing more than coaxing her to smile. But that didn't mean she was getting pie for dinner. Fish stew would have to do. "Let's make a nice *kenchinjiru*, shall we? You can help me by watching."

Lily eagerly agreed and settled onto the bench to watch, Zuzu still clutched in her arms. "Watching" was usually how Lily helped him in the kitchen. The entire stove got hot as he cooked, and he didn't want her getting scorched, so she quietly watched him from the safety of the bench.

"What's kenchin . . . kenchin-whatever-you-just-said?" Jenny asked.

"A Japanese vegetable soup, but I usually add some fish or crab-meat. I like to start with a nice fish-based stock to give it a little more heft."

Finn groaned and Jenny looked skeptical, but Ryan loved Japanese cuisine, and the only way he was going to get it in this country was to make it himself. Which was not a problem, since he enjoyed cooking.

In short order he had diced up carrots, a few potatoes, and burdock root. He was in the process of mincing bean curd when the front door slammed open.

Boris was back, his face flushed as he staggered into the kitchen, out of breath and with panic in his eyes.

"Ryan, there was cyanide in the apple brandy you drank," he said.

14

Jenny asked Boris to repeat himself three times to be certain she had heard correctly. Cyanide? *Cyanide?*

Boris quickly relayed everything he learned at Dr. Keselowski's office. After examining the grit at the bottom of the bottle, the doctor determined it was apple seed sediment. Apple seeds carried trace amounts of cyanide and could be toxic if accidentally ingested. The doctor said that if Ryan had drunk the entire bottle, it might have killed him.

To her amazement, Ryan shrugged off the incident, assuming it was just a bad batch of brandy. He'd had the bottle for over a year and suggested that it had taken a while for him to begin ingesting the apple seed sediment accumulating near the bottom. It seemed a dangerous assumption, but when she tried to talk sense into him, he shut down the conversation.

"Not in front of my daughter," he said, calmly mincing bean curd into the soup.

How could he be so nonchalant about this? He'd just been poisoned and couldn't even be bothered to interrupt dinner preparations. She and Finn traded worried glances, but Boris was taking items out of the pantry and rolling up his sleeves to help with the meal.

"Perhaps Lily could go outside to play so we can get to the bottom of this?" she tightly suggested.

Ryan frowned. "I want Lily to learn how to make authentic Japanese food. We both enjoy it, and she likes watching me cook."

He didn't raise his voice, but the tone carried a hint of curtness she wasn't used to hearing from Ryan. It immediately caused her to stop arguing, but it couldn't lessen her growing sense of panic. Ryan had been poisoned, and he didn't seem overly concerned as he expertly chopped a sheaf of green onions.

Jenny and Finn sat fuming at the dining table while Lily happily watched her father cook, her feet swinging from the bench. The little girl watched Ryan with hero worship, following his every movement with her gaze. It was oddly appealing to watch Ryan confidently dice, simmer, mix, and season the food. He had an apron tied around his hips, but not a drop of food stained it as he moved through the kitchen with ease. He soaked dried mushrooms in warm water until they expanded and gave the entire kitchen an odd but not unpleasant odor. Then he diced other strange vegetables, mixed up a bean paste, and added some soy sauce to the pot. It took an extraordinarily long time to simmer, and by the time he added crabmeat and a bottle of dried kelp, the entire house smelled peculiar, and Jenny didn't know if she could eat even a bite of it.

Finn seemed equally daunted. He'd been battling opiate withdrawal all day and had been pale and shaky even before the fish stew filled the house with its pungent aroma.

"I'm going to pass on this one," Finn said.

"No you're not," she said. "You need to keep up your strength, and everything that went into that pot has the makings of a good, nourishing meal. At least try it."

"You try it for me. Rumor at the Presidio claims you're the toughest nurse on base. Prove it."

She didn't feel very tough as Ryan set large bowls of kenchinjiru soup at each place setting. She swallowed hard. It was late and she was famished, but this soup didn't look like anything she wanted to eat.

After Simon led them in a prayer, they all picked up their spoons. Anyone who grew up in San Francisco was familiar with the scents and seasonings used in Chinese cooking, but this seemed altogether different. The fermented soy sauce was the only seasoning she recognized, and she watched as Lily happily used a spoon almost as big as her mouth to dig in.

Finn met Jenny's eyes across the table. "Go on," he taunted. "I dare you."

It was the inspiration she needed. "Those are fighting words," she said, dipping her spoon in the soup. She could feel the weight of Ryan's gaze on her as she took her first mouthful. Oh, this was odd. She wasn't certain if it was disgusting or something she could get used to. She tried the broth again and got this swallow down easier.

"Well?" Ryan asked, awaiting her verdict with a cautious expression.

"I've never had anything quite like it," she said truthfully. It had a strange flavor, but she could grow to like it.

Finn smirked. "You ought to be a politician. Come on, tell us what you *really* think."

"I '*really* think' you ought to eat something," she replied.

❦

Jenny hoped to reopen the conversation about the cyanide after dinner, but Ryan disappeared upstairs for an hour while he put Lily to bed.

Finn was twitchy and took out a pouch of tobacco to fill a pipe. Before he got very far, she smoothly lifted the pouch of tobacco from his hands and touched, smelled, and even tasted a bit of the finely cut strands. She grimaced at the noxious taste, but there was nothing more than tobacco ground into the mix. Finn rolled his eyes but permitted her inspection. Tobacco was a mild vice compared to what he would prefer to be smoking right now, so she gave a nod of consent, then disappeared into the kitchen to rinse the taste from her mouth.

By the time she returned to the parlor, the sun had set and a few ship's lanterns illuminated the room with a warm glow. She got right down to business.

"Boris, do you know anyone in Summerlin who would want to hurt Ryan?"

The cook shook his head. "Everyone in town likes Ryan. That's just the way he is."

She glared up the darkened staircase, willing Ryan to appear. How long did it take to change a child into a nightgown, tuck her under the covers, and walk away? They had important business to discuss, but first Ryan lingered over preparing a meal, and now it seemed he was engaged in the world's longest bedtime story. It had been more than an hour since he disappeared upstairs.

When he finally emerged, he seemed surprised to see them gathered in the parlor. "I'm sorry. I didn't realize you were all waiting for me. I should have warned you that settling Lily down for the night usually takes a while."

"Why don't you just order the girl to bed?" Finn asked.

Ryan's mouth hardened. "It's actually my favorite part of the day. So no, I would not simply 'order' Lily to do anything."

Ryan's back was turned, so he didn't see Finn pantomime the slow wrapping of a string around his little finger. Jenny didn't laugh. The generosity Ryan showed his daughter was both moving and painful to witness. She never had a parent love and fuss over her as a child, but it was obvious Ryan was a good father. Maybe a little overprotective, but it was Ryan's wholesome, unabashed kindness that had always appealed to her.

"Ryan, we need to talk about the cyanide," she said.

"Not that again." He sighed as he picked up a few of Lily's toys and deposited them in a chest beside the hearth. "I think it was a naturally occurring incident. The brandy had gotten old, the bottle was untouched for months, and the sediment gathered on the bottom. It was just a bad batch. I'm sure it happens."

"And the man who stabbed you last month?" Boris asked. "He was a stranger in this town, and Summerlin is far off the beaten path for vagabonds looking for a quick dollar."

"Probably just a coincidence." Ryan cast an annoyed look at Finn's pipe and opened a window. "Could you please remember to open a window if you must smoke inside?"

He seemed more annoyed at Finn for smoking in the house than at a possible murder attempt. The beginnings of a headache gathered, and Jenny rubbed her forehead. How could he be so nonchalant about two potentially fatal incidents within the past month? It was difficult talking to a man who refused to see.

"Who would have cause to want you dead?" she asked.

Ryan's eyes lit with pained humor as he met her gaze across the room. "You're the only person I can think of."

Finn choked on a burst of laughter, and even Jenny had to stifle a smile. A few weeks ago she could never have jested about Ryan's infidelity, but getting to know Lily had dulled some of the pain.

"Well, it wasn't me, so dig deep and think of someone else. Come on, Galahad. Who has cause to hate you?"

He shrugged as he stepped onto the front porch and returned with a large wire crab trap. It was the size of a horse saddle, with openings, ramps, and a bait box. He set it on the floor and began brushing rust from the hinges with a stiff brush. The soft rasping sound was rhythmic in the quiet room.

"The MID was annoyed when I resigned my commission, but they wouldn't kill me over it." He seemed indifferent as he continued brushing away the rust. If anything, he was more concerned with gathering the rust scrapings into the dustpan in order to spare the braided floor rug than the possibility that someone might be trying to murder him.

"Most crimes are rooted in either sex or money," Finn said. "You don't have much money. From what I can see, almost everything you own is happily living beneath the waves out by that rotting dock of yours. That leaves women. Have you been consorting with anyone in the village?"

Jenny froze. Abigail's pretty blond image immediately sprang to mind, for the girl certainly seemed comfortable waltzing in and out of Ryan's house. And Ryan was no monk, that much was obvious.

He flushed and cleared his throat before finally speaking. "There has been no one since my wife died."

"You sure?" Finn pressed.

Ryan shot Finn an exasperated look, then went back to working on the trap. "That isn't something I'm likely to forget."

"Yes, but I know you," Finn said. "Some fisherman's wife could be swooning over you, and you'd never notice. That sort of thing can make a man jealous. What about that girl who lives down the beach?"

Ryan shook his head. "Abigail sometimes looks after Lily. That's where it begins and ends. Trust me, there is no one."

"She seems mighty attentive," Simon observed, but Ryan was dismissive.

"She's too young. And too American."

"What's that supposed to mean?" Simon asked, but Jenny had to smother a laugh.

She knew all about Ryan's crippling shyness around American girls. He'd confessed it to her back when they were courting, saying American girls were so flirtatious and he had no experience with that sort of thing. He said Jenny was the first American girl he felt comfortable with. Maybe he was simply too sick when they met to be shy, because they established an immediate rapport when he arrived at the Presidio.

"It means I have no interest in Abigail Mayberry, nor she in me. None whatsoever."

The tension gathering in Jenny's shoulders released, and her headache eased. Abigail didn't seem like a good match for Ryan. Not that it was any of Jenny's business, but she didn't want him taken advantage of by an adolescent hoyden.

"Then that leaves money," Finn said. "Have you cheated anyone? Stolen? Come into an inheritance that might cause resentment? A business deal gone bad?"

Ryan was such a straight arrow that it was hard to imagine him locking horns with anyone, but given the way his mouth compressed into a hard line as he stared into the distance, he was giving the question serious consideration.

"I don't suppose the Japanese scientists I worked with would be overjoyed to know I'm trying to develop cultured pearls," he finally said. "The technique is not patented, and I'm under no legal obligation to abstain from pursuing this research, but I learned a lot from them. All of us are groping blindly in the dark to see who can be the first to develop a round pearl."

"Would they kill you over it?"

Ryan reached into a toolbox for a pair of pliers and began loosening the hinges on the cage door. "When perfected, the technique will be worth a lot of money," was all he said, still maddeningly disengaged from the conversation as he fiddled with the crab trap.

But Ryan was up to more than just pearl research while in Japan.

"Is it possible someone in Japan learned what you were really up to?" she asked. "If they suspected you of spying, they'd have cause to . . ." She let the sentence dangle, unwilling to even speak the word. Espionage was serious business, often punishable by death. Although he hadn't been assigned to carry a rifle or engage in battles, Ryan's activities were far more dangerous than that of an ordinary soldier.

"Nobody suspected," Ryan said.

"Are you sure?" she pressed. "They might not confront you to your face, but that doesn't mean they wouldn't take action behind your back."

"I'm sure. They would never have let me leave the country if they suspected." He twisted a wire on the trap, not even looking up as he addressed them. "I don't think the Japanese are out to get me, and what happened with the brandy was just a result of a lousy batch of liquor. Some apple seeds got into the mash at the distillery. It happens. There is no big conspiracy here."

"Ryan, it's happened twice within the past month!"

"And I'm telling you, there's nothing to worry about. No jealous fisherman, no foreign spies out to get me. This conversation is spinning into the ridiculous. Does anyone have any idea how to get the hinge on this bait box to swing? I'm not sure it can be repaired."

The way he shrugged away her concerns was maddening. He was so naïve. He thought the American involvement in the Philippines would be over in a few months, and yet American troops were still mired in the rebellion six years after the war. He thought Abigail Mayberry's visits were all about Lily, blind to the adoration in the young woman's gaze. Jenny had come here to save Finn, but it looked like she might need to save Ryan instead.

She crossed the room and grabbed the pliers from his hand. "I need you to take this seriously," she said, her anger gathering steam at the stunned expression on his face. "You have responsibilities!

You are responsible for that girl upstairs. For getting Finn trained and ready to go to Japan. To Boris and his ten percent stake in the pearl farm. And all you can do is fiddle with your crab trap while pretending the world is a safe and cozy place."

"Trust me, Jenny, I am well aware of my responsibilities."

"Then act like it! Quit fiddling with your fishing equipment and stand up to defend yourself and your family."

Ryan went still, and the room fell silent. Even without looking she could sense the weight of Finn's and Simon's disapproval, but they didn't know Ryan as well as she did. Ryan was raised by loving Christian parents and was too innocent to suspect the worst of anyone.

He closed the lid on his box of tools and set it aside. "It's been a long day, and I think we're all overtired. Perhaps tomorrow we'll be able to discuss this more calmly, although I assure you . . . this is simply a case of a few coincidences."

The mild tone in his voice contrasted sharply with her screeching, and it made her feel even worse. He did not meet her eyes as he left the room. She glanced at the three other men in the parlor, all of them looking at her through somber eyes.

"Am I the only one who thinks he's in real danger?"

Boris shifted uneasily. "The doctor thought it could easily be a batch of bad brandy. And Ryan isn't the sort to collect enemies. Even in the navy, no one ever had a bad thing to say about him. He's just too nice."

Simon seemed equally skeptical of her fears. She looked at Finn, surely the most sharp-witted man here. He clenched his pipe in a fist shaking from tremens, the tip of the pipe clattering against his teeth.

"Maybe he is, maybe he isn't," Finn said. "But a man as trusting as Ryan probably won't notice anything until it smacks him between the eyes. It's best to be on guard."

And Finn wouldn't be much help there. He was twitchy, miserable, and had run for the outhouse three times this evening. His eyes were dilated and streaming with tears so heavily it was unlikely he could even see clearly.

That meant Jenny was the only one who could be relied on to keep Ryan safe from his own unsuspecting nature.

15

The next morning Jenny woke feeling sick at heart for grousing at Ryan. Even if she was right and danger lurked around every corner, she should not have attacked his character in front of the rest of the household. But her apology would have to wait until she checked on Finn, who sat on the back porch and sucked on his pipe as though it were a lifeline.

"How are you feeling?" she asked as she stepped into the bright morning.

He glared at her. "I'd feel better if I didn't have to smell the reek of whatever is growing in those pots on the window ledge. And if paint flecks didn't keep dropping on me from the overhang."

She glanced overhead and saw that bits of paint had begun to curl on the underside of the porch roof, but it wasn't that bad. And the fact that Ryan grew Asian herbs for his cooking was oddly charming.

She sat in a vacant seat beside Finn, bracing herself for another long day of his grumbling. "Finn, I know your entire body is aching and miserable right now, but the constant stream of nastiness you've been indulging in isn't helping. Why don't you tell me one thing you're looking forward to after you make it out of this rough patch? I want an honest answer, not a backhanded insult."

His response was immediate. "I want to be a better man."

The statement was shocking in its simplicity. Finn was normally so arrogant that for him to admit he was anything less than a gift to humanity was refreshing.

He nodded toward the pier, and Jenny was surprised to see that Ryan was already out tending to his oysters. He was bare-chested, and water glinted on his sunbrowned shoulders as he lugged a cage onto the pier.

"Look at him," Finn said. "He doesn't have to struggle to be good, it just comes naturally to him. Not me. I started butting heads with my parents before I was out of the nursery, and I *liked* it that way. My entire world shifted when I was thirteen and read a book about the samurai warriors of Japan. I was spellbound. The samurai were a living embodiment of raw strength and valor, and I wanted it for myself. I devoured everything I could find about them. I fell in love with Japan and learned its language and history. I want to join that society, but at heart I'm still an American. I'm loyal to this country and want to fight for it, especially if it means I can go to Japan to do it. I want to throw every ounce of my strength, talent, and skills toward this mission. The fact that I'm one of the few people in the world who can do it makes it even more appealing. I want to become an American samurai."

An American samurai. The first time she'd seen Finn, he'd been sporting a flowered paisley vest and had just come from frolicking on a sailboat, but appearances could be deceiving. If he could shake this opiate addiction, she had no doubt he could indeed succeed in becoming an American samurai.

Her gaze trailed to Ryan, whose attitude toward Japan was so different. Ryan wanted nothing more than to come home and be an American for the rest of his life. He was a good man who had never been cut out for subterfuge. Finn surely had the makings of a better spy.

She leaned on the porch railing, watching Ryan dive beneath the waves like a dolphin. While he was underwater, she found herself holding her breath. He stayed down so long that she feared for him, but just when her own lungs started aching, he emerged again. He swam back to the dock, dragging a cage behind him.

"I wonder what he's doing with those oysters," she said.

"Go ask. I can survive on my own without a nursemaid standing guard."

Finn would still be in sight, and she desperately wanted to apologize to Ryan without the rest of the household listening in.

Warm sand squished between her toes as she padded toward the pier. The grit was rough beneath her feet as she walked onto the dry planking. Ryan noticed and swam to meet her. He reached the pier and held on as water swirled around his chest. Droplets rolled from his deeply tanned skin as he looked up at her.

"Good morning, Jenny," he said, still panting a bit from all the diving and swimming. "What brings you out so early?"

She sat on her haunches to see him better. "I came to apologize for the way I acted last night. I'm sorry."

It was hard to read his mood, especially since he sank lower in the water, finally submerging his entire head and then bringing it up and shooting a stream of water from his mouth in a graceful arc.

"Don't worry about it," he said casually, but his tone sounded resigned and not particularly forgiving.

"Ryan, I'm afraid for you." Her voice was devoid of the frustration from the night before. This had to be handled calmly and with compassion. Ignoring the splotches of water and sand on the deck, she clambered to sit down on the pier and dangled her feet in the water. "I think there may be real danger, and you aren't taking it seriously. You see the world through rose-colored glasses, always looking on the bright side. It's what makes you so wonderful to be around, but I worry you won't spot danger until it walks up to you, introduces itself, and knocks you flat."

For some reason he seemed pleased by her comment. His teeth gleamed white against his tanned face as he grinned at her. "I like my rose-colored glasses. I refuse to look at the world through cynical eyes. And if the world sometimes disappoints me? That's okay." He launched backward to tread water a few feet from the dock but still close enough to see her easily. "I promise not to take foolish risks with my health or safety, and I thank you for your concern." He stopped treading water and stood up. The water came only to his abdomen, and he executed the slightest of bows while still maintaining eye contact. "I accept your apology, Nurse Bennett," he said in a formal tone but without an ounce of mockery. "The incident is behind us and will not be stirred to life again."

It seemed such an odd way to phrase things, and she looked at him in confusion. Was she supposed to say something? Bow in return?

Ryan must have noticed her bewilderment, for he smiled and continued talking. "That's how a genuine apology is accepted in Japan. I sometimes find that Americans treat apologies too carelessly, which gives them permission to drag out old offenses when convenient. That should never happen once an apology is accepted. The offense is in the past. The rift is mended. It will not be brought up again."

Ryan's openhearted acceptance of her apology seemed as pure as the morning sun. Relief trickled through her. "That seems remarkably civilized," she said.

"I agree. One should not accept an apology until one is prepared to consign the offense to the past. Otherwise it will fester like a splinter beneath the skin and continue to cause problems in the future. So I accept your apology, Jenny. It's in the past."

"*Galahad*," she muttered, her tone a mixture of admiration and exasperation. It was just like Ryan to behave in such a flawlessly pure and generous manner that it was impossible to live up to his example.

He interpreted her teasing correctly, and his laughter was like warm chocolate. He slid back beneath the water and moved toward her in a languid breast stroke.

"You look very pretty in the morning sunshine," he said as he drew up alongside the pier.

"And I don't look pretty at other times?"

"Lately you've been scowling at me. It's hard to appreciate a woman's beauty when she looks ready to cleave the head from my shoulders."

Instinctively, her gaze dropped to where water lapped around the base of his tanned neck. "Very attractive shoulders," she said before she could help herself.

She shouldn't be flirting with him, but six years seemed to have dissolved, and they slipped into the natural banter of happier times. Even with his tan, she could see the flush heating Ryan's skin, and he disappeared under the water again, an embarrassed but pleased grin across his face when he emerged.

"Are you feeling well enough to be diving like that?"

"I'm fine," he said. "Well enough to check on my oysters, anyway."

"How exactly does one 'check' on an oyster?"

"I'll show you."

And before she could move aside, he launched up onto the pier, twisting to sit beside her. Droplets of water flung on her, and she couldn't help laughing. His trousers were sopping wet, but the rest of him was all sleek, sun-warmed skin. He swiped a towel over his chest and head but casually tossed it aside as he reached for one of the tall cages already on the dock.

Opening the top of the cage, he filled his palms with a couple oysters, their rough, knobby shells mottled in shades of black and gray. "I give them a brush down about once a month. Otherwise algae can grow on them and cause problems. At least, that's what the scientists in Japan said. The oysters don't seem to mind, but we worried the algae might give rise to disease. So I brush it off."

"Can I help?"

"Have at it." There was only one brush, but he handed it over along with an oyster.

The lumpy shell was oddly comforting in her palm as she swiped away the faintest trace of algae forming in the craters. Then she handed it to Ryan, who dunked it in a bucket of seawater, then set it aside and handed her another.

Water dribbled on her skirt, and there would surely be salt stains, but she didn't care. It was nice to be away from Finn's surliness, even if only for a few minutes. While she cleaned, Ryan described the slight variations he used in each cage in the hope of stumbling across a technique for coaxing the oysters into making round pearls. In one cage he was going to allow the algae to grow in case it somehow triggered an immune response within the oyster that proved beneficial.

She could sit here forever, listening to Ryan talk about the subject that clearly held him enthralled. Was there anything more attractive than a man who loved what he did for a living? She was sorry when they finished cleaning the oysters and returned the cage to the water. She lowered it over the side, and Ryan flashed her a grin as he took it and then swam with a one-armed stroke as he hauled it to the far end of the buoys.

Once again she held her breath as he sank beneath the waves to reattach the cage to a submerged line. What lungs he must have! She gave up and breathed twice before he finally broke the surface again.

"Are you game for another?" he called out, and all she could do was nod.

He disappeared again, but soon he was swimming toward her in that one-armed manner as he lugged another cage behind him. This time she was better prepared when he launched up onto the dock and moved well back from the spray.

"Are you confident these have pearls?" she asked as she began brushing the next batch of oysters.

"I'm sure of it," he said, and to her surprise, he unfolded a small pocketknife from his tool kit and began prying open an oyster. He cradled the splayed shell on the palms of both hands and held it out for her inspection. All she saw was the pale, wet muscle tissue gleaming in the sun. It looked remarkably ordinary to her.

"I don't see anything."

"Look closer." The eagerness in his voice prompted her to lean forward, scrutinizing the slippery blob of tissue. With the tip of his knife, Ryan pressed down on a spot near the rim of the shell, and a little silvery stone popped into view.

She gasped. "That's a pearl?"

"That's a pearl," he said in a voice brimming with a combination of pride, excitement, but tension as well. He nudged the pearl free of the shell and balanced it on the tip of his finger. It was the size and shape of a grain of rice. "It's a disappointment. A puny little thing, but it's only a year old, so it's on target for size. But the shape is a problem. This pearl will never be round. All the oysters in this cage were treated with the same technique, so they'll all produce rice-shaped pearls."

She glanced at the oysters in the cage. "What will you do with them?"

"I'll keep them growing for another two, maybe three years. It won't cost anything to let them come of age because most of the real work has already been done. Simon believes he can still make jewelry from them."

He flicked the tiny pearl into the ocean and she startled in dismay.

He looked at her curiously. "I'm sorry, did you want it?"

"It was my first pearl. I kind of liked it."

"I know where you can get forty-nine others just like it." His voice was wry, and it was impossible to tell if he was truly disappointed or not.

Ryan so often took things in stride. She supposed it was those rose-colored glasses. Even now he was casually brushing the algae from the next batch of oysters, his face mild as he performed the simple task.

"I think it's amazing. This pearl farm of yours," she said softly.

"You do?" He swiveled to look at her. "Yesterday you didn't seem very impressed."

"Yesterday I didn't understand how it all worked. Now I do, and I think it's extraordinary." He seemed to grow two inches taller at her words.

"It's not a very practical profession," he admitted. "Not like being a nurse."

She gazed out over the lines of rope and buoys that marked his oyster cages. "No, it's not very practical," she admitted. "But it's a beautiful dream, and I hope it works for you. The world would be a very boring place if no one ever dreamed outside the boundaries of what was practical and useful. So I love the idea of what you're striving for. It's amazing and inspiring. I hope someday you find a way to make your perfect American pearl. I'll be rooting for you."

The expression on Ryan's face was captivating. He looked overjoyed, like he had just swallowed the sun and rays of hope were shining from his eyes.

"Thank you for that," he finally said.

They went back to brushing the oysters, and Jenny could not remember a more enjoyable morning. It would be better if she could stay angry at Ryan. When she resurrected his offenses and infidelity, it was easy to keep him at arm's length, but this kindhearted optimist with big dreams was hard to resist.

His acceptance of her apology was humbling. He delivered full-throated forgiveness with no hesitation or hint of a lingering grudge. He made it look so easy. Would she ever be able to forgive him for what happened in Japan? It would be hard to forget those six years of anxiety and confusion, but it would be wonderful to have that bitterness removed and recapture the halcyon days when Ryan was the sun, the moon, and the stars for her.

That longing terrified her.

"I'd best get back to Finn," she said, scrambling to stand up.

Ryan offered a hand to help, but she dared not take it. The closer she let herself come to him, the more he could hurt her.

❧

Ryan set a wireless telegraph transmitter on the table before the sofa. It was smaller than a loaf of bread but the most dangerous piece of equipment Finn would take to Japan. It was essential Finn be able to break it down and hide the components with only a moment's notice. The wires, binding posts, brass rods, and jump-spark coil looked like ordinary scraps of hardware when disassembled. When hooked together, they turned into a transmitter capable of sending messages to the U.S. Army base in the Philippines. Such a piece of equipment was enough to get a man arrested for espionage.

"You have sixty seconds to break it down," Ryan said, eyeing the clock carefully. "Go!"

Finn unhooked the wires from the dry cell battery, but the tremor in his hands made him clumsy. When he unscrewed the first post from the wooden platform, the screw rolled from his grasp and bounced on the floor with a tiny *ping*. He muttered a curse beneath his breath as he worked to release the second post, but his hands were shaking even worse. The most difficult step was releasing the battery from the transmitter, and Finn didn't even come close.

"Time's up," Ryan said. The transmitter was still easily identifiable.

"You were distracting me," Finn muttered. "If you sat on the other side of the room, I could at least breathe."

"And if someone is pounding on the door while you're breaking it down? You won't find that distracting?" The MID would be far more rigorous. It wouldn't surprise Ryan if they ordered Finn to break down the transmitter while blindfolded.

Finn shot off the sofa and paced the small confines of the parlor. "Where's Jenny?" he demanded. "She's late with my medicine."

She was late because Ryan had asked her to stay away. Since arriving in Summerlin, Jenny had been giving Finn a mixture of tea steeped with an herbal concoction to soothe aggravated nerves. Ryan wanted to know what would happen if Finn did without the tonic, and it hadn't gone well.

He headed out to the back porch, where Jenny sat with Simon and Lily as they played with one of the cats. "Jenny? Finn needs his medicine."

Finn had gone back to taking the transmitter apart, but from the corner of his eye, Ryan watched Jenny move about the kitchen, her manner calmly efficient as she prepared tea laced with the tonic. Had it only been this morning they had sat on the pier, laughing as they cleaned the oysters? It suddenly seemed more imperative than ever to get Finn healed and trained so that he and Jenny could have more sun-kissed days of happiness. A lifetime of such days.

But Finn was a long way from being healed. When Jenny gave him the tea, it sloshed in the cup as he raised it to his mouth.

"Do you like music?" Jenny asked. At Finn's nod, she gestured to the stringed instrument displayed on the far wall of the parlor.

"Maybe Ryan could take that thing down and play it for us. It might help you relax until the tea can take effect." She turned to Ryan. "What is it, anyway?"

"It's a Japanese *koto*," he said stiffly. The last thing he wanted was to play it for her. The koto resembled a long, thin harp, but it was laid on the floor while playing. He and Akira had played it together often, for there was nothing more lovely than a duet between two koto. It had been Akira's fondest wish to someday teach Lily to play, which was the only reason he still kept it. He had failed Akira in so many ways, but at least he could ensure their daughter learned to play the instrument they both loved so well.

"Well," Jenny prompted, "take it down and play something for us. Maybe it will even lull Finn to sleep. He could use it."

"I'm sorry, I don't know how to play," Ryan said. It was a lie, but it seemed every time he spoke about his life in Japan, it only saddened Jenny.

She looked at him curiously. "Why do you have an instrument you can't play?"

"Perhaps someday Lily will learn. I'm keeping it for her." He bent down to scoop up the screw Finn had knocked to the floor, anxious to divert the subject. "Let's see how fast you can put that transmitter back together," he said. Maybe Finn would do better once the tonic took effect and his fingers didn't shake so badly. If Finn passed the necessary tests in September, Ryan would be free to pursue Jenny with a clean conscience. He could hope, at least.

It seemed most of his life was spent hoping.

16

Two weeks passed, and Jenny's attraction to Ryan grew increasingly uncomfortable. He was impossible to avoid, however, since they were trapped in the same room most days as he drilled Finn in various means of sending coded messages via overseas telegraph cables.

Throughout it all, she kept a careful monitor on Finn's withdrawal. He was fidgety, rarely slept, and was weak from exhaustion. She tried a number of mild herbal remedies to soothe his exacerbated nerves and finally settled on a tincture of *avena sativa* as the most effective treatment. She suspected that if he could make it through a few more days without a drop of opiates, he might finally turn the corner.

Today she was determined to help Finn get at least a few hours of sleep. He was having difficulty retaining Ryan's lessons on Baudot's 5-bit code, which he would need in order to transmit messages to an army base in the Philippines.

Jenny shooed Ryan and the others outside to ensure absolute quiet as she attempted to read Finn to sleep. Finn insisted his upstairs bedroom was too warm, and he sprawled on the sofa in the parlor, where the shades had been pulled to block the sunlight that irritated his overly sensitive vision. A compress soaked in chamomile water rested over his eyes as she began reading.

With his eyes covered, it was impossible to tell if Finn slept, but she monitored the hand that held the compress. At first it was twitchy, but by the time she reached the second chapter of *Madame Bovary,* his hand had relaxed. His breathing deepened, but she dared not slow her reading, as it finally seemed to be working. More than anyone, Jenny understood the restorative blessing of sleep and prayed Finn would find it. She lowered her voice, softening it to a mild cadence as she continued reading *Madame Bovary*, which struck her as a terribly sad story. It was one of the few novels on the bookshelf in the parlor.

"You mispronounced *lycée,*" a chirping voice pointed out.

Jenny startled, the book slipping from her lap as she shot to her feet. Finn tore the compress from his eyes and jerked into a sitting position. The past half hour of soothing reading was wasted as Abigail Mayberry smiled at them from the kitchen. She must have come in through the doorway from the beach, but who wore a satin dress to walk along the beach?

"I what?"

"You mispronounced the *Lycée of Rouen,* or 'the school of Rouen,' if you don't speak French." Abigail moved farther into the room, smelling like lavender and smugness.

Fancy lessons in French had never been part of Jenny's education along the wharves of San Francisco, and she didn't want one now. A glance at Finn revealed he was sitting up and blinking against the dim light in the room. It would take at least another hour to get him calmed down again.

"What can I do for you?" she asked Abigail tightly.

"I bought some lemons in town today. I've come to make Ryan some raspberry lemonade. He's been out in the surf all day and could surely use some sustenance. He loves my efforts in the kitchen.

That man simply goes weak at the knees when he sees me coming with a big pitcher of raspberry lemonade. It's actually a little embarrassing, but I do what I can."

The way Abigail preened didn't look embarrassed, it looked like a fireworks display.

Finn's voice was cynical. "Abigail, you are a martyr on the altar of feminine self-sacrifice. Were I a Catholic, I'd put your name in for sainthood."

"You would?" Abigail beamed.

Finn shrugged. "Sadly . . . not a Catholic."

"Oh well," Abigail said. "I think I'll bake a cake while I'm here. It's Ryan's birthday tomorrow. Didn't you know?"

Jenny blinked. She didn't, and it was disconcerting that this flirtatious girl knew something like that about Ryan. It stung a little, especially since Abigail continued to ramble on about it.

"Last year I made him a batch of gingersnap cookies, which are his favorite. After dinner we walked along the beach, and he told me how much I mean to him with all the cooking I've done and looking after Lily. I expect it will be the same this year." She smiled and shivered a little. Actually shivered!

"Here's the thing," Finn said tightly. "I don't like the idea of an outsider using Ryan's kitchen."

Jenny immediately understood Finn's line of thinking. They both suspected that someone had tried to poison Ryan, and letting an outsider into the kitchen was a problem.

Abigail's laughter was the perfect blend of delight and condescension. "But I'm not an 'outsider.' My goodness! Didn't Ryan tell you about me? We're practically engaged."

Without another word, Abigail twirled away and headed to the kitchen.

Jenny handed the compress back to Finn. "Wait here," she said quietly. "Some things are better handled between women."

Finn flashed her a wink. "I shall listen to every word with breathless anticipation."

Jenny didn't doubt it. By the time she arrived in the kitchen, Abigail was already slicing lemons.

"If you are practically engaged," Jenny said, "I'm sure you will understand Ryan's request that Finn have as much rest as possible. I appreciate your visit, but we have been struggling along fine, even without the benefit of raspberry lemonade."

Abigail set down the knife. "Are you asking me to leave?"

"Yes."

Silence descended on the kitchen. Abigail's pretty blue eyes grew hard as she drew herself up to her full height. She picked up the knife and went back to slicing lemons.

"I'm not leaving," she said calmly. "I think I need to make something clear. For the past eighteen months, Ryan and I have been inseparable. When he was new in the village and didn't know a soul, I was the one who took him to church and introduced him to everyone. I talked to all the ladies in the village and made sure no one would breathe a bad word about his little Asian child. He's got *me* to thank for that. I am practically a second mother to his daughter. *You*, on the other hand, are a nurse who earns three dollars a day." Abigail's smile was as tart as the lemon scent in the air. "My father used to handle medical law, and he said that is the going rate for nurses. The good ones, anyway."

Abigail twisted half a lemon over the cone of a citrus juicer, humming as though she didn't have a care in the world.

Jenny narrowed her eyes. As a child she got into plenty of back-alley brawls and usually won. But she didn't pick fights needlessly, especially when the competition was this mismatched. Jenny could spot blinding insecurity when she saw it, and at the moment it was juicing lemons and trying to stake a claim in Ryan's house.

"Shouldn't you be helping with your father's clamming business?" Jenny asked.

Abigail lifted her chin. "I am exactly where God wants me to be. Taking care of a man and his motherless child."

Jenny fought the temptation to roll her eyes. Finn wandered into the kitchen and spared her the need for a reply.

"God wants you to make Ryan raspberry lemonade?" he said. "Then don't let us stop you. Maybe the Lord will also ask you to make us some batter-fried clams and scalloped potatoes for dinner."

Abigail narrowed her eyes. "I think the two of you are being very rude. I have always been welcome in this house."

Probably because Ryan was too polite to ask her to leave. Jenny looked at Finn. "I don't suppose there is any chance of lulling you back to sleep?"

"Not a prayer. Every nerve ending is firing again." He clenched and flexed his fists, then scratched his neck and forearms. He looked as anxious as a bumble bee trapped in a jar.

"Let me get you another dose of *avena sativa.*"

She poured three teaspoons from the dark brown bottle and mixed it into a glass of water. Finn swallowed it dutifully, but her supply of the tonic was getting dangerously low. Ryan had already promised to take her to town tomorrow to buy more at the apothecary shop.

"Come on," she suggested. "Maybe a walk along the beach will help."

Jenny headed to the kitchen door, but Finn paused before leaving, sending Abigail one of his devilishly charming smiles. "Can I see the inside of your satchel?"

Abigail looked confused. "Why? All I've brought is lemons and a bit of raspberry syrup."

"I've never seen raspberry syrup. Show me."

The girl bloomed under Finn's attention, but Jenny knew exactly what Finn was doing. He unscrewed the cap of the syrup jar and sniffed the contents, tasted a drop on his finger, and offered it to Jenny as well. It was perfectly innocent syrup. Abigail happily juiced lemons, singing the praises of her famous raspberry lemonade, never noticing how Finn poked through the remaining items in her satchel.

"Harmless," he silently mouthed to Jenny.

She nodded, and they headed out the back door to the beach. To her surprise, Simon wanted to accompany them on their walk. He had been on the patio, sketching designs to turn Ryan's lopsided pearls into something that could be used for jewelry, and heard the entire conversation through the open window.

"That girl is trouble," he said once they were out of earshot of the house.

"That girl has the intellectual complexity of a bowl of mashed potatoes," Finn said. "She's harmless."

"I'm afraid it's not a laughing matter," Simon replied. "I met Chester Mayberry, the girl's father, while walking along the beach a few days ago. He asked me to notify him if Abigail ever showed up at Ryan's house unannounced. Apparently there have been some incidents."

"What sort of incidents?" Jenny asked.

"Last summer she asked Ryan to marry her," he said bluntly.

"What?" Jenny shrieked, startling a pair of gulls into flight. Ryan had dismissed the possibility that Abigail was infatuated with him, but he'd already had a *marriage proposal* from her?

"Her father says she had been reading one of those overblown novels by that dreadful Lavinia Styles, the one where the plucky heroine rescues the sad widower from his grief. Ryan let the girl down as gently as he could, but he told her father everything. Chester was mortified and insisted Abigail stop reading that tripe if it was going to plant ideas in her head. In any event, he's worried

Abigail still has notions of becoming the next Mrs. Ryan Gallagher, and he asked me to keep an eye out."

Jenny felt heat gathering inside. Ryan had told her not to read anything into Abigail's behavior, and yet he *knew* the girl fancied him. It wasn't that she was threatened by Abigail, but Ryan's omission made it hard to trust him again. He seemed so kindhearted, but time and again he hid things from her.

Abigail was proof that Ryan knew how to keep secrets, and he was keeping a lot of them.

Jenny set out for town with Ryan first thing in the morning to buy more tonic for Finn. Ryan smiled as he helped her into the wagon. It was an eager, boyish smile that cut straight to her heart and made her feel like the only woman in the world.

Except for Abigail. And Akira, of course. How many other women had basked beneath Ryan's heart-stopping grin and imagined they were the only one?

"Happy birthday," she said tightly.

He laughed a little in surprise. "I didn't realize you knew. Thank you."

She was silent as he flicked the reins and began the two-mile ride into Summerlin. He tried to make conversation, but all she could manage were curt, one-word responses. It was hard to be chatty when Abigail Mayberry and her delicious raspberry lemonade were constantly on her mind, and yet sulking wasn't going to solve her problem. It was only fair to give Ryan a chance to explain the situation.

"Abigail seems quite taken with you."

One corner of Ryan's mouth turned down, but he said nothing as the horse continued its plodding walk.

"Aren't you going to say anything?"

"I already said everything I have to say about Abigail. She looks after Lily. That's all."

Pressure began building inside Jenny. Ryan had been living in Summerlin for eighteen months. That was a long time to be isolated in a rural location with a woman as attractive as Abigail Mayberry making frequent and adoring appearances at a man's doorstep with her windblown blond hair and raspberry lemonade.

"And yet I've heard rumors of a marriage proposal."

She scrutinized him closely. The only sign that he heard was a flushing of his cheeks. When he refused to respond, she pushed harder.

"Why didn't you tell me about that?"

"Because there was nothing to it. It all came about because of some silly novel Abigail took to heart. Jenny, it didn't mean anything. She's moved past it."

"Then why does she say catty things to me every time we meet?"

"She does?" He seemed genuinely surprised. "Oh. Well, don't worry about it. I'll tell her to stop." He flicked the horse into a faster pace and nodded toward a screen of shrubs lining the road. "Look at that tree swallow over there in that bush. Did you know tree swallows lay pink eggs?"

"Don't change the subject. Why didn't you tell me about Abigail?"

"Because there is nothing to tell. Nothing! I'll speak to Abigail about being rude to you, so that should be the end of it. I have no serious intentions toward Abigail and never will."

His voice was so annoyingly rational. Why wouldn't he get into a good loud fight with her? It would make her feel better, but all she heard was the rhythmic clopping of the horse's hooves on the dusty road.

This wasn't about wounded feelings from Abigail's barbs, it was the fact that she couldn't trust Ryan. He was accustomed to keeping secrets, and it was going to be impossible to rebuild her faith in him unless he quit.

She squeezed the edge of the bench. "When you shade the truth, it makes it hard for me to trust you," she said tightly. "When Abigail said that she—"

"I can't believe that girl is coming between us. She means *nothing* to me."

"What about Akira? You never talk about her, and I don't understand how you can claim to love me and then marry another woman. That one is hard to forget, Ryan."

He looked away. "What do you want me to do about it? Tell me how to fix it, and I'll do it, but I can't rewrite the past."

He didn't sound angry. He sounded tired and defeated as he urged the horse to speed up, his demeanor cold and closed. It was his sign that the conversation was at an end. She couldn't force him to talk about Akira, and he seemed unwilling to offer the least insight into his marriage.

They maintained a stony silence all the way into town, and for the first time Jenny saw Summerlin by the light of day. It had a dry goods store, a bank, a church, and a post office. A few other stores and houses lined the street that led down to the wharves, where a two-story fish cannery seemed to be the only business of any size.

It was so quiet compared to San Francisco. There were no noisy automobiles chugging along the streets, no vendors hawking their wares. At least the apothecary shop seemed well-stocked. A bell dinged above the door and the scent of menthol and peppermint greeted her as she entered. One wall was filled with dark glass bottles, all carefully labeled and with their own measuring scoops tied around their necks. The other side of the shop contained an assortment of soaps, jars of ointments, and tins of imported tea.

To her relief, the pharmacy had everything she needed to help

Finn last through these final, difficult days. The pharmacist not only had plenty of *avena sativa,* but he had sodium bromide with a little ground ginger to help ease Finn's troubled stomach.

While the pharmacist prepared the bromide, Jenny wandered down the counter, trailing her fingers along the cold glass and feasting on the cornucopia of sights and scents surrounding her. She missed San Francisco. It had been a long time since she'd indulged in the sheer normalcy of window-shopping as she sniffed wrapped packages of almond oil soap, lavender bath salts, and fingered the soft bristles of a shaving brush. She sniffed six different perfumes before settling on an orange blossom scent to sample on the inside of her wrist.

"Would you like anything?" Ryan stood directly behind her, leaning over her shoulder, his voice conciliatory. It was obvious he was doing his best to smooth over their quarrel in the wagon, but buying her a bottle of perfume wasn't going to do the trick.

"No, thank you," she said, setting the bottle back with the others.

Ryan purchased the tonic for Finn, then said he wanted to see if he could find a new crab trap at the pawn shop across the street. The shop had all manner of used goods, including furniture, fishing tackle, and everything else under the sun. Jenny was amused to see a prosthetic arm for sale in the front rack.

She looked at Ryan with a question in her eyes. "I guess the original owner doesn't need this anymore?"

"That belonged to Jack Brewster," the shop owner said. "He got fitted for a fancy new arm up in Los Angeles last month. I'll sell it to you cheap, if you're interested."

Ryan shook his head. "I'm afraid you may be waiting a while to find a customer in need of that arm. I'm hoping you have a crab trap in decent condition. One of mine can no longer be repaired."

Ryan and the shop owner chatted while Jenny drifted over to

a shelf of children's toys. Would any of them be suitable for Lily? It might be nice to buy something for the child, especially since they'd gotten off to a rocky start.

A little wooden doll caught her attention. It was one of those brightly painted Russian dolls with a stylized face and scarlet cloak covering most of its round body. A nesting doll? The painting on the doll was strange. It looked like a jolly old man, but with only one eye. The artist had left a blank white space where the other eye should be. How odd that the doll had been sold when the painting wasn't complete, but perhaps no more unusual than seeing a disembodied arm for sale. She tossed the lightweight doll in her hand, looking for a seam, but she couldn't figure out how to open it to see if there were smaller dolls inside.

She held it up before the shopkeeper. "Is this one of those Russian nesting dolls? Does it open?"

"I haven't been able to open it," the shopkeeper said.

When Ryan saw the doll, he nearly choked. "Where on earth did you get a *daruma* doll?"

Both Jenny and the shopkeeper gave him a blank look. "A what?" the shopkeeper asked.

"That's a Japanese daruma doll. I've never seen one in the United States."

"Nonsense," the shopkeeper said. "It's a Russian nesting doll. I think the seam got painted shut."

Ryan shook his head. "No sir, it's a daruma doll, I'm sure of it. See the white space where the eye should be?" He smiled as he took the doll from Jenny and explained how the wishing dolls worked. They were purchased with two blank spots where the eyes should be, and then the owner made a wish. If it came true, both eyes were painted in. If the wish came partially true, only one eye was painted.

"So someone out there has a partially filled wish," he explained.

"Only if the rest of the wish comes true can the other eye be painted."

Jenny studied the doll curiously. Did wishes ever come completely true? It always seemed as if the happiest times of her life were still tinged with longing.

A commotion from outside interrupted her thoughts. Yelling came from down the street, and a few of the villagers ran past the shop window. Ryan set the doll back on the shelf and dashed outside. So did the shopkeeper.

By the time Jenny got outside, the shopkeeper was grinning from ear to ear. "The O'Malley brothers are in!" he roared. He threw down his cap and went running down the street toward the docks.

Ryan seemed just as delighted. "Are you game?" he asked.

"For what?"

"The O'Malley brothers are in! They always bring in the best seafood but only dock in Summerlin a couple times each year. Come on, we have to hurry!"

He grabbed her hand and pulled her down the street at a hearty clip. She still had no idea what had prompted the stampede toward the dock, but it seemed all the women of Summerlin were out of their minds with delight as they picked up their skirts and ran toward the pier, ankles kicking up and empty baskets at the ready.

As they drew near the wharf, Jenny could understand the excitement. The deepwater fishing schooner looked grand and magnificent, its sails towering over the squat structures in the harbor. She was out of breath by the time they arrived at the rope fence protecting the pier, but a handful of men scrambled over to help haul the catch ashore.

Three fishermen on the ship lowered baskets brimming with fish to the upraised hands below. Jenny recognized yellowfin tuna, white seabass, halibut, and plenty of others she could not begin to identify. Ryan's laughter rang out over the dockside as he helped hoist the baskets onto dry land. A gasp of excitement rose from the crowd as a net bulging with lobsters was hoisted up on a crane and lowered toward the people below.

It felt good to be alive. This spontaneous celebration of a good catch seemed abnormally exuberant, but Jenny didn't care. Sometimes God gave them glimpses into the sheer joy of the ordinary, and this was one of those times. Friendly people, a bountiful catch, and a beautiful summer's day.

"Stay here," Ryan urged. "I'm going to try for some of that lobster. It won't last long!"

Plenty of other people trailed after the men carrying the bulky net of lobsters. Who could have guessed the modest structures in this small town housed so many people? It seemed the entire community came out in force to greet the arrival of the O'Malley ship. Men wearing white aprons came from the fish cannery to take most of the haul, but plenty was being sold directly to women with their baskets at the ready.

A thump and a cry of pain came from a cluster of people near the ship. Men on the dock knelt to help someone on the ground, but the sounds of anguished whimpering were plain. Sailors on the ship had a perfect view of the commotion below, and the pained expressions on their faces didn't bode well.

Jenny angled her way through the crowd. "I can help . . . I'm a nurse." The words were like magic as the crowd parted and allowed her through.

The boy curled against a post couldn't have been more than ten or twelve years old. He clutched his forehead, and his face was covered in blood, his eyes terrified.

She knelt beside him. "What happened?"

"A crate hit him in the head on the way down," a man beside her said. There was a lot of blood, but head wounds usually bled profusely.

"Let's get you down," she said, supporting the boy's back as she lowered him gently to the dock. His eyes followed her the whole way, which was good. If he were seriously injured, his eyes wouldn't be able to track her like that.

"What's your name, lad?"

"Jacob," he said through clenched teeth.

She balled her handkerchief and pressed it to the wound above his brow. "Well, Jacob, look at you, hogging all the attention for yourself," she said in a lighthearted tone.

For a moment he seemed ready to laugh until she applied pressure with her hand. He groaned but held steady.

"Good boy," she said approvingly. "How many fingers am I holding up?"

"Two."

"And now?"

"Just one."

"Good! So your noggin didn't take too bad a hit, did it?"

"It hurts pretty bad, ma'am."

Jenny pulled an exaggerated frown. "You look a lot better than the halibut I just saw coming off this ship."

Once again, the hint of a smile threatened to break through his pain, and other men circled them to murmur encouragement. The best thing would be to wait here until the bleeding stopped.

"Do you need anything, Jenny?" Ryan's voice came from directly behind her. His hand rested on her shoulder, then he squatted beside her, concern in his eyes.

"Can you go back to the pharmacy and get some bandages and a bottle of hydrogen peroxide?"

He squeezed her shoulder before heading off. Strange how that simple squeeze communicated such reassurance. This wasn't a challenging case. Over the years she'd dealt with dozens of wounds on men who fell from bed or slipped using their new limbs, and head injuries always looked the worst but rarely caused lasting damage unless there was a concussion. She would sit here with her patient for twenty minutes before trying to move him. It put a damper on the joyous unloading of the fishermen's haul, but no one seemed too taken aback. The unloading continued a little farther down the ship and at a more measured pace as the townspeople cut a wide swath around her.

It turned out the boy's father was Mr. Cuthbert, the pawn shop owner who had been about to sell Ryan a crab trap when the arrival of the boat cut the transaction short. Jenny's arm was getting tired from applying pressure, so she passed the task off to Mr. Cuthbert, who looked to her and Ryan with gratitude.

It was another hour before Jenny was sure the bleeding had stopped, allowing her to thoroughly clean and bandage the wound. They moved the boy to the bench outside the hardware store while Ryan and Jenny made casual conversation with Mr. Cuthbert, but she kept an eye on Jacob, looking for any sign of confusion, nausea, or light-headedness. All the while a continuous stream of villagers wandered over to check on the boy and introduce themselves to Jenny, who had suddenly become the newest luminary in town. She supposed the arrival of anyone new in a town this small was cause for curiosity, for she certainly hadn't done anything extraordinary in treating a simple head wound.

A man set a basket of lobsters beside them and disappeared before Ryan could offer thanks or payment. A few minutes later, a tin of sea scallops packed in ice appeared as well.

Mr. Cuthbert insisted Ryan take the crab trap he had been about to buy earlier. "Your money is no good today," he said. "My boy is safe, and the two of you provided comfort for Jacob when we were both terrified."

A sense of well-being flooded Jenny. It felt good to be a nurse again. Despite her insistence that she became a nurse only because the pay was good, that wasn't it at all. When she extended comfort to people, it felt like she was doing what God put her on this earth to do. Was there any more worthy feeling than that?

The ride home was so different than the ride out. Caring for the Cuthbert boy had forged her and Ryan together in a common cause, cutting through the petty resentments of the morning. Looking at the fresh fish in the wagon, she knew they would have quite a feast tonight. A *birthday* feast, she teased Ryan.

He slanted her a curious smile. "Were you really mad because it's my birthday?"

"I was mad that Abigail knew and I didn't."

It felt good to be able to confess her pointless anger and even better when Ryan reached over to squeeze her hand. It was only for an instant, but she knew he bore no grudge for her surly mood.

Even as she enjoyed the ride home, she sensed herself falling back into Ryan's life. It was obvious he would welcome her, and there was even a place for Simon here should he wish to continue working with pearls.

But something warned her that it would be a mistake to stay. She had come far in the world by trusting her instincts, and they were screaming that she was wandering into beautiful, dangerous territory that could destroy the stability she'd fought so hard to earn.

17

Ryan sat at the picnic table with Jenny, shucking sea scallops, while Lily played in the grass a few yards away. Hope warred with desperation as he watched the woman he still loved make tentative overtures to Lily. Jenny and his daughter got off to a bumpy start, but today was unfolding perfectly. Lily chattered about her cats as she played with the discarded seashells, trying to stack them into a tower.

"And how do you say sea scallops in Japanese?" Jenny asked Lily.

Ryan hid a smile. Jenny's willingness to broach the subject of anything Japanese meant that maybe, just maybe, she was ready to acknowledge his life and failings in Japan. It would be impossible to mend the rift between them unless Jenny could accept Lily, the most obvious symbol of his infidelity in Japan.

Lily answered Jenny's question, her little voice eager to please as she smiled bashfully under Jenny's attention.

"Wrong," Finn growled from his position in a lawn chair a few yards away. "The way to say 'sea scallops' in Japanese or any other language is 'bland, flavorless rot that stinks in the sun.' I wish you people would finish so I can try to relax without that stench reeking up all of humanity." He tugged a straw hat over his eyes, and Ryan stifled an impulse to ask him to leave until he could behave decently.

Jenny had already warned everyone in the house that people moving deeper into withdrawal often suffered from heightened sensitivity of smell. In a perfect world, Ryan would have time alone with Jenny and Lily as the two got to know each other, but Jenny's job as Finn's nurse meant there was no avoiding him. Finn was an annoying and irritable presence, but it was a small price to pay if they could get him straightened out and ready to undertake the assignment to Tokyo. Always hovering at the back of Ryan's mind was the fear that Finn might be unable to take over the Japanese assignment.

And that would be a disaster. Sitting with Jenny and Lily beneath the cottonwood trees, with the crystalline ocean in the distance, Ryan felt like he finally had a family again. This was his home. He built this oyster farm with his own two hands, and he wanted to spend the rest of his days in this sun-drenched American dream. But it would only happen if the surly, twitchy man sprawled in the chair nearby could cross the finish line and get to Japan.

Ryan scooped up a handful of shells and laid them on the grass before Lily. "Count them into groups of ten, sweet pea."

"Out loud?" she asked.

"Yes, out loud. First in English, then in Japanese."

Lily began dutifully counting out shells and mounding them in a pile. Then she dismantled the pile in Japanese.

"Why groups of ten?" Jenny asked.

"No reason," he said too quietly for Lily to hear. "She's too young to do any meaningful help with the oyster farm, but I want her to know that she's important, that she's a part of things."

Jenny seemed to understand, a wistful smile curving her mouth as she gazed at him. He had loved every moment of this afternoon, even with barbs flying from Finn. This was how life was supposed to be.

Boris came out of the house, the screen door slamming behind him as he headed toward them. "I almost forgot," he said, handing a fat packet of letters to Jenny. "You got a lot of letters sent to you from the Presidio. I guess they miss you back home."

Boris collected the bucket of freshly shucked scallops and headed back to the house, but Jenny stared at the packet of letters on the table before her. They were tied with a simple piece of white string, but she seemed oddly unnerved, staring at the letters almost as if she were afraid of them.

And there were *a lot* of letters. A niggling seed of jealousy flared to life, for there was so much about Jenny that Ryan knew nothing about.

Finn whipped the hat from his face and leaned forward to scrutinize the letters. He instantly transformed into an alert man with mischief in his eyes.

"My, my," he purred. "It seems Box 2356 continues to be popular."

Ryan didn't know what to make of the bizarre comment, but it was enough to snap Jenny from her momentary daze. She snatched the letters, hiked up her skirts, and ran toward the barn. She ran so fast the white fabric of her petticoats kicked up behind her.

"What was that all about?" he asked Finn.

"I believe our Nurse Bennett is a woman of mystery," Finn said as he reclined back into the lawn chair. He settled the straw hat over his eyes again, but the smug, self-satisfied smirk on his mouth was still visible.

"What does Box 2356 mean?"

"Ask Jenny. Maybe you'll have more luck than me, but I doubt it. She's been paying to lease Box 2356 for years, so whatever it means must be important for a woman as tightfisted as Jenny to keep shelling out for it."

Ryan stared after Jenny as she made a beeline for the barn. He wanted to follow, but leaving Lily alone with Finn wasn't a good idea.

He reached for her hand. "Come on, sweet pea. Let's go see if Boris needs help in the kitchen."

And then he would find out what kind of mysterious hold Box 2356 had on Jenny.

❧

Daylight filtered through the grimy window in the barn. It was dim inside, but there was enough light to read by. Jenny held a single unopened letter in her hands. The rest were scattered on the floor where she had dropped them.

The answer to her question was written in large block letters across the back of the envelope. *Knickerbocker.*

It was the name of the parrot belonging to the sailor with the scar. It had been almost twenty years since she'd seen him, but every detail of his face was still etched in her memory, including the way he played with his pet parrot.

This letter could be from Oliver himself or merely someone who once knew him. In any event, she had been looking for news of the sailor with the scar for years, and this letter was her first solid lead.

She didn't want to open it. Her life would be so much easier if she could scrub that man from her memory and continue with the new life she had created for herself.

Easier, but not better.

She closed her eyes, drew a deep breath, and prayed to God that she was doing the right thing. She opened the letter.

It was short, a mere three paragraphs, but her hands shook too badly to read it. She plastered the letter against the windowsill, holding it steady so she could make out the words.

With every line, her heart sank. The letter was from Oliver's wife. She correctly identified the parrot as Knickerbocker and even the name of the Mexican port where her husband bought the parrot from a Portuguese ship captain more than twenty years earlier.

The woman wrote that she was a widow. Oliver had been dead for eighteen years.

It was the worst news imaginable. Jenny curled over, certain she was about to be sick. Heat washed through her even as goose pimples chilled her skin.

The creak of a latch broke the silence, and the door opened. "Jenny? What's going on?" It was Ryan, and within an instant, his arm encircled her. "Come, sit down. You're going to pass out leaning over like that."

She was going to pass out anyway. Of all the things for the letter to say, this was the worst. There would be no easy healing or redemption for her now.

A crate thumped on the dusty floor as Ryan turned it over, then guided her to sit. "Jenny, tell me what's going on. What has you so upset?"

His voice was tender in the dim interior. He squatted beside her and tried to take her hand, but she jerked it away. She couldn't even bear to look at him. Ryan Gallagher was a good man. Not perfect, but his crimes had been so paltry compared to hers.

"It's nothing." The danger of being sick was gone, but now a headache roared to life as uncertainty swamped her. So much of the past few years had been devoted to finding the sailor with the scar, but now she didn't know what to do with this terrible news.

"That's clearly not true. I've never seen you so rattled. Tell me what I can do to help."

Ryan couldn't rewrite history, so continuing this conversation was pointless. Worse than pointless. If she told Ryan the truth about her early years, the warm admiration in his eyes would be replaced by pity or revulsion, and she didn't want either.

"What is Box 2356?"

"I gather you've been talking to Finn. You should know better than to swap gossip with an opium fiend."

"This isn't about Finn. This is about something causing you a great deal of pain. Tell me."

She swallowed hard. All these years she had taken such pride in the new image she had created for herself, but it was all just vanity. She had painted over and disguised this part of her past, and until five minutes ago was prepared to bribe her way into a clean conscience.

"Shall I ask Simon?" Ryan said.

"No!" Simon was well acquainted with her past and where she'd come from, but even he didn't know about the sailor with the scar.

"Who is Matilda?"

Too late, she realized Ryan had been reading the letter in her hand. She yanked it away. "She's the widow of someone I knew a long time ago."

Ryan waited for her to continue, but she couldn't. To go any further would be peeling away the scar tissue she'd built to insulate herself from those terrible years along the wharves.

Ryan's sigh cut through the silence of the barn, but he dragged another crate over to sit opposite her. His face was open and waiting. It was hard to look at him. How ironic that it was easier to deal with someone angry and judgmental than this soft-hearted kindness. Ryan was, and always had been, far too good for her.

"Your life before Simon has always been a blank page," he said. "I never pried because I didn't think it mattered. You were generous and funny and shining with optimism. I loved that woman, and her past didn't matter to me. It does now."

She glanced up, prepared to run if he pushed this any further.

"It matters because it continues to haunt you. Something is filling you with shame and regret. Trust me, this is something I know about. I want to help you if I can."

She stood, crossing to the window to see the pure swath of bright ocean in the distance. It was hard to believe this was the same ocean that lined the grimy docks where she'd been born.

"My mother worked as a dancing girl on Maiden Lane," she began, keeping her face averted from Ryan. "To call her a 'dancing girl' is a polite word for what she did. I don't remember much about my early years. For a while I was at some kind of orphanage run by nuns, but at other times I was at the saloon where my mother worked."

Even speaking of those times brought to mind the reek of her mother's perfume. Back then Jenny loved the smell, for the flowery scent of roses was so much nicer than anything else in that section of town. The rules at the saloon were never clear to her. Sometimes she was allowed to sleep in her mother's tiny room, other times she was woken in the middle of the night and told to leave.

"When I was seven, my mother got sick and couldn't work at the saloon anymore. When she got too sick to leave her bed, she asked one of her friends to look after me. His name was Jake Malone, but most people called him Shanghai Jake." Even saying the name left a sour taste in her mouth. She risked a glance at Ryan. "Have you ever heard of him?"

"No."

No, of course not. Someone like Ryan would have no cause to cross paths with a man like Shanghai Jake.

"Jake owned a nice hotel over a restaurant at Buena Vista Cove. It was much nicer than where my mother lived, and at first I was happy there. But, um . . . Jake was a crimper. Do you know what that is?"

Ryan's eyes darkened, and it was clear he knew the term. No matter how clean-cut, any man from the navy knew about crimpers. It was hard to find qualified men to work on the thousands of trading vessels that sailed from San Francisco, and drugging

225

unwary sailors on shore leave was an easy way to earn a fast dollar. Crimpers were paid a hefty bounty for every sailor delivered to a ship. The practice was outlawed in 1872, but it still continued beneath the tables.

"Most crimpers work by drugging ignorant sailors who went into a bar for a drink, but Shanghai Jake was shrewder than that. Bars were sometimes watched by the police, but nice restaurants rarely were. He used children to lure sailors to his restaurant. Sometimes I pretended to be hungry and begged a meal, but usually I told the sailor that he'd be treated well at Jake's hotel. Some of these men were vile. I knew why they followed a little girl to a hotel, so I didn't feel bad turning them over to Shanghai Jake. But other men were perfectly nice. I had no business leading them into Jake's trap, but I did."

"Jenny, you were only a child. You didn't know."

It was typical for Ryan to think the best of her. He was so earnest, his eyes full of compassion. She could agree with him, but it would be a lie.

"I knew, Ryan. I knew and I didn't care. On nights I brought a sailor to the saloon, Jake let me sleep in one of the upstairs rooms. Normally I slept on the street or under a bridge, so I wanted that room. On the rare occasions I was able to bring a second sailor, he gave me a big slab of Italian salami. I loved salami and worked hard to win it."

It had once been her favorite food, but now even the scent of salami was revolting. It awakened memories of a greedy, soulless child who would do anything—literally anything—for a mouthful of food.

"I can't remember all the men I duped," she continued. "They all seemed alike, you know? They dressed the same, looked the same. But the sailor with the scar was different. He was younger than most, and he had red hair, but what I remember the most is the scar splitting one eyebrow. And a parrot. Like any nine-year-old, I loved animals, and when he noticed me staring at the parrot, he invited me over."

The sailor with the scar had been with a group of men who'd been kicked out of a bar on Pacific Street when they ran out of money. They loitered on the benches outside the bar, and the sailor with the scar kept them entertained by coaxing his parrot to perform tricks.

Jenny had hidden behind the trash barrels and watched the parrot, perched atop the sailor's head, take a bow for the others. She stifled a giggle, and that was when the sailor noticed her. He was surprised to see her, for it was past midnight, but he recovered quickly.

"Hey, kid, have you ever seen a parrot wave hello?"

She hadn't, and he beckoned her forward for a better view. "What's your name, kid?"

"Jenny Malone." In those days she used Jake's last name because she didn't have one of her own, and it was as good a name as any.

"Hi, Jenny Malone, I'm Oliver. Isn't it past your bedtime?"

"I'm not a baby," she said so defensively that all the sailors laughed.

Except Oliver. He squatted down to be at eye level with her. "This here is Knickerbocker." He stroked the parrot's bright yellow feathers.

The bird gave a little bow and repeated its name in a weird, squawky voice.

"Wave hello to my new friend," Oliver prompted, and the parrot shifted its weight to one leathery claw and rotated its other leg in a little circle.

Jenny covered her face to hold in a giggle.

"Seriously, kid, shouldn't you be in bed? It's not safe for a girl like you to be out on the streets at this time of night."

So Oliver wasn't one of the men who liked little girls. That meant she had to use a different trick to lure him to Jake's. She bit the tip of her tongue to make a sheen of tears pool in her eyes.

"I'm hungry," she said plaintively. It was easy to sound pathetic because it was true. She hadn't eaten since lunch, and the thought of a big salami sandwich clawed at her.

Oliver's face softened. "I don't have any money, kid. How about tomorrow morning you and I go in search of a church where they give out food to poor folks for free, eh? Maybe they'll even throw in something for Knickerbocker, since he doesn't eat much."

She shook her head. "I know a restaurant where they give out food, but I'm afraid to go there by myself. Could you take me?"

After that it had been easy. Oliver even held her hand as she led him straight to Shanghai Jake's. She'd been rewarded with a pound of Italian salami and a warm place to sleep, but she never saw Oliver or his parrot again.

Two days later she met Simon, and her world changed forever.

That was when she began to grasp the horror of the crimes she had committed. Men shanghaied into the Merchant Marine were brutally treated. They were drugged, robbed, and awoke aboard ship with little but the clothes on their back. Rumors of vicious hazing and malnourishment were rampant. Ships sailing from San Francisco were usually bound for Asia, meaning it could be close to a year before the sailor would be able to send a letter back home. Many simply vanished, never to be heard from again.

Oliver had been her last victim. In her mind, the countless victims she'd lured to Shanghai Jake all morphed into the only man she could distinctly remember. The sailor with the scar embodied all her victims. She became desperate to find him and beg his forgiveness. If she could win his forgiveness, she could finally close the ugly first chapter of her life and move forward with a clean conscience.

It was easier to stare at the dusty spider webs in the corner of the windowsill than look at Ryan. Nothing could be worse than seeing the disillusionment on his face as he learned what sort of person she truly was.

She drew a ragged breath. "Oliver's widow said he died eighteen years ago in Hong Kong. That means he died within a year of being shanghaied. My guess is that he got stuck on one of the rougher ships and didn't survive to make the return voyage."

Ryan picked up the letter, and she watched his eyes travel across the feminine handwriting. His face was closed and impassive.

"And what did you hope from this letter?" he asked.

"I've saved two hundred dollars, the equivalent of a year's worth of sailor's wages. I wanted to find the sailor with the scar, give it to him, and beg his forgiveness. Now that's hopeless. I'll send his widow the money and be done with it."

"You can't *buy* forgiveness," Ryan said. "If that was possible, I'd give you two hundred dollars this instant."

"Don't make this about us." Her skin prickled and her headache roared, and she just wanted this conversation to be over. Oliver was dead, so this whole search had been a pointless and expensive endeavor. Squatting down, she began scooping up the discarded letters.

"Would it work?" Ryan pressed. "Tell me. If I could stuff a wad of bills in your hand and ask you to forget what I did in Japan, would it work? Because I'd do it, Jenny."

"Just shut up. You're being ridiculous. I don't know what else I can possibly do other than try to forget the first decade of my life."

Even talking about it was mortifying. It was horrible to be naked and exposed in all her shame, and all she wanted to do was get away from Ryan.

She pushed on the barn door, but it was sticky. A solid kick at the bottom caused the door to shudder open.

Finn and his unrepentant grin stood on the other side. He'd been eavesdropping and didn't even have the decency to look embarrassed.

"I always knew you were an interesting person," he said.

She hauled back to punch him, but Ryan grabbed her fist. She swung her other fist, but Ryan scooped her up from behind, lifting her from the ground to pull her back from Finn's smirking face.

"If you breathe one word of this to another soul," she said, "I'll rip you to pieces and feed your sorry carcass to the sharks!"

Finn assumed the look of a choir boy. "But I'm your patient," he said in mock dismay. "You can't abuse a patient. It would be contrary to the ethical standards of nursing."

So was shanghaiing sailors, but she'd been good at it. She swung a leg to kick him in the shin, but again Ryan hoisted her away, his arms clamped around her middle like a vise.

He gave her a solid shake. "Have you calmed down? No more swinging fists?"

He wasn't going to let go until she could prove herself. She scowled at Finn, wishing her glare could send a blast of fire at that smirk. She jerked again, but Ryan wasn't letting go.

Drawing a steadying breath, she relaxed her muscles. "He deserves a thrashing, but he's not worth losing my job over."

Ryan still did not release her. "Finn? What do you have to say for yourself?"

"I'm bored out of my skull, and this is the most fascinating conversation in all of California. Only a saint would have had the fortitude to resist listening in, and I'm no saint. But you've got my respect, Jenny, and I promise not to tell anyone. Spies are good at keeping secrets."

"I'll hold you to that," Ryan warned.

Jenny glared at Finn. Over the past weeks she'd recognized a small kernel of decency buried deep within him, but she didn't want him knowing her most shameful secrets. Not that she had any choice in the matter now.

It took a while, but her racing heart returned to a normal pace. Ryan's arms eased their hold and he took her hand. "Let's head inside. Boris is cooking scallops, and they don't last long in this heat."

Even as they walked back to the house, Ryan kept her hand clasped in his. Did he fear she was going to take a swing at Finn again? They passed the picnic table and a few buckets of discarded scallop shells. Was it only an hour ago they were opening scallops and laughing at Lily's chatter? Her muscles were drained of energy and every step felt like a slog. She'd once read that emotional struggles could sap a body's energy, and she was experiencing that strange phenomenon now.

Their footsteps thudded on the porch steps leading up to the house. Finn kicked at a wicker chair, toppling it over and exposing some rotting material on the canes.

"Look at the lousy shape of this wicker," Finn said, hoisting the lightweight chair up with one hand. "You see that? Salt damage. You're a terrible property owner, Ryan."

Instead of retaliating, Ryan's brows lowered with concern as he leaned over to scrutinize the underside of the chair. "Salt damage?" He ran his fingers along the white grit gathering between the canes.

"When was the last time you rinsed the wicker with fresh water?" Finn asked.

"Never. I didn't realize I was supposed to."

Finn rolled his eyes, then kicked the side of the house, knocking a few chips of paint free. "And you didn't realize you ought to be sanding and painting the house to prevent this sort of thing," he said with another kick.

"No, I didn't," Ryan said, bewilderment in his voice. There was worry in his gaze as he scanned the house, the porch ceiling, and the warped steps.

"If you let it go much longer, the whole house is likely to rot and fall down around your head. Isn't it just my luck? I'm ordered to a beachside property to regain my health but end up in a decaying shack on the verge of becoming a deathtrap."

Ryan straightened, annoyance creeping onto his handsome face. "You know what? I'm tired of listening to you complain about everything in creation. I don't know how Jenny has tolerated it as long as she has. You can insult my house and my oyster farm to your heart's content, but you are to stop insulting Jenny immediately. Lounging around hasn't improved your attitude, so I want you to sand and paint my 'deathtrap' of a house. When you're too tired to lift another brush, go translate a chapter of Japanese philosophy. Your days of lounging in the sunshine and hurling insults like Zeus from the mountaintop are over."

Jenny's eyes widened as he spoke. This was a side of Ryan she'd never seen before, but she liked it. The confidence in his voice was both exciting and attractive at the same time. He didn't have a mean bone in his body, but it was nice to see there were limits to his tolerance.

"I'm not here to be your houseboy," Finn declared, then let out a stream of curse words that turned the air blue as he kicked one of the empty scallop buckets.

"First of all, stop swearing in front of Jenny," Ryan said tightly. "She's the closest thing to a saint you will ever meet. She radiates decency and compassion and deserves more respect than you've been showing her. And if you ever breathe a word of what you overheard to anyone, there won't be enough of you left to scrape off the ground."

And then Jenny witnessed something she never expected of Finn Breckenridge. He backed down.

❧

Jenny headed to the shed to gather sanding and painting supplies, anxious to get away from the others at the house. It didn't matter that Ryan and Finn treated her gingerly, they knew *everything* about her, and never had she felt so vulnerable. Both Ryan and Finn had huge moral failings in their lives, but they'd never led dozens of men to their ruin. She would run to the ends of the earth if it meant escaping her past, but the best she could do today was flee to the shed to regain her equilibrium.

Dust swirled in the air as she rummaged through a bin to find a coarse wire brush, sheets of sandpaper, and plenty of rags. There were paintbrushes and canvas drop cloths too, but she probably wouldn't need those for a while. It seemed the previous owner of this property understood the importance of regular sanding and repainting.

The shed door creaked open. Ryan stood silhouetted in the doorway, the late afternoon sun making it hard to see his expression.

"Did I overstep with Finn?" he asked softly.

He had, but she couldn't resent him for it. As the nurse responsible for Finn's health, it was her decision what sort of physical activity was best for her patient, but rest and relaxation clearly weren't working. Finn's mind was too restless to settle down, and perhaps a monotonous chore would keep him occupied.

"It will be fine," she said. She set the wire brush into a bucket, the clang echoing in the quiet of the shed. She couldn't look at Ryan's face as she curled sheets of rough sandpaper in the bucket as well. "Thanks for what you said about me back there. About me being a decent person."

"It's true. And you don't have to feel bad about what you told me. God forgave you long ago."

Maybe God could forgive her, but she didn't really believe it. No matter how hard she worked or how many starched collars she wore, she still felt polluted. The respectable nurse was only a pretty shell built up to disguise the sordid grit at her core.

She turned away from him. "I just want to forget it ever happened, plaster over it somehow. I want to pay my debt to the sailor's widow and go back to the rest of my life. I don't know how you can even look at me."

She heard his footsteps and then felt his warmth as he stood directly behind her. Warm hands turned her to face him in the dimness of the shed. The look on his face took her breath away. With two fingers he tilted her chin up. Only two fingers, and yet a thrill raced through her entire body.

He lowered his head and kissed her.

She stood frozen, but after a moment she rose on tiptoes to return his kiss. He treated her with the care of delicate, handblown glass, and she felt as if the last six years had dissolved.

At last he lifted his head, smiling down at her. "I can still look at you," he said gently. "If I had my way, I'd look at you for the rest of my life."

She couldn't even speak, only stare at a man who knew the darkest secrets of her life and still gazed at her with tenderness.

"Jenny, I am in awe that you found your way out of that life," he said. "I think those old wounds made you what you are today. Compassionate, giving . . . and yes, a little tough. You've been tested and hurt since childhood, but instead of turning you bitter, it has made you luminous and strong. A pearl. A radiant pearl that adds beauty to the world even though it had a tough beginning. That's who you are to me."

He pulled her against him, hugging and rocking her gently in the dim light. Her muscles relaxed as she sank into him, savoring the beauty of this brief moment. She knew it couldn't last.

As idyllic as Summerlin seemed, there was still too much uncertainty here, for if Finn failed his tests, she had no doubt Ryan would be on the next ship back to Japan.

18

Ryan rose early the next morning. Despite his words the previous evening, he feared for Jenny. She wanted to make amends to the sailor's widow, and that might cause problems. Some secrets were better left undisturbed.

The rasp of sandpaper greeted him as he stepped outside onto the back porch. Jenny and Finn must have gotten an early start, for already a third of the plank flooring was scraped and sanded. Finn sat on the top porch step as he attacked a patch of decking with a wire brush. Jenny was at the far end of the patio, down on all fours and using sandpaper to finish the process.

"I meant for *Finn* to scrape the patio, not you," Ryan said.

Jenny looked flushed but beautiful as she sat back on her heels and swept a strand of hair off her forehead. Her smile could light his whole day. "I like a little manual labor."

"I'm helping too, Papa," Lily chirped, appearing from behind Jenny's skirts. She delicately traced a wad of sandpaper on the patio.

He winced. "Has she been in the way?"

Jenny smiled. "She's no bother."

Another seed of hope took root, for the growing affection between Jenny and Lily grew by the day. He loved the way Lily was fitting in seamlessly alongside Jenny, whose easy acceptance of his daughter gave him hope that she might be ready to forgive him for what happened in Japan. "I'm heading over to the Mayberrys' for a bit. Can you look after Lily while I'm gone?"

Jenny raised a pointed brow. After their kiss in the shed yesterday, how could she think Abigail meant anything to him?

"I'm just going to ask Chester's advice on what sort of paint to buy," he said. "I doubt I'll see Abigail at all."

Jenny shrugged and went back to scraping.

He wasn't really going to ask advice about paint, but he needed an excuse to visit Chester. He left the back porch and started the walk down the beach to his neighbors' property.

Chester Mayberry was a lawyer who'd fled from the drudgery of his legal practice more than a decade earlier and had been living the simple life of a crab trapper ever since. After spending the past ten years beneath the sun, Chester's skin was as ruddy as his ginger hair. This morning he stood on his pier, scrutinizing something in a large bucket.

"Caught something interesting?" Ryan asked as he walked up the wooden boards and onto the pier.

"I found an octopus in one of my crab traps. Come have a look."

Coiled in the bottom of the bucket was a splotchy, brown- and rust-colored octopus that must have gotten too curious about the contents of Chester's bait box. Chester wasn't much of a cook, especially with an exotic animal like an octopus, but Ryan hoped he wouldn't release it back into the sea. A curious octopus was perfectly capable of getting into one of his lantern cages and wreaking havoc among the oysters.

But he wasn't here to discuss oysters. He needed advice.

"How is your memory of civil law?" he asked.

Chester grunted. "I spent seventeen years bickering in courtrooms all over California. Civil litigation is indelibly burned into my mind and can never be erased, no matter how long I bask in the cleansing sea spray. Why?"

Ryan had no business discussing Jenny's case without her permission, but he was quite certain she would never give it to him. So long as he couched his question in hypothetical and anonymous terms, he could glean the insight he needed.

"Let's say I had a friend who committed a crime when he was a child." Switching genders would surely keep Jenny's involvement obscured. "Let's say he was only nine or ten years old when these crimes occurred, but they were bad ones. Serious enough that a lot of good men were ruined. I know the statute of limitations will prevent criminal prosecution, but could someone still sue him in a civil court? Perhaps a widow or family member of a victim? Could an employer dismiss him for moral turpitude?"

Chester rubbed the small of his back as he squinted into the distance, causing creases to fan out from the corners of his eyes. "The thing is," he slowly drawled, "I quit the practice of law because even thinking about all that verbal nit-picking gives me a headache. Maybe if I was promised one of those elaborate, fancy Japanese meals you cook, I could be persuaded to lend my advice."

Ryan hesitated. His household was tense enough with Finn's surliness, but he needed to know the answer to his question. He didn't want Jenny approaching the sailor's widow. God forgave her long ago, and awakening a sleeping dragon was never a good idea. If trying to make amends with the sailor's widow could expose Jenny to danger, he needed to warn her.

"What did you have in mind?"

Chester nudged the bucket with his toe. "I remember those tasty dumplings you make with octopus. I'll happily send this one home with you in exchange for a decent meal."

A *takoyaki* dinner was a small enough price to pay in exchange for Chester's legal insight and discretion.

Ryan sat on the pier and helped Chester rig his traps with bait as he listened to his friend's assessment of the situation. Even the possibility for civil litigation expired within eight years, so Jenny was completely safe of any legal actions the widow might bring. He didn't understand her compulsion to make amends to the widow, but if it helped soothe her conscience and there was no danger, he would help her do so.

❦

The spicy fragrance of minced ginger filled the kitchen as Ryan prepared the takoyaki feast. Normally Boris was responsible for kitchen duties, but Boris didn't know much about Japanese cooking, so he'd been sent to tend to the oysters while Ryan cooked. Octopus meat rolled in spicy-sweet dough and fried in a hot skillet was a treat they all enjoyed, but most of the work came in preparing the seasoning sauces. His arm began to ache from mincing mounds of green onions, dried seaweed, and octopus meat, but he loved this aspect of cooking. Combining sweet, salty, and spicy ingredients was both an art form and a challenge.

Lily sat on the kitchen bench, dragging the tines of a fork through some beaten eggs in a small bowl. The way she scrutinized the mixture made him suspect she was merely playing with the egg whites as they separated from the yolks, but that was fine. He wanted her to feel involved. The last time he'd taken her into town, he overheard a few women whispering about her "cute little slanty eyes." Summerlin was small enough that most people knew he had a mixed-race child, and soon Lily was going to understand the whispered comments and sidelong looks. It wouldn't be as brutal as it would have been in Japan, but he ached, knowing the pain that was heading toward his sweet girl.

"Let's have the eggs, Lily," he instructed. "You can pour while I whisk."

Lily clambered up on a stool, then carefully tipped the eggs into a larger bowl of broth, soy sauce, and minced ginger.

From the open kitchen window came the voices of Jenny and Finn as they continued stripping paint off the porch. From what he could hear, it was good-natured bickering over the rules of a yacht race. It was a relief to hear them getting along.

He was about to ask Lily to return to the bench so he could fire up the stove, but a commotion outside caught his attention. Boris was running toward the house at full speed, sand spraying out from beneath his bare feet as he sprinted up the beach. He was waving his arms and shouting something, but was too far away to hear.

"Stay here," Ryan instructed Lily, darting to the back door. Both Jenny and Finn stood on the porch, bewildered by the agitation in Boris's mad dash.

"The oysters are spawning!" Boris shouted.

At last! Joy filled Ryan at the knowledge that his oysters were healthy and on their way to supplying him with a future harvest. He raced down the stairs and straight at Boris, hugging, laughing, and clapping him on the back.

"What now?" Boris asked.

Good question! Ryan had been preparing for this day for months and was exhilarated and terrified at the same time. In the past he'd always worked with plenty of Japanese scientists who knew what they were doing in their carefully secluded hatcheries. Everything was different here, where the water was choppy and the nursery several acres away.

"We get the mesh nets and the buckets," he said.

"Can we help?" Jenny joined them on the sand and looked at him with curious eyes. Finn stood beside her, looking pale but alert.

"Can you swim?" Ryan asked.

They both could, but Jenny didn't want Finn going in the water while he had so much medication in his system. No matter, there was plenty of work for everyone. There would be no takoyaki feast tonight, but if he played his cards right, he would capture thousands of oyster spawn.

The future of his farm depended on it.

❧

Jenny stripped down to her cotton camisole and bloomers. Sunlight warmed her bare shoulders, and it felt odd stepping out so scantily dressed, but she could hardly go into the surf fully clothed. Boris had gone to prepare the nursery cages in the lagoon, so all the swimming work would be handled by her and Ryan.

Simon and Finn stood on the pier, buckets at the ready, while she and Ryan headed into the sea. She gasped as a surge of water rushed around her knees. It was so cold! Goose pimples bloomed on her skin, and she shrieked as she pranced in the water.

"You'll get used to it," Ryan shouted, his teeth flashing white against his suntanned face before he dove beneath the waves. He emerged with a good-natured whoop and started slogging toward the buoys.

She followed, overwhelmed by the cold water as it penetrated her hair and scalp, but within a few minutes her body adjusted to the temperature. The water lapped her ribs by the time she reached the first row of oyster cages.

Ryan showed her what to do. He dove under and unlatched a lantern cage, then removed the compartment at the top that had been covered by layers of cheesecloth. What looked like tiny flakes of pepper filled the compartment. They had been prevented from floating away by the cheesecloth.

"This is called oyster seed," Ryan said, running a finger along the cloth. He turned his finger so she could see the dozens of specks clinging to his skin. "Judging by the size, they're probably a couple days old, but they were too small to notice until now. If you looked at them under a microscope, you would see they're already tiny bivalves with the fragile beginning of a shell and a little dark spot at the belly."

Bursting with the pride of a new father, he carefully peeled the cheesecloth away from the lid and passed it to her. "Take this to Simon, and I'll get the next cage."

She held the cheesecloth well above the water as she trudged through the surf toward the pier, then handed it over to Simon and Finn. Simon lowered the cheesecloth into a bucket of seawater and gently swirled it to release the clumps of seed.

"Are they really oysters?" he asked as he stared at the specks floating in the water.

"Ryan says so."

What a miracle of nature. There must be hundreds of specks in this single bucket alone. Finn carried the bucket to the lagoon, where Boris would transfer the contents into the waiting nursery frames. Jenny swam out to the far end of the buoys, where Ryan had reattached the first cage and worked to free another. It was the securing and freeing of the cages that took longest, so she learned how to dive down and feel for the metal clips that held the cage anchored to the submerged rails.

It didn't take long to sink into a routine. Ryan bore the brunt of the cage work, while Jenny carried the cheesecloth to the pier for Finn and Simon. Lily helped by filling buckets of fresh seawater she lugged onto the pier. As soon as they had two buckets filled with seed, Finn carried them to Boris at the lagoon.

It went on for hours, and Jenny loved it all. It was a physically challenging but exhilarating task as she worked in the surf alongside Ryan. They were capturing the future of his oyster farm. She swam and dove and lugged oyster seed so long that her lungs ached and the skin of her fingers became wrinkled and waterlogged, but she could not remember a more perfect day.

❧

The next week was the happiest of Jenny's entire life. The seed had been moved into the lagoon nursery, where it was now big enough to be considered spat. It was amazing how quickly the spat grew in only a few days. What initially looked like tiny specks of pepper were now the size of poppy seeds. One afternoon Ryan brought out a magnifying glass so she could get a better look at the developing oysters. Under closer examination, the seeds were tiny, pear-shaped beads with a dark spot visible through the developing shell.

The spat needed a lot of tending. Baby oysters pooped plenty, and in such a confined space, it was important to keep them clean. Each day she and Ryan lifted the frames onto the shore to rinse the seed of what looked like mud but Ryan said was oyster waste. They couldn't use lagoon water because it wasn't as clean as Ryan liked, so they lugged five-gallon buckets of fresh water from the pump near the shed.

Jenny never realized how spoiled she'd been at the Presidio, where getting clean water was as easy as turning the handle of a faucet. Here they tested their strength daily by cranking the lever of the water pump, then lugging buckets to the nursery. She felt new muscles developing in her arms, but it was a good sort of ache. The kind that came from being useful and tending her baby oysters.

The next step was for Ryan to heft a frame onto a pair of sawhorses, and Jenny used a watering can to shower the oyster spat clean. It took several cans before the water draining from the bottom of the frame was clear, then they carried it back to the bay and lifted out the next frame.

Sea gulls dived and swooped overhead, a little too curious for Jenny's comfort, but Ryan warned to expect plenty of gulls, crabs, and fish waiting for an opportunity to pounce, should any spat escape the mesh-lined frames. Ocean tides would sweep some away, and natural die-off would claim others before they grew large enough to be used on the pearl farm. Despite the losses, Ryan expected they would still have thousands of oysters by the end of the summer. Jenny worried over them like a mother hen and loved every hour of it.

Simon was fascinated by the entire process of pearl creation, and Ryan set him to making the nuclei that would be used for seeding next season's batch of pearl oysters. They would experiment with scallop, mussel, clam, and even lobster shell to serve as the irritant in the quest to create the conditions for a round pearl. Simon's experience as a jeweler came in handy as he clipped the shells down to tiny chips and then used a sander to smooth away the rough edges.

Several times a day, Jenny went to check on Finn, who continued studying for his tests in September. He was past the worst of his withdrawal and was making excellent progress in memorizing a stack of code manuals and Japanese history books.

Lily was usually underfoot. It amazed Jenny how Ryan was able to find something meaningful for her to contribute in almost every task. Sometimes he asked her to sit on the grass a few yards away while they rinsed the spat and report when the water ran clear. Other times he asked her to scare sea gulls away when they hovered over the nursery. It was in these daily interactions that Jenny developed a genuine affection for the girl who was always so eager to please.

At the end of each day, she was tired and windblown but still exhilarated as she and Ryan headed home. Boris worked his magic in the kitchen, and there was always a delicious meal awaiting them, usually fresh seafood with corn bread or some greens picked from the field across the way. Simon always said the prayer before the meal, and as others bowed their heads, Jenny couldn't help scanning the group.

What an odd assortment they were from such different walks of life and backgrounds, and yet they fit together perfectly, even the annoying Finn, whose health rallied by the day. Chester and Abigail joined them more often than not, and not even the girl's hostile presence could mar Jenny's contentment.

After dinner, most of the adults relaxed in the front room while Ryan took Lily upstairs for the nightly ritual of coaxing her to sleep. Jenny and Finn placed bets on how long it would take each evening, which she usually won. She'd spent enough time with Lily to predict how much difficulty Ryan would have getting her to settle down. It was always amusing to watch him tiptoe down the stairs after finally succeeding, trying not to laugh as the others made grand gestures in silent pantomime, welcoming his return like a conquering hero.

This must be what it felt like to be part of a real family, something Jenny had never known. With Simon she found a safe harbor, but she'd never had a family before, and it would be hard to leave it.

⁂

As the final days of July drew to a close, Finn's recovery was complete, and it was time for Jenny to think about returning to San Francisco. The rent on Simon's shop was due, and she had less than a month to return to the Presidio, or she would lose her coveted transfer to the day shift.

She approached Simon while he was grinding mollusk shells. The steady rasp of the grinder was comforting as she joined him at the picnic table overlooking the shore.

"Rent is due at the end of the week on the jewelry shop." Even speaking of mundane realities like a rent payment seemed profane in this sun-kissed paradise.

Simon did not even look up as he moved another bit of shell against the grinder. "I am well aware," he finally said.

"Are you going to pay it?"

He paused, then set down the shell. "Has it been so bad here? I thought perhaps you and Ryan . . ."

The phrase trailed off, but she couldn't miss the hope in his eyes. Simon loved it here. If Ryan's pearl farm worked out, Simon could live out his days crafting jewelry and spinning his far-flung dreams in a safe and protected world.

If Ryan's pearl farm worked. *If* they got married. *If* she could trust him not to hurt her again.

"Staying with Ryan isn't a safe bet. If Finn doesn't pass his tests, Ryan will be going back to Japan. Probably for good."

"Nonsense," Simon retorted. "He's invested his life's savings in this piece of land. He wouldn't leave it. Let the MID find another man to send over."

Simon didn't understand Ryan's bone-deep sense of loyalty to the United States, but she did. Ryan had turned his back on her and a life here once before. She couldn't trust him not to do it again.

"I can wire the rent money to your landlord. I have to go to town on an errand anyway."

She didn't want to tell him about Oliver's widow. Ryan was the only one who knew the full story of her attempt to buy a clean conscience, and she wanted to keep it that way. He had agreed to drive her into town, where the bank could wire the funds to the widow. It would be simple to wire Simon's rent money at the same time.

Simon let out a sigh of frustration and gestured to the expanse of ocean behind him. "Look at it here! It's paradise. This is what we've both dreamed of. Why would we leave it?"

Because she had a day job waiting for her back home, and only a man who might leave her for Japan here.

"Simon, we live in a world where rent needs to be paid. Where jobs fall through and men cheat on the women they supposedly love. I'm not going to tell you how to live your life, but I can't afford to be a dreamer. Do you want me to wire the rent or not?"

In the end, he conceded.

She stayed up late that night, thinking of the perfect note to send along with the guilt money to the widow.

Mrs. Swinton,
   Your husband once tried to do me an act of great kindness, and I responded badly. I would like to repay the debt I owe him, and I hope God will bless your family.

That was it. No details or confession of guilt. Most importantly, nothing that would identify her or let the widow seek Jenny out should she even want to. Would the sailor with the scar leave her in peace now? Would the nightmares stop? It was impossible to apologize to a dead man, but his widow was the next best thing.

She and Ryan set out for town early the following morning to send the wire. It was obvious Ryan did not understand her sense of urgency in paying off the widow, but he was a good sport about taking her to the Western Union office. He vouched for her good character, which seemed to be enough for the bank manager to initiate a withdrawal of funds from her San Francisco bank. She even paid extra to have a courier take the wired money directly to the widow's house. Her debt was paid.

Jenny rode in silence beside Ryan on the journey back to his home. She was surprised and dismayed that instead of a sense of peace, paying the debt left her feeling curiously empty.

19

As Finn's recovery continued, Ryan redoubled his hours mentoring him for the September tests. Lily could be a distraction, so he often took Finn to the almond grove across the road to study in peace. They had hundreds of pages of military armaments and munitions to memorize.

Sitting on a blanket beneath the shade of the almond trees, he began drilling Finn from a fat stack of pages documenting various ships and artillery. He held up a page with a drawing on one side and text on the other.

"What's this?" he asked.

"An American-made Whitehead torpedo, complete with an Obry gyroscope. Very deadly. Probably the last thing a naval man ever wants to see headed his way."

"And this?" Ryan held up another page.

Finn's eyes narrowed, and he took his time scrutinizing the drawing. "It looks like a Dutch trading vessel, but the rear tween deck is too tall. It could have been modified to hide a gun turret."

Excellent. With each training session, Ryan grew more confident of Finn's abilities. He was about to reach for the stack of pages documenting weaponry when a movement in the distance caught his eye.

"What's Jenny doing out here?" he asked.

She carried a pitcher between both hands and wore a radiant smile. Dressed in her loose-fitting, pale blue gown, she looked the epitome of wholesome womanhood striding through the almond grove.

"I've brought you some raspberry lemonade," she said as she approached.

"Is Abigail about?" Ryan asked, worried at the flare of jealousy Jenny still seemed to harbor over the girl.

"No, but she left her bottle of raspberry syrup last week. I peeked while she made it so I could prove that I'm not completely hopeless in the kitchen."

"So we aren't the only spies here," Finn said with a snicker.

Jenny flashed a guilty smile as she passed them both a cup of cool lemonade, and Ryan was secretly pleased. This was a sign Jenny was fighting for him. These past weeks had only confirmed his determination to stay in America and win Jenny back. Somehow he knew that neither of them would ever be truly happy unless they found their way back to one another.

"I love almonds," she said. "Would it be horrible to pick a few?"

"I don't own this grove," he said, but he didn't want her to leave. He never wanted Jenny to leave. "Stay and keep us company. I'm sure Finn would enjoy showing off for you." He picked up the stack of pages documenting weaponry. "Name this rifle."

"A Mosin-Nagant carbine rifle," Finn said. "Made by the Russians. Imported mostly to Austria and Latin America."

"Why do you need to know who makes it?" Jenny asked Finn.

"Because if I see a crate of them being off-loaded at a port in Tokyo, it's important to know who they've been keeping company with. Honestly, Jenny, you'd make a terrible spy."

"Why do you say that?"

"Because every iota of your thought process is spelled out on your face. You keep glancing up at those almonds, wondering if it's possible to pick a few."

Jenny shrugged, but her forthright honesty was one of the things Ryan found most appealing about her. From childhood he had been trained to lock down and cover his emotions, a trait that was only reinforced by the MID. Jenny was the opposite, and it was refreshing.

He drilled Finn on dozens of ships, weaponry, and military apparatus. It was mind-numbingly dull, but Finn needed to be able to identify this equipment on sight and from a distance. Throughout the drill, Ryan's attention kept straying to Jenny. She lay flat on her back, the dappled sunlight playing across her face as she gazed at the almond buds overhead.

They'd been studying for twenty minutes when Jenny suddenly rolled to her side. "Boris said if you shake the branches, the ripe almonds will drop right off. Shall we try it?"

"Why not?" Finn tossed down a pamphlet as he leapt to his feet. Jenny joined him and reached for a low branch.

Ryan stood. "We've got at least another hour of studying before we can break."

"Don't be such a killjoy," Finn said as he reached for a branch.

"It's hardly being a killjoy to buckle down and prepare for a demanding test," Ryan replied. "Besides, this property does not belong to me, and these aren't my almonds to harvest."

Jenny ignored him as she grabbed a branch and tried to shake it. The limb did not budge. Finn joined in, standing beside her and throwing all of his body weight into the task. The limb moved, but no almonds fell. They coordinated their moves to jump in tandem, hauling on the limb with all their might, but there was still no sign of fresh almonds dropping from the tree.

"Are we doing it right?" Jenny asked.

"How should I know?" Finn laughed. "Don't quit! We have not yet begun to fight!"

Ryan felt ridiculous standing aside while the two of them played like children. "You're tampering with someone else's private property."

Jenny's smile did not falter as she jumped alongside Finn. "You're such a wet blanket," she giggled.

He'd been called a lot worse, and the taunt didn't bother him. It was watching her shriek with laughter alongside Finn that hurt. Why couldn't she be that carefree with him? They had been that way before . . . well, before he went to Japan.

The two of them battled the tree, leaping in tandem like idiots, but none of the budding almonds looked ready to drop to the ground. Beneath their laughter, another voice shouted in the distance.

Ryan turned to see Boris striding toward them, waving a hat to get their attention. "Where have you been?" he hollered. "I've been looking everywhere for you."

"What's going on?" Finn asked, all hint of humor gone.

"Colonel Standish is here. He needs to see you. *All* of you," he said, and alarm shot through Ryan like the flash of a hot blade. These unexpected visits from the MID rarely boded well.

Cattails snagged at his boots as he strode toward the house, Finn alongside him. At least Finn seemed to appreciate the seriousness of this event, his face stern and all hint of laughter gone.

The colonel waited for them in the sitting room, his back rigid as he paced the small space. He got straight to the point the moment the door closed behind them. "Mr. Breckenridge, how are you feeling?"

"Never better, sir. Fit as a fiddle."

The colonel's steely eyes turned to Jenny. "Do you concur, Nurse

Bennett? Is he indeed 'fit as a fiddle'? I need to know if he is back to his normal state."

Jenny paused for too long, and tension gripped Ryan. Finn was clearly through the worst of his withdrawal, but neither he nor Jenny knew Finn before his addiction, so it was impossible to testify if he was back to normal.

"I have seen no symptoms of body tremors or heightened sensitivity in almost a week," Jenny finally said. "He is able to sleep and is clearheaded."

"Has he indulged in alcohol or opiates while under your care?" the colonel asked.

"Not to my knowledge."

The way the colonel narrowed his eyes made Ryan nervous. He thought of the hours when he and Jenny were working with the oysters. Finn was usually studying on the back patio during that time, but they were so busy, it would have been possible for Finn to slip away.

The colonel continued to press. "Have you ensured that he does not have a stash of intoxicants? Think carefully. Addicts can be quite clever in protecting their supply."

The way the colonel spoke seemed to imply he knew something they didn't. Perhaps Finn had been indulging in such a way as to take the edge off his symptoms, thus failing to shake his dependency? Panic started to set in, especially since Jenny did not look at all confident.

"I *think* I would be able to spot it," she said, "depending on the severity of the—"

"I'll make this easy for you," Finn interrupted. "I have been stone-cold sober for twenty-eight days. I have not sniffed, smoked, swallowed, or injected anything."

The colonel's smile was thin and cold. "And yet the bottles of opium we planted in this house have disappeared, and Nurse

Bennett says she did not discover them. And since you are the only known addict in this house, I can only assume you are responsible for their disappearance."

Ryan reeled at the news, but Finn only smirked. "Is that all you've got?"

"You don't consider the disappearance of two bottles of opium a significant issue?" the colonel demanded.

"I might if they actually disappeared," Finn said. "In this case, I found them within twenty-four hours of arriving here, and they've been upstairs in my bedside table ever since. Untouched, by the way."

"Why didn't you tell me?" Ryan sputtered.

Finn's glare did not waver from Colonel Standish. "Because I wanted the MID to know that I could spot their tests. I want them to know I've had those drugs within arm's reach for the past twenty-eight days and did not falter a single time."

"You know we will need to verify that," Colonel Standish growled.

"I would expect no less."

Finn led them all upstairs to his bedroom beneath the slanted roofline. Ryan and Colonel Standish both had to stoop, but they crowded close as Finn withdrew the dark glass bottles from a drawer and handed them to Colonel Standish, who scrutinized them closely. Jenny was able to confirm it was indeed opium, and the bottles were full.

Colonel Standish pocketed the two bottles while Finn looked triumphant.

"I'll admit, planting your wife at the Presidio took me by surprise, but ever since, you've been pathetic. I knew someone as straight-laced as Ryan would never keep snorting opium around his house. And the beachcomber you've had wandering past the house for the last week to spy on us? He's completely out of place. No one who lives along the sea would have a complexion that lily-white."

Pride surged inside Ryan. He hadn't even noticed the beach-comber, but Finn had, and never had he felt so confident of Finn's suitability for the Japanese assignment. Finn was cunning, dedi-cated, and had the natural makings of a brilliant spy. His ability to sleep beside a generous supply of opiates without touching it was proof he was well on his way to recovery.

Which meant that maybe, just maybe, a future with Jenny was within his grasp. He met her gaze across the dim interior of the bedroom, hope warring with caution. Jenny had no hesitation about showing her joy. Her smile was jubilant, and it cut straight to his heart. For the first time, there was no shadow of caution in her eyes.

The future he longed for so badly was now within reach.

⧉

Jenny shouldered the bulk of the oyster work while Ryan and Finn spent all their time preparing for the September tests.

Chester Mayberry had been visiting the house a lot lately, and Jenny recruited him to help rinse the spat. They lugged buckets of clean water from the well toward the sawhorses near the lagoon, and she let her gaze wander to his house farther down the beach.

"Doesn't it get lonely living out here with only Ryan and Boris for neighbors?" she asked.

Chester filled the other watering can, then dropped the bucket to the sandy ground with a thud and wiped the perspiration from his brow. "Not really," he said. "I was worried at first, because Abigail seemed to have set her cap for Ryan. Puppy love, I suppose, but she'll grow out of it."

There had been no sign of it so far, and Jenny scrambled for a diplomatic way to suggest Abigail still seemed to be planning an assault on Ryan's heart that would rival Hannibal's attack on Rome.

"She seems eager to settle down and set up housekeeping," Jenny said as she lifted the watering can to start rinsing the spat.

Chester nodded. "I'm hoping to send her to finishing school come September. She'll find a more appropriate suitor eventually. Ryan is too old for her, and besides, he's still mourning his wife. Any fool can see that."

Jenny looked up. Ryan was still mourning Akira? He'd told her they married because Lily was on the way, so she assumed that meant he didn't really love her. Didn't it?

Chester scooped up a pair of buckets and headed back to the water pump. Jenny snatched up her two pails and scurried after him.

"How so?" she couldn't help asking.

The pump's arm squeaked as Chester started filling his bucket. "Ryan is usually so stoic," he said, "but if you catch him at the right time, the floodgates open, and there's no stopping it. One night he'd invited us over for one of those fancy Japanese meals he likes to make. Boris was visiting family in San Francisco, and Ryan said he didn't want to be alone. That night he outdid himself, with seafood wrapped in leaves and strawberries cut to look like little rosebuds. There were almond cookies shaped like lotus blossoms, and lanterns lit all over the house. It was magical. Afterwards I helped him clean up in the kitchen, and he said it was the anniversary of his wife's death, and he made the feast to honor her memory. He started crying as he said it. He said Akira was the kindest person he ever knew and that he wasn't worthy of her. I gather she still looms large in his heart."

Jenny felt sick. Ryan hadn't married Akira only because she was pregnant. He married her because he *loved* her.

Chester filled the last of the four buckets and grabbed a pair to head back to the lagoon. Still dazed, she lifted the other two buckets, feeling every ounce of the fifteen pounds of water as the handles cut into her fingers.

Chester filled the watering cans while she retrieved another frame of oyster spat. The frame wasn't heavy, but the size made it awkward to carry. Her back hurt, and she was damp and filthy before she got it propped on the sawhorse. How different the job seemed today. There was no joy in her heart, only drudgery as she hefted the watering can up to rinse the spat.

Chester upended the final bucket into the watering can, then sat on it like a stool, worn out from his labors. He nodded to the row of frames tied to the dock. "This is quite the operation he's got here."

If she had the energy, she would shrug. It was hard not to be proud of what Ryan had accomplished, but right now she just wanted to run upstairs and hide in her bedroom. Except that Lily was napping, and Akira's lovely photograph would be framed on the nightstand. A beautiful, serene person whose memory would forever be in Ryan's heart.

"Maybe tonight we can persuade Ryan to take that Japanese harp down from the wall," Chester said. "A little music is a perfect way to end a hard day of labor."

She looked at him blankly. "I don't think he knows how to play it."

"Of course he does. Why would he keep an instrument he couldn't play?"

Jenny remembered the conversation perfectly. She'd thought it charming that Ryan was keeping the odd-looking instrument so that one day Lily could play it. "He's keeping it for Lily, but Ryan can't play it at all. He told me so."

"Nonsense! He plays it beautifully," Chester countered. "It's a strange sound . . . like a cross between a harp and a guitar. He said he and his wife each had one, and they played duets together."

But Ryan had looked her in the face and told her he didn't know how to play the koto. "I don't believe it," she said.

Chester shrugged. "Ask him. He's played it for me a time or two. I'm sure he'll play it for you."

Jenny felt sick. Ryan had denied that he played the koto, but that was just another of his lies. It had been so easy to delude herself into imagining she was the only true love of his life, despite what happened in Japan. But he loved Akira. Probably more than he loved her, for Akira had given him a child. Akira was the kindest person Ryan had ever known, while Jenny was a tough girl from the wrong side of San Francisco.

She gazed back at the house. All her life she had longed for a sense of security, and she had it at the Presidio. Yes, she was lonely, but that was alright. For a brief time she'd deluded herself into thinking she could be part of Ryan's world, but Akira's ghost was in every room of that house, and Jenny hadn't even realized it until this moment. Even now Ryan was bracing himself for a return to Japan if Finn couldn't pass those tests. How could she feel safe with a man who could put her aside so easily? He did it once, and he could do it again.

Finn didn't need her anymore, and the longer she stayed here, the more she fell under Ryan's spell. He gave her the illusion that she could have a safe and permanent home here, but all she really needed to feel safe was for a man to love her, wholeheartedly and without reserve. A man who would be honest with her instead of shifting and evading. How could you love a man you did not trust?

❧

Ryan and Finn started buckling the harness on the horse and preparing the wagon. They needed to drive into town to buy more fish meal for the baby oysters and would use the ride for an opportunity to practice the proper cadence when speaking Japanese. Finn's accent had been atrocious when they first met, but he'd made considerable progress in both cadence and inflection. They'd gone over these drills a thousand times, but Finn never tired of it, always eager for more help minimizing his accent.

The front door of the house slammed shut, and Ryan turned to see Jenny marching across the front lawn toward him. Splotches of seawater, sand, and dirt marred her skirt, but most worrisome was the expression on her face.

"This doesn't look good," Finn murmered, and Jenny's tone confirmed it.

"I need to talk to you," she said.

"Is something wrong?" Ryan asked.

"Can you play the koto?" she demanded.

He blinked, taken aback by the hint of anger underlying her words. "No. I don't play the koto."

"Chester says you do."

Panic clouded the edges of his vision. Why was she questioning him about such trivialities? And why had he just deceived her over something that mattered so little? "What is this all about?" he asked cautiously.

"I just want to know if you can play the koto."

"I know *how* to play, but I prefer not to," he clarified.

"Why?"

He considered his answer carefully. Jenny's mood seemed bizarrely volatile, and he didn't want to have this conversation in front of Finn. His relationship with Akira was complex and something he rarely liked discussing, even in the best of circumstances.

"It was something I enjoyed doing with Akira. It no longer brings me joy, but I know she wanted Lily to learn. That is why I keep it."

Jenny's lower lip started to wobble. This was *exactly* why he didn't like talking about Akira. All it did was hurt Jenny when he only wanted to protect her.

"Shall I make myself scarce?" Finn asked with uncharacteristic sensitivity.

Ryan nodded gratefully. "Jenny, I need to head into town for more fish meal. Perhaps we can discuss this on the way." Whatever it was that had set Jenny off, he needed to fix it. Now.

Five minutes later the horse was harnessed, and he set off for the main road with Jenny beside him. He swallowed hard and tried to form the right words. "I'm sorry I misled you about the koto," he said, beginning to suspect this was about far more than just the koto.

"Tell me about you and Akira," she said.

He tensed. "Not that again."

"What happened between the two of you? Why did you throw me aside for her?"

No good could come from this conversation. He flicked the reins to prompt the horse to move faster and scrambled for a way to divert the topic. "All this is in the past. I don't see any purpose in digging it up."

"How about because I asked you? Isn't that a good enough reason to respond?"

He looked away. Akira was the deepest shame and regret of his life, and it hurt to relive the memories.

Jenny's voice was sad and tired as she continued. "A part of me wants to hate Akira. Every instinct in my body wishes I could kick her to the moon and back, but she did nothing wrong. She never made any promises to me. She probably didn't even know I existed. It was *you* who turned your back on me. You who broke a promise."

Tension coiled in his muscles, and he hoped his frustration would not leak into his tone. "Everything you say is correct. It is the biggest regret of my life. I wish there was more I could say, but I can't rewrite the past."

"I'm going back to San Francisco." She twisted on the seat and gathered her skirts as though about to jump off the buckboard.

He pulled on the reins to slow the horse and reached out to grab her arm. "You can't!"

"Finn doesn't need me anymore, and it hurts to be around you. I want to trust you, but I can't. You lie about stupid things like the koto and if Abigail has a crush on you."

He swallowed hard. The woman he'd always loved was about to leave him, and he had to think of a way to stop her. As soon as Finn passed his test, there was no reason he and Jenny couldn't build a life together. "Don't go. Tell me what you need, and I'll give it to you."

She stopped trying to jump out of the wagon. Whatever else happened, he had to keep her from leaving him. He guided the horse to the side of the road and halted. He turned on the bench to look at Jenny.

"Did Akira know about me?" she asked.

"No."

"Did you love her?"

He'd rather talk about anything other than this. "Why do you want to know these things?"

"Because when a wound is infected, it must be lanced, sterilized, and drained of puss. It hurts. It isn't easy, but it's got to be done before it can heal."

He hung his head. There was no escape. He'd lance the wound and hope for the best, but he knew that all it would do was hurt Jenny.

"Yes, I loved her," he admitted. "It was different than how I feel for you, but of course I loved her."

He told Jenny everything. Akira was quiet and demure, very Japanese in all things except for her insatiable curiosity about America. During the painful years of his youth, they had been inseparable. He now understood that Akira carried a torch for him during those years, although he'd been too blind to see it until he returned to Japan as an adult. Akira and Jenny could not be more different, and he'd always kept them separate in his mind.

"When I first went back to Japan, I thought about you all the time," he said. "I counted the days until the war would end and I'd be free to go back to California and to you. I looked at the sun rising, and I knew it was setting in San Francisco. I wondered if you were looking at it at the same time, and somehow I knew you were."

Jenny looked away, gazing across the almond grove but not denying his statement. "I can be such a fool sometimes," she said in a sad voice. "I convinced myself you had a marriage of convenience, but no. You simply chose your career and Akira over me."

He longed to close the space between them and comfort her but sensed that she needed to talk and he needed to hear it.

"Deep down, I know I'm not a very good person," she continued in a voice heavy with dejection. "You tell me Akira was kind and didn't know I even existed, but I still despise her. I know how much you loved your father, but I delighted in selling his watch because I knew it would hurt you. I sold it for a piece of glass and a steak dinner. That makes me no better than the girl who sold a sailor to the crimpers for a piece of salami."

"Jenny, stop. You *are* a good person. You wouldn't be human if you didn't have these feelings. We've both done things in the past that we regret, but it is past. Can't we just move forward?"

The look on her face made him want to weep, for it was devoid of hope. "I tried to fool myself into thinking I could live with what happened in Japan because you had a loveless marriage. But it was more than that, wasn't it, Ryan?"

"I never stopped loving you. Not for a single day—"

Pain ripped through his arm, knocking him sideways. The report of a gunshot sounded a moment later. He dropped the reins, and the horse broke into a panicked gallop. The jostling knocked him to the floor of the buckboard.

"Ryan? Are you alright?" Jenny's voice sounded like it came from a long way off, but she was hunched over him on the floor of the buckboard.

"I've been shot," he choked out.

"I know," she said grimly.

She stayed crouched on the floor but reached for the reins. Each rock and bump of the wagon as the horse careened away brought fresh agony. Blood trickled between his fingers, and he tried to squeeze his arm to stanch the flow.

Mercifully, the horse quickly slowed, and Jenny pivoted to reach beneath the seat for the pistol he kept to guard against cougars.

"Probably a hunter," he gasped. "Pheasant season . . ."

"Do we look like pheasants?" she roared.

He wanted to reassure her, but the ferocious pain made it hurt even to breathe. With his head wedged on the floor of the buckboard, he couldn't see what she was doing, but he heard the cocking of the pistol, then a deafening blast as she fired the gun.

"That's to let whoever's out there know we aren't sitting ducks," she said grimly. A moment later she was leaning over him. "Let go of your arm."

"Can't."

"Do it, Ryan. It will hurt, but I'm going to tie it off until we get home."

It hurt to let go, it hurt when she tied a handkerchief an inch above the wound in his bicep. Everything hurt, and he was so thirsty he'd give anything for a drink of water, but the pain got worse when Jenny grabbed the reins and drove the horse into a canter, bumping and jarring on the rutted path toward home.

20

The bleeding had stopped by the time Jenny got Ryan settled into bed. The bullet had lodged deeply in the bicep tissue, and while waiting for the doctor to arrive, she cleaned the lacerated skin and used tweezers to remove fragments of lint from the wound. Ryan groaned each time she probed for bits of thread, but it was nothing compared to the agony he suffered when Dr. Keselowski dug out the bullet.

She'd assisted with the surgery, handing over tools and bandages as a fresh gush of blood flowed from the wound. She did her best to maintain a tough shell of professional detachment, but it was hard as Ryan suffered. Dr. Keselowski was better at maintaining an impassive mood, calmly telling Ryan it was barely a flesh wound.

Maybe he intended to comfort Ryan, but it wasn't true. The round in his arm had traveled almost two inches into the muscle, stopped only by the humerus bone. Not until after the surgery did the doctor permit sedation, and Ryan had finally drifted to a restless sleep.

Dr. Keselowski collected his supplies, gave Jenny instructions for changing bandages, and took his leave. She stood motionless at the foot of the bed, saddened to see Ryan's face darkened with pain even in sleep. At least now he could no longer deny that someone was trying to kill him.

She glanced around his room, her gaze drawn to the slim, locked drawer in his dresser. Aside from a flimsy latch on the front door, it was the only lock in the entire house. There was something important in that drawer, and it might relate to a motive behind the attempts on Ryan's life.

She stepped toward the dresser and gave the drawer a tug. It was still locked. She rummaged through the garments in the neighboring drawers in search of a key but came up empty.

It would be easy to pick the lock. All it would take was a hairpin and a little patience. Ryan was deeply asleep, and she could get into this drawer in a few minutes. Whatever paper work or correspondence he kept in there might point a finger toward their mysterious assailant. Or maybe it would simply shed more insight into his life. There might be something about Akira in there.

Or another woman. Ryan claimed there hadn't been anyone since arriving back in California, but how could she believe that? He hid a lot of things from her, claiming he did it to avoid hurting her.

She worked a finger into her neatly coiled bun, wiggling until she latched onto a hairpin and tugged it free. She fitted the hairpin into the lock but glanced over her shoulder to be certain Ryan was still asleep.

He was. He also looked impossibly vulnerable, and here she was preparing to prowl through his private belongings in an attempt to reassure herself he had no other woman in his life. She withdrew her hand.

She either had to trust Ryan or get out of his life. She would wait until he was awake and discuss the drawer in person.

Jenny stood in the corner of Ryan's front parlor, arms folded across her chest and still wearing her bloodstained clothes as she studied the people crowded into the room. News traveled quickly in a place like Summerlin, and villagers had started arriving even before Dr. Keselowski finished surgery. A couple men from the local hardware store arrived to offer help, as had a minister and the fishmonger who sometimes bought crab from the Mayberrys. The baker's wife agreed to take Lily to her home for the rest of the day, as the girl started sobbing the moment she saw her father stagger through the door in a blood-soaked shirt.

The sheriff arrived, and Jenny was surprised to see he was Mr. Cuthbert, the owner of the pawn shop where she'd seen the fake arm for sale. It was troubling to know this crime was going to be investigated by a man who knew more about prosthetic arms than tracking criminal behavior.

She scanned the crowd. Who had the most to gain? Chester Mayberry had been coveting this property for a long time, and maybe he'd manipulated documents so he would have a straight shot at it in the event of Ryan's death. What about Boris? Ryan had given him ten percent ownership of the oyster farm, but it wouldn't be worth a dime until Ryan sold it. Might Boris have gotten impatient?

Sheriff Cuthbert asked everyone in the room if they'd seen any strangers in town or anyone loitering along the old orchard pass, where Jenny believed the shooter must have been hiding when they rounded the bend. The last time anyone could remember seeing strangers was at the arrival of the O'Malley brothers' fishing vessel, which always had a rotating crew of sailors. The sheriff took a few notes, but Jenny heard nothing useful, and it seemed the sheriff was completely out of his league. He suggested it was time for everyone to leave, claiming the family needed peace and privacy. The hardware store men didn't take kindly to being asked to leave and made a point of offering their services to Jenny should she need anything in the coming days.

When Chester Mayberry rose to leave, the sheriff stopped him. "I'd like a few words, Chester."

It took a while to clear the house, but once all the visitors were gone, the sheriff asked Chester to go outside with him for a moment. He took the precaution of closing all the windows so they wouldn't be overheard. The kitchen door to the beach was tugged shut behind them.

"Upstairs," Finn silently mouthed, and Jenny nodded. All the windows upstairs were still open, and it would be easy to eavesdrop.

They darted into Finn's bedroom, a tiny room with nothing but a bed and chest of drawers. The slant of the ceiling was so low that they both had to crouch next to the open window.

Perhaps Sheriff Cuthbert wasn't so dim-witted after all, for he seemed to suspect Chester as well. As Jenny listened, the sheriff accused Chester of planting crab traps in Ryan's cove and selling the catch to the local fishmonger. Chester did not take the accusation lightly.

"I set those traps twenty yards outside of the cove. Ryan gave me permission to add them back so long as they didn't drift into his nursery."

"To feed your family," the sheriff said pointedly. "Does he know you're selling crabs in town again? It will be easy enough to ask him when he wakes up."

"How should I know what Ryan knows and doesn't know?"

"What about your daughter? Where is she today?"

The lawyer's voice was angry. "At this very moment? I have no idea. I know one thing she hasn't been doing—toting a gun around and firing random shots at Ryan Gallagher. That girl would more likely throw rose petals at him than shoot him."

Jenny never underestimated the wiles of a determined woman, but trying to pin this on Abigail did seem farfetched. The sheriff had other questions, but Chester was a lawyer, and after providing minimal insight into where he'd been that day, he dried up and refused to answer any more questions.

The sedative kept Ryan asleep through the night, but the following morning Jenny helped him come downstairs for breakfast. He put on a brave face for Lily but was clumsy wielding a fork with his left hand, blobs of scrambled eggs continually slipping off. Finally he surrendered and used a spoon.

After breakfast, Jenny and Finn coaxed him out to the pier to talk. It was the only place they could be certain they wouldn't be overheard. It felt terrible to suspect Boris, but he'd been in the vicinity for all three attempts on Ryan's life, and they'd be foolish to overlook him.

Ryan moved slowly as they crossed the beach and headed toward the pier. It creaked as their footsteps thudded on the dry planking.

Ryan paused, squinting at the line of buoys. "Ha! This is the third time I've seen that same sea gull perching on that buoy. I think he knows what's right below and is trying to think of a way to get at my oysters."

She sighed. "Ryan, could we please discuss who might have reason to shoot at you rather than worry over predatory sea gulls?"

"Go ahead," he said. "I admit it's getting harder to ignore the coincidences, so tell me what you're thinking."

"You said that ten percent of the farm belongs to Boris. What happens to the rest of it if you die?"

"It goes to Lily."

"And who have you designated as a guardian for Lily?" Finn asked.

"Boris." Ryan swallowed hard. "But I have a will, and everything is spelled out very clearly. Boris won't be able to profit from it. He'll have access to what I own to pay some bills, but it's a very comprehensive will with lots of safeguards."

"Who drafted the will?" Finn asked.

"Chester."

Another set of warning bells went off in Jenny's mind, but Ryan was dismissive.

"Both Chester and Boris know what is in my will, and quite frankly, it isn't much. I spent everything I had to buy this place, and they wouldn't know how to operate a pearl farm. Yes, there is value in the land and the house, but it's not worth killing over."

"Chester has wanted this property for years but couldn't afford it," she said. "Could he be driven by resentment? Or something else entirely? It seems so odd for a man his age to have retired from a lucrative profession, especially since he seems chronically short of funds."

"It's not Chester," Finn said. "He couldn't have fired that shot yesterday. He's going blind."

She and Ryan both swiveled to look at him. "How do you know that?"

"Haven't you noticed the way he makes his daughter sort the clams he catches? He can't tell the different varieties apart anymore. It also explains why he had to quit the law."

"Blind?" Ryan asked, looking as though he'd been poleaxed.

Jenny's heart sank. She'd been annoyed with Chester for taking advantage of Ryan's generosity by nudging his crab traps ever closer to the cove, but blindness wasn't something she'd wish on anyone.

"I think this has something to do with Japan," Ryan said. "Between the MID work and the pearls, there are plenty of people in Japan with cause to resent me. And I can't stop thinking about that daruma doll at the pawn shop. One eye painted in, the other still blank. It didn't bother me at the time, but how did it get here? I've never seen one in America. They're simply too strange. Ugly, really. Whoever brought in that daruma doll had probably been in Japan."

The pawn shop was owned by Sheriff Cuthbert, and if he could remember who sold him the daruma doll, they might have their first solid lead.

❧

The ride into town sapped Ryan's strength. He felt like a weakling as Finn drove the wagon and Jenny walked alongside. It was flat-out wrong to make a woman walk while he sat on the bench like an infant, but she refused to listen to his protestations.

"No arguing, Galahad. I don't know how to drive, and the horse can't pull a third person, so it's you and Finn on the bench."

At least the trip into town was not in vain, for the pawnshop owner remembered the man who sold him the daruma doll.

"He came in with a whole raft of stuff to pawn," Sheriff Cuthbert said. "Silk fans, ivory carvings, some jewelry in onyx and jade. He had a big box of opium he said came direct from Shanghai. I couldn't help him with the opium, but I took everything else."

"Did he sell it or put it on consignment?" Finn asked.

"Consignment. He wanted me to buy everything outright, but I don't have that kind of money lying about. I've already sold the fans and some of the jewelry, but no one wanted that strange doll. I'm due to send him a payment at the end of the month."

"How long ago was he in here?" Ryan asked.

"It was right after the cherry harvest, so around three months ago."

Ryan felt his heartbeat pick up. That was when he was assaulted coming out of the hardware store. He would never forget the sight of the man charging straight at him.

"Do you remember what he looked like?" he asked.

Sheriff Cuthbert scratched his head. "Not really. He was a large man, dressed like a sailor. The only thing I really remember was that he had a big gap between his two front teeth."

"That's him," Ryan said. "The man who attacked me had a gap just like that."

"You're sure?" Jenny asked.

It wasn't something he was likely to forget. He saw that face in his nightmares for weeks afterward. "I'm certain." He straightened, savoring the rush of energy that suddenly powered his body.

Finn asked to see the other items on consignment from the gap-toothed man, and a quick glance revealed they all came from the Far East. Thousands of sailors made the Pacific journey, so that was nothing unusual, but the daruma doll could have come from nowhere but Japan. Why would the gap-toothed man want Ryan dead? He and Finn could speculate endlessly, but the easiest thing would be to get their hands on the gap-toothed sailor and pressure him to talk.

The address on the consignment slip gave the man's name as George Boylston of San Diego. Given the value of the goods he had on consignment, it wouldn't be hard to lure him here for payment. And then Ryan would get answers.

He clenched his fists. An uncomfortable sensation roiled inside. It wasn't fear but anger. If something had happened to him, Lily would have been left alone. He had no family, no one who would swoop in and raise her with the loving, protective care she deserved.

He had so much to live for. His daughter, his pearls. He glanced at Jenny, a woman he'd longed for since they exchanged their first words.

Jenny glared at the consignment slip and George Boylston's signature with such ferocity he thought it might burst into flame.

"Don't kill him, Jenny," he said, trying to smother the laugh that threatened to break loose. He'd worked alongside hardened soldiers and sailors for years but had never seen such militant determination. She looked like a Valkyrie ready to spring into battle.

"This needs to be planned carefully," Finn said, and Ryan agreed. It wouldn't be long before they had their answers.

21

It took several days to set up the operation to lure the gap-toothed man to Summerlin. A telegram had been sent to George Boylston in San Diego, suggesting that all his items had been sold and he needed to come to the store for the $165 he was owed. Sheriff Cuthbert insisted it be done on the following Friday, claiming he would withdraw the money from the bank specifically to pay the bill. He didn't like keeping that much money in the shop over the weekend, and he could not guarantee it wouldn't be spent if Boylston didn't come get it quickly.

Sheriff Cuthbert lived in a set of rooms over the pawnshop, and Ryan and the others waited there on Friday until the sailor arrived for his money. It was going to be a long day. They had no idea when Boylston would finally appear, but when he did, they would be ready to spring the trap.

Chester Mayberry loitered downstairs with the sheriff while Ryan, Jenny, and Finn waited in the apartment. The plan was to pressure Boylston into making a full confession, and Chester knew enough lawyer-speak to put on an impressive show.

The apartment was cramped and warm. Finn and Jenny played poker at the sheriff's compact dining table, using raisins in lieu of poker chips, but Ryan felt too anxious to join them. His gut told him that his cover in Japan had been blown. This wasn't about pearls. Other people were trying the Japanese technique in Australia and Mexico, and none of them lived in fear for their lives. This had to be about the MID.

Which would be awful. He'd given six years of his life in an effort to secure American safety in the Far East. If their intelligence network had been compromised by something he did or failed to do in Japan, it would be devastating.

The mound of raisins in the middle of the dining table was growing large as Finn drove the stakes ever higher. Finally Jenny folded, and Finn swept the raisins toward him with a gloat of triumph.

"I thought I had you going," she said in frustration. "I was working so hard to project subtle confidence."

Finn smirked. "Jenny, you're as subtle as a punch in the mouth. Don't ever play for real money. Anyone who knows human nature can read you like a dictionary."

Jenny's face hardened in determination as she scooped up the cards and dealt another hand. "I can do better," she muttered. "I *will* do better."

But Ryan hoped she would never change.

A quick series of thuds on the water pipe broke his concentration. It was the signal they'd been waiting for. In short order Finn shrugged into his jacket, and Jenny grabbed the parasol she'd borrowed from the shop downstairs. The three of them slinked down the staircase and into the alley behind the pawnshop.

Ryan ignored the pounding of his heart as he rounded the shop and sidled up to the plate glass window at the front of the store. He could only see the back of the man at the front counter, but he had the same beefy build as the gap-toothed man.

Ryan strolled inside, Finn and Jenny close behind as they wandered around the store like casual window-shoppers.

Sheriff Cuthbert stood behind the counter, reading from the list of items placed on consignment and the price he'd earned for each. The man's back was to them, his hands braced against the counter as he leaned over to scrutinize the consignment slip. Chester stood behind the counter as well, meeting his gaze and giving them a quick nod.

It was time. Ryan cleared his throat and spoke in a polite tone. "Mr. Boylston?"

The man straightened and swiveled, his eyes growing round in surprise, but he masked it quickly. He flicked a quick glance at the sling on Ryan's arm but gave no other sign of recognition.

"Yeah?" Boylston responded.

"I was wondering why you shot me the other day. And why you stabbed me a few months ago."

Finn moved to stand near Boylston, and two men from the hardware store who'd been loitering near the back of the shop stepped forward to make a ring around Boylston. He was surrounded.

He crouched low into a fighting stance, both hands fisted. "I don't know what you're talking about," he growled, a flush darkening his ruddy complexion. "Besides, you can't prove anything."

Ryan fought to maintain a cool tone. "Other than testifying that you attacked me in front of the hardware store? I would probably be dead if Harlan Caruthers hadn't intervened."

"Like I said, prove it."

Ryan glanced at one of the men surrounding Boylston. "Harlan? Does this look like the man you pulled off me?"

"Sure does."

Chester stepped forward. "I'm afraid you're in a tight spot, my friend. A lot of eyewitnesses can testify they saw you stab Mr. Gallagher in the middle of a public street. Back in my days practicing law, we'd call your situation 'a gallows case.' Silly, because we don't really use gallows anymore to execute men. Firing squads are the preferred technique, but I suppose there's a certain poetic ring to it. It hearkens back to our collective memory of swift, certain justice, no?"

Boylston was sweating and breathing heavily, his gaze darting around the ring of six men surrounding him. Chester might be laying it on a bit thick, but his technique was effective.

"Of course, you have some bargaining chips on your side," Chester continued. "What we really want to know is who paid you to harm Mr. Gallagher, because he doesn't know you and suspects there must be someone else involved. How about it, Mr. Boylston?"

"I ain't sayin' nothin'."

One of the men recruited to help spoke up. "Hey, Harlan, do you have some rope at the hardware store? I say we just string him up right now."

Sheriff Cuthbert's brow furrowed. "I'm an officer of the law. I can't take part in that kind of rough justice."

"Then step over to Martha's and have a piece of pie," Harlan said. "We can take care of business all on our own." He flexed and cracked his knuckles while grinning at Boylston. "We can save the town the cost of a trial, and everyone knows the sheriff is a big fan of Martha's apple-plum pie. He's the only officer of the law in the whole town, and I don't expect anyone else will come riding to the rescue."

Ryan kept a keen eye trained on Boylston, who swallowed repeatedly during talk of a hasty hanging. Ryan had no idea if this sort of intimidation was legal or not, but he needed to know who was trying to kill him and why. He couldn't raise Lily in a household where a stray bullet or poisoned drink could turn her into an orphan. George Boylston could be neutralized, but unless they learned who was behind this plot, another man would be hired to complete the job.

The bluster continued from the hardware store men, but perhaps it was time to shift tactics.

"Who gave you the daruma doll?" Ryan asked.

Boylston stilled. So did the others. "I want a lawyer," he said.

They had already planned for such a contingency. There were no lawyers in Summerlin, but a lawyer from Gleaner's Point had been asked to Summerlin for precisely this event and had been kept out of the advance planning in case Boylston asked for a lawyer. He was waiting at the café across the street.

An hour later Ryan, Finn, the sheriff, and the lawyer sat at a table with the gap-toothed man. An offer of immunity had quickly been drafted and signed by all the relevant parties. Ryan agreed not to press charges against Boylston pending a complete and verified confession of who hired him. When Boylston started talking, the story came out quickly.

"A crazy old man in Yokohama gave me that creepy doll with the blank eyes. He said he needed someone in America killed and was asking sailors coming through the port at Yokohama to do the job. As soon as I agreed, he painted in one eye on the doll and told me to paint the other once the job was done. The doll gave me the willies, so I sold it as soon as I got here."

If the man who wanted him dead was from Yokohama, and he was old. . . . A rush of acid filled Ryan's stomach and clouded his vision. He physically recoiled, for he hadn't seen this coming. He feared he knew exactly where this conversation was headed.

"Who was it?" he asked.

"He wouldn't tell me his name. I've only got an address for some lawyer in Yokohama who will pay me once I send proof. The crazy old guy didn't care how it was done, but he warned me there would be a little girl underfoot. At all costs, I was warned not to harm the little girl."

Ryan's eyes closed. It was as he feared. Akira's father was trying to kill him.

"I was here for weeks trying to get a clear shot when the girl wasn't around. Finally I gave up and poisoned some liquor, since I figured it was the one thing the girl was in no danger of drinking. The bottle sat on the shelf for weeks, and I got tired of waiting, so I charged him with a knife. Then he was gone and I couldn't figure out where he went."

This was hard to hear, even though Ryan knew his father-in-law hated him. Harue was from an old family that held tightly to traditions of the past. To have a foreigner taint his bloodline was anathema to a man as proud as Harue.

Sorrow filled Ryan, but he forced himself to keep listening to details of the plot. Boylston said that once the Yokohama lawyers had proof Ryan was dead, arrangements would be made to have Lily sent to Japan to be raised by her grandfather.

That would never happen. Ryan didn't doubt that Harue loved Lily and had legitimate cause to resent his son-in-law for taking her from Japan, but the old man had grown too unstable to be trusted. Over time, Lily's foreign blood might start to grate on Harue. In any event, Lily would remain in America and grow up in a world where she had a chance to pursue whatever wild dreams she could envision.

All that remained was figuring out how to neutralize Harue from five thousand miles away.

❧

Saving face was everything in Japan, and Ryan suspected he could use that to his advantage with Harue. Japan's hierarchical society was built upon relationships, and a public embarrassment was not easily forgotten or forgiven. Harue was a man of high status and was accustomed to bowed heads and murmurs of admiration when he walked down the street. All that would come to an end if it was known he had tried to murder his son-in-law. It didn't matter that Ryan was a hated foreigner. In a society that valued harmony, elegant manners, and saving face, Harue would do anything to avoid public exposure.

As of five o'clock that afternoon, Ryan had a written confession from a man hired by Harue to murder a member of his own family. He had contact information for the Japanese lawyers who would pay off Boylston. Ryan recognized the names of the lawyers, men who had been employed by Harue's silk factory for decades. Somehow the fact that the lawyers participating in his planned murder knew him personally was another wound. Had he been *that* despised?

The miracle of the transpacific cable, completed in 1903, made communication shockingly swift. Ryan's message to Harue would first be wired to San Francisco, where a telegraph operator would send a message on the undersea cable to Honolulu, then on to Midway, Guam, the Philippines, and finally to Yokohama. The entire transmission would take less than fifteen minutes. The last step was for a telegrapher to write the message out on paper and hand-deliver it to Harue.

It was dinnertime in California, which meant the servants in Harue's household were just beginning to rise and prepare breakfast. It was the perfect time to begin negotiations. Summerlin's only telegraph station was in the back of the apothecary shop. Chairs, sandwiches, and a deck of playing cards were brought in. It was going to be a long night.

The first message to Harue was lengthy. It began with a standard Japanese salutation, then inquired after Harue's health, followed by Ryan's hope that his silk factory continued to flourish. Then he spoke of his own poor health of late, describing the failed attempts on his life. Finally, he relayed Boylston's full confession, the names of the Japanese lawyers, and the arrangements for Lily's return to Japan. The message closed by humbly asking the older man's advice for a resolution to the problem.

Ryan stopped short of accusing Harue of being the mastermind. At all costs, it was essential that Harue be allowed to save face.

The telegraph operator's eyes bulged when he saw the lengthy message. "This is going to cost a fortune," he said. "There's no need for this fancy greeting. And I can help you shorten your sentences so it won't cost so much."

Ryan shook his head. He was not a wealthy man, and it irked him to spend so much on a telegram, but this had to be handled correctly. He had one chance to defang Harue, and he would not bungle it with blunt American efficiency.

"Keep every word," he said.

"Make Boylston pay for it," Jenny said. "He's got goods on consignment at Sheriff Cuthbert's shop, doesn't he? I'll bet most of it was a down payment from Harue, and he shouldn't be able to profit from criminal activity, right?"

Ryan hid his smile. Trust Jenny to see straight to the most logical solution. Both lawyers seemed willing to accept her suggestion.

The sight of Ryan, the sheriff, and the others settling in at the back of the apothecary shop captured attention. Townspeople began congregating to watch. Asking for privacy was hopeless. By now everyone in town knew of the three attempts on Ryan's life, and soon the cause would leak out as well.

It took three hours for Harue's reply to arrive. As Ryan expected, it began with formal salutations, blessings for the coming season, then a mild rebuke for suggesting a man of Harue's stature would know anything about dishonorable and regrettable attempts to harm a family member. It closed by wishing continued health for his granddaughter and son-in-law.

Rehashing the evidence would serve no good. Both parties knew exactly what had happened, but it was going to take a while for Harue to acknowledge it. Negotiations were an art form in Japan, and these steps could not be rushed.

Ryan drafted a reply, beginning with another elaborate greeting, followed by compliments on Harue's continued success in his silk factory, then respectfully asking his advice for how to solve this dilemma.

Jenny looked ready to explode. "Respect? You are *respectfully* asking for advice? I wish I could reach through that telegraph wire and respectfully wring his neck."

"Then it's a good thing I'm doing the negotiating," he said. "Trust me. I know what I'm doing."

Which gave him the advantage. He understood the Japanese, but Harue would never understand America, so Ryan was able to manipulate the situation toward the outcome he needed. It was just going to require patience.

Three more exchanges occurred in the coming hours. By two o'clock in the morning, even from a distance of over five thousand miles, Ryan could predict exactly what was happening on the other end of the telegraph wire. The first reply from Harue took three hours to arrive, probably because it had taken the old man by surprise and he needed to consult with his attorneys, but now the messages were flying quickly. Replies came in less than an hour.

Each new telegram contained the fraction of a budge. Harue acknowledged Ryan had cause for concern, but claimed to know nothing about Boylston. Ryan suggested he had been hasty in ascribing such terrible motives to Harue but stood firm in his belief that the gap-toothed sailor had been commissioned by someone in Japan. He asked the older man's wisdom in finding a solution that would avoid taking the matter outside the family. It was a carefully veiled threat, but he was certain Harue would understand it. With each message, Ryan left the door open for saving face.

Jake, the young telegraph operator, catnapped between

messages, but the others had wandered off to sleep in their own homes. Only Jenny and Finn stayed awake to keep him company as the long night progressed. Finn was as alert as a live wire, a savage grin on his face as he strategized alongside Ryan to frame the perfect response blending elegant diplomacy and pointed barbs.

"Are you certain you don't want to go sleep on Sheriff Cuthbert's sofa?" Ryan asked Jenny. "You look exhausted."

She smiled. "Nonsense. I'm accustomed to staying awake through the night."

He was grateful for her support. The apothecary shop was eerily quiet, and it felt like the three of them were the only people awake in the world. He didn't want to admit it, but Harue's attempts on his life had knocked Ryan off balance. Having Jenny and Finn's resolute support was a lifeline on this long, dark night.

The sun had begun rising on the horizon when the telegraph wire began pulsing out an incoming message. Jake roused and scrubbed a hand over his face, gave himself a good shake, then began decoding the message. He handed it over.

Ryan's eyes glided past the obligatory salutations and went straight to the heart of the matter.

I wish a peaceful life for my granddaughter but hope she continues to study the Japanese language and customs. I look forward to letters from her written in her own hand, using the Japanese language and traditional kanji characters. Should my granddaughter wish to visit Japan on her eighteenth birthday, she will be greeted warmly. Until then, my son-in-law shall have access to Akira's inherited portion of the silk factory to be used in providing for Lily. There is no need for this to be taken outside the family. I know nothing of a gap-toothed sailor.

It was enough.

He would never get Harue to acknowledge the murder attempt or the underhanded scheme to win Lily's return to Japan, but this message gave him all he needed. Harue's end of the conversation required several telegraph operators and lawyers, meaning the old man would not be able to go back on his word without losing honor. Ryan was safe. He could raise Lily in peace and would honor the request to teach her the language and customs of Japan. Exhaustion sapped his energy as he instructed Jake to send a final reply, agreeing to the terms and wishing Harue a happy birthday next month.

"I can't believe you're letting him get away with this," Jenny said on their journey home. She walked alongside the wagon while Finn managed the reins and Ryan struggled to keep awake. It was almost noon, and he'd never been so fatigued in his life.

"I don't think I ever appreciated how hard it must have been to work the night shift until this very moment," he said.

"Don't skirt the issue," she retorted. "Harue is getting away with attempted murder, and you're simply accepting it."

"Not everyone is like you," he said gently.

He didn't mean it as a criticism or in judgment. It was simply a fact. Perhaps being raised in an entirely different culture had given him the perspective to accept differences without trying to push a person into a mold that didn't fit. Jenny was a fighter. She always had been, and he admired that about her. But he was different. He'd lived too many unhappy years to dive into battles he could never win.

After all, his normal life was challenging enough. He was beginning a decades-long battle with the oysters on his improbable quest to produce a round pearl. As Lily grew older, he foresaw challenges fighting for her acceptance in a society where she was distinctly different. Foremost in his mind was the battle to get Finn sent to Japan, and then the fight to win Jenny's heart and trust again. These were battles he welcomed. He had no interest in pursuing revenge when his other aspirations required every ounce of his heart, intellect, and resolve.

And even then, it might not be enough.

22

It was possibly the strangest day of Jenny's life. After returning to the house after the marathon night, Ryan and Finn both staggered up to bed, but downstairs the others rejoiced at the news that a peaceful resolution had been found. Boris began preparing a feast for dinner, marinating kabobs of chicken in a ginger sauce. They would gather on the beach at sunset and grill the meat around a bonfire. Simon took Lily out to gather firewood, and even Abigail was unusually pleasant by offering to bake cinnamon apples for their dessert. Chester, inspired by his brief foray back into the law, kept them all entertained with stories of litigating trivial lawsuits in San Diego.

Jenny felt sick at heart. It was time to make a decision. Ryan was out of danger, Finn was healed, and she no longer had an excuse to remain in Summerlin. Unless she was prepared to take the plunge and marry Ryan, it was time to return to San Francisco.

Could she ever wholeheartedly forgive Ryan? Trust that he would never be dishonest with her again? Time and again her mind strayed to that morning on the pier when Ryan accepted her apology so beautifully.

"The incident is behind us and will not be stirred to life again,"

he had said after she groused at him before the others. And he had been true to his word. He never once raised the issue again or held it over her head. Could she forgive his infidelity with such wholehearted honesty? Move forward and never revisit it again? Until she could do so, it would not be right to marry him.

She knew she was nowhere close to genuine forgiveness, for the pain of his betrayal still flared to life at the least provocation. She needed to believe she was the foundation of Ryan's world, but he had not been able to make her feel that way. He hid things from her. He evaded her questions, and she could never be certain when he was telling her the whole truth. She sensed that any moment the rug would be yanked from beneath her again.

But she loved it here, and she loved him. Could she walk away when it was obvious he so desperately wanted her to stay?

The question haunted her all afternoon as she helped Boris prepare the feast. They set bits of chicken to marinate in soy sauce and grated ginger, and the scent of baked apples filled the kitchen.

Late in the afternoon, Ryan finally woke up and joined them in the kitchen. Still sleepy-eyed but with a contented smile, he looked so loveable that she had to fight the temptation to finger-comb his messy hair.

As the afternoon grew late, they gathered on the beach. Boris and Finn rolled stones into a large ring while Simon piled wood and kindling inside it.

She glanced at Ryan. "It's a little breezy. Will it be too windy for a bonfire?"

"It's always windy on the beach. We'll make do."

She loved that he never complained. "It might be cold for Lily after the sun starts setting. I'll run upstairs and fetch her sweater."

It was dim inside the room she shared with Lily, and she tried to avoid the photograph of Akira on the bureau as she opened a drawer to get Lily's sweater. She didn't need to look at the picture, as she'd already memorized every facet of Akira's serene, flawless image.

Jenny found Lily's sweater quickly and draped it over her arm. Everyone was outside preparing for the barbecue, and she was alone up here. It was so quiet that her own breath sounded loud in the silence.

Ryan's room was empty. She drifted toward it and stood in the doorway. This would be her bedroom if she chose to stay. Could they be happy here? Could she truly put the past behind her and move forward with an open heart?

The late afternoon sun gave the room a warm, yellow glow. His bureau was spartan, with only a hairbrush, a razor, and a little bottle of bayberry cologne on the surface. The room carried a hint of that scent, and it drew her deeper inside, surrounding her with a sense of well-being.

She trailed her fingers across the top of the bureau, but her eyes were drawn to the tiny brass lock on the top drawer. What did he keep in there? Maybe it was just boring paper work, but maybe not.

If he hadn't betrayed her, she wouldn't feel this nagging sense of distrust. These warring emotions were his fault, and he hadn't done much to alleviate her anxiety. It seemed he always had secrets buried beneath secrets.

Perhaps if she could reassure herself that there was nothing to be worried about in this drawer she could slay these traitorous feelings for good. She didn't even feel guilty as she tugged a hairpin free of her upswept hair, twisted it open, and began working the lock. It was no challenge, and she lifted the mechanism with ease. With trembling fingers she slid the drawer open.

Grade cards from the Naval Academy. A copy of his last will and testament. She pushed the papers aside and a flash of gold caught her eye. She stared at it, dumbstruck.

It was his father's watch.

The metal was smooth and cold in her palm. She flicked open the cover just to be certain and saw that the corner of the ivory on one side was a little discolored. There could be no doubt.

Ryan had his father's watch all along and hadn't told her about it. She slipped it into her pocket and closed the drawer silently.

❦

Dinner was torture. Everyone basked in the celebratory atmosphere on the beach, the sky lit by streaks of purple and orange as the sun sank low on the horizon. Flames crackled and snapped in the bonfire as the elderberry brambles burned. Laughter peppered the hearty conversation as everyone devoured the perfectly seasoned meat grilled over a quick flame. None of it could penetrate Jenny's confusion over finding the watch. While the others ate and laughed, all she could feel was the cold weight of the watch in her skirt.

"Are you planning on eating that?" Ryan's amused voice cut into her dreary thoughts.

She blanched when she saw the disaster she'd made of her chicken, which had burned down to little blackened lumps. She pulled the skewer from the fire and tossed it aside.

"I'm not really hungry," she mumbled.

He looked taken aback, but she couldn't summon a smile to reassure him. No one else noticed her glum mood as Boris kept them amused with stories of his days as a navy cook. As the evening wore on, Jenny's confusion morphed into anger. Couldn't Ryan have taken *one minute* to tell her he'd gotten the watch back? He took twenty minutes that afternoon to carve an apple into the shape of a turtle for Lily!

Eventually the cooling temperatures sent them all inside. Jenny waited until all the others were in bed before tapping quietly on Ryan's door. She counted heartbeats while she waited, but finally he opened the door. He wore a robe loosely knotted and had concern in his eyes.

"Jenny?"

She held up his father's watch, letting it swing from its thin chain like a pendulum. "I thought you might want to tell me how you came to possess this."

He looked away.

She pushed inside and closed the door softly behind her. "Why didn't you tell me?" she whispered fiercely, knowing the others slept in rooms only a few yards away. When he didn't immediately respond, she continued. "I've been torturing myself over this watch. I felt guilty from the moment I sold it. You *knew* I felt horrible about it, and you didn't even try to tell me you got it back."

"It never seemed to be the right time."

"How about during the fourteen-hour train ride down here?"

He opened his mouth to speak, but no words came. He looked like he'd rather have a tooth pulled than continue this discussion, but she'd had it with his evasive answers and refusal to crack open the door on his past.

"I need an answer, Ryan. Why didn't you tell me about this watch?"

"I got it back under less than honorable circumstances." He pressed his mouth together in a hard line, and the silence stretched between them.

She raised a brow. "I'm waiting."

He shifted his weight and had the grace to look embarrassed as he began speaking. "After you told me it was sold to a pawn shop, Finn and I went looking for it. We found the right place, and the pawnshop owner said he'd be willing to sell it to me for an additional twenty dollars over the price he paid for it. When we returned with the money, I guess he sensed how much I wanted it, and he tripled the price. I didn't have that much on me, so we had to leave. The whole thing rubbed Finn the wrong way, so that night he broke into the pawn shop and stole the watch."

Jenny said nothing, so Ryan continued. "I never would have authorized stealing the watch, but I wasn't going to give it back, either. I sent the original price to the pawnshop in an anonymous note."

"And the shame of the incident was so overwhelming you preferred not to tell me?"

He tipped his head in acknowledgment.

Maybe it was her bad nature, but Jenny didn't think what Finn had done was all that horrible. Reckless and stupid, yes, but she wished Ryan had put her need to have her guilt absolved over his own shame in participating in the theft of the watch. Was it so wrong to want to come first in a man's heart? There were a lot of areas she wished Ryan would put her first. She raised her eyes and asked for the biggest.

"If Finn doesn't pass the tests in September, are you going to leave me again?"

Ryan grimaced. "I think you already know the answer to that."

"Say it! I want to know if, for once in your life, you will put me first. Ahead of your job. Ahead of your desire to avoid difficult conversations. Ahead of disclosing painful facts about Akira or how Finn got that watch back or whether Abigail Mayberry continues to fling herself at you behind my back. Can you do that?"

Ryan folded his arms across his chest. "I think you're being a little irrational. There is no comparing a man's love of country to dealing with an infatuated teenage girl."

Well, then. She had all the answers she needed. Oddly, instead of anger, it felt like a weight had been lifted from her chest.

She deserved better than this. From the moment she encountered Ryan again, she wanted to believe she was the foundation of his world, but he hid, evaded, and disguised his real emotions from her. If she wanted more of the same, she could stay here and beg him to change.

Or she could leave. She had a good life in San Francisco—not perfect, but good. She deserved better than what Ryan offered.

She grabbed his hand and slapped the watch into his palm. "Take it. I'm leaving in the morning."

He tossed the watch on the bed and grabbed her elbows. "Don't go. I made a mistake, and I should have found a time to tell you about the watch. I'm sorry! I know I'll make more mistakes, but you can't doubt that I love you."

He'd had all summer to prove he loved her. He said it often but never managed to make her believe it.

"Maybe you love me," she said, "but not enough to tell me you had that watch. You didn't love me enough to risk the hard conversations and the messy, tangled emotions they stir up. And you know what? I have a perfectly good life without you. When I walk into my ward at the hospital, I see eighteen men who are glad I'm there. Do you know how good that feels? And when I'm here, I feel sick at heart, wondering what secrets you're keeping from me this time. So this is the end, Ryan."

She closed the door and didn't look back.

Even more telling, he didn't follow her.

23

Jenny left Summerlin without saying good-bye. She left a note for Simon so he would not be alarmed by her absence, but it was time to get away before her resolve faltered.

Before she could go to San Francisco, however, she had a mission to accomplish. Just as Ryan had failed to be completely open and honest with her, so she had failed the widow of the sailor with the scar. Sending money without explanation or begging forgiveness was the cowardly way out.

And Jenny wasn't a coward. Frightened, apprehensive, ashamed— she was all of these things, but only a coward would give in to those impulses.

By ten o'clock the train was on its way to Los Angeles, and Jenny gazed out the window at the cultivated valleys rolling past. Apprehension knotted her stomach as the train drew closer to the city with each passing mile. Was it possible to give herself an ulcer in the space of a few hours? The sprawling groves of avocado and orange trees gave way to smaller garden plots and chickens pecking in fenced yards. Houses were built closer together, and telephone poles lined the streets. Two boys on bicycles raced alongside the train, laughing and trying to keep pace, and she watched them until the train finally won and they fell back in the distance. Had she ever been that young and carefree?

It didn't matter. Five minutes later the train pulled into the first of many stops within the city. She'd already showed the porter the widow's address, and he'd instructed her to get off at the third stop near Spring and Fourth Street.

She bowed her head. Was this the right thing to do? Perhaps the widow had put Oliver's disappearance behind her long ago and would not welcome learning the terrible details of what happened to her husband. It wasn't too late to buy a ticket and simply proceed on to San Francisco.

But that would be running away from her past, and this was a wound that needed to be lanced.

When the train stopped at Spring Street, she rose on legs still numb from sitting motionless for the past two hours. The glare of the sun was blinding as she stepped into the late morning. Los Angeles had trolley cars that looked just like the ones in San Francisco, powered by a network of electric cables running down the center of the street. She stopped a newspaper boy and asked which trolley would take her to McNamara Street.

"Ouch, that's a bad part of town," he said, but he gave her directions nevertheless.

Jenny could see what the boy meant as she drew closer to McNamara, filled mostly with dilapidated boarding houses and secondhand shops. She swallowed hard and got off the streetcar, then headed toward a small cluster of houses near the end of the street.

At least her two hundred dollars had gone to a household that needed the money. The widow's house was a compact, one-story cottage with peeling paint and a few chickens strutting in the tiny lawn. The fence was latched, and she set her hands atop the dry, cracked boards. Shame welled up inside her. She'd confessed her sin to God, but it was time to complete the mission and ask forgiveness from the one person she'd hurt most in the world.

"Can I help you?"

Jenny looked up at the front door, which had opened to reveal a woman with fading auburn hair and a curious gaze. "I'm looking for a lady named Matilda Swinton. Does she live here?"

The woman stepped outside and closed the distance in only a few steps. "I'm Matilda. Can I help you?" she asked again. A spray of lines fanned out from her eyes, and her skin was weather-beaten. The moment their gazes met, Jenny looked away.

This was it then. She twisted her hands so hard they hurt. "I was the person you contacted about the parrot."

"It was you?" she asked with a startled gasp. "What on earth was that all about? None of us could imagine what prompted such a strange request. Come inside."

The widow pulled open the gate, shooing a chicken out of the way. "I take it you knew Oliver?"

"Yes. Mr. Swinton was a very kind man."

The widow looked confused for a moment. "Swinton is my second husband's name. I remarried long ago."

"Oh, I see," Jenny said, already feeling better knowing that this woman had not lived the past nineteen years in lonely widowhood.

It was dim inside, and a woman about Jenny's age tatted lace at a table in the corner. It was such a modest house, with threadbare furniture and a board nailed over a broken window. A small crucifix hung on the wall over the fireplace. That had to be a good sign, right? It was a cool morning, but perspiration trickled down the small of Jenny's back, and it was a struggle to control her breathing.

"This is my daughter Cathleen," Mrs. Swinton said. "I've got two younger boys with Mr. Swinton, but they are both in the navy now. Cathleen is Oliver's daughter."

Jenny's mouth went dry. She hadn't realized she would need

to ask forgiveness of both a wife and a daughter. It was hard to look at them. Cathleen had the same carrot-colored hair as Oliver.

"How did you know Oliver?" the widow asked. "You must have been very young."

Jenny nodded. "Yes. I was nine years old when I met him. He did me a great kindness."

"So your letter said. Come, you look pale. Sit down and tell us what's going on."

She didn't realize how badly her legs were trembling until she sat. The daughter left the table and pulled a stool alongside the sofa, but the widow remained standing, looking at her with a mixture of curiosity and confusion.

"When he was in San Francisco, Oliver fell victim to a man named Shanghai Jake," Jenny said in a shaky voice. "I would give anything to deny it, but I was in league with the crimpers and played a role in leading Oliver straight into their trap."

Silence greeted her statement. Jenny stared at the crucifix over the fireplace as she spoke, anything rather than risk looking at the two women whose lives she had so drastically altered. She spilled the entire story, granting herself no mercy as she recounted how Oliver tried to help her while she only betrayed him.

When she finished, she drew a heavy breath. "I didn't realize he was dead until I got your letter. I can't tell you how sorry I am for my part in what happened to him. It is the biggest regret of my life."

The sofa sagged as the widow sat beside her. "Thank you for telling us. We knew he'd been shanghaied. He was able to post a letter from a port in Bangkok. I gather the conditions on the ship were poor, and he was in bad shape when he arrived. He got consumption while aboard ship, and, well . . . he died a few months later."

Jenny doubled over. "I'm sorry. Oh, I'm so sorry."

"It's in the past," the widow said. "Oliver is long dead and not in pain anymore. For all we know, he already had consumption before he ended up on that ship, so he might have died anyway."

"He wouldn't have been mistreated but for me," Jenny said quietly, staring at the braided rug on the floor. It was time to do what she came here for. She raised her eyes to the widow, who looked old and tired. "I'm sorry for my role in what happened to your husband. It is a regret I will always carry with me." She looked at the daughter, who watched her with hard eyes. "You grew up without a chance to know a loving father, and for that I am deeply sorry. And Mrs. Swinton, you were robbed of a good man. Both of you have every right to throw me out of your house and hate me forever." She swallowed hard. "But I hope you can find it in your heart to forgive me."

She looked the widow in the eyes, shaking, vulnerable, and sick to her very soul.

Mrs. Swinton moved first, her warm hand covering Jenny's icy one. "There is no doubt in my mind you are genuinely sorry. You are forgiven, dearest."

The breath left Jenny in a huge rush. The daughter was a tougher case. When Jenny looked at her, all Cathleen did was shrug. "I suppose so," she said in a sullen voice.

It was enough. Forgiveness could not be demanded, nor could it be rushed. It could only be freely given.

"Come. Lunch is ready, and you must share a meal with us," Mrs. Swinton said.

Jenny would rather run to the train station and put this difficult hour behind her forever, but she could hardly refuse the invitation. Shortly after sitting down to a small bowl of stew, Mr. Swinton came through the door. Jack Swinton worked at a packing plant a few blocks down and listened in amazement as his wife recounted Jenny's story.

"You didn't have to send us that money," he said. "Not that

we're in a position to give it back. We've bought supplies to add another room onto the back of the house. There's a baby on the way come December."

Jenny nearly choked on her stew, but a glance at Mrs. Swinton's expanding waist gave truth to the words.

A note of humor lit the widow's eyes. "I thought those days were behind us, but God had other plans."

"I'm hoping for a girl this time," Mr. Swinton said.

As Jenny prepared to leave, both Mrs. Swinton and her husband gave her a hearty farewell embrace, though Cathleen offered only a stiff nod.

Although Jenny had been reluctant to stay for lunch, she was glad she had, for she'd learned something very important. Jack Swinton discussed his wife's first husband openly and without resentment. Even though his wife clearly loved Oliver, she loved her current husband as well. The two of them laughed, teased, and in light of the coming baby, they obviously still enjoyed a vibrant marriage. Was Jack tormented by jealous imaginings of his wife's first husband? He showed no sign of it.

But as she stood on the train station platform, a ticket to San Francisco clutched in her hand, Jenny knew her situation was drastically different than the Swintons'. Jack Swinton seemed to be an open, straightforward man. He and his wife spoke frankly and with honesty. In such circumstances, it was easy to imagine that they'd be able to work through whatever bumps and setbacks were in their path.

That sort of automatic trust and openness was something she'd never had with Ryan.

24

Jenny moved to the day shift upon returning to the Presidio, and it was a balm to her body and spirit. Her sojourn to Summerlin had been bittersweet, but she would be forever grateful to Ryan for her ability to savor a decent night of sleep every day of the week. At long last she had her private room back and kept it spotlessly clean. There were no toys strewn about, no sticky fingerprints on the windows or a little girl who liked to chatter long after the sun went down.

The men of the amputee ward welcomed her onto the day shift. "You look even prettier during the daytime, Jenny."

"Nurse Bennett, please," she said as she carried in a set of canes and crutches.

Each day she coached the patients as they struggled to find a new center of balance while taking tentative steps on artificial limbs. It felt good to be a nurse again. When she whispered encouragement to struggling men, she felt like it was what she'd been put on this earth to do.

Two weeks after leaving Summerlin, she got a letter from Simon, telling her not to renew the lease on his jewelry shop, as he would be staying with Ryan indefinitely. There was plenty of work to be done, not only in grinding seeds for the oysters, but in turning Ryan's lopsided pearls into something of beauty. She tried not to let it hurt. She and Simon had been a team since he picked her up off the streets almost twenty years ago. Now he was siding with Ryan.

As summer drew to a close, she had to admit that moving to the day shift had not made her magically happy. Although she now had the opportunity to mingle with people on base rather than merely tend to sleeping patients, she was still lonely.

She missed Ryan. She missed living at the beach and Finn's irreverence and watching baby oysters grow in the nursery. She even missed sharing a room with Lily.

But mostly she missed the dream she'd hoped to create with Ryan at her side. When they were together, it had been easy to imagine a life of moonlit walks along the beach, raising children, dreaming and hoping that someday one of his oysters would produce a perfectly round pearl.

But that dream could not be built on a foundation of sand. She wished Ryan had been able to help her repair their beautiful but broken relationship. He hadn't. And if she tried to ignore his unwillingness to mend their past, she'd be like the foolish builder who erected his house upon sand rather than undertaking the more challenging task of preparing a foundation on rock.

She didn't want to be alone for the rest of her life, and it was time to move on. There were other good, honorable men with whom she might be able to build a future, and this evening she'd agreed to meet a young doctor at the mess hall to share dinner. If it went well, perhaps they'd take an evening walk in the eucalyptus grove or watch the sunset over the bay.

Ryan was her past, but Dr. Weber might be her future.

She had met him several times in the hospital kitchen. Dr. Weber's interest was digestive issues, and he was fascinated by the possibility of different nutritional components helping speed a patient's healing. They'd only spoken about nutrition on the few times they'd met, but tonight she'd have a chance to get to know him better.

Dr. Weber had potential. He was an intelligent man with a head of thick brown hair, well-formed features, and a neatly groomed mustache. He was a fine-looking man, if only she could get used to the idea of letting another man court her.

He was waiting on the bench outside the mess hall and rose as he saw her walking toward him. "Hungry?" he asked politely.

She was too nervous to be hungry, but she returned his smile with ease. "Famished. I'm glad you suggested this. It will be nice to dine with someone besides the other nurses."

There were still ten minutes before the dining hall opened, and Dr. Weber was entertaining as he talked about a consultation he had with the hospital cooks about the preparation of healthy food.

"Do you enjoy cooking, then?" she asked. If she could imagine Dr. Weber in a kitchen preparing a meal with competent expertise . . . well, already he seemed a little more attractive in her eyes.

"Naturally," he said. "Any doctor who wishes to make the alimentary canal the focus of his research should understand everything about food, from the moment it enters the mouth until it completes the digestive path. Cooking plays an important role in that. The effect of heat and acidity on meat and vegetables helps break down the enzymes. One can hardly appreciate the process from a textbook, and actual experience in the kitchen is essential."

Dr. Weber's discourse on food preparation was quite interesting, and he spoke about it nonstop until the mess hall opened its doors.

This was going to be just fine. Maybe she hadn't felt the immediate sort of attraction she had for Ryan, but that didn't mean Dr. Weber couldn't be a perfectly charming man. She liked people who had a passion for their profession.

He was courteous as they entered the cafeteria line. It was always crowded and noisy in the cavernous dining hall, but as they moved through each station, he asked what she would like and then repeated her requests in a confident voice to the kitchen attendant. It was flattering. She had been ordering her own meals for seven years, but it felt nice to have a man perform this simple courtesy for her.

They found a spot at the end of one of the long dining tables. She liked the way he bowed his head and murmured a prayer before dining. He had a large glass of milk, while she was drinking hot tea, and he offered her a little milk for her tea.

"Thank you, yes," she said.

"Not at all." He spooned some into her tea, laughing as he stirred it in. "You should drink as much milk as possible. It's an excellent lining for the stomach. The digestive juices are a powerful force not to be taken lightly. Did you know the stomach has the ability to consume itself? One must be on guard against that."

In her entire professional career, Jenny had never once worried about the danger of her stomach beginning to consume itself. "How interesting," she managed to say without breaking into laughter.

He continued discussing digestive issues, but Jenny was beginning to feel like she was back in nursing school. Perhaps Dr. Weber was as nervous as she was and just needed a little prodding to discuss something outside of medicine.

"I gather the San Francisco Yachting Club is hosting a regatta next weekend," she said. "Do you ever watch sailing races?"

"It's not how I choose to spend my free time," he replied.

She perked up. "And what do you enjoy in your time away from the hospital?"

"Mostly I grow tapeworms," he said. "I keep them in jars lined up on my windowsill. Some people grow herbs or roses. Not me! I fancy myself a tapeworm expert and have quite a collection. Possibly the finest in America."

His smile was broad as he described his hobby. Jenny tried several times to divert the conversation, but unless the subject related to digestive issues, she never got more than a monosyllabic answer. The ultimate irony was that nonstop discussion of the human stomach caused her to completely lose her appetite.

And to think she had hoped to extend the evening by watching the sunset over the bay. She'd rather not spoil one of the prettiest views in all of California with a discussion of tapeworms.

After they finished their meal, she allowed Dr. Weber to escort her to the barracks.

"I've enjoyed our dinner immensely," Dr. Weber said. "Might we do this again sometime?"

She politely declined. As much as she'd hoped Dr. Weber might help her move forward, she found herself missing Ryan more than ever.

Ryan sat at the kitchen table, watching Lily's face screw up in concentration as she traced the kanji characters with an uncertain hand. He hadn't intended to teach her the Japanese writing system, but the deal he'd struck with Harue would be honored. That meant one hour of kanji training each day. Finn had been helping Lily as well, but the first of his tests would take place next week, and he had retreated to his bedroom for uninterrupted study.

"The stroke goes the other direction," he cautioned.

Lily tossed down the pencil. "I don't like these letters. I want to play with the pearls."

Across the table, Simon smiled as he continued grinding a lopsided pearl into something suitable for a brooch. "Pearls aren't a toy," he said. "And think how proud your grandfather will be when he gets a letter written in your very own hand."

"Can I write a letter to Jenny, too?" Lily asked. "I want to tell her that if she comes back, I won't eat cookies in the bed anymore."

Ryan's blood heated. There were plenty of reasons he resented the way Jenny had left in the middle of the night, and the fact that Lily seemed to blame herself was near the top.

"Jenny didn't leave because of a messy bed," he assured his daughter. "She has very important work in San Francisco and needed to get back to her hospital patients. Right, Simon?"

The older man pulled the pearl away from the grinder to send him an ironic glare. "Oh yes, I'm sure it was Jenny's work that called her away. Nothing else," he drawled.

Ryan put the pencil back in Lily's hand and guided it to form the strokes of the Japanese characters. His first impulse on reading Jenny's terse farewell note had been to race to the train station to intercept her. He'd panicked, desperate to have another try at convincing her to stay.

Halfway to the train station, he thought better of it. Marriage involved two people willing to make sacrifices, work through problems, think and act rationally. He wouldn't go dashing off into the wild to drag back an unwilling woman. If Jenny could not forgive him for what happened in Japan, it was best they found that out now.

"You need a little more space between those two characters," he said to Lily. He rubbed the marks away with a rubber wedge, then slid the paper back to her. "Try again, sweet pea."

"I don't want to. It's too hard."

"You're doing beautifully," he assured her. "Just four more words, and then you'll be finished."

Lily completed the letter with a mighty sigh, her little body collapsing on the table in a grand display of exhaustion. He folded the page into an envelope and addressed it, using both English and Japanese lettering, for this envelope was going to travel across thousands of miles before it reached its destination.

"Sit up, sweetie," he said after setting the envelope aside. "We have ten more minutes of learning new kanji words before we can quit."

"Nooooo!" she moaned.

He remembered using that same tone with his own parents years ago. Now he was grateful for their insistence that he learn both writing systems, but at the time he thought it terrifically unfair that he should be required to learn two forms of writing while everyone else at school needed to learn only one. He hoisted Lily upright and slid the page of Japanese vocabulary words before her.

"Can we step outside for a moment?" Simon asked.

Ryan glanced up. Simon stood by the kitchen door, an annoyed expression on his face. Things had been tense since Jenny deserted them, but Ryan couldn't recall ever seeing Simon this annoyed.

He patted Lily's shoulders. "I'll be back soon, sweet pea."

It didn't take Simon long to get to the point once they stepped a few yards away from the house. "How many hours have you spent drilling those Japanese characters into Lily's head?"

"Plenty. And it will take plenty more before she learns them."

"It's no business of mine how you raise your daughter, but by my count you've spent days torturing that girl, all to make an old man on the other side of the ocean happy. And you couldn't spare the time to have one decent conversation with Jenny to calm her nerves about what happened in Japan."

Ryan was flabbergasted. "I apologized until I was blue in the face! *She's* the one who ran away without giving us a chance."

"She didn't trust you not to hurt her again."

"That's ridiculous. If my actions haven't convinced her I'm a man of honor, no conversation will ever be able to change her mind."

Simon peered through the kitchen window at Lily, then back at him. "You're a practical man. You give Lily everything she needs, even when it isn't pleasant for either of you. Teaching her the

Japanese writing system is proof of that. You were different with Jenny. Somehow you thought she was too fragile to handle the hard things, so you kept secrets, more than were necessary. If you'd trusted Jenny to shoulder the hard things, she wouldn't have feared you were hiding something else from her and that at any moment her world might come crashing down again."

Ryan swallowed hard, absorbing the truth of Simon's words. In trying to protect Jenny from things he knew would hurt her, he'd only dug himself into a deeper hole, making her distrust him even more.

He could have done better, but why did she insist on dwelling in the past when they could have such a grand future if she would just be brave enough to step forward into it?

He gripped the railing of the porch and stared out to sea. "I don't understand how she can possibly think I don't love her."

"You're thinking like a man," Simon said. "Start thinking like a woman whose greatest need has always been to feel safe. She's strong enough to handle bad news and tough times, but she dreads the unknown. Unless you're entirely open with her, she's going to keep suspecting the worst."

It was in his nature to protect people, be it Lily or Jenny, but what Simon said was right. In trying to protect Jenny, he'd stoked all her old fears. Somehow he needed to prove that she meant the world to him, but he had no idea how, or if it was too late to undo the damage he'd created.

❧

The letter Jenny had been waiting for arrived in the first week of October. As she went about her duties in the amputee ward, all she could think about was the letter's contents and how quickly she could race across town at the end of her shift. The moment the clock struck five, she dashed down the hallway, not even stopping to remove her cap or apron. It was going to be a challenge to catch the 5:15 cable car to the pier at the Embarcadero.

She gathered her skirts and hoisted them out of the way as she ran down Lyon Street, but the cable car was already pulling away. She ran faster, chasing after it. A couple passengers noticed her and hollered encouragement as she redoubled her effort. She had to catch that cable car! Her cap fell off, but she couldn't stop for it as she gained on the car. She drew near, and a young man leaned out to extend a hand. She reached for it and hopped aboard.

"Thank you!" she gasped as relief flooded her. Missing this cable car would have been a disaster.

She arrived at the pier in the nick of time, hurrying along the crowded boardwalk and searching through the throngs of people. The scent of warm pretzels mingled with the salty tang in the air, flags snapped in the breeze, and gulls swooped overhead. Jenny moved quickly, praying she wasn't too late.

"Dear me," a disapproving voice said directly behind her, "I don't believe I've ever seen such an appallingly scruffy nurse."

She whirled around. "Finn! I was afraid I missed you."

Over his shoulder he carried a seaman's pack, and he flashed her one of his irreverent smiles. He dropped the pack and held out both arms.

She raced into them. "Congratulations," she said. The note in her pocket said that Finn had passed the last of the MID tests and would sail for Japan on the evening tide.

She stepped back to get a better view of him. He looked quite fine, with a smartly tailored jacket and shiny new boots.

He noticed her glance. "They bought me new clothes," he said. "Quite fitting for a wealthy man setting up trade with his family's shipping company."

There was no need to mention who "they" were. Even the name of the MID was something that couldn't be said in public.

Finn's voice was full of energy. "My ship has been delayed for half an hour while an oversized freighter maneuvers into port. Come on, let's get something to eat. It's likely to be my last decent meal until I get to Japan."

A few minutes later they were at a table with warm sourdough bread and fried clams. Finn's appetite was healthy as he mopped up garlic butter with his bread.

"How's Ryan?" she asked politely.

"Vastly relieved he isn't headed to Japan."

She laughed a little. "I can imagine." She was happy for Ryan, even though one of the reasons she left was that she couldn't bear to come in second place again should he return to Japan. Now that didn't matter anymore.

"And Lily?"

"Growing like a weed. I almost forgot—she asked me to give you this."

Finn handed her a folded piece of paper with a drawing Lily had made for her. It showed stick figures of Ryan, Simon, Finn, and Lily standing on the porch, all waving. "We miss you" was carefully printed in childlike lettering at the top. Her heart squeezed. Lily had drawn herself so tiny compared to Ryan, who towered over the rest of the group.

Her gaze narrowed. "Why did she draw a smudge on Ryan's face?"

"Abigail gave him a black eye," Finn said bluntly. At her sputtered outrage, he went on. "Immediately after you left, Abigail started making a pest of herself again, showing up before the crack of dawn to start breakfast and ingratiate herself into the family. Ryan finally realized the problem he had let fester. He took her for a walk on the beach to talk it out, and I gather it didn't go over well with Miss Abigail. He came back with a world-class shiner."

Jenny stifled a gasp of horrified laughter. It wasn't funny, but

Abigail's sense of outrage wasn't entirely misplaced, either. Ryan was well-intentioned, but his kindness could have a downside, too. In trying to spare the girl's feelings by ignoring her embarrassing overtures, Abigail's fantasies were allowed to spiral out of control.

"Poor Ryan," she said in fond exasperation. "How a man so reticent could have such problems with the women in his life is baffling. Has Abigail stayed away?"

"More or less. Her father plans to send her to college soon, so that ought to give her something more appropriate to focus on." Finn swiveled in his chair to peer at her in speculation. "What would you say if Ryan showed up at the Presidio and begged you to take him back?"

"I'd tell him to take a flying leap into the Pacific."

"That's what I like about you. You're usually so tough."

She lifted a single brow. *"Usually?"*

"Usually," he repeated firmly. He waved a crust of bread at her, wagging it like a finger. "You couldn't take Ryan on, now could you?"

She straightened her shoulders and raised her chin. "What's that supposed to mean?"

"It means that women can be irrational," he said. "Ryan couldn't think of the magic combination of words to put you at ease about Akira, and that drove you batty. Then there was Abigail with her raspberry lemonade who stirred up jealousies that you took out on Ryan, not Abigail. Typical scorned woman behavior. They can misinterpret a comment, a glance, a well-intentioned compliment—"

"A child with another woman?" she asked pointedly.

"A gift from God."

Heat flooded her body, and she looked away. As painful as Ryan's betrayal was, it had brought Lily into the world. Lily was a miracle, so beautifully and seamlessly woven into the fabric of Ryan's life that it was impossible to think of Ryan without Lily alongside him.

Lily *was* a gift from God. Maybe there was a beautiful rationale to Ryan's betrayal in Japan, but she'd been too closed-minded to look for it.

Finn finished the last of the bread, then flashed her a conciliatory smile. "Your leaving was probably good for Ryan. Fleeing before dawn was a little overly dramatic, but it got his attention. So I'll ask again . . . if he showed up at the Presidio and could think of the magic words, would you take him back?"

"I don't need *words* from Ryan, I need actions that prove what I mean to him, and he never delivered on that when I was in Summerlin. Ryan will make a decent husband someday—"

"Decent? That's the best you can do?"

"Alright, an exceptionally decent husband," she affirmed. "He's nowhere close to being perfect, but all in all, he's a good man. I just don't think he can give me what I need. In case you hadn't noticed, I'm gun-shy when it comes to men, and Ryan's secrets set off all my warning bells."

Finn laughed, stood, and hoisted his pack over his shoulder. "Look, if you think Ryan loves you, then marry him. If you think he's nothing more than a sweet-talking womanizer, cast him aside. But know this—I think you are one in a million and deserve only the best. Don't settle for anything less."

She walked him to the gangway. It was hard to imagine that in a few minutes Finn would be gone forever. They reached the end of the line of passengers preparing to depart, and she turned to face him.

"Good luck, Finn. I'll be praying for you every day," she said, surprised at the sudden lump in her throat.

He must have noticed, for he flashed her a wink. "Don't worry about me. I've been waiting to do something like this my whole life."

The lump in her throat threatened to sink her, but she swallowed it back. She knew what the MID expected of him, and the mission had no end date. It was a dangerous assignment, for the Japanese would not take kindly to a foreign spy living in their midst.

"Are you sure you're in good shape?" she asked. "No lingering cravings?"

He shook his head. "Everything is under control. I never did thank you for helping me through that rough patch. I wasn't always the easiest patient, but I'm grateful you put up with me."

"You were a howling pain in the neck, Finn."

His laughter rang out over the pier. "Indeed I was."

"I'm going to miss you. Now don't take this the wrong way, but I hope I never see you again."

His eyes brightened. "Me, too." He dragged her into a bear hug, then bent down to pick up his pack. "Take care, Jenny."

She waited on the pier until the steamship sailed. He stood on the main deck, waving to her. Her American samurai. It was hard to look at the ship as it headed into the glare of the sunset, surrounded by a blaze of orange and red, but she watched and prayed until she could no longer see Finn.

25

Jenny scooped up an armful of bandages still warm from the drying racks. Despite the chilly October air, it was sweltering inside the laundry building.

"Have you got any more?" she asked the attendant. Rolling bandages was usually done by laundry staff, but it was an easy chore to foist off on Skeeter. As part of the agreement to operate on his eyes, Captain Soames insisted the boy volunteer at the hospital twice a week for an entire year. Although Jenny understood his reasoning, it was up to her to provide tasks a twelve-year-old boy could perform, and it was a challenge. The bandages wouldn't take even half an hour to roll.

"That's all I've got," the attendant said.

Jenny nodded. She'd just have to find something for Skeeter to clean during his remaining time.

Skeeter was waiting for her when she returned to the amputee ward. He looked stiff and uncomfortable standing in the corner, and relief washed over his features when he saw her.

"I thought you forgot about me."

"Never!" Jenny cleared a space at the dining table. He'd once confided in her that he was terribly intimidated by the men in the ward, all of them battle-hardened soldiers. She set down the basket of bandages. "Take your time. When you're finished here, I have some straightening up you can do in the storage closets."

"Thanks, Nurse Bennett." Skeeter sprang up only a moment after sitting down. "I almost forgot. I'm supposed to give you this." From his pocket he passed her a box. Her name was printed on the brown paper wrapping, and it was so light it felt empty.

"Where did this come from?"

Skeeter shrugged. "A man gave it to me."

She took a chair at the table to open the box. Could it be medicine from the dispensary or something for one of the patients? She opened the box and her eyes widened in stunned disbelief.

It was a pearl brooch in the shape of a snowflake. The pearls were tiny and oddly shaped, held together by delicate silver wires to create a brooch of stunning beauty. Simon's whimsical artistry shone in all its glory in this lovely pin, but the pearls were Ryan's. Was it a gift from Simon or from Ryan?

There was a note inside, and her fingers trembled as she opened it.

Dear Jenny,

It is only right that the first piece of jewelry from my pearl farm should go to you, as you were who I dreamed of during the long months in which I dug out the lagoon and seeded the oysters. I am sorry we were not able to come to an understanding, but that was my fault, not yours. I now understand that my reluctance to talk only exacerbated your wounded feelings. I hope you can accept this brooch as a peace offering.

Ryan

She traced her fingers along the delicate arrangement of silver and pearls. Ryan's farm was going to succeed, for even if he never figured out the technique for making round pearls, this was still a lovely piece.

Had she been right in walking away? Her fear that he would return to Japan had come to nothing, but the wounds she carried from what happened with Akira were so deep, and Ryan hadn't been able to cure them.

Finn was right. She had run away rather than stay and work through the pain.

"What's wrong?" Skeeter asked. "Your face looks all screwed up."

She forced the muscles in her face to relax. She folded the note and tucked it back in the box. "I'm fine. Sometimes it's a little scary to face the past."

Skeeter snorted. "You're the bravest person I know. If you hadn't been with me, I never would have had the guts to let that doctor cut on my eyes."

She wasn't so brave. She'd run away because she was afraid of wounded feelings. Ryan had apologized repeatedly to her. She didn't doubt that he would be a loyal and faithful man. It was her *feelings* that got the better of her. She felt like she came in second after Akira. After his loyalty to the MID. Even the pearl farm seemed to take precedence—

A new thought struck. "Who gave this to you?"

"Some man. I've never seen him before."

Her heart started to pound. Was it possible that Ryan could actually be here in San Francisco? "What did he look like?"

"He was really old."

"Oh." Probably just someone from the local post office, then. It was foolish to think Ryan would have come all this way just to deliver a brooch, especially since she'd left him in such a rude fashion.

That evening she walked along the bay, sinking tighter into her coat. Ryan's infidelity would be with her forever, but that didn't mean she couldn't forgive him. Forgiveness was a choice, and if she withheld it until the wound vanished without a trace, she would wait until her dying day. She had seen the pain carried by Oliver's widow, but Matilda still forgave her. Jesus forgave them all, even when he was in pain. She knew Ryan would never be unfaithful again, and by nurturing the old wound, she was only hurting them both. She wished he had managed to find a way to make her feel more secure in his love, but that was a sign of her own deep-seated neediness.

It was time to put this behind her for all time. It was time to choose forgiveness.

Tomorrow she would write a letter to Ryan thanking him for the brooch, apologizing for the way she left, and letting him know that he was forgiven. Would they have a future together after that?

She did not know. She went home and pinned the brooch onto the front of her gown, feeling a little foolish, but enjoying it nevertheless. She'd never had a piece of jewelry so fine. A girl from the wrong side of San Francisco really shouldn't wear something as fine as pearls, but she wore them anyway.

❧

It rained the next day, so instead of wheeling patients to the courtyard for therapy, Jenny was forced to work with the men inside the ward. She began the day with a new patient still struggling with the amputation of his leg high on his thigh. She sat beside Sergeant Lansky on a hard bench as they practiced standing up from a sitting position. Even such a simple activity was a challenge for a man whose center of gravity had been destroyed by having thirty pounds of his body removed from one side.

Sergeant Lansky toppled to the side, but she supported him. "You're doing fine," she assured him as they lowered to the bench again.

He glanced at a group of patients playing cards at the far end of the ward. "I'm a clumsy idiot," he mumbled.

Tiny dots of perspiration broke out on his skin, and she knew he was worried his awkward attempts to sit and stand were being witnessed by the men who'd already learned to walk. There would never be a more sympathetic audience than the people in this very room, but he didn't understand that yet.

"You're doing better than most men only two weeks out from an amputation. By next month I expect you'll be walking over to play cards at that table, but the first step is learning to stand. Let's try again."

Jenny silently cheered as he lowered his head in determination, shifted his weight as she'd taught him, and they rose together.

"Well done!" Major Kinnear shouted from across the room.

One of the orderlies approached the bench. "Nurse Bennett? You have a visitor waiting outside. Ryan Gallagher."

She froze, not certain she'd heard properly. She sat down on the bench. "Who?"

"Gallagher, ma'am. He says you know him."

Her mouth went dry and her heartbeat picked up pace.

One of the patients in a nearby bed sat upright. "Gallagher ... wasn't he that fella we wrote a letter about a few months ago? The deserter?"

"He wasn't a deserter," she defended, but when every eye in the room turned to stare at her, she clamped her mouth shut. To say any more could draw attention to something better left unspoken. Talking about this could even endanger Finn, but it was still hard to sit here and listen to Ryan's reputation be smeared.

"Our letter was sent to General Dwyer," Major Kinnear said. "He dismissed it out of hand, so there's nothing behind this but idle speculation." The major turned his attention to the young hospital orderly. "I take it Lieutenant Gallagher is back on base?"

"He's back," the orderly confirmed. "He wants to see Nurse Bennett. Can I send him in?"

"No, I'll go out and see him."

Why was Ryan here? He must have delivered the brooch personally to Skeeter, and to a twelve-year-old, Ryan probably looked "really old." A smile threatened. Could he have come all this way just to see her?

Before she even took a step, she noticed Ryan standing in the doorway, looking at her in a combination of expectation and worry. She'd forgotten how tall he was. And how quickly she could fall for that cautious, hopeful look on his face. A drop of rain clung to the end of a lock of hair, and she had to clench her hands to avoid reaching up to brush it away.

"Let's head outside where we can speak privately," she said.

"Private?" One of the patients smirked. "Like his mysteriously absent service during the war? That kind of private?"

"Don't get too close to him, Nurse Bennett, or some of that yellow-livered stink might rub off on you," someone shouted.

She shot the soldier an angry glare, cutting off the heckling. "Come on, Ryan. We don't have to stand for this."

"No, I want others to hear what I have to say." Ryan stood motionless, a burning appeal in his gaze.

"Don't have anything to do with him, Nurse Bennett. He's a coward."

She whirled around. "He's many things, but he's not a coward."

"No, he's right, Jenny." Ryan spoke softly, but every man in the ward heard, and the grumbling immediately ceased.

Her gaze flew to his, confused by this startling admission.

"I've been a coward from the moment I saw you again," he continued, heedless of the eighteen men listening in. "I should have paid more attention to what you were asking of me. You are the foundation I want to build the rest of my life around, and I should have been willing to do whatever it takes to make you happy. I'm sorry it took me so long to hear what you were trying to tell me. I want to say this in front of as many witnesses as possible, because all my life I've covered and disguised and evaded. I'm tired of it. I want to live a simple life with a woman I love, and I desperately hope that woman is going to be you."

He held up a sealed envelope. "This is a contract I am ready to sign that will put my house and land up for sale. I care more for you than for little pieces of calcium carbonate—"

"But Ryan! You can't sell it—"

"I will, Jenny. I know you love San Francisco, and we can build a good life here. All you have to do is say the word."

She swallowed hard. "You would walk away from your pearl farm for me?" Moving to San Francisco would mean a complete break with the world of pearls, for the ocean here was too cold to support oysters.

His eyes gentled. "Yes, Jenny, I would, and with no regrets. Whether I become a fisherman or a scientist or a pearl farmer, you are the one I want walking beside me. In my eyes, you are perfect. I love you and want to heal the wound I gave you. Jenny, will you forgive me?"

Her heart turned over. Ryan was an imperfect man who had stumbled and sinned, but who was without sin?

"You're too good for him, ma'am!" one of the patients shouted.

She shook her head but did not pull her gaze away from Ryan. "I'm nowhere close to being perfect, and if for a single second I pretended I was, I was a fraud and a liar." She tugged off her starched collar and threw it on the ground. It was easier to breathe without it, even though it felt strange to be stripped of its reassuring mask of propriety.

"Ryan, I forgive you," she said, and the bitterness that had been dammed up for years evaporated. It wouldn't poison her anymore.

"Thank you for being brave enough to ask. The incident is behind us and will not be stirred to life again." The words flowed easily because she meant them.

He swept her into his arms and kissed her. She dimly heard a combination of cheers and boos from the men.

"Don't sell your pearl farm," she whispered against his lips.

His arms tightened. "Are you sure?"

"I am." Knowing that he was willing to move to San Francisco made her heart sing. It was enough. He was willing to give up everything for her, but she didn't need him to follow through to be happy.

The men howled as she excused herself to take her break early, but she and Ryan had a lot to discuss, and she didn't want to do it in front of rowdy soldiers who couldn't keep their opinions to themselves.

The rain kept most people inside, so they had the courtyard to themselves. They sat in the rocking chairs and smiled at each other like idiots.

"How long have you been in San Francisco?" she asked.

"Since Monday."

"Monday? And you're only now coming to see me?"

"I couldn't be sure I'd be welcome until Finn told me you thought I'd make an exceptionally decent husband."

She looked at him in confusion. The only reason she'd poured her heart out to Finn was because he was sailing to the other side of the world, taking her secrets with him. But that was the exact phrase she'd used to describe Ryan, and somehow it had gotten back to him.

"This doesn't make sense," she sputtered. "I *saw* Finn get on that boat and sail away. How could you know anything about that conversation?"

"Finn has a wireless transmitter, and he knows Morse code."

Ryan pointed to the ridge of buildings visible over the hospital wall. "What do you think that antenna on top of Roberts Hall is for? He sent me the message less than an hour after he left port."

She straightened in her chair. "First of all, I have no idea what an 'antenna' is. And secondly, I'm not thrilled you've been talking about me behind my back."

He sobered. "That's why I told you. From this moment forward, I will have no secrets from you. If you ask me a question, I will answer it honestly and fully . . . whether I think it will hurt you or not. I know you're strong enough to handle whatever is on the horizon or even in the past."

She squeezed his hand. "Thank you for that."

"I'm sorry if you feel betrayed by the way Finn pumped you for information to pass back to me. Frankly, he's a far better spy than I ever was."

That was certainly true. At heart, Ryan really was Galahad, a kind and generous man who only wanted a simple life in America.

She held Ryan's hand as she gently rocked and let her eyes scan the courtyard. She loved it here. She loved her work as a nurse and feeling useful. She did not want to leave the hospital, but she was no longer free to make decisions based on her will alone. She was part of a family now.

"Are you going to make an honest woman out of me when I go back to Summerlin?"

He grinned. "I was hoping we could get that taken care of here in San Francisco. It seems like a nice place for a honeymoon."

She wanted to leap out of her chair and dance in the rain but kept herself carefully contained. "That sounds really great."

His gaze tracked the outline of the courtyard. "I'm sorry to take you away from a job you love—"

She cut him off. "I'll be fine. I'm ready to build a new life with you."

She would miss her work at the Presidio, but she was smart enough to figure out a way to use her medical talents in a village with no doctor. Summerlin was the right place for them to begin their family. Ryan had always been alone as he sailed to the farthest shores and back again, but from here on out, they would undertake their journey together.

Epilogue

WASHINGTON, DC, 1928
U.S. FEDERAL TRADE COMMISSION BUILDING

Ryan sat on a hard bench in the hallway, rubbing his palms against his trousers. Nervous habit. Jenny had been trying to calm him down all morning, but it was hard to be calm when the future of the entire pearl industry was being decided behind the closed door at the end of the hall.

Jenny sat beside him, flipping through a guidebook to the city. She'd never been to Washington and was determined to see everything. Yesterday they'd visited the Naval Observatory where he worked all those years ago. With luck, they would have time to visit the Smithsonian this afternoon, but that would depend on the outcome of the case.

"Relax," Jenny soothed. "Everything will be fine."

He swallowed hard. Everything *ought* to be fine, but the decision was being made by a panel of stuffy government bureaucrats who knew nothing about pearls or marine biology.

It had been more than twenty years since the first round pearl had been cultivated in Japan. It took Ryan a little longer to develop a workable technique, but he would never forget that warm August afternoon in 1911 when he opened an oyster to see it—the culmination of so many years toiling to create a perfectly round pearl. He'd cupped the oyster in his hand and sprinted back to the house, shouting, laughing, and weeping in elation. Jenny had just put their youngest son down for a nap and frowned as he bounded into the nursery and woke up the baby, who started crying at the sudden commotion. It didn't take her long to recognize what he held in his wet, grubby palm. She shrieked in joy and leapt into his arms. The pearl clattered to the floor and rolled away. It took them twenty minutes to find it again, but that pearl had been made into a necklace that even now rested around Jenny's neck.

In the years that followed, they expanded the pearl farm from one to five piers, where their three sons worked alongside him to harvest thousands of pearls every year. It would have been nice if the boys could have come with them to Washington, but it was spawning season, and the pearl farm needed them.

Cultured pearls still had legal hurdles to clear. The price of natural pearls plummeted as soon as cultured pearls entered the market, and the public loved them. For the first time, a strand of pearls was within reach of ordinary Americans, but powerful jewelers' syndicates fought against the newcomers in courts all over the world. They lobbied the government to demand that anything from an oyster farm be labeled an "imitation pearl."

It was going to take a nation-by-nation battle to win acceptance of cultivated pearls. The British finally had allowed them to be traded as authentic pearls in 1921, and the Japanese won that right a few years later. Last month the American National Jewelers Board finally recommended that cultivated pearls be recognized as authentic in the United States. It was a huge step, but it would only go into effect if the Federal Trade Commission signed off on it. That decision would come down today, and lawyers, scientists, and trade regulators had been closeted all morning in one of those fancy conference rooms.

"What is taking them so long?" he groused. "Can't they understand that there's no difference between a cultivated pearl and one grown naturally? It would be like suggesting an apple raised in an orchard isn't a real apple because it wasn't found in the wild."

"You don't need to convince me," Jenny said. "The good news is that we have the best possible lawyer on our side. How can we lose?"

Jenny was right. Their lawyer was an expert on pearls and had a front row seat in Tokyo during the Japanese court case to win recognition for cultivated pearls. Ryan would just have to trust that the government bureaucrats would see reason.

The door down the hall opened, and he stood, heart racing as their lawyer left the conference room and began walking toward them. Her slim skirt showed a shocking display of ankle, and the click of her high heels echoed down the marble hallway as she drew near. Her smile was radiant.

"We won, Dad."

He scooped Lily into his arms and swung her in a circle. The lump in his throat made it impossible to speak, but Jenny didn't seem all that surprised.

"I never doubted it for a moment," Jenny said as she embraced Lily. "Can we please go to the Smithsonian now?"

"Absolutely," Lily said. "A biologist from the Smithsonian was at the meeting, and he said he would give me—I mean, *us* a personal tour."

His paternal instincts awakened. "A nice young man, I hope?"

"Yes, Dad, he's a nice young man," she said with a roll of her eyes. "American, too."

Ever since Lily began making regular trips to Japan to oversee the silk factory she'd inherited from Harue, Ryan suffered a paranoid fear that she might one day fall in love and stay in Japan forever. It was her decision, of course. One of the reasons he fought so hard to raise Lily in America was because he wanted her to have the freedom to follow her dreams wherever they led.

For himself, he never had any doubt where home was. He and Jenny had worked hard to build their kingdom by the sea. Harvesting pearls from the ocean was not an easy way to make a living, but the freedom to make his own choices in life was a blessing he gave thanks for each day of his life. There would always be stormy times and disappointing harvests, but for the most part, their days overflowed with summer-bright happiness and dreams of tomorrow.

Historical Note

The Military Information Division was established in 1885 as a branch of the U.S. Army and was one of several organizations charged with gathering intelligence about foreign nations. These units were not integrated until the creation of the Central Intelligence Agency in 1947.

The world's first cultured pearl is credited to Kokichi Mikimoto in 1905. Mikimoto was the son of a noodle-maker, a humble profession in Japan. His first stroke of good fortune came when he married Ume, the wealthy daughter of a master Japanese swordsman. Ume's fortune allowed them to pursue Mikimoto's fascination with pearls. The husband-and-wife team toiled for decades in search of a technique for creating round pearls, and bad harvests almost drove them into bankruptcy several times. Ume resorted to making and selling noodles to support the family while her husband continued his quest to cultivate a perfectly round pearl. Ume died in 1896, leaving Mikimoto with five young children and a struggling pearl farm. When Mikimoto's farm finally produced a perfect pearl in 1905, he carried it to his wife's grave and wept.

In the coming decades, Mikimoto's pearls became a favorite

of the Japanese emperor, and his wildly successful store in Tokyo spread his fame throughout Asia. As his reputation surged, Mikimoto opened stores in Paris, London, New York, and Chicago. When Mikimoto died in 1954 at the age of 96, his name had become synonymous with the world's most elegant pearls.

The only reliable way to tell a cultured pearl from a naturally occurring pearl is to use an X-ray, where the artificially created nucleus looks different than a natural irritant. Although early cultivated pearls were grown in salt water with various types of oysters, the most affordable pearls today are freshwater pearls grown in mollusks.

Questions for Discussion

1. Ryan withholds information from Jenny because he wants to protect her feelings. Ironically, this has the opposite effect as it reinforces her inability to trust him. Have you ever tried to protect people by withholding information?

2. Jenny tries to buy peace of mind by sending Oliver's widow an anonymous gift but still feels unsatisfied. Why did she feel compelled to take the next step and apologize in person?

3. Have you ever worked an overnight shift? What effect did it have on your body and spirit?

4. Ryan claimed that apologies are often given and accepted too easily. When he accepts Jenny's apology, he says, "The incident is behind us and will not be stirred to life again." Do you believe this is possible for a serious offense? What are the consequences of bringing offenses back to life once an apology has been accepted?

5. Harue gets away with attempted murder, and Ryan makes it clear he has no intention of pursuing the matter further. Was this wise? Are there some battles that aren't worth fighting? How do you know the difference?

6. Should a Christian feel obligated to forgive an offense? Are there circumstances in which forgiveness is not warranted?

7. Jenny's obsessive need for security and Ryan's tendency to hide his feelings are both an outgrowth of their childhoods. Do you have any defense mechanisms from childhood that are still with you?

8. Had Finn not passed the MID tests, Ryan would have returned to Japan. How do you feel about that?

9. Ryan compares Jenny to a pearl when he suggests her difficult childhood made her a deeper, more compassionate person. Have you had struggles you've tried to turn into a positive factor?

10. Jenny quit a job she loved to follow Ryan to his pearl farm. Have you ever made a similar career sacrifice for a spouse? How did it work out?

Elizabeth Camden is the author of nine historical novels and two historical novellas and has been honored with both the RITA Award and the Christy Award. With a master's in history and a master's in library science, she is a research librarian by day and scribbles away on her next novel by night. She lives with her husband in Florida. Learn more at www.elizabethcamden.com.

Sign Up for Elizabeth's Newsletter!

Keep up to date with Elizabeth's news on book releases, signings, and other events by signing up for her email list at elizabethcamden.com.

Catch Up on Elizabeth's Books!

Artist Stella West has moved to Boston to solve the mysterious death of her sister, but she is in need of a well-connected ally. Fortunately, prominent magazine owner Romulus White has been trying to hire her for years. Sparks fly when they join forces, but will her questions cost him everything?

From This Moment

BETHANY HOUSE

More From Elizabeth Camden

Visit elizabethcamden.com to see a full list of her books.

National Weather Bureau volunteer Sophie van Riijn has used the abandoned mansion Dierenpark as a resource and a refuge for years, but now the Vandermark heir has returned. When old secrets come to light, will tragedy triumph or can hope and love prevail?

Until the Dawn

When a map librarian and a young congressman join forces to solve a mystery, they become entangled in secrets more perilous than they could have imagined.

Beyond All Dreams

United in a quest to cure tuberculosis, physician Trevor McDonough and statistician Kate Livingston must overcome past secrets and current threats to find hope for their cause—and their futures.

With Every Breath

◊ BETHANYHOUSE

Stay up to date on your favorite books and authors with our free e-newsletters. Sign up today at bethanyhouse.com.

Find us on Facebook. facebook.com/bethanyhousepublishers

Free exclusive resources for your book group! bethanyhouse.com/anopenbook

an open book

ore Historical Fiction

Hope Irvine always sees the best in people. While traveling on the rails with her missionary father, she attracts the attention of a miner named Luke and a young mine manager. But when Luke begins to suspect the manager is using Hope's missions of mercy as a cover for illegal activities, can he discover the truth without putting her in danger?

The Chapel Car Bride by Judith Miller
judithmccoymiller.com

Miss Permilia Griswold, the wallflower behind *The Quill* gossip column, knows everything that goes on in the ballrooms of New York. When she overhears a threat against the estimable Mr. Asher Rutherford, she's determined to warn him. Away from society's spotlight, Asher and Permilia discover there's more going on behind the scenes than they anticipated.

Behind the Scenes by Jen Turano
APART FROM THE CROWD
jenturano.com

The Boden clan thought their troubles were over with the death of a dangerous enemy. But with new evidence on Cole's shooting, Justin can't deny that the plot to steal their ranch was bigger than one man. While the doctor and his distractingly pretty assistant help Cole, Justin has to uncover the trail of a decades-old secret as danger closes in.

Long Time Gone by Mary Connealy
THE CIMARRON LEGACY #2
maryconnealy.com

◊ BETHANYHOUSE